REQUIEM FOR PRIVATE HUGHES

A NOVEL

By Chip Tolson

Requiem for Private Hughes is a work of fiction.
© Chip Tolson 2015.

Published by Createspace Independent Publishing Platform, 2015.

ISBN-13: 978-1517354176
ISBN-10: 151735417X

Chip Tolson has asserted his right to be identified as the author of this work in accordance with the Copyright, Designs and Patents Act 1988.

Front cover: Three miles distant Second Lieutenant Peterson heard an explosion, later a thump, and saw a billowing column of dark smoke rise above the rolling jungle landscape.

Dedication

For Clare, whose patience over my disappearing to the other end of the house, and her many comments, have encouraged me to write this novel.

CONTENTS

Foreword .... page 5

PART ONE:

Chapter 1 .... page 7
Chapter 2 .... page 16
Chapter 3 .... page 24
Chapter 4 .... page 27
Chapter 5 .... page 35
Chapter 6 .... page 44
Chapter 7 .... page 56
Chapter 8 .... page 67

PART TWO:

Chapter 9 .... page 80
Chapter 10 .... page 95
Chapter 11 .... page 105
Chapter 12 .... page 111

PART THREE:

Chapter 13 .... page 121
Chapter 14 .... page 131
Chapter 15 .... page 140
Chapter 16 .... page 151
Chapter 17 .... page 164
Chapter 18 .... page 176

PART FOUR:

Chapter 19 .... page 183
Chapter 20 .... page 195
Chapter 21 .... page 205
Chapter 22 .... page 214
Chapter 23 .... page 227
Chapter 24 .... page 241
Chapter 25 .... page 255
Chapter 26 .... page 263
Chapter 27 .... page 266
Chapter 28 .... page 276
Chapter 29 .... page 280
Acknowledgements, about the author .... page 285
Other works by Chip Tolson .... page 287

Foreword

ARCHIE Middlebrook, a Somerset lad studying at art college, is called up for two years' national service in 1953. With many others of his generation, he is posted overseas to serve in a British infantry battalion during the Malayan Emergency.

With some variations over the years, national service – conscription into the armed services – was introduced for the Second World War and continued afterwards for men aged 18 to 21. It ended in 1963; over two million young men served as conscripts after the war.

The Malayan Emergency was the period in the late 1940s into the mid 1950s during which ethnic Chinese communist terrorists in Malaya, known as CTs, having fought a guerrilla campaign opposing the Japanese forces occupying Peninsula Malaya, continued their struggle against the returning colonial British rulers and then against the Federation of Malaya, the forerunner of Malaysia and Singapore.

British forces – including many national servicemen – Commonwealth contingents and the early Malaysian armed forces combined to defeat the communist terrorists.

One hundred and four national servicemen died serving in Malaya.

This novel celebrates the endeavours of all those called up for national service at home and abroad.

PART ONE
1955

Chapter One

SITTING at a trestle table facing down the stifling barrack tent, Archie Middlebrook drew the shapes and colours of the deep jungle, twisting rattans woven round stretching trunks, scant light filtering down.

On patrol they knew there were things unseen all around, small beasts, a myriad of insects, aware of their progress. All the time they prayed there was no terrorist lurking close by, no communist watching the patrol working its way into a trap; always on guard, their weapons held ready, looking for any sign that warned of the enemy, nervously checking the man ahead and the man behind.

'Not another jungle picture, Archie?'

'What do you think, Geraint?'

'I'd have thought you were sick of the bloody jungle by now.'

'And lie on my pit all day with my thumb in my bum and mind in neutral like this idle lot?'

'Sod off' was the only retort that came from the figures lying under the sweltering canvas, its sides rolled up to capture the slightest breeze.

'Now then, now then, that's no way to address our illustrious corporal.' Geraint's singsong tones rang out and he winked at Archie, whose second stripe had only been sewn onto his sleeve that morning. 'Let's have a bit of respect in the ranks.'

'Sod off, Geraint. When's the poxy rain coming?'

'Language, Bevan. What would your dear old mother be thinking if she could hear you now? Language fit to curdle milk in a bowl.'

'A dollar says seventeen minutes.' Archie checked his watch 'Seventeen minutes from... now' and he pencilled "15:22 hrs" at the top of his paper.

Geraint went out onto the grass and looked round. 'I'll buy thirteen minutes.'

'Eight effing minutes – sooner the better.'

'Twenty.'

'Eleven minutes.'

'Come on, money up front, I don't trust you buggers.' Geraint went up the line of beds. 'Come on, dollar-a-diddle.'

'I'm skint; take it out of my winnings.'

'No chance, cash on the nose or you're not in. First drop on the canvas, none of this, "I heard thunder" bullshit.'

Archie went out into the glare of the sun. Huge thunderheads were building in the west, coming in from the Strait of Malacca, the sky blackening as lightning flickered high in the clouds. He'd been too cautious; ten minutes looked nearer the mark.

It was 15:19 when the first drop hit and in seconds the deluge drummed down, water-shoots cascading off the canvas, everyone up from their beds, the temperature dropping, fanned by wind blowing through the barrack tent.

'Who won the sweep?'

'No bugger did. Roll it over to tomorrow,' replied Geraint.

'Who was nearest?'

'Doesn't count.'

'At bloody last.' Private Shorthouse pulled off his vest, stripped off his shorts, dropped his baggy army issue drawers and strolled out towards the Padang, bollock naked, holding out his arms, letting the pummelling rain drum over his bare flesh.

'Come back, Shorty,' Archie commanded.

'I can't for the life of me see why we call him "*Shorty*".' Geraint watched the young man jumping up and down, legs apart, legs together, arms swinging out, in to the side and out again. Then others stripped off and soon a dozen bare-arsed young squadies, their arms flailing were running round the Padang as the deluge washed down.

'How about it Archie?'

'And lose my second stripe on the first day?'

'Can't lose it if there's nowhere to pin it.' Geraint stripped and ran out, jumping the already flowing monsoon drain to catch up with the others, all shouting at the top of their voices, wheeling round in large circles.

The Padang, the battalion sports field of mown tropical grass, was adjacent to the accommodation block for married regular NCOs.

Sergeant Brewer's wife, Joyce, had two friends in her flat for tea and something stronger. She was bored; sweat stuck her floral dress to her body, her straggly hair to her scalp. She heard the shouting and looked out the window, feeling the spray blowing in from the teeming rain.

'Well, just look at this, girls. Did you ever see such a well-equipped patrol in your lives? My God, Lindy, look at that chap in the front.'

'Take that man's name, I say,' giggled Lindy.

❈ ❈ ❈ ❈ ❈

'What is all this, Mr Peterson?' asked Major Willocks, the Company Commander. High up a ceiling fan turned teasing the papers on his desk, papers held down with an array of stone weights collected by his children as mementos from family picnics on beaches thousands of miles away.

'I'm sorry, Sir. Fuss about nothing really; Sergeant Brewer is up in arms about it. He says his wife was deeply offended by the chaps running round the Padang yesterday in the rain, Sir.'

'What offence is that for heaven's sake?'

'They were naked, Sir.'

'And Mrs Brewer was offended? That must be a first.' Second Lieutenant James Peterson caught the older man's eye. 'Forget I said that, Peterson.'

Requiem for Private Hughes

'Yes, Sir.'

'I want to get on with the scout car briefing. Why were they naked?'

'High spirits, Sir; they've had a pretty rough time recently.'

'That's as may be.' Major Willocks pushed back his chair and looked at the national service subaltern standing in front of his desk, not quite cutting a military figure. Young Peterson, a Platoon Commander, hadn't got the hang of looking neat in uniform. He would far rather be deep in his classical studies; another few weeks and he would be, his national service over and up at Oxford on a scholarship.

'Do I need to do anything, James?'

'Bit of a dressing down, perhaps; I've persuaded Sergeant Brewer it isn't a hanging offence, but he insisted I bring the matter to you, Sir.'

'It's a bit personal between those two: Brewer and Middlebrook. I suppose Brewer wants me to take away Middlebrook's second stripe.'

'Something of that sort, Sir.'

'Well, I know which of the two I would want to be with on a sticky wicket. Can't we post Brewer and his missus off somewhere?'

'Corporal Middlebrook is due out in a few weeks.'

'He's a good chap. No chance of persuading him to sign on, I suppose?'

'He's off to art school when he gets out, Sir. He's a dab hand with a pencil and brushes. I got him to do a picture of a jungle patrol for me. Good to have it on the wall when it's snowing back home.'

'You know his father was decorated in Italy.'

'Military Medal, wasn't it, Sir?'

'It was posthumous; many said he should have got more than the MM. You'd better get him in.'

Archie stood as straight as he could in front of the Company Commander's desk, reaching up half an inch under six foot, his hat off and pinned to his side by his elbow, beads of sweat trickling down his reddened forehead from close-cropped fair hair, his thumbs pointing down the crinkled seam of his shorts. The ceiling fan wafted heavy air round the office, sending a chill through his sweat-soaked shirt.

'Not a good start this, Corporal. I don't give a damn if your men do run about naked, but not in front of the ladies.'

Archie stood to attention, his eyes on the wall opposite. A gecko ran out from a corner, flicked up a small insect, and shot across the ceiling. How did they do that? How could geckoes defy gravity? He watched as it scurried back onto the wall, to a place behind a faded framed photo, a line of smartly uniformed young men celebrating a pass-out parade on a snow covered square. He guessed the Major was one of the young men in the picture.

'Right, that's enough.'

'Sir.' Major Willocks had said something else, but Archie hadn't heard it. Mr Peterson would tell him if it was important.

'I want all the men together at noon, Peterson.' The Major turned to Archie still standing to attention. 'At ease, Middlebrook. Have you heard we're going to get a squadron of scout cars to play with? Our cavalry friends are off home and there's no armoured regiment due out for six months, so we're going to take the scout cars over for a while.'

Archie relaxed. 'I've heard rumours, Sir.'

'Ferret scout cars, nifty things, and we've got just a week to learn how to drive and deploy them. Then it's for real, escort work on supply convoys. Do you reckon the lads will be up for it?'

'They'll jump at a chance to sit on their backsides on a set of wheels. If there are any jungle patrols going, I'd like to be included, Sir.'

'You like the jungle, don't you, Middlebrook?'

'Yes, Sir, I liked being in the woods at home and it's the same here, only huge and mysterious.'

'And a damn sight more dangerous, too. Right, noon in the Mess Hall for the Ferret briefing, Corporal Middlebrook; pass the word round.'

※ ※ ※ ※ ※

Requiem for Private Hughes

Geraint was thrilled with his new charge. They'd spent a week driving the Ferrets, at first within the camp perimeter, later out on the road in a non-hostile area. Geraint settled into it, easing himself into the restricted space, sitting secure in the cramped driving position, with the steering wheel tilted toward his shoulders like a ship's wheel, getting used to looking through the viewing prisms with the steel hatch shut, building up speed, enjoying the whine of the transmission running off the Rolls Royce engine. It was hot, bloody hot, but who cared? He'd written a letter to his folks, telling them he was driving a 'Rolls', not letting on it was only a Rolls engine. Still the Ferret was built by Daimler, and that wasn't bad.

'Who would think it? Me, Private Geraint Haydn Hughes, in charge of a Rolls-bloody-Royce? Marvellous.'

In the morning they had to arm up, fill the magazines, check-out the Sten and the sub machine gun from the armoury, then make for the rendezvous with a supply convoy from a depot outside Ipoh.

'Come on, Geraint. You'll be sleeping with the bloody thing next. I'm parched, let's get to the NAAFI.'

It was light by seven in the morning. They were greeted by a blood-red sun climbing above the jungle into clear sky, and were driving by a quarter-past the hour – three scout cars, each with two-man crews, for convoy duty. There should have been four, but one broke down before they were out of the camp gates. They couldn't wait and left Sergeant Brewer behind to cope with repairs. The laden convoy had to leave its depot at eight. And it did.

Archie soon learned the good thing about escorting supply convoys; the new places they found. As the sun rose higher in the sky, they passed by crowded kampongs. Archie raised a hand in greeting, but even the children gave no reply, looking away as the army churned by throwing up a cloud of dust. They passed rubber plantations on cleared jungle land, the rubber trees planted in straight lines across the landscape, dappled light filtering through. Dark-skinned Tamil rubber-tappers moved through the plantations to check the gathering cups, collecting the oozing white latex gum from scars cut on the trunks.

Requiem for Private Hughes

The convoy made good progress to wheel in through the forward camp gates after two-and-a-half hours on the road. Geraint climbed down from the Ferret red faced, his sweat-soaked overalls sticking to his back.

'Hot, Geraint?'

'It's easy for you with your head stuck out in the wind.'

'Let's get some chow.'

'I could murder an Anchor, Archie.'

'Tonight, promise, I'll buy you a beer tonight.'

The journey back to Ipoh would be quicker with the wagons empty. They'd been going for an hour when four of their six wagons started overheating. The drivers had failed to check radiator levels at the forward camp. Archie might have monitored their readiness, but a Service Corps corporal was travelling in the lead truck and the drivers were under his charge.

Peterson worried. They were vulnerable. He decided to rest the convoy, post sentries, let the radiators cool, then top up from the jerry cans they had with them for emergencies. An eerie pause fell on the column of vehicles; sentries stared into the jungle, listening out for strange noises, with nervous fingers hovering over safety catches and hands checking and re-checking their loaded magazines.

'Mr Peterson, I've spoken with the front two drivers. They're in good nick, Sir, no problems. Why don't I take them down the road, best speed, then you can nurse the others back. Once we've got these to the depot, we'll retrace the route to meet up with you again,' said Archie.

Geraint egged him on, fancying a spin along the highway into Ipoh. He stood behind the young subaltern, gesticulating at Archie.

Peterson hesitated. There'd been no reports of insurgents in the area yet word can spread like wildfire, runners slip away from kampongs, disappearing into the jungle to make contact. Would it be wise to split up? Corporal Middlebrook was competent and at least some of the column would be back at their base before dark.

'Okay, but proceed at a sensible speed. None of Private Hughes's Stirling Moss notions. And keep in touch while you're in range.'

Requiem for Private Hughes

The column was split. The small group set off with Archie's Ferret in the vanguard and the two Bedford trucks following. The Service Corps corporal stayed with the overheated vehicles, the other two Ferrets and Mr Peterson.

The laterite track rolled out twisting through the landscape, the same red as Somerset's fertile soil. But for the heat and the overhanging greens of the jungle piled up high on either side, Archie might have been at home.

On their way outward in the morning, they'd come across elephant droppings on the track. The column had halted as they warily looked for a booby trap. Mr Peterson had gone forward for a nervous couple of minutes before they got underway again, word passing back – "just a pile of shit".

Archie laughed to himself; horse dung maybe on a Somerset lane, not a great pile like that. He watched the jungle fringe. He wanted to see wild elephants; he'd seen captive ones in Bristol Zoo, never in the wild. There were occasional reports of big cats. They'd had a scare on one of their foot patrols, huge pugmarks by the bivouac in the morning.

Geraint sang into his mike, alternating *Men of Harlech* with *Bread of Heaven,* which he called *Cwm Rhondda,* sung in Welsh. He claimed a forebear composed the tune, but no one believed him. If he'd sung the songs once he'd sung them twenty times. He revved the Ferret, changing gear flamboyantly to tackle the rising track.

A flock of yellow-crested parrots gazed down from the trees as the scout car breasted the brow of the hill, getting ahead of the two wagons churning along in a blue haze of petrol exhaust.

The explosion shattered the late afternoon still of the jungle.

Screaming parrots clouded into the sky. The Ferret reared up from the track to fall back, half in, half out of the crater in the road, lying over on its side, clattered by a rain of stone blasted from the track. Archie, flung out from his observation hatch, hit a tree and crashed to the ground, his ears ringing, glaring white light in his eyes, blood running from his split scalp.

Requiem for Private Hughes

Geraint yelled out as the dust swirled round the battered scout car.

'Shit, Geraint.' Archie staggered back to the ambushed Ferret.

'Get me out, for Christ's sake, get me out of here.'

Archie hauled on the steel hatch handles. 'Bloody thing, it's stuck.' Archie pulled hard, superhuman strength came to him, but the buckled steel wouldn't budge. Petrol poured out of the ruptured fuel tank. The crack of gunfire rang out from jungle cover. Geraint screamed.

'Geraint, get back to the turret. I can't budge the bloody hatch...'

There was a metallic thud as a hand grenade hit the scout car's armoured cladding falling like a ripe fruit into the crater; Archie stared at the projectile, the world standing still in terrifying silence, before more bullets struck and the fuel exploded in a massive ball of flame. Archie was hurled back, his overalls ablaze, falling heavily into the jungle edge to roll by instinct on the ground to smother the flames. As he struggled to get back to his feet, the hand grenade exploded, a savage scream coming from the Ferret.

Archie, his overalls charred and smoking lay unconscious face down in the blood-soaked dirt of the jungle.

Three miles distant Second Lieutenant Peterson heard an explosion, later a thump, and saw a billowing column of dark smoke rise above the rolling jungle landscape.

Chapter Two

SWATHES of twisting rattans reached down clasping his limbs, as the herd of elephants charged, the trees shook and clouds of dust billowed into the air. There were dozens of them all round him, in the jungle and in the rubber plantation, and the Ferret wouldn't budge, its four wheels spinning. The elephants careered on into the sea and a tiger leapt from its stalking place, ripping into his arm.

He heard voices, quiet voices, soothing voices. Someone held him and there was a gentle breeze.

It was light. The red mist faded. There was a face looming close, gentle blue eyes looking into his.

'Where's the tiger?' He heard his voice. She held his arm; it was wrapped in bandages, smelling of antiseptic. A ceiling fan turned, stirring the air.

'I'm checking your dressing, Corporal.' A hint of a sweet smile, a blonde curl sticking out from her starched white cap, a bead of sweat running down her temple. 'Don't move, Corporal, you're all right. You've had an operation.'

'Has the tiger gone?'

'Yes, it's gone. I'm going to fetch Sister.'

Later there were more people standing round the bed while a doctor checked the dressings on his shoulder, his right arm and his right leg.

'You're lucky, Corporal. This could have been worse. There will be scarring. You have a gash on your scalp and broken ribs, nothing else broken.'

'Where am I?'

Requiem for Private Hughes

'This is the British Military Hospital in Penang. How's your head?'

'Groggy,' Archie's head ached and his ears throbbed with the sound of a muffled drum.

'You've been sedated for a long time. It'll wear off. You'll be all right.'

'Sick.' He felt a spasm in his throat, it dribbled down his chin, bitter tasting. His stomach churned.

A tall, starched figure looked down. 'Nurse, clean him up.' And they were gone, moving off down the ward.

The cloth cooled his bitter lips. She cradled his head and held a mug to his mouth. Sweet liquid cleansed his throat, trickling down, refreshing. He sensed other beds, other people in them, in lines on both sides of the ward. On the far side shutters were thrown back, there were flame trees of startling orange and beyond a deep blue sky. Everything was painted white in the ward, the lofty ceiling, the walls – even the metal bed frames were white. There had been screens round his bed when the doctor spoke, now wheeled away by an orderly. Archie looked at his arm, bandaged right down to his hand. Just his fingertips and the thumb poked out. There was a sickly sweet smell and myriad pins stuck into his limb as he tried to move it.

The nurse had gone.

'You with us, Corp?' A figure in striped pyjamas stood beside the bed.

'I suppose so.' The man came into focus.

'Back to your bed, Hastie.'

'Sorry, Blondie, just saying hello. No harm in that, is there?' The man had a Scots accent.

'Nurse, where's Geraint?' asked Archie.

'Geraint?'

'Private Hughes. Where is he?' Archie tried to sit up, but she gently pushed him back.

'There's no Private Hughes here, Corporal. Was he with you?'

'He was driving. Where is he?'

17

'He must be somewhere else. You have burns. This is BMH, Penang. You were transferred here two days ago.'

Later they moved his cot into a small room. They changed the dressings on his arm and shoulder; his leg was in plaster; there was ligament damage. It hurt, but they said that was good, the nerves ends were in place. They told him he'd be in the small room for a day or two. The room was taller than it was wide, and sparse, with only his cot and a tin locker, again painted white, its surface chipped. The shutters were closed against the night, the room lit by a single bulb in a metal holder sticking out from the wall above his bed. There was no fan.

'Hello, Corporal. It's Archibald, isn't it?'

'Archie, Padre.' The dog collar distinguished his visitor from other officers. He'd come silently into the room.

'Ah, Archie, I've only your official records to go on. National service and you have made it to corporal, that's quite an achievement.'

The Padre talked on for a while. Archie wondered whether he would say a prayer. He didn't want to pray; he'd been to Sunday school, all the village children went to Sunday school - but he hadn't been to church much after that. There were regular church parades in the battalion; they were sing-a-longs with the lads trying to out-blast each other. Geraint was the best singer – no one could out-sing Geraint.

Then the Padre said it. He'd guessed it, the Padre spoke it; Geraint was dead, killed in the ambush. The Padre said it was quick; Archie knew it was not.

He lay in his bed, with the rhythm of the tropical night pulsing outside the shutters, and wept while the Padre said a prayer. Archie wasn't listening, and shutting his mind to the Padre, he heard Geraint scream. No-one else heard it, only he knew the truth. He should have seen the mine in the track, there had to have been some disturbance

The nurse came in before the Padre left. They spoke in whispers for a moment. She was the one the Scotsman called 'Blondie'; her name was Mary. She came over to tidy the already neat bed. Gently she held his good hand.

'I'm so sorry, Archie.' Very softly her lips kissed his forehead. There were tears in the corner of her eyes, the most beautiful blue Archie had ever seen. 'I'm so very sorry.'

* * * * *

Six weeks passed as Archie came to understand what his arm and thigh were going to be like – nothing missing, just healing skin to carry his scars and ligaments knitting back. They told him it would always be with him. The wound on his head where he had smashed into the tree had healed, leaving a place on his head where his hair had burnt off. It was growing back, a snow-white patch above his right ear.

He told Mary he wanted to draw. She found him paper and pencils and told him it would be good exercise for his hand and arm, getting him to flex his sore muscles. The skin on the back of his hand was not badly burnt, but it looked fragile, even old, like his mother's.

Archie spent days sitting out in the gardens under an awning, with other recovering patients. Frangipani and hibiscus were flowering; a column of ants wound its way through the coarse leafed grass, a mynah bird picked up the whistles of the soldiers, mimicking them back across the gardens.

Archie looked up, squinting in the noonday light. A familiar figure was coming across the grass. The Padre pointed to another part of the garden and the tall man with him crossed to a bench in the shade, while the Padre came over to the group of resting soldiers.

'You have a visitor, Archie.'

'Give him extra prayers, Padre. He's been having naughty thoughts about the nurses.'

'I'm sure that isn't true, Hastie. And I doubt your plate is as clean as it should be.' There was a ripple of laughter round the lads as Archie gathered up his things and went over to the seated figure. Archie straightened up in salute. James Peterson stood and acknowledged him.

Requiem for Private Hughes

'Sit down Archie. It's good to see you up and about again.'

Nothing was said as the two young men swallowed their emotion at seeing each other, both staring out over the hospital grounds. Peterson, six months older than Archie, was two months ahead of him on call-up. For a brief overlap they'd both been Privates in the training battalion before James Peterson went to Mons, the Officer Cadet School in Aldershot. If they'd met in training neither remembered it. They'd come out to Malaya on different troopships and it was only when Peterson became his platoon commander that Archie got to know him. They worked well together, given the divide that existed between the Officers' Mess and his tented barracks.

'Food all right?'

'Can't complain, doesn't change much.'

A lizard worked its way along the wall. Archie watched it hunt, nosing into every crevice, its tongue licking up small insects. When it was still he could hardly make out its outline against the stone. High up, two black kites wheeled in from the sea, the tips of their wings splayed out, feeling for every breath of thermal.

'I'm here for the night, staying at The Penang Club. Would you be allowed to come out and have dinner with me, Archie?'

'If you requested it, Sir. I don't know what uniform I've got here. I've only seen what I'm wearing.'

'No problem, I've brought up your stuff. I'll fix it. We need to have a chat. There's going to be an Inquiry, Archie.'

Archie watched the kites, remembering buzzards circling in Somerset air, watched for hours as he'd lain back in the heather, wishing they would swoop down to lift him up high above the moor, knowing they could see every detail of him from their great height. In late summer there were squadrons of buzzards, families joined with others, flocking, sometimes ten at a time, in the sky, mewing to each other in lazy circles. One of the great birds would encroach too close to a crow's tree and the black birds would scramble from their perches to see off the intruder, the buzzard turning over, talons grabbing, as a crow swept past.

Requiem for Private Hughes

'It's bad about Private Hughes: young Geraint. We got him out, but it was too late. He was buried with full military honours.'

The garden was silent. The other men had gone in for lunch. The sun was high in the sky, almost overhead, and even the small birds were silent in the shrubs.

'Geraint was a good friend to you. Rotten do for you, Archie. We all liked him.'

Archie stared at the hospital across the garden, blinking tears away, gripping his fists tightly and not daring to open his lips.

'I've written to his parents in Cardiff.' Peterson stared toward the hospital, tapping his leather bound cane against a shoe.

* * * * *

James Peterson did better than ask permission for Archie to come out to dinner at the club - he booked a bed for him to stay overnight. At dinner they reminisced about the good times there had been since training days at the depot. James had brought Archie's 'civies', as well as his uniform. It made them less conspicuous in the club without their respective ranks on display. Archie hadn't drunk alcohol while he'd been convalescing, but they consumed a bottle of claret, Peterson most of it, on top of the Tiger beer they'd had at the bar beforehand.

Over Nasi Goreng and Gula Mulaka, Archie told Peterson what he remembered of the ambush; there had been no other witness, just Geraint and himself, until the driver of the first Bedford came over the brow of the hill to find the desolate scene.

'There has to be an Inquiry. It was a fatal incident and a vehicle was destroyed. We both have questions to answer.'

The Inquiry was bound to query why Archie drove into the ambush – there were those who suggested proper diligence would have spotted any disturbance on the track – and why Peterson allowed the convoy to split. It was a bad mistake. There was also the question of why they had set off without all the wagons being checked. That was down to the Service Corps corporal. They both knew they should have double-checked.

'The Colonel is of the view that there is fault, but not blame. He has to lay the evidence before Brigade. Hopefully, with us both due out soon and with otherwise good service records, it will be a black mark and that will be an end of it.'

'I didn't see anything on the track because I wasn't looking.' Archie played with a broken bread roll on the starched white tablecloth. 'I was trying to see into the jungle, to see if there were elephants in there. It was my fault. I should have seen something. Geraint was singing; he was singing *Bread of Heaven* and *Men of Harlech*, telling me I ought to know the words. He said they sang *Men of Harlech* at the mission post when the Welsh soldiers were besieged by the Zulus at Rorke's Drift.'

Once Archie had started he couldn't stop. Peterson looked on hoping nobody was listening, sensing Archie needed to have his say.

'I don't even know where the hell Harlech is. Geraint said I would regret my ignorance one day. I told him I was elephant spotting, then the thing exploded.'

'Now shut up and keep that to yourself, Corporal. Remember this is strictly between us – not a word to anyone else. Just say your recollection is a blank.'

Archie looked at him. 'Geraint is dead.'

'Saying any of that won't bring him back, Archie. You aren't to blame. If anyone is, I took the wrong decision. You and I, we'll have to live with it, it happened. It's the bloody Emergency, that's the beginning and the end of it.'

Peterson was flushed; the wine and the naivety of Middlebrook's outburst had got to him. He paused looking at the young artist who applied himself so diligently to his duties. He reached over to Archie putting his hand on his good arm. 'He was a close friend. I understand.'

Peterson told Archie he would not be returning to the battalion. On discharge from BMH Penang, he would cross over to Port Butterworth and take the train to Singapore to stand by for embarkation home.

'It's not that we don't want to see you back, Archie. We're active and your release date comes too soon to get you fit for duty. I'm off, too, at the end of the month. For some reason best known to the top brass they want me to go on a course in Delhi, a joint project with the Indian Army. It means I'll be flying home, which is a welcome change. I can't see any point in my going on the course, I'll be up at Oxford by October, but it's a great chance to see India. You going back to the art school, Archie?'

'I don't know. I didn't pass my exams.'

'Bugger exams, they just get in the way. Do what you want. You're a damn good artist. Remember the picture of the jungle patrol you painted for me? I'm going to have it framed, have it on the wall back home.'

Chapter Three

THE troopship *Empire Georgic* sailed from Singapore in November, bound for the Mersey by way of Suez, expecting to get its burden of returning servicemen and many families home for Christmas.

Archie was fortunate. Classified as a *Non Commissioned Convalescent*, they gave him accommodation on the Junior Officers' deck, a cabin shared with three others that had a porthole. If he'd been fit, he would have been below the waterline in a sweaty ten-berth dormitory.

Singapore had not been the exciting place he and Geraint had long dreamed of visiting. Isolated from the men he'd served alongside, he was adrift amongst all sorts due for return to the UK. Those in charge had no idea what to do with the waiting men; by and large they could do what they wanted so long as they didn't draw attention to themselves.

With no mate to share adventure out on the town, he stayed close to his quarters. On Sundays after church parade at St George's garrison church, he took a stroll into the Botanic Gardens, wandering on his own, looking at plants, admiring the bright colours and dyed batiks worn by the women strolling in family groups, wearing sarong kabaya.

The anticipated visit to The Lotus Bar, their planned coming of age, was never going to happen. He opted for educational classes – French and maths. French because he couldn't speak a word of it, maths because he was always top in arithmetic at school. On a few days he went to the Bukit Timah NAAFI for a change of scene. Once he went to The Globe cinema, they were showing *East of Eden*, starring James Dean. He'd been killed just months earlier in a collision driving his Porsche, dead like Geraint who had talked about Dean as the coming film star.

The cinema was where he saw the woman, and she'd come on to him, he'd seen her before some place – late twenties, large breasts and always in a tight dress. She was with another woman and knew his name.

'Hi, Archie,' she said as the audience turned out.

The next day he was buying envelopes and writing paper at the NAAFI, when she appeared from nowhere, smiling at him.

'Hope you blokes didn't get into trouble.'

'What for?'

'Running starkers round the Padang.'

Then he remembered. She was Sgt Brewer's wife. Her hand, sticky from the heat, was holding his arm and she pressed against him in the packed shop. She smelt of soap, there were beads of sweat on her lip above bright lipstick

'Don't worry, Archie, the silly bugger is still up country, and can stay there for all I care.'

Archie reddened, his chest prickled and his dick pushed his shorts against her as she pressed her pelvis onto him. He couldn't speak, his throat swelled as if a fruit was stuck in it. He stared at her simpering face – she was going to kiss him. He broke away, fleeing from the shop letting his envelopes and paper drop to the floor.

* * * * *

After many long days *Empire Georgic's* voyage ended through grey seas and steady rain. By the time they surged up through the Irish Sea many of the ship's passengers were sick.

Liverpool Pierhead was a sea of confusion. Streams of military in tropical uniform edged through rain, trailing in crocodiles and lugging kit bags down the gangways. They wandered about, getting wet, as disembarkation sergeants tried to match the headcount to buses lined up for the short journey to Lime Street Station.

Out of the busses, harassed NCOs paced round the railway station, allocating uncooperative groups to chartered trains and reserved carriages. The station bars filled, as soldiers made up for lost time, rekindling their taste for warm English beer.

Archie's detail changed at Crewe Junction, travelling on through the night, changed again at New Street, Birmingham, then at Temple Meads in Bristol, each time losing a few men reaching their destinations. Only three soldiers travelled on the last leg to Tonecastle.

It was daylight by the time the train ran over the flat Somerset farmland looking out over the sea, the familiar contrasting shapes of Steep Holm and Flat Holm lying far out in the Bristol Channel. Archie looked further to the Welsh shore, to where he guessed Cardiff might be, to the City with a grieving household, where a son was not coming home for Christmas, not ever coming home. In spring he must go to find Mr and Mrs Hughes. Would they want to see him?

'You OK, Corp?'

Archie turned blinking eyes to the soldier in the far corner. He couldn't hold the man's gaze and turned back to the distant smudge of the Welsh coastline without saying a word.

'Gets you, don't it, seeing Blighty again; couldn't stand the heat, myself.'

Chapter Four

HIS mother was moving about downstairs, going through remembered tasks, as if his two years away had never happened. Dorothy Middlebrook followed her routine every day; the dog out into the garden at half past six, cat fed, the Esse stove's overnight ash riddled, a hod of coke filled the evening before tipped into the stove, the kettle moved onto the hottest plate and a pot of tea set to brew. The Esse burned all year, the heart of the house, the source of hot water, baked bread, roast weekend joints, and on winter days the haven where his dog found heat from floor tiles. Patch was forever in the way.

Archie wasn't stirring. His mother would bring him a mug of tea, but he would feign sleep, leaving the mug untouched, to be retrieved when she came up again after her breakfast. It had been the same every day for the past week. It would be midday before he was downstairs.

Ivy Benson came to clean at Hawthorne Cottage every Tuesday and Friday. This was Tuesday, the day to do the sitting room almost untouched since she'd done it the previous week. Cushions off the sofa and chairs, taken out and beaten, a stiff brush in every corner over the slates, the Ewbank worked back and forth, picking up dust from the carpet. Nothing had changed at Hawthorne Cottage, fixed in its routine. The training depot, the troopship to the tropics, jungle patrols, the ambush and the weeks in hospital had all happened in Archie's life, and on every Tuesday and Friday Ivy had come to Hawthorne Cottage on her bicycle.

He'd rung his mother from Jellalabad Barracks, the depot in Tonecastle, but Dorothy already knew he was back from an earlier call from the stationmaster.

'Mrs Middlebrook?'

'Yes.' Dorothy was always brief. The telephone on a table in the slate floored hallway was no place to dally on drafty winter mornings.

'Mr Sanderfoot here, Tonecastle Station.'

'Hello, George.'

'Dorothy, just to let you know your son is back. The military contingent got in on the 9.22 from Temple Meads, met by Sergeant Hackett, and off to Jellalabad Barracks double quick. I saw Archie was with them. He's a grand lad, your Donald would have been proud of him.'

'Thank you, George.'

'Will you come in by train?'

'No. I'm getting Mr Horsfield to bring me in by taxi. Thank you, George.'

Dorothy put down the phone and wondered again, as she had ever since first hearing of the ambush, how her lad was looking. He'd been a long time in the hospital; the sea voyage would have done him good.

Then Archie rang.

'I'll get the bus home, Mother.'

'Not a bit of it, I've got Mr Horsfield standing by; he'll bring me in to collect you, Son.'

They met at the Jellalabad depot gates. Dorothy was thrilled to see him in uniform, with his corporal's stripes.

'You're home for Christmas, Son.' She hugged him, his military dignity ebbing away.

Mr Horsfield drove through town, along Bridge Street and out past the railway station where Archie had arrived three hours earlier. Since then he'd handed in his tropical kit, had an interview with the base commander, who told him he would be made up to sergeant after six months if he signed TA papers and attended regular parades, and he'd been for his final medical.

'All seems well, Corporal, healed nicely, not too much scarring.' For a while the MO scribbled on his papers then gave him a letter for his doctor.

They drove past familiar shop fronts, unchanged since he was a boy. There were decorations, a few cotton wool snowstorms hanging on strings in shop windows, a jovial Father Christmas stood by the main doors of Harptree & Ellis, the town's department store. Occasional trees stood out on the pavement, but Archie knew that at Hawthorne Cottage they would bring in their potted tree from the garden on Christmas Eve – it never came in a day earlier. He wanted the tree, two seasons older, to be much taller than he remembered it, tall enough to reach the dining room ceiling. Pot bound, it looked no taller.

Ivy and her daughter, Jilly, joined them for Christmas lunch. During Archie's two-year absence, Dorothy had gone to Ivy's cottage to share her Christmas. Mr Benson wasn't at home; he drove a wagon and drank heavily. In the end Ivy had thrown him out and he hadn't come back, not even for Christmas, or for Jilly's birthday.

Jilly was seven years old. She sat quietly, near the fireside, working with a box of colouring pencils Archie had found in a drawer and wrapped for her present.

'What are you drawing, Jilly?'

'Church, and that's the school and the conker tree.'

'Are you going to put the flag up on the church tower? They fly the flag on Christmas Day.'

'What's it like?'

'Didn't you see it when you went to church this morning?'

'You do it, Uncle Archie.'

So he drew a flagpole with the Cross of St George flying from it with wavy edges.'

'Look, Mum. Uncle Archie has drawn a flag blowing in the wind.'

'He's an artist, Jilly.' Ivy watched her daughter tugging at Archie's sleeve. He'd been awkward in the few days he'd been home, saying little. He looked happier kneeling by Jilly's chair. Ivy had wondered if they should come over, it being his first Christmas home.

'Draw me a picture, Uncle Archie.'

He started to draw holly and a Christmas tree then he stopped. 'You put the berries on the holly, Jilly. I'll get some more things.'

'Uncle Archie, why have you got white hair above your ear? You look like Patch.'

'Shush, Jilly. That's not your business.' Ivy glared at her daughter.

'But he has.'

Archie went to his bedroom, fetched out pastels and a quarto drawing board, found good paper and clipped it to the board. Back downstairs, with Jilly looking over his shoulder, he started to cover the sheet. Soon a multitude of greens were winding over the paper, flashes of yellow and pale pinks to pick out orchids high in the jungle trees, while speckled blue sky lit the canopy.

'What're you drawing, Uncle Archie?'

'This is Christmas Day in a country a long way away, where it's very hot and you can sit out in the open in just your shirt and shorts to eat your Christmas lunch.'

Archie kept drawing. Figures sat round a table, dressed in khaki, eating and drinking. The young girl watched, he drew an elephant hiding in the jungle, but she was puzzled as he covered over lines already drawn with more colour, working fast, using his fingers to smudge the pastel lines together. And in the corner there was a fire, bright orange and black smoke building up until it licked out over the whole page, consuming the jungle, burning up through the trees, burning the elephant and all the soldiers, until there was no jungle left, just a black orange sheet of paper on his drawing board.

Jilly started to cry.

Archie, his knuckles clenched, felt sick. He threw down the drawing board and ran out to the garden.

* * * * *

At lunchtime on Boxing Day, Archie walked the two miles to the Star and Garter in Helecombe. Familiar drinkers propping up the bar asked about Malaya, they'd mostly served in the war. Word had gone round about his wounding. He said nothing of the ambush. He drank down a pint of beer and left walking the long way home, hoping to meet no one in the narrow hedge-banked lanes, wishing he hadn't gone to the pub.

Requiem for Private Hughes

Back home he called Patch out for a walk up the lane. Twelve years old she was slow, lagging behind as he walked. Patch had always been Archie's dog. He chose her from a mongrel litter, spent hours with her in the orchard, his nine year old high-pitched commands training her to sit, to come, to go out and to come back. To young Archie she was the best sheepdog in the county, even without sheep.

'Come on old girl.' The tail wagged and the dog quickened her pace for a few strides.

'Dog getting slow, Archie?'

He looked about to see where the voice came from, knowing it was Zed. There was no mistaking his tones. Zebedee Vellacott farmed eighty acres off the lane up from the village road. Archie had spent many childhood hours playing round his yard, climbing the stacks, pushing his hands through pyramids of grain on the barn floor after thrashing time, searching for eggs when hens were laying out in the summer, getting a pecking when he found them nesting in the hedge and took their eggs. Zebedee had taught him to milk a cow, had shown him how to shear a sheep, but his boy's hands couldn't grip the shears and the blades kept crossing.

Zed was a big man in those days, now he looked small as Archie stood at the gate and grasped his hand.

'How's the soldier, then?'

'I'm all the better for seeing you, Zed. There isn't much stock about.'

'Tidn't worth it, sold m'sheep last backend.'

'Still milking?'

'Only eight mind, got them in-by. No labour to help these days, does it all myself, but I'm as slow as that ol' dog o'yourn.'

There had never been a Mrs Vellacott. There was no child to follow Zed on the farm. Archie had heard tell of a woman that lived-in before the war, but she left Zed. She went to work in an aircraft factory, married a Yank and was gone.

Zed could sing. His rich tenor voice would soar away in church and there was many a poem he'd learned by rote as a child and could recite word perfect as he worked the land. It wasn't Zed that folk thought about as much as his eighty acres. Dorothy Middlebrook was sometimes mentioned when Zed was spoken of in the village. Dorothy still grieved for her man killed in the war. Archie's father had been older than Dorothy. He was the stationmaster at Helecombe Halt before the war, always immaculate in his uniform, determined every branch line train would run on time – or he would want to know the reason why.

'Shall I come over at four, see if I can still milk a cow?'

'I could do with a hand, truth be told. It's like a bike, Archie, once learned you don't forget.'

'I'll see you, Zed,' and Archie strode down the lane with a purpose in his step leaving Patch lagging far behind.

* * * * *

The first cow knew an unpractised hand was at work; she turned her head in the stall and flicked her tail to give Archie a sting on his ear. But the comfort of sitting on the squat stool, with his head pressed against her flank, hearing giant gurgling within her vast body and smelling the warm milk fizzing into the pail, soon carried Archie into it. He managed to do three cows to Vellacott's five.

Next morning, to Dorothy's surprise, Archie was up at six. She heard the stove being charged and the dog let out in the dark. He called upstairs.

'I'm off to Greenings Farm to do the milking. I'll be back for breakfast.'

He wasn't back for breakfast, it was more like lunch. That was how it began. Archie came home past noon, covered in dirt with a smile on his face. 'Mum, I'm ravenous.'

'I was going to do you a big breakfast.'

'Just what I want; I've got a pocketful of eggs.' He delved into a bulging pocket and brought out a dozen large brown Maran eggs.

'Get yourself washed up, Son. You can put all that stuff in the wash.'

'I'm going back, Mum. I've promised to do the evening milking.'

'Is Zed paying you?'

'I doubt it,' and they laughed – happiness was payment enough.

'There's a load to do up at Greenings. It's getting beyond old Zed. I'm going to help him lay the long hedge, the one that touches our orchard.'

'And what about going back to art school, Son? They're holding a place for you. I said you'd be in to see Mr Jennings.'

'I can't, Mum. Not yet. Drawing has gone dead in me. I had drawing things at the hospital. It was all rubbish, like on Christmas Day.'

'I know, Son, but you've always wanted to paint, since you were small you wanted to paint.'

'Well, I don't want to paint now. Give it a rest, Mum. I'm not going back to college in January – and that's final.'

Dorothy turned to the stove took the pan from its hook and put it on the heat. Only the low rhythm of Patch snoring in her basket under the stairs broke into the silence.

'I'm sorry, Mum, you do go on about it. If I work for Zed for a while I'll be able to sort things out. Maybe I'll go back to the art school in the summer.'

In the last week of 1955 Archie's days fell into a new pattern; morning milking at Greenings, back to Hawthorne Cottage for a fry-up, then the day under Zed's guidance laying the long hedge. At four o'clock the hedging stopped to get the cows into the parlour for afternoon milking.

Zed laid out his hedging tools; a favoured billhook with his father's initials burned into the handle, kept sharp with an edge keen enough to shave a chin and balancing easily in the hand, a slasher on a long handle, a heavy cross cut saw, with each tooth sharpened by hand, and a newly bought hand saw.

The young man and his old mentor worked the daylight hours along the grown hedge, stripping standing timber, choosing the stands to lay, those to cut out and the best growth to leave standing as occasional hedgerow trees. Archie soon had the hang of it and worked on down the hedge bank. Zed, lacking the strength of his young years, pulled back the cut timber, taking the billhook to pare down the cordwood to set aside for logging. By afternoon milking time they had cleared a good run and had enough brashings to start a fire burning in the field.

It was dimpsy by the time they returned to the hedgerow after milking. Archie watched the old man build a base; he'd brought with him a bag of wood shavings and dry kindling; he let the flames catch before he put the first damp cuttings from the hedgerow onto the fire. Gradually he built it up until twenty minutes later great flames leaped up, sparks jetting skywards. Archie hung back, uncertain, not wanting to be close. Vellacott worked round the fire, pushing the burning boughs into the flames his gnarled hands feeling no pain from the hot wood.

Archie watched the flames. His leg and his arm itched, involuntarily he rubbed his sleeve over the scarred skin, but he kept his eyes on the flaming pile dancing shadows across the field. Zed piled the brashings high until he was satisfied it would burn through the night.

Archie walked home late along the lane, feeling a snap of frost. The smell of burning wood wafting on the breeze caught in his work clothes, on his hands and in his hair.

Dorothy smelt the smoke and worried.

'I need a bath, Mum.'

'There's plenty of water, Son. Fish pie, do you later?'

'Great, I won't be long.'

'Take as long as you like, Son. It won't spoil.' Dorothy relaxed.

1956
Chapter Five

ARCHIE sprawled asleep in the kitchen chair, Patch lying at his feet, as exhausted as her master. There were burrs in the dog's fur, dirt on Archie's boots, which he should have taken off at the back door. His cap was held in his lap, his face weathered under stubble on his chin, while his forehead showed pale under where his cap fitted.

Dorothy looked at her son; what was in his mind? All day he worked in the fields, throwing himself into farm work. Calloused hands, arms scratched by thorns, torn pockets and mud caking his trousers bore witness to his labour. Why wouldn't he talk, tell her about the accident, tell her all he had seen, all that had happened? He clammed up the moment their talk encroached.

There'd been a Christmas card from somebody called James Peterson. Dorothy was proud of the card, a white card embossed with a coat of arms and a ribbon in it holding a picture of an Oxford college. '*Archie,*' it said, '*hope you got back home for Christmas all right. I was late up to Oxford after India, but reckon I've caught up with it all. Very strange here in my cold room after the tropics – it's snowing! Keep in touch, regards, James.*' Archie said James was another national serviceman, he didn't reply to the card.

'Wake up, Son.' Her hand rocked his shoulder. The dog opened an eye, the end of her tail flickered. 'Sleep on, Patch, it's Archie I want moving.'

'Sorry, Mum; I must have dozed off.' He pulled himself forward in the upholstered chair, the fabric of its arms worn thin. 'By the end of the week I'll have that hedge done.'

'Supper's just on ready, steak pie, last of the winter cabbage and potato. I'll mash the spuds.

Requiem for Private Hughes

'Gravy?'

'I wouldn't do you a cooked without gravy, Son. Now, are you going to have a bath? There'll be plenty of hot water.'

'I'll just wash, have a bath later.'

'Is Zed paying you, yet?'

'He will, when we need it and he's got a few bob coming in. Don't fret, Mum. We'll have all the logs for burning next winter, they'll last us an age. I'll use his old horse and butt to bring them round.'

Archie lay in his bath after they'd eaten, hot water stinging his scratched arms and bruised legs. Candlelight flickered shadows onto the walls, casting huge hands onto the ceiling, hands with his fingers stuck up to show a rabbit shadow, then a butterfly with his two hands together, as he lay wondering what his mother would think about his plan. He was doing most of the farm work anyway. The hedge looked good now he'd started banking up. It was hard work and good was coming from it. The pain had gone from his tight muscles under the burn scars. He moved easy now, digging out with the mattock, spading up the earth to re-build the bank where beech, ash and thorn were laid along the hedge bank. More tall timber left standing as hedgerow trees than Zed had wanted; Archie enjoyed trees and a well timbered hedge.

Zed had told him he wanted to ease up with the farm, hinting he had money put by. Archie guessed he had a fair bit squirreled away over the years, even if he hadn't offered him a wage. Mother and he could rent the land from Zed, informal for a year to see if he could do it all, build it back up, get a few sheep, more cows to milk and even buy a tractor. Would Mother want it? Why not? The old man could still live in the farmhouse. It was a mess in there, but he did for himself, never went upstairs, just used the kitchen and the room close by where he had an old press and a bed, which the whole family had slept in when Zed was a child with a brother and a sister – all dead from the 'flu almost forty years back. All in the churchyard, brother, sister, mother and father as Zed laboured on alone at Greenings.

There had been Mario. He'd come over to the farm each week, staying in the house, going back to the prison-of-war camp at Cross

Requiem for Private Hughes

Keys for a night each week for routine's sake. Archie had been told he mustn't talk to Mario; he was an enemy, a prisoner of war. They said he couldn't speak much English; Archie knew he could speak quite a few words. He was a sad man missing his own children far away; he got few letters in the eighteen months he worked on Zed's farm. Mario was happiest out in the fields and when milking cows; he'd never wanted to be a soldier.

When he was told Archie's father had been killed in Italy he painted a picture on cardboard cut from a box, a scene of his native countryside with an angel praying, and he left it on the doorstep for Dorothy, with a letter written in Italian. She never had the letter translated; kept it pushed into the frame she found for the picture to hang over the big bed she'd shared with her stationmaster husband before he went off to fight. Dorothy missed Mario when he went back to Italy.

The bath water had grown cold. Archie lay looking down his torso, flexing the muscling of his stomach. Despite weeks in hospital he was as fit as he ever had been, probably ever would be, unless they got the farm. His hand moved down to his dick lying limp in the tepid water, fiddling with the waking flesh and wishing he had done it. They'd had their plan, Geraint and himself, to get to Singapore before they embarked for home, have a few pints then go for it with the girls at the bar. It was bloody ridiculous to be twenty, twenty years and almost six months, and still to be a virgin.

Then he remembered Brewer's wife who'd come on to him in Singapore. Silly sod, he thought shivering from the cold of the bathwater, it was there on a plate for you, an older woman to teach you how, and you ran away, you idiot. No bloody good having it erect like a pikestaff now, it's too late.

* * * * *

The trodden ground had grown muddy with February's rain, but now the footing was hard from a week of frost. Archie lugged cord timber to the saw table. Zed had set up the Lister engine, its single cylinder thumping a rhythm spinning its flywheel, the belt bouncing as it drove the circular saw; the rattling scream of the cut reducing the timber to logs in seconds. Overnight frost in the valley had built up crystal strands in the grass, cold on idle feet, but Archie worked in his shirtsleeves, sweat running from his head to dribble into his shirt as he handled the timber. Later he loaded the butt, the single axle farm cart built in the village forty years before and still as good as the day it was delivered, only a couple of floor boards replaced. He threw the logs from the ground as Zed's old cross-bred horse chomped oats from his nose-bag. When he'd finished each load, the horse followed him across the field and out into the lane, the four-foot-high, metal-tyred wooden wheels trundling easily over the hard ground, the horse's feathered feet thumping on the lane as the cart rumbled behind.

He tipped the logs at Hawthorne Cottage, the sweetly balanced butt rotating on its axle thick as a railway sleeper. After the last journey, Archie took an axe and split the widest logs, then built a store piled high as his shoulders under the lean-to against the outhouse; fuel for many good fires next winter.

* * * * *

Dorothy posted her letter without telling Archie. Maggie might not come down to Somerset. There was a letter back from her god-daughter within the week.

7B, Queen's Gate Terrace
London, SW7
Phone: KEN 401

Dear Aunt Dorothy,
Super to get your letter. London has been wretched this winter, fog before Christmas smelling of soot and making everything filthy, and for weeks we've had rain. I get wet every day going to work and have to sit at my typewriter in damp clothes. It's horrible.

Yes, I would love to come down to see you and grown up Archie back from his adventures. I loved it when I came to Hawthorne Cottage in the summer after the war and we picked bilberries up on the hills.

I have a week of holiday in April, (3rd – 10th) and no plans, can I come then?

Love, Maggie.

Dorothy put her reply in the post and told Archie about their visitor.

'And you make sure you shave every day when she's here, Archie Middlebrook. I don't want you looking like a ragamuffin all the time. And take time away from the farm. You'll need to show Maggie around.'

He took the bus into Tonecastle. Dorothy made him wear his sports jacket, given him to go to college when he was seventeen. He thought it would split at its seams. She said he must wear a jacket; Maggie was from London and would be smartly dressed. As the bus laboured into town along the winding road behind a cattle truck – it was market day – he hoped he had enough money to get a taxi back, but could only find sixteen shillings and nine pence in his pockets. A taxi would be more for twelve miles and back.

He was half an hour early for her train from Paddington. He paced along the platform, automatically picking up a marching step and counting strides. Four hundred and fifty-nine, end to end, one of the longest platforms on the Great Western. He stood and watched the clock hand creeping nearer to time. He could just make out the minute hand moving.

'I thought it was you, Archie, when I saw you pacing out the platform. Back from Malaya, then?' The man stood erect, smart in his stationmaster's uniform. He called sometimes at Hawthorne Cottage, an old friend of his father's.

'Hello, Mr Sanderfoot. Yes, home for four months now.'

'And Mrs Middlebrook, is she well?'

'Yes, thank you.'

'And you back at art school?'

'Thinking about it, I'm working on Mr Vellacott's farm at present.'

'Railway is a good job, Archie. We may be nationalised now, but it's still the Great Western at heart. It was in your father's day and it is now.'

Why did everyone want to know what he was going to do? All except old Zed, he was just pleased to have Archie working on the farm.

'Meeting the London train?'

'Yes, my mother's goddaughter, don't know how I'll recognise her. I haven't seen her since we were children.'

Mr Sanderfoot looked at his watch pulled from a waistcoat pocket. 'Three more minutes, it'll be on the dot.' Then with hardly a pause he called over to a man in uniform with a trolley: 'Look lively, Lyons, there'll be folk wanting porters off the London train.'

As the stationmaster had said, the train pulled in 'on the dot'.

'Look at that, Archie, 6000 King Class, that's a true steam locomotive, thirty years good service and more to come. I'll retire the day they go.' Archie had never been that keen, despite his father's employment.

Mr Sanderfoot made his way along the platform. Archie stood nervously at the head of the stairway. He had no idea what Maggie looked like, for certain she wouldn't be like the growing girl who had filled their cottage with laughter all those years ago, three years older than Archie, a foot taller and further on in life, she had stuffed two tennis balls into her already swelling vest and told Archie she was a movie star. He'd blushed and run into the garden.

Passengers were getting down, doors slamming back, people were greeting travellers, taking bags, there was a shout of 'porter' and the man Lyons set off up the platform with his trolley.

Mr Sanderfoot spoke with the guard, a whistle blew, the locomotive woke from its brief pause with a powerful shunt of billowing steam; the train edged on into its westward journey. The stationmaster addressed a young woman with a large case. She was wearing jeans, mosquito boots and a duffle coat.

'Are you being met by Mr Middlebrook, madam?'

'That's right.'

'This way please, madam.' He picked up her case, setting off along the platform. 'Here's your guest, Archie.'

'Wow, Archie, can it really be you?' Maggie stood wide-eyed.

'Hello, Maggie. This is Mr Sanderfoot, the stationmaster.'

'You people certainly know how to greet a girl in Somerset.'

Archie stared at his mother's goddaughter. Fresh faced, her hair windblown, not dressed at all how his mother had predicted. She reached up and kissed Archie on his lips hugging him tight in her embrace; her scent wafted on the air.

Archie carried her case out of the station and mumbled about getting the bus; a few passengers from the train were already waiting at the signboard. Two taxis were waiting, a few cars moved away. For a moment there was an awkward pause.

'Let's take a cab, Archie. I'll pay since you've all given me such a wonderful welcome.'

Dorothy Middlebrook was picking primroses to put in Maggie's bedroom when they got back earlier than expected. The grown-up Maggie – much her own height and not in the London clothes she'd anticipated – had the look of her mother, Dorothy's school friend, Rita. She was the one who had the eye of the village boys, until her parents moved to the Midlands. There had been letters as Rita worked her way through teacher training to emerge with a good job, and a baby.

For her first few years, Maggie was brought up by her grandmother while Rita worked, then did something secret through the war. Dorothy had been surprised when Rita wrote asking her to be a godmother to the ten year old; she couldn't get to the christening with the war time travel restrictions.

She first saw Maggie when Rita brought her to Somerset after the war on her way to her honeymoon in Cornwall; the newlyweds had served together in security operations.

Now here she was, a London girl, elegant even in casual clothes with her mother's smile reminding Dorothy of schooldays.

Dorothy hurried to get tea things ready – the best china, the silver teapot, cake, scones, raspberry jam and clotted cream from Greenings Farm's milk.

Requiem for Private Hughes

Maggie unpacked, and responding to her godmother's lead she changed into a skirt and jersey and remembered to wear the necklace Dorothy sent her for her twenty-first birthday, to show it wasn't forgotten.

Archie, feeling spare, wandered down to the orchard, where the apple blossom was breaking. Maggie watched from the bedroom window fascinated at the exciting young man who'd grown from the timid boy she'd had to put up with on her last visit.

'Archie is gorgeous, Aunt Dorothy. He was a pip-squeak when I last saw him; he's quite a dish now. Can I call you Aunt?'

'Call me Dorothy, dear.'

'I know you aren't actually an aunt, but I think of you as one: one of my three aunts. The others are only just aunts, they're my step-father's sisters, one lives in America, the other in France. I don't ever see them.

'Archie is a fine lad, but he's shy. He's finding it hard to settle down now he's back.'

'I wondered. He didn't say much in the taxi. He was in Malaya, wasn't he? I sometimes wish girls did national service. I went to France on an exchange from school, but that's the only travel I've ever done, and I was sick on the boat both ways. It wasn't much fun.'

'Archie won't talk about it; he was wounded in an ambush. Be careful what you ask him.'

As soon as tea was finished Archie was off to do the evening milking.

'Can't you leave it to Zed today? He can't always have you at his beck and call.'

'I said I would do it.'

'What about Maggie? She's our guest.'

Maggie watched as Archie said nothing, the small boy of years ago now a strapping farm boy. He was uncomfortable, uneasy in her company. You'd think he was used to female company, there being no other male in the household.

'I promised him. I'll come straight back. I'll just do the milking.'

Archie wanted to be away, to get out of his uncomfortable clothes.

'I'm fine, Dorothy. All I want to do is relax. Can we look round the garden later? I bet you grow your own vegetables.' Maggie smiled.

Archie was soon into his rough clothes and off to Greenings. He asked on the way out if Maggie would like to see the cows. She smiled the way Dorothy remembered her mother smiling when asked to do something not uppermost in her mind.

'Tomorrow, perhaps, Archie.'

'I'm up at six for the morning milking.'

'Oh, good heavens, I can't be up for that, Archie. That's worse than getting up for work. I'm on holiday; can I come in the afternoon?'

Archie felt good as he ran up the lane. Tomorrow he would show Maggie how to milk a cow. He would give the parlour a full hose down after morning milking.

Chapter Six

BACON smells wafted upstairs as Maggie lay in her bath, reminding her of schooldays rush to be downstairs to eat a full breakfast – her mother never let her leave the house without one – then racing to be at school before the assembly bell.

Maggie had been downstairs, bleary-eyed in pink flowered pyjamas and heeled slippers.

'Can I have a bath, Dorothy?'

'I'll just go and see Archie left it clean last night.'

'I can do that. I just wondered about the water.'

'There'll be plenty, dear. Did you sleep all right?'

'I was cold. Can I have another blanket for tonight?'

'I can give you a hot bottle, if you want. There's plenty on the shelf.'

Maggie remembered the earthenware bottles; as a child she had lain in bed all night with a wet patch. She looked at the kitchen shelf lined with the bottles with their doubtful tops.

'A blanket will do fine.'

'Go and have your bath, dear, then it'll be breakfast. Archie should be back soon.

Maggie was down again warm at last from her deep bath, dressed in slacks and a sweater which she thought right for the country. She ate toast and jam. Dorothy urged her to have butter and a fry-up. Ivy Benson made the butter at home, always bringing a wedge of it over to Hawthorne Cottage – golden yellow, salty and delicious with toast.

They were on their second pot of tea by the time Archie got back. There was a roar and a spluttering engine as he drove into the yard, parking outside the kitchen window, his hands and face streaked with oil.

'Did you know Zed still had his car, Mum?'

'Where did you find it?'

'He started talking about it, said he'd been tinkering with it; it needed two of us to start it. And it's mine.'

'You've borrowed it?'

'No, he's given it – it's mine to keep. He hasn't paid me, now he has. It needs things doing. I've been over to Hake's. They had a quick check, put in a new battery. Where shall we go today?

'What is the car, Archie?' Maggie looked out through the window at the old fashioned saloon.

'Morris, 1936, almost the same age as me. It's been on blocks for years; it hasn't been far, not five thousand miles yet.

'In twenty years?'

'Been in a shed most of it; he's looked after it.'

'Your breakfast will be frazelled up.'

Dorothy knew the car. The woman who'd been at Greenings before she went away to the aircraft factory, had persuaded Zed he should have a car, but he never took to it. The woman shipped off to the States and the car stayed on its blocks after the war. 'Get yourself cleaned up, Archie.'

'Don't you want to come out and see it?'

* * * * *

Archie got up speed along the Esplanade at Northhill. Maggie shouted that a policeman was watching. Archie slowed the car and they parked up opposite the New Pier entrance.

'It must have done more than thirty-five,' said Archie, knocking the speedometer dial on the wooden dashboard. 'It seemed much faster – the needle must have stuck.'

Dorothy hadn't come with them, in truth there was not a lot of room. Maggie was keen, as he'd promised to let her drive some of the way. There were hardly any cars on the Esplanade, the longest flat straight Archie could think of close to home.

Nor'hill, as locals called it, was carved out in foot high stone letters on the façade of the Town Hall in full as 'Northhill by the

Sea', spelt with the double 'h'. Over the years there had been impassioned arguments amongst local scholars that it should be hyphenated: 'Northhill-by-the-Sea', and by others that Nor'hill was the acceptable abbreviation. Whatever its name might be, the town looked out from the West Somerset coast across the Bristol Channel to the smoking chimneys of the South Wales's steel plants.

Northhill had enjoyed a late Victorian elegance. When the railway reached the sea it brought adventurous middle-class visitors from the industrial Midlands for summer holidays. Rich manufacturers built turreted Balmoral look-a-likes on land at the top of the hill above the town, from which the cliffs dropped into the sea. The town's greatest importance had been centuries earlier, when the small harbour had been a staging post for Cromwell's forces to take ship to Ireland. Its importance as a sea port waned with the years and even its once busy fish dock held fewer boats as each generation passed. It was in a limbo, with holiday makers preferring the milder climate of the south Devon and Cornish coasts, and the railway bringing fewer passengers every year.

Archie decided over breakfast that Northhill Esplanade was the place to give his new-found transport its head. At top speed it had taken a distance to brake the car to proper speed after Maggie shouted out the constabulary were watching.

Maggie looked over at the pier, which stepped on steel legs over the sand to the low-tide sea. The pier still rejoiced under its early billing of 'The New Pier' six decades after it was named to celebrate Queen Victoria's Golden Jubilee. Its life reflected the rise and fall of Northhill's fortunes. Archie was surprised to find it open at all in April. He bought entrance tickets, regretting the two half crowns it cost him, which wouldn't contribute to the lunch he planned for Maggie.

'Race you to the far end,' Maggie was off, running so fast they were almost at the end of the pier before he caught her up, grabbing her to stop her falling as she ducked to evade him. She wriggled round then relaxed against him. He was panting from the sudden exertion.

'You're meant to be fit, farmer lad.'

'I was paying the man, and you're out of breath, too.' She was and her blue eyes were laughing with a dare in her stare.

'Come on, Archie. What's in here?' She broke free and went into the white paint-peeled wooden hall close by. It smelt of cheap scrubbed floor boards. There were electric lights directing them past unmanned booths, waiting for next weekend's visitors. A man was taking down shutters to reveal murky pock-marked ringed targets, where airgun pellets had connected. A woman was busy with a brush and turning on lights.

'Have a go, Archie.'

'You first.'

'I don't know how to do it.'

Archie stood close behind her, pulled the butt of the air rifle into her shoulder, eased her head to aim along the sights, told her to breathe steadily and gently squeeze the trigger. The end of the barrel flipped up and the pellet lodged in the woodwork, away from the target. They broke the gun, his hand grasping hers to lever the air charge for the next pellet.

'Nearly. Did you see it Archie?'

'Close, you'll hit it with the next shot.'

He stood back, the air rifle waved and there was a ping as the pellet clipped a light shade.

'Oops, sorry.' She looked at the attendant. 'You do it Archie.'

With the next five pellets he knocked down the five standing targets.

'Let me try again, Archie.'

The attendant stood the targets back up and Maggie took aim. With a pleasing thud a target fell; the remaining pellets hit the back board.

'At least I got one.' She took his hand. He chose a wooden clothes peg doll from the prizes and gave it to her.

'It can be a mascot for the car, Archie. Let's see what else is open.'

A sharp wind greeted them as they came out of the amusement hall perched on the end of the pier. They had wandered through a Hall of Mirrors, had witnessed *What the Butler Saw*, its worn grey photos flickering with a hint of undergarments from years past.

Maggie had put her hand on a machine plate that rippled small rods along her palm to tell her fortune, but she didn't let Archie see what it said. And he won her a Bakelite necklace with a grinning pixie hanging from it, for a direct hit on the coconut shy. Maggie shivered in the breeze as he snapped the clasp of the trophy round her neck.

Gulls hung on the wind waiting to see if they had sandwiches, then banked away to swoop on to the rubbish floating on the waves beneath the pier.

Maggie looked around. 'There must be something exciting to do here.'

'There's a ghost train; it's a bit pathetic.'

'Where?'

Maggie squeezed as close as she could to Archie, as they set off alone into the ghost train tunnel and once in the darkness she twisted round, hugged and kissed him.

'What happened to you in there, Archie Middlebrook? You've got lipstick on your cheek and I swear you're blushing.' He wiped his hand across his face. 'Did a ghost kiss you?'

'Yes, and it told me to pass it on,' he pulled her close.

'You'll let me drive the car, won't you?'

'Have you got a licence?'

'No, but I've driven my stepfather's car.'

* * * * *

For milking that afternoon Maggie wore one of his old army shirts over her sweater as an overall and Dorothy's rubber boots. Together they gave the milking parlour another hose down before they called in the cows. The first four ageing beasts trudged into their customary stalls, leaving the juniors to wait their turn. Each beast looked at Maggie as she stood waiting where Archie had told her to stand. He clipped tethers round their necks, giving each beast a scratching on its forehead and a squeeze of its ear. He brought a bucket and sponge round to rinse off their tails and back ends before getting the warm water he'd brought from the farmhouse to clean off their udders and teats.

Requiem for Private Hughes

Maggie watched in the dull light, Archie crouched on a three legged stool, a milking pail held between his knees, working the teats in tandem. Dulcie, as he called the lead cow, munched from the manger of hay, letting down her milk, soon frothing in the pale. Archie, his cheek pressed against the cow's round belly, smiled at Maggie as he chatted to the beast.

'I'm just easing it down. You don't pull at it, she'll let it flow if she wants, and keep talking to her. Have a chat with Peggy, this next one. Then you can have a try with her. She's easy to handle, but she has to know you.'

Archie started her then Maggie tried, her small hands soon aching from easing the big teats. She thrilled at the drill of the milk into the pail and was encouraged by the close hug of Archie reaching round to guide her hands, trying to keep her aim true to the pail. Peggy's huge belly rumbled as Maggie pressed her head against it, and what seemed like gallons of gas rolled through the cow's inner workings, then just as they were finished, she arched her back. Archie pulled away the milk as her tail lifted and she let fly.

'Oh, no. Archie you should have warned me,' Maggie turned, surprise in her eyes, then burst into giggles.

When all was done, the milk put through the cooler and into the churns trundled out to wait overnight on the lane-side collection stand, the parlour hosed down again and the cows back out into the pasture, Maggie and Archie walked to Hawthorne Cottage their arms linked happy with their day.

'Six o'clock in the morning and its all to do again.'

'I'll be in my bed, Archie. But I did get some milk, didn't I?'

'You did; some of it in the bucket, too.'

'Don't be mean.'

'Are your hands all right?'

'They're sore.'

'You got plenty of milk, and nearly a lot else.'

'You're rotten, Archie Middlebrook. You knew she was going to do that.'

'We all learn the hard way.'

Requiem for Private Hughes

'Not funny. And where was Mr Vellacott? I never saw him.'

'He was in the house. Truth is I don't think he's too well. I'd better get Mum or Ivy round to see him. He always refuses the doctor.'

* * * * *

Someone was calling. A small voice, miles away, urging, calling; someone was shaking his shoulder. It couldn't be the nurse, he'd taken his tablets, and it was night time, they never gave tablets in the middle of the night. A dark black, cold night. How could it be cold? The ceiling fan was turning for the tropical heat?

'Archie, can you hear me? Please wake up, Archie'

'Maggie? What is it?'

'Archie, I've been trying to find a blanket, or a spare eiderdown. I'm frozen, I can't sleep. I'm sorry, I didn't want to wake you, but I'm freezing.'

He sat up, the bedclothes falling from his naked shoulders, and looked at the luminous clock. It was just after three o'clock. A cold hand was on his shoulder.

'Hell, you are cold. Get in here, Maggie; warm yourself, I'll go and find something for you.'

'Where's the light switch, Archie.'

'No, don't turn it on. I know where things are.'

As she slipped into his bed, wearing her pyjamas and her thickest sweater, she felt his hot, naked body get out into the cold room. Maggie lay under the warm covers and shivered. She heard Archie open a cupboard on the landing. She could still hear snoring from Dorothy's room. Then he was back by the bed, even in the darkness she could sense him there, could smell him beside the bed and feel his glow.

'Here you are.'

'Can I stay here a bit, till I get warm?'

He was silent, she heard him pull the blanket round his shoulders.

'I can't get warm on my own, Archie.'

She reached out and her hand touched his thigh – muscled, warm and silky. Then his hand was on hers, a rough farmer's hand, yet one that could delicately flow milk to a pail. She held his hand and pulled him back into his own bed.

'God, your feet are like ice blocks.' Archie got out again, pulled open a drawer of his bedroom chest and was back at the bed with thick woollen socks. 'Put these on,' and he held her feet, slipping the scratchy army wool over her ice cold toes.

They lay still, hugging each other, till she stopped shivering and drifted into sleep. Archie lay near to heaven – Maggie's body, soft in his arms, clad in her wrappings, snug against him.

Archie didn't sleep through those small hours, willing every minute to stretch out into hours, each brief hour to be a day, wanting to emboss every breath she made on his memory to dream of on future nights. His mother always slept heavily, but he knew he would have to be up and off to the farm before she was moving about.

Maggie stretched in his embrace. Warm now, her socked feet pushed down the bed against him, her body turned to nestle her back against him. Her drowsy hand held his, guiding it under her sweater and pyjamas to hold the softness of her breast, cupping his hand, her nipple hardening against his fingers. Her breathing settled again, her back pressed into him, there was a tingling in his stomach and he hardened against her, but she slept and he hardly dared to breathe.

Early light mingled with the dark. Archie, his face buried in a soft sea of her curls, listened for his mother in her room down the corridor. He'd slept late for morning milking. He slipped from the bed, feeling for his clothes in the grey light.

'My gorgeous white knight, I swear you saved my life.'

Archie didn't mind her watching as he slipped on his farm clothes. 'Keep warm,' he whispered, kissed her forehead and crept downstairs without a sound.

The dog was dozing, just the tip of her tail knocking against the wainscot beside her rug, he bent and stroked her head.

'Don't say a word, old Patch, it's our secret.'

Requiem for Private Hughes

The latch on the back door gave its familiar clunk as he went out; he set off up the lane to Greenings with a jaunty step.

It was as good as having done it - he had slept with a woman.

Dew glittered in the last of the moonlight on spiders' webs along the hedgerow, and the cows left trails through the damp grass as they came to wait his summons to the parlour, feet squelching deep into the mud of the gateway. The eastern horizon glowed pink, reflecting off morning clouds. Pink in the morning, a warning for shepherds, was it a warning to cowherds, an admonishment to lovers? He'd said under his breath: a 'lover'. He was a lover, and why should there be any warning? There could be nothing to fear for him, fresh from his lover's bed.

The cows were wet from the grass, but warm as he leant against their thick flanks, drilling the milk into the pail, hearing the note change as it foamed deeper. He hoped Zed wouldn't come over from the house too soon; he wanted to be alone with these contented beasts.

Could he persuade Maggie to come again to his bed tonight? Would she want to be with him again? Nothing had happened, but had she wanted him to take her? Did she think him a poor thing clutching her all night? She said he had saved her from the cold, it must have been what she wanted. Now he wanted more; he had to make love to her. How could they? Not in the house with his mother only a room away, however well she slept.

They would have to drive somewhere. He had the car, they could go up to the moor to find a woodland, get a blanket and a groundsheet to put in the car, and he had that packet of French Letters, a packet of three, well only two as he had put one on for practice. They had been in his wash-bag for months, available from the NAAFI on medical advice in the hope of keeping young soldiers one step away from problems when they went on leave in Singapore.

He and Geraint had made the first of their preparations in their plan to 'do it' by getting the Frenchies at the NAAFI. Strange how they were called 'French'. Those who knew such things said Frenchmen called them 'Capeau Anglais'. He'd kept them for a long time, and in the heat of the tropics. Did they go off? Archie thought he ought to check when he got home.

That was it; he would suggest they both went out for a drive into the country. Surely there wasn't going to be only one chance. Had he blown it? Had she done it before?

Maggie lived in London in a flat with other girls, so they must have boyfriends. He guessed she had done it. But did she have a boyfriend? Was it just that she was cold and wanted to get warm? She had put his hand on her breast, but was she asleep, did she think it was her boyfriend who was holding her? Did she sleep with her boyfriend in London?

'You doing all right, boy?'

'How you feeling this morning, Zed?'

'Not bad, soldier boy. Joints is better with the sunshine.'

'You should see the doctor. He'll give you something to ease the pain.'

'Don't want to go bothering him, and it will cost.'

'I keep telling you, Zed, it's free with the National Health, it won't cost you anything. Mum will take you if you want someone with you, and I can drive you in the car. It went a treat, Zed. You should have seen us down the Esplanade, it must have been forty, even more.'

'That with your lady friend.'

'She had a go at the milking last night; she did well. She wants to meet you.'

'Rita's girl?'

'Did you know her mum?'

'Lived over Ralph's Cross. Moved away sudden, they did.'

When Archie reached home the two women had planned the day and were eating breakfast. Maggie had been persuaded to have bacon and egg eating it on toast, foregoing the fried bread Dorothy offered her. Archie sat down and looked across at Maggie; there was a bloom on her face; she was happy.

'Dorothy and I are going into town. I'm trying to persuade her to buy an electric blanket for the spare bed.'

Requiem for Private Hughes

'It sounds dangerous to me.' Dorothy was not convinced. 'I'll get a new eiderdown. I'm sorry you were cold again, dear.'

'Archie saved me.'

His heart missed a beat; she would never say, surely not?'

'I put another blanket on your bed, dear.'

'Archie got me another one, and a pair of his army socks. Then I was fine. Electric blankets are quite safe, I promise. I've got one at my flat, just to warm the bed up. Once it's warm I turn it off.'

'I thought we might go for a drive, onto the moors. It's a fine day and you can see for miles,' said Archie.

'You can drive us to Tonecastle, Archie. I'll sit in the back and your mum can go in the front.'

There was going to be no moorland drive.

'If you promise to take it slow, Archie. I'd as soon use the bus.'

'No. I'll take you, Mum.'

'Can you drive, Dorothy?' asked Maggie.

'I've got a licence, but not that I can drive.'

'Did you pass a test?'

'Not in my day.'

'I drove the car yesterday, but Archie had to help me with the gears.'

'You two be careful, mind, or that car will get us all into trouble.'

'I might buy a decent jacket. I could do with one that fits.' Archie thought he had better make the most of a bad job.

'I'll come with you.' Maggie wanted to get him up to date. 'I could help you choose.'

Archie tried to read her signal. She was warm, but she wasn't leading him. She was going home the day after tomorrow. He would have to take her out to the moors before then.

'Thanks.'

In the end, both women were with him at Harptree & Ellis, the only place he had ever been to buy clothes. They had been to the bedding department, leaving an eiderdown to pick up on their way out – and Maggie had bought herself a rubber hot water bottle with a fabric cover, saying she needed a new one at home – they'd paused for coffee on the third floor and were now in the men's wear department. Archie was glad Maggie was there.

His mother favoured a sombre cloth, but Maggie picked out a louder check with leather ball buttons, two slits at the back in a military cut. It was Harris Tweed and cost more than he'd expected, but with Maggie's approval he was happy to buy it.

She ran her hands over his shoulders, her fingers feeling the cloth and the set of his shoulders. Dorothy watched her goddaughter. She'd wanted her to be the watershed to help her son, to lift him from his ruminating; now she felt uneasy. Maggie lived a different lifestyle from their quiet life in the country.

That night, Archie was wakeful, sleep coming only in restless snatches. He listened, but there was no sound from Maggie's room, no soft tread, no click from her door latch. She was probably cocooned in her sweater and his army socks, snug under the new eiderdown and clutching her hot water bottle.

However they were going to be together all next day. Archie had forgotten the Women's Institute outing to Wells Cathedral Choir Festival; it'd been planned for weeks. Dorothy was going with Ivy and the charabanc was due to pick her up at the end of the lane at eleven. At supper Dorothy asked Maggie if she wanted to come with her to Wells, Archie held his breath. He'd promised not to linger at the farm after milking, suggesting they could drive out and see the moors. And she'd agreed.

Archie lay awake planning which road to take, worrying about the hills, wondering whether the car would be able to cope. The road was steep up over Elworthy.

It was early, still dark, he needn't go to Greenings for another hour, but he got out of bed. He was tempted for a moment to open Maggie's door, but went downstairs to the kitchen. The dog opened an eye, wagged her tail a few beats and went back to her dozing.

Chapter Seven

DOROTHY, dressed in her best tweed skirt, brogues, lisle stockings and a pale blue twin set under her usual winter coat and this year's red hat – her hats were always red – had walked down the lane with her son ten minutes early for the charabanc; the coach with Ivy amongst those already on board was five minutes late. With no shelter at the main road she and Archie got wet. He'd suggested they drive down, even if it was only half a mile from Hawthorne Cottage, but she would have none of it. So they'd walked together, as they had many times in years gone by for the bus to town, admiring the primroses and catkins hanging in the hedgerow.

Archie walked back along the lane in a light drizzle. Maggie, wisely, had stayed behind in the warmth of the kitchen.

'I told you to take an umbrella.'

'It's broken. Anyway country folk aren't afraid of a drop of rain.'

'Tell me about your father, Archie.' A smile hovering on Maggie's lips, answering the questioning look he gave her. 'I was looking at the wedding photo in Dorothy's bedroom.'

'Why did you go in there?'

'Being nosey.' She held his gaze. 'Do you mind?'

'No.' But he wondered why she had gone into his mother's bedroom; he seldom did.

'Do you remember your father?'

'I remember him... not well.' Archie recalled their last day together; it had rained that day. They'd laid out his father's kit round the border of the pattered rug in his parents' bedroom in the stationmaster's house at Helecombe Halt. It had been his job to pick up the army clothes, the shirts, trousers and wash things as his father called them out to put into his kitbag. It was a happy morning, even though his father was going off on the afternoon train. It never crossed his six year old mind that his father wouldn't come back. It was what they all knew; fathers went away.

At the end a parcel was delivered to Hawthorne Cottage, a few personal possessions, strangely his shaving kit, photographs of the three of them standing on the station the day that royalty had passed through the halt, and his watch.

From the depths of the armchair Maggie looked intently at the tall farming boy. 'You have many of his looks, Archie.'

'He always wore uniform; for his wedding he wore his stationmaster's uniform.'

'I wondered what he was wearing. Your mum looked happy; he must have been quite a catch for her.'

'He was smart, freshly cleaned boots, and he bothered about his official railwayman's hat. He kept it in his station office where it had to be brushed every day after he arrived. He wore a bowler for the short walk from the house. I wasn't allowed to touch his hat when I was there.'

'Poor Archie, he sounds very strict.'

'I often went down to see the trains.'

'Is it far away, the station?'

'Three miles by the road; it isn't a station any more. It's derelict. The trains still go through on the branch line to Northhill; they say the line will close next year.'

'Have you got other pictures of him?'

Questions about his father, Donald, the decorated war hero, made him uneasy. A destroyed scout car with its driver killed – that was the only memento of his army service. He wanted Maggie to stop talking about his father. Archie wanted to move the day on, this last day of her stay. They had been so close, and she can't go back to London with nothing more happening.

'Have you had coffee, Maggie?'

'Yes.' She gave him an unrelenting look. 'You're lucky, Archie. You knew your father; you can remember him. I know nothing about my father.'

'You've got a stepfather.'

'It's not the same.'

'You don't know anything about your real father. Your mum must...'

'She won't talk about him. When I press her she says it was horrible, that I'm selfish to want to know about him. I will find out one day.'

'I'm sorry, Maggie. I... I thought we might go out for a drive in the car.'

'It's a horrible day, Archie. Let's just stay here.'

'It's stopped raining.' Archie stood at the kitchen sink looking at his car, standing ready in the yard. Rain had splashed over its polished paintwork; he'd cleaned it twice already. Everything was worked out in his mind. Take Maggie for a drive, then a walk in the woods.

'Do you remember the games we played in the summerhouse when I stayed here that summer? It was my house and you had to be the delivery man?'

He remembered. Maggie had bossed him around. It always had to be her game they played. He was glad when she went away and he could be on his own again.

'Is the summerhouse still there?'

'Yes. I used it as a studio to paint in when I was at art school, before I did national service.'

'Do you still paint?'

'Not much.'

'Why don't you do a picture of me? I'll model for you.'

'I'm not much cop at portraits.' His mind screamed at him; say yes! Did she mean she would take her clothes off? The life models at college were nude; did she mean that?

'I'm best at painting landscapes.' Of all the stupid things to say.

Maggie came over and put her arms round his neck, looking into his eyes. 'Some people think a woman's body is a landscape, Archie Middlebrook. Let's go to the summerhouse.'

He had to get to his bedroom, get his long held pack, the packet of three which now had one missing.

Requiem for Private Hughes

From the front of Hawthorne Cottage the lawn sloped gently to a long herbaceous border, Dorothy's year-round floral workshop. She spent hours working the border in all seasons. Carefully staked plants were already putting on their first growth for summer; the bare winter border would transform itself in a few weeks into a tall riot of greens, picked out with flowering colours. At the far end of the border was the wooden summerhouse, with a pitched shingle roof and large glazed double doors off a small veranda.

It had been Donald's great joy, bought from a house sale soon after they married, taken down and rebuilt at Hawthorne Cottage with a group of friends. They'd come over from the stationmaster's house to the cottage on summer days bringing a picnic. The whole structure was set on a large iron ground wheel, which in its heyday had let it be turned by a winding mechanism to face the travelling sun through the day. Now the clinker-board cladding was warping in the weather; the turning gear was stuck unused for years, and there was a leak in one corner of its roof.

Maggie shivered. 'Grief, it's cold in here.'

'There's a paraffin stove, it soon warms the place through.' Archie pushed aside the clutter in the summerhouse to pull the stove into the centre of the floor, ruffling the old patterned carpet put out from the house years back. He looked for matches and had to strike three before he found a dry one.

Tennis racquets with broken strings, a cricket bat with tape round its blade and a broken sunshade, were stacked together in a corner. Against the back wall there was a sofa, a once elegant Edwardian design where you could release a catch so that one of its end arms dropped down.

'It's just as it was when I stayed. Have you got your drawing things here, Archie?'

'There's some in the cupboard, or there should be.'

'Thank God, it's warming up. Do you want me to take my clothes off?' Maggie burst out laughing as Archie tried to speak. 'Archie, you may have been a gallant soldier away fighting wars for Queen and Country, or whatever you were away doing, but you don't know anything about girls, do you?'

The windows of the summerhouse were steaming over; Maggie took both his hands in hers, looked at his bright red face then kissed his lips. 'I'm going to have to teach you, aren't I?'

There was panic in his mind. All he could think of was the packet of two, in his pocket. Maggie put her arms round his neck and pressed against him. His stomach muscles tightened and from the pit of his belly he grew hard.

'Are you going to take my jersey off?'

Archie fumbled for the hem of the jersey, pulled it up over her back, she wriggled to ease it up, holding her arms above her head. The fabric snagged the chain necklace round her neck and was stuck, her face pressing against the wool.

'Sorry, Maggie.'

'Hang on,' she slipped her arms free, released the gold charm that had been hidden under the jersey and tossed the garment onto the sofa; she pulled herself against him, one hand easing down his chest. 'Did you like holding my breast when I came to your bed?'

'Of course.'

'You didn't say anything.'

'You were asleep.'

'I wasn't.'

'Sorry.'

'Archie Middlebrook, don't keep saying you're sorry. I want you to make love to me.' Her hand was pressing against his trousers. 'And you want it too.'

His hands reached under her camisole and undid the hook of her brassiere.

'You've done that before, or have you?'

'I haven't.'

'Archie, you're so sweet. I didn't mean you to give everything away. You do want me, don't you?'

'Oh, God, yes I do.'

In seconds their clothes were piled on the floor and Archie fumbled for the packet in his discarded trouser pocket; he pulled her down onto the sofa, not bothering to release the catch to fold the arm flat. Her hand held him and he trembled as he struggled with the rubber, but Maggie guided his endeavour and he felt the heat of her body as he pushed into her depth, her arms holding tightly round him, pulling a surge of strength to brace his body. In seconds his baptism was complete.

They lay locked together on the old sofa as his pulse slowed. He lifted his body to look at her, sweat on her forehead, her hair tousled and eyes smiling.

'There's got to be more, Archie.'

And there was.

They stayed in the summerhouse as the day passed. At times their congress was wild far outlasting the supplies from his wash bag – not that Maggie cared. At times they dozed together as the paraffin fire spluttered and condensation ran down the windows. Maggie had questioned him when she realised the packet was one short, astonished he had experience. He confessed his virgin curiosity; it didn't bother her that they took no other precaution.

'I wish there was another blanket or something here. I'm getting cold, even with the fire.'

'I'm hot.'

'Hardly surprising; you could go on all day if I let you. I thought you were going to squeeze the life out of me. You must be gentle, Archie.'

'Sorry. I...'

'No more, sorry, Archie. You have nothing to be sorry about. You are quite a lad and your... your you know what, is quite a lot for a girl to take.'

'I could go up to the house and get a rug if you want.'

'Just hold me.'

There were so many things Archie had not known when he had woken that morning. His fingers roamed over her silky, damp skin, fiddling with her nipple, teasing it to stand up, letting it fade back

Requiem for Private Hughes

to rest, only to tease it again. He combed his fingers through her hidden hair, thicker and darker than he had expected, darker than the hair on her head that was now lying in strands on the cushion under her head. The little hedge of dark hair reached up towards her navel across her slim tummy, not the few wisps he remembered from the art school models in life classes. She reached down and held him again, squeezed him and he responded.

'You're insatiable, Archie Middlebrook.'

Later at the cottage he ran her a hot bath, found a fresh towel and embraced her again before she climbed into the water. She lay back to let it flood over her, enjoying his gaze.

'Can I get you something to eat?'

'When will Dorothy be back?'

'Not for ages. Mum left a stew in the bottom oven for tonight.'

'It's almost four o'clock, Archie. I thought she said she would be back about five.'

'I thought it was three.'

'Time flies when you're enjoying yourself. You did enjoy it didn't you, Archie?' His beaming face said it all. 'What I would really like is a cigarette and a glass of wine, red wine.'

'I don't think we've got either. There's some whisky.'

'There are ciggies in my handbag, Gauloises Bleu; and a glass of whisky, why not?'

'I don't smoke.'

'It's not all you didn't do, until today, young man.'

'I'll have to go and do the evening milking, I didn't realise it was late. I don't think Zed is up to it.'

'Archie, do you mind if I don't come with you? I'm aching all over, I feel as if I have been in a rugger scrum,' she laughed. 'Go and get me a glass of whisky, and my fags, then strip yourself off and get in here with me. I've never made love in a bath.'

*****

It was a long night – Zed was ill. Archie rushed back to Hawthorne Cottage to get his mother, just back from Wells, running her up to

Greenings in the car. While he did the evening milking Dorothy got Zed on to his bed and phoned Doctor Perkins. The doctor was unhappy with the state of things at Greenings and took the old man direct to the Cottage Hospital. Dorothy said she'd wait at the farmhouse for Archie to finish in the milking parlour.

She went to the foot of the farmhouse stairs then slowly climbed to the landing sweeping dust from the unused handrail. Floorboards creaked as she went to a door and pushed it open. Nothing had changed; the iron bedstead, the plain chest of drawers and the picture of Mario's village on the wall. It was all as she remembered it.

Over late supper Maggie told her godmother how they had gone out for a drive and a walk on the moors where they got soaked in the rain. Maggie had still been in the bath when Dorothy got home. Nothing was said, but Archie sensed his mother was unconvinced. Dorothy noticed things; she would have noticed the car was standing in exactly the same place as when she'd left.

The evening had been quiet after supper, Maggie went to bed early.

'Do you think Zed will get better, Mum?'

'I can't see him getting back to the farm, not to farm work. You've been doing the lot in recent weeks. I've seen it before with his sort; work all hours for years then when they stop they go downhill fast.'

'What did Doctor Perkins say?'

'He's worried for him.'

'Mum, I've been thinking. Do you think we could take the farm over? On a rental from Zed for a while to see if we could run it. He's taught me a lot in recent weeks and I'm sure I could do it; there are so many things that could be improved up there.'

'The trouble is it is Glebe land, son.'

'I thought Zed owned Greenings.'

'No, it's the Church that owns it. His family has rented for generations.'

'But we could rent it from them, just the land.'

'You'd like that, Son. I guess you would farm it better than poor old Zed. He's just edged along since the war years when he had Mario to do things for him.'

Archie thought of the Italian, dark hair turning grey, his funny way of saying words, his singing - he was always singing as he worked the daylight hours.

'I wonder if Mario will ever come back to see us.'

'It's a long way, Son.' Many a night Dorothy thought of her two men in Italy, her stationmaster buried in that distant soil and Mario the POW farmhand who sang as he laboured far from his home, now perhaps a grandfather, amongst the olive trees in his mountain village.

'What do you think, about Greenings, Mum?'

'I think it will go to Barrow Farm; they want more land and have a common boundary on the far side. Maybe the house will be sold, when Zed goes.'

'But we could rent the land and the house and sell Hawthorne Cottage.' But he knew as he said it Dorothy would never do that, not sell her home, the place of her birth and widowhood.

That night Archie lay in bed wanting to sleep. Too much had happened for one day. Was it five or six times they had made love? It was the sort of thing you should know yet he wasn't sure. Geraint would think him a fool for doing it without a French letter. This was different, Maggie wasn't bothered and he loved her.

But how could he see her again once she was back in London? Would she come down to Somerset again in the summer? She must get holidays from her job or come down to stay over a weekend, but there wouldn't be any easy chance of their having the house to themselves. A job in Tonecastle, that's what he needed. Get some digs – no, a small flat – then Maggie could come down to stay with him at weekends.

But Zed was in hospital and he wasn't going to get back to the farm. Archie would have to run it himself, even if there wasn't going to be a chance it could be theirs. There must be some way they could take on Greenings. Would Maggie want to be a farmer's wife?

He'd said it: Maggie, his wife.

Would she want to be his wife if he was a farmer? She was a town girl. He needed to have a town job. What could he do? They shouldn't have made love without taking precautions. She must want his baby.

Archie knew what he had to do. In the morning he would ask Maggie to marry him. It didn't matter that she was three years older. What about an engagement ring?

Archie sat up in his bed. He fumbled for the torch on his bedside cupboard, shone it for a moment on the clock dial; five to three. Should he go and wake Maggie? Creep into her room, slip into her bed then when she wakes ask her to marry him.

Archie lay back on his crumpled pillow searching for the right words before sleep caught him up.

The next morning it looked as though they were going to be late at the station. Maggie had procrastinated, wanting to take daffodils from the orchard then wanting to get mud off her shoes. They set off with only forty minutes to spare before her train.

He wanted to ask her, but he couldn't get the words sorted as he drove. At the station he carried her case up the steps to the platform. She went to buy a magazine at the station bookstall and only then could he get her to himself.

Mr Sanderfoot stood outside his office as a porter called out down the platform. 'London train, London train, stand back, please; London train.'

Archie held her arm. 'Maggie.'

'Archie, it's been wonderful. Everything, it's been such fun.'

The train bore down, steam belching from its pistons as it slowed into the station. 'Maggie, I want to marry you,' he almost shouted over the hiss and clatter of the train. He'd meant to ask her with the right words; it came out wrong.

'Archie, you are so sweet. You really make a girl feel good.'

Doors were opening; she looked away to the train.

'But, Maggie...'

She turned back to him, put her arms round his shoulders and kissed him, pushing her lips to his, leaving her lipstick on his mouth.

She pulled away clutching her daffodils, grabbed her case and got into the train, the door slammed and whistles blew. Her face was at the corridor window. She mouthed 'thank you,' and a tear ran down her cheek.

It was yes, it had to be yes. The train pulled away. Archie lingered, then as it disappeared round the distant curve in the track he ran down the steps, out of the station to his car and sat gripping the steering wheel. Now he had to buy a ring for Maggie.

He wondered about his mother. Maggie was her goddaughter, she would be pleased, she must be pleased. Maggie was wonderful and he loved her, yet there had been hesitation in his mother's look last night. She was wary, something wasn't right.

Chapter Eight

DOROTHY fixed it; on the second Monday in May Archie took a bus into Tonecastle for his first day at work, employed in the Hardware Department at Harptree & Ellis. Archie thought about using his car, but there was a problem with the distributor, besides the bus would stop outside the main door of the department store.

Dorothy had seen the Reverend Bartholomew. He'd told her Barrow Farm had already laid their claim to Greenings's acres on the Church Commissioners table, and she realised it was a dead-end. Barrow Farm had been asked to manage Zed's land and his livestock while matters were sorted.

The old man was out of hospital and moved to the convalescent home in Northhill. Wearing a suit, his hair cut, his weathered face shaved, he was a neat, if sickly, figure amongst the grey-haired residents sitting in the dayroom as he told his stories. Archie took his mother over to see Zed, parking the car where Zed would be able to see it. They talked, but Zed didn't ask about the farm. It was ended, he didn't want to know.

There were shades of the army in the hierarchical structure of Harptree & Ellis. With the Ellis family no longer in the business, Oscar Harptree, the sole owner, worked long hours from his wood panelled office on the fourth floor, presiding over layers of time-served departmental heads, hoping at least one out of his two daughters and young son would follow him into the family business.

But disappointment was looming. Archie had known Jane, the elder of the two girls, at college before he was conscripted. He'd heard she'd gone to live in a French commune, painting and sculpting with an all-over tan. Her sister, Mary, was nursing in

London and the boy, Andrew, was still at boarding school, repeatedly absenting himself from classes to travel to weekday race meetings; his scholastic studies neglected, his knowledge of the horse racing world growing every day.

Oscar Harptree, older than Archie's father, was Donald Middlebrook's company commander at the outbreak of war and held rank now as an Honorary Colonel in the Territorial Army. It was to Colonel Oscar Harptree that Dorothy had addressed the letter on her son's behalf when it became clear there was no chance of the land at Greenings.

Harptree & Ellis was undergoing much needed refurbishment when Archie joined. An escalator was being installed to serve the first and second floors; a single flight that was to carry their customers up; they would still descend by one of the two Edwardian lifts, their open mesh gates controlled by lift boys – men in their fifties – who called the floors, or by walking down the carpeted central stairway. Disruption in many of the sales departments was fraying nerves as dust and noise disturbed the routine of the store.

Archie was into his second week at Harptree's when he was summoned to the fourth floor.

He climbed the 'staff only' stairway, to report as instructed to Mrs Mayfair, who controlled the comings and goings of the top floor with the tenacity of a French concierge. She greeted him as he pushed open the glass swing doors off the lobby.

'Good morning, Mr Middlebrook. Is your mother keeping well?'

To his knowledge he had never met Mrs Mayfair. She didn't wait for any reply flipping an intercom switch at her desk. 'Colonel Harptree, Archie Middlebrook is here to see you.'

'Bring him in, and I'll have my coffee now, Mrs Mayfair,' the Colonel's voice crackled from his inner office.

Archie had bought a new suit before he started at Harptree's. There were generous staff discounts to apply to his next purchase, which should be soon, as with daily wear his suit was already losing shape. He wished he'd pressed the trousers over the weekend.

'You have Donald's look about you.'

Requiem for Private Hughes

Archie stood a short distance from the large Partners' desk. Colonel Harptree, tall and thin with a trimmed moustache as white as his full head of hair, sat where his father had sat, the chair on the other side of the desk unoccupied. In the Twenties Colonel Harptree's father and his uncle, such is the complexity of families at work, had sat on the two sides of the desk without speaking, communicating only in notes written longhand and passed to their co-owner through Mrs Mayfair's predecessor.

Patience Mayfair came back into the room bringing a tray with the coffee, but only a single cup. She moved an upright wooden chair from the panelled wall and placed it beside Archie. He stood waiting a further word.

'Sit down, young man. It is good to have you with us. I knew your father well. He was a brave man.'

'Yes, Sir.'

'And you did well in Malaya. I hear you were skilled in jungle craft.' He looked at Archie then looked away, through the window, to where the tower of St Mary's reached above the rooftops. 'It was a rotten business about the ambush and Private Hughes. You did your best; you showed great bravery.'

There had been no witness; this man could not know what had happened on that laterite track deep in the jungle. Archie's throat was tight, he could not speak. He could hear Geraint singing *Men of Harlech*, revelling in the power of the Ferret scout car before the shattering crash of the explosion. Geraint might have taken up a job in a department store, but he would have told Archie to go painting, not to stand at a counter serving customers. Geraint would have told him for the fool he was, told him to get out of his suit, get his paints and go out into the countryside. But Archie couldn't do it, painting was gone.

He cleared his throat. 'Thank you, Sir. Geraint Hughes was a good friend.'

'I know. Don't blame yourself, Archie.' He took a sip from his coffee, just a hint of it marked his moustache. 'These things happen in war. It's never fair. It wasn't fair in your father's generation; it wasn't fair when I was a young man in the mud of Flanders.'

Then he talked about the store, how he wanted Archie to learn the business on the shop floor, understand what customers wanted, then if all went well he would move him to work behind the scenes in the office.

Archie's mind raced away down the twisting tracks of the Malayan jungle, sun flickering through breaks in the canopy, a muddy stream with leeches ready to grab hold as they waded through the water.

'In the circumstance you don't have to follow up with the Territorials, it's up to you.'

'I'll give it thought, Sir.'

'I understand you are good with figures.'

'I got my 'O' level in Additional Maths.'

'Splendid. You'll see me on the floor from time to time. I make a point of knowing all the staff. If ever you want to talk with me, just let Mrs Mayfair know.'

Archie had been told the Colonel, known by all the senior staff as 'Mr Oscar', was often to be seen inspecting the store, checking the sales floors, always with a word to the staff. Word had it that on one occasion, a young sales assistant who didn't recognise him had sold him a bottle of perfume for his wife before he used the assistant's name and congratulated her on her sales prowess. At the end of the week there was a ten shilling bonus in her pay packet.

Sensing the interview was at an end Archie stood up.

'Did you know Jane at the art college?'

'She was a year ahead of me, Sir.'

'I don't think she did much work while she was there; she lives in France now, loves to paint, but she doesn't sell anything.'

Archie went back to the sales floor feeling awkward, frustrated in his ambitions to paint, or to be a farmer, now smart-suited to wait on the whim of the customers. But he was in love, nothing else mattered.

It was eight weeks since his adventure with Maggie; he hadn't seen her again, nor spoken to her on the telephone. He didn't like speaking on telephones, but the one time he'd rung her flat in London she was out. The flatmate who answered had giggled when he told her who was calling. Maggie had not returned the call – perhaps she hadn't got the message. There had been letters – well, his four letters to her and the one she sent to him in the same envelope with her thank you letter to Dorothy.

It wasn't a long letter; he still puzzled over it after many readings. It was warm, she'd enjoyed her holiday, he was fun to be with; she mentioned the thrill of driving his car, remembered the pier in Northhill, but the letter didn't say 'yes', it didn't say 'I will'. There was a postcard from Paris, just a scribble to say she was enjoying a weekend with a friend. What sort of friend? She didn't say – that made it worse.

At breakfast one morning, shortly before he had to go down the lane to catch the bus to work, Archie told his mother he wanted to marry Maggie. Dorothy was not surprised. She worried for her son. She was fond of the girl, recognising much of the girl's mother, Rita, in her knowing looks. Archie's announcement confirmed her suspicion over their relationship; perhaps it had been a mistake to ask Maggie to stay. Life in London was too far removed from their style at Hawthorne Cottage. She couldn't imagine Archie in London, or Maggie in Somerset.

Archie wanted his mother to be thrilled. She just asked him if he was sure. Of course he was sure, why should he stagnate in the country? Beside Maggie was going to have his baby, but he didn't tell her that.

He had to run the last yards of the lane seeing the bus coming along the main road.

Then a letter came. There was to be a party at the flat. Could Archie come up to London?

Everything was good again; there were things to do; did he have the right clothes? Had he got the cash to buy a ring? There was a jewellery department at Harptree's. He looked round their display on the pretext he was getting to know what was on the sales floors. He would get a discount in the store, but word would go round if he bought an engagement ring. He went out to a town jeweller in his lunch hour and chose a small diamond in a gold band that cost him his wages for the first three weeks at Harptree's. All that afternoon he kept feeling for the red leather box in his pocket.

❋ ❋ ❋ ❋ ❋

The London train slowed passing the flower fields of Sutton's Seeds outside Reading, tilled acres with a web of planted rows pushing into summer growth. As the train got up speed again small figures worked with hoes along the growing lines. Every February Dorothy received her order from Sutton's in a brown paper parcel, the outcome of her careful ticking in the autumn catalogue; seeds for summer and winter vegetables, for the herbaceous borders and her herb garden.

It was a while since Archie had been to London, five years since he and his mother had travelled to London to see the Festival of Britain Exhibition on the South Bank. Sixteen year old Archie had tired his mother that day, studying exhibits in the Dome of Discovery, marvelling how the Skylon balanced in its delicate wire cradle, then into the 3D cinema where, clad in red and green Perspex glasses, they'd ducked into their seats as the swinging ball on the screen shot out into the audience. It had been a long day, not home on the charabanc until well into the small hours.

Light rain was drizzling as his train pulled into Paddington. He lifted his grip holding his overnight things down from the rack, left his newspaper on the seat and set off down the platform. Arching spans of grimy glass roofed the station, echoing the bustle of its business; the engine driver, his peaked cap pushed back over greying hair, stood on his footplate watching the passengers depart.

Archie caught his eye, the driver nodded, neither of them sure who the other was, yet thinking they had met before. Was he one of the drivers who had taken the stationmaster's young son up onto the footplate from the platform at Helecombe Halt so many years before?

Archie went to the café on Platform One, got out his London street map, as he had many times in the past few days, to plan the remainder of the day. He traced the direct route to Maggie's flat. Down to Lancaster Gate, into Hyde Park, the bridge across the Serpentine, turn right along Kensington Gore to find Queen's Gate running south from the park then Queen's Gate Terrace would be off to the right. It wouldn't be hard to find, he had the number written down, a basement flat. Maggie's invitation mentioned a gate in the railings and down stone steps.

There was time to kill. The invitation said half seven, he judged that meant eight o'clock. It was just after four. He decided to go to the National Gallery. The notes on his street guide suggested he take the Bakerloo Line or a Number 15 bus from Praed Street outside the station. He would see more from a bus.

Archie felt in his jacket for the red leather case housing the engagement ring. It was still there. It was all he could afford. One day he would buy her a better ring.

He went to the café counter and ordered a cup of tea with an Eccles cake.

* * * * *

Four hours later Archie approached the Queen's Gate Terrace flat as noise from the basement boomed out onto the street. A duffle-coated figure, waving a tankard, stood at the top of the steps shouting down to an unseen companion.

'No, I bloody well didn't. It was that stupid sod, Biddle. He broke it.'

Archie stopped a couple of paces away, sizing up the youth.

'Are you coming to this party?' The youth, unsteady on his feet, stared at Archie.

'I am.'

'Waste of time if you ask me. All the birds are taken and they're running out of beer.'

Archie regretted putting off his arrival, sitting in a pub down the road for the last forty minutes, lingering over half-a-pint of beer. He clutched his overnight bag expecting to spend the night with Maggie, but faced with the immediacy he was anxious. Music thumped from the stairwell.

'Where're you from?' The youth demanded.
'Somerset.'

Archie smelt beer on the youth's breath 'Is that far?' The freckle-faced student giggled. 'I'm from Timbuktu, but I think the trains have stopped running.' With that the tipsy student meandered off down the road.

Inside the flat, in the half light, the partygoers pressed close. There was no sign of Maggie, just a crowd of people talking, shouting, some jiggering about as drums, a guitar and a muted trumpet drowned out the chance of conversation. He edged through a doorway; someone put a glass into his hand. 'Keep hold of this for me, I'm going for a pee.'

There was a girl beside him. 'Do you live here?' he asked.
'No.'
'Do you know where the hosts are?'
'Haven't a clue; it's just a party. We've come for the booze. Have you brought anything, it's running dry here.'

'You can have this if you want.' Archie gave her the glass that had been put into his hand, then eased his way past into another room.

'Hello.' A young woman, wearing a cocktail dress in contrast to the sweaters and jeans, stood beside him. 'You look too well dressed to be another of the invading students. We're swamped.'

'Do you live here?'

Yes, but we've made a hash of it, we all invited different people and there's a load of gatecrashers. Now we've no food and the beer is running out. We got two firkins in for the night; you would think that would be enough.'

'Should be enough,' Archie almost shouted to be heard. 'It's a huge flat, how many of you live here?'

'Ten, at the moment, but there's room for twelve if we all share rooms. It makes it very cheap.'

'I didn't realise. I'm looking for Maggie.'
'She's about. Is she a friend of yours?'
'Yes. My name is Archie.'

The girl looked up. 'I'm Lynn.'

'Do you know where Maggie is?'

Lynn held his gaze, her blonde head pushed against his shoulder as people pressed past them. 'You're her cousin, or something, aren't you? Didn't she stay with you in Devon?'

'Somerset. My mother is her godmother.'

'Let me get you a drink, if I can find any. Do you mind what it is?'

'I'm not really thirsty.' He was still clutching the grip, it was getting in the way, but he didn't want to put it down.

'Got any booze in there, old fruit?' A stranger prodded his bag.

'Lynn, I must find Maggie.'

'She's wearing a blue dress, rather dashing even for Maggie,' Lynn smiled. 'She was with a bloke, but they've disappeared.'

'Gone out?'

'No. She'll reappear soon. Meantime I'll have to do. Tell me about yourself.'

Archie's eyes roamed the room. There was no blue to be seen, just a blurred mass of dully-clothed people, shouting to be heard, or standing silent as the party passed them by.

'Come on, Archie, don't ignore me.' Lynn reached up and kissed his cheek. 'Where have you been hiding all my life?'

'I must find Maggie.'

'Suit yourself, then.'

Archie forced his way past people. There was a corridor with doors off it. He pushed the first door open. The room was dimly lit, with people in a huddle and a sweet smoky smell. 'Come in or go out, and shut the door,' he was commanded. He pulled the door to, stepping back into the passageway. If Maggie had been in there he hadn't seen her.

A guy pushed past him. 'Christ, where's the piss house in this place,' and blundered on to the end of the passageway. Archie opened another door. In the dim light couples were entwined on two beds in the room, long stockinged legs wriggling, and a glimpse of a figure in a blue dress. The man on top looked round.

'Bugger off, can't you see we're busy.'

For a second he saw her face flushed as he had seen it before in the summerhouse in Somerset. He slammed the door, forcing his way through the throng in the hallway. There was a shout behind him, but he made for the door. The girl Lynn looked at him. 'Are you going?'

'Yes, I bloody well am going.' Archie barged up the steps, angry tears flooding into his eyes as he ran blindly into Queen's Gate towards the traffic lights. 'You stupid, stupid idiot,' he cursed as he ran. On Cromwell Road a bus came abreast, slowing for its stop. He clambered onto the platform, mounted the stairs, stumbling to the front as the bus surged forward. Seated he stared ahead at the London traffic, oblivious of the bus's journey.

Only when they crossed the river did he wonder where he was going. There were few people around; the bus sped on before braking to a juddering stop. Archie stumbled down the stairs, clutching his bag. The conductor was uninterested when he offered his sixpence.

Along the wet pavement there were a few shops, boarded up for the night, a laundrette, people staring silently at a rank of machines and music coming from a pub. He pushed open glass doors embossed with *Watney* and its familiar Red Barrel. Stale smoke hung in the air, a hush descended round the bar. He put his grip down on a chair and went to the bar to order a pint.

'Watch your case, son,' the barman said, 'someone will nick it.'

'They can for all I care.'

'Don't say I didn't warn you.'

An hour later Archie stood leaning against the parapet of Battersea Bridge, watching the rippling black water swirling below to be cleaved in two as a thumping tug, its stack and mast hinged back to clear the underside of the bridges, battled against the tide towing laden barges.

'I'm just one person in the queue.'

He crossed over the river with no idea where he was. He was going north, that was right, it must be to get back to Paddington. His second pint had been a mistake. At the pub he'd wondered whether to go back to the party, speak to her. But he couldn't face the prospect of finding her with someone again. Why hadn't she told him? Said no when he'd asked her, they could have been friends. Why did she invite him to London? He had to get home – this was no place for him. What if she was carrying his baby; she could be, or it could be whoever took her to Paris, or the bloke at the party, or nobody at all. Had he had made the whole thing up? There was not going to be any child.

'Good evening, Sir. Going far?'

Archie stopped and stared at the policeman in front of him.

'I'm trying to get to Paddington.'

'A bit of a journey from here; had a drink have you, Sir?'

'Been to a party, well a pub; a couple of pints.'

'Do you mind if I look in the bag, Sir.'

'Just weekend things.' He held the bag up and pulled the zip. The policeman shone a torch inside.

'Thank you, Sir. You'd be surprised what people carry about with them at this hour of the night.'

The policeman gave him directions to Paddington. It was too complicated to follow, but he got the drift of it knowing in which direction he should be headed. A light drizzle was falling.

It was midnight, a wretched midnight when he might have been warm in bed with her soft body curled against him, wanting to caress her stomach where his child lay.

Shut up about it for heaven's sake. He cursed stepping into a puddle off the kerb.

'Hello, love. You're out late.'

He hadn't noticed the woman, leaning against a doorway, the dim glow of a cigarette showing in her hand.

'Looking for someone, are you, love?'

'Not really. I'm trying to get to Paddington.'

'No trains for hours, love. Come back with me and have a bit of fun. You look like you want cheering up.'

'No. I'm just damp from the rain. I haven't got a mack.'

'Come back to the warm, love.'

Requiem for Private Hughes

The woman came over and hooked her arm through his.

'Come on, love. It's late. My place is only just round the corner.'

They started walking, but when she stopped at a paint-peeling door and started to pull a key out from the letterbox on a string, he knew he shouldn't follow. Yet he walked behind her up the threadbare stairs as the timer light switch ticked behind them.

The room was dimly lit, drying washing hung over a clothes horse, a bed was against one wall, its bedclothes rumpled, a gas fire spluttered, half of the stained white ceramic glowing red. There was a movement behind a screen.

'Don't worry, love. It's my mother, but she's asleep.'

He stood rooted to the floor, the enormity of where he was filtering into his muddled brain.

'I must go.'

'What do you mean, go? We've only just got here.'

'I'm sorry. I shouldn't have come here with you.'

'Well, you're here now. You can't just go.'

'I haven't got any money.'

'What yer mean no fucking money. I can't go back out on the street now.'

She was older than he'd thought. In the street, with little light and with her perfume he'd thought she was his age, she was much older, but it wasn't that. He didn't want it and he only had a ten shilling note in his wallet.

'I've only got ten bob.'

'What you take me for?'

'Sorry. I'll pay you for a cup of tea.'

'A cup of tea. You think I run a fucking café, or something.

'Sorry.'

'Christ I've never met one like you. Sit down; I'll put the kettle on. My feet are bloody killing me.'

'If you're making tea, I'll have a cup.' There were sounds behind the screen and an old lady emerged with a dressing gown pulled loosely about her.

'Mum. You're meant to be asleep.'

'You're making too much noise for me to sleep, and your language. He looks a nice young gentleman and he doesn't want to hear you swearing like that.' The old woman turned to Archie. 'I didn't bring Maureen up to swear like that.'

Over a pot of tea he told the two women about Maggie, Greenings and the cows, his trip to London and his humiliation at the party. Archie reached into his pocket and pulled out the small diamond ring. No one else had seen it since he bought it, not Dorothy after she had been so subdued when he told her he wanted to marry Maggie. Yet he put it on the table in its case and showed it to Maureen and her mother.

'It's not much; it cost me three weeks wages.'

'Stupid girl if you ask me,' said Maureen stifling a yawn.

'It's a proper ring, don't you worry, son. You'll find the girl for it one day.' The mother patted his arm.

'I'm not even going to look. It's a mug's game.'

'You'll get over it, Archie.'

He shut his eyes and the tears rolled down his cheeks. Maureen put her arms round his shoulders and gave him a hug.

'You'll be all right. There'll be someone else for you, a lovely lad like you, Archie.'

In the early hours he woke, fully dressed, lying on the scruffy bed against the wall with a blanket thrown over him. His watch said twenty to six as light was coming into the room through the unlined curtain. Archie swung his legs off the bed. His shoes, still damp, were side by side on the floor, next to his grip. The ring sat in its box on the table.

He laced his shoes and peered round the room. The two women were sleeping, breathing noisily on the bed behind the screen, lying back to back. There was a pile of clothes on a chair.

He found a piece of paper, the back of an old envelope, and wrote. *Thank you for understanding, Maureen. Please keep the ring; I won't need it now.* He hesitated then added: *Best wishes, Archie.* He slipped the envelope under the ring, picked up his bag, turned his back and let himself out of the room.

Archie walked fast, almost at a jog, in what he hoped was the direction of Paddington.

PART TWO
1984

Chapter Nine

THE wooden perpetual calendar on his office wall, reset every morning by the caretaker before Archie was in to work, displayed *Monday 3 April*. The calendar was made from an oak brought down in summer gales; a brass plaque confirmed the date the storm blew: July 1935. Oscar Harptree gave Archie the calendar on the day he was promoted from the sales floor to the management team noting the tree fell in the month Archie was born.

The calendar had been in the office years before Archie began work at Harptree & Ellis. Only Tommy Henshaw hidden in a basement workshop making bespoke doll's house furniture had been on the staff longer than Archie. Tommy's doll's house furniture had started as a hobby, but was then used in a window display. Through a circuitous route it led to a request to supply pieces year by year to Queen Mary's doll's house at Clarence House, gaining Harptree's a coveted Royal Appointment. Their warrant lapsed when she died, the replica Royal coat of arms remaining as a trophy on the boardroom wall.

Tommy, growing old with his craft, worked a full day making items to order for customers worldwide, who wrote him longhand letters with precise specifications. Archie often dropped in on Tommy for a chat in his basement lair, with its smells of wood dust and formula glues.

Now there was work to be done. Files were heaped on Archie's desk. The programme was tight, the next set of annual trading figures was important. Every year Harptree's management accounts became more complex to estimate how the full trading year had progressed. Archie got queries sorted with section heads and the overall summary into a standard format by the fourteenth of the month after the year end and posted out to the directors for their late April board meeting.

'Problems, Archie?' Lorna Curtis poked her head round his office door.

'Not yet,' he pushed his chair back looking round. 'There will be before it all gets sorted.' Almost twenty-five years his junior, recently appointed as the first in-house qualified accountant of the company, Lorna intrigued Archie. Always dressed in dark jerseys, tailored skirts and low-heeled shoes, her mousy hair cut short, she wore dark framed glasses she had to keep pushing back on her nose. Her work was quick and skilled. 'I'll get there, Lorna, one way or the other.'

She smiled, much as a niece might smile at her reliable uncle. 'I don't doubt it for a minute, Archie. Next year, it will all be on the computer.' Lorna had her agenda to move the store forward getting point-of-sale systems installed on the sales floors. 'The figures will be at our fingertips for analysis in any way we want.'

It wasn't that he didn't want change, but he'd seen nothing to persuade him the costs of change were warranted.

'I'll believe that when I see it. Till then I'll keep my paper systems running, just in case', he grinned.'

A breath of fresh air in the office looking younger than her mid-twenties, her accounting knowledge was sound and she had an uncanny knack of asking a question that put her finger on a problem. Archie had enjoyed his months working with Lorna, his years in the store on the sales floors, then as cashier before building the management accounting system for the business, coupled with her expertise on accounting and tax matters made them a happy team. It was hard to believe in a couple of years it would be thirty years he had worked at Harptree & Ellis.

Archie drove in every day from Hawthorne Cottage. It had rained the childhood day they'd moved in to live with his grandmother at the cottage, moving from Helecombe Halt Station House. Their goods were piled up on Zed Vellacott's cart – beds in pieces, the chest of linen and the old sofa, a treasure of grandmother's given to her daughter, being brought back to Hawthorne Cottage and was still there today in the summerhouse more than forty years later.

On the journey their goods were sheltered from the rain under a tarred tarpaulin; the linen and the sofa smelling for weeks afterwards. The chickens protested in their coop as the cart, pulled by two lumbering horses, bounced along the potholed lane.

Time melted away, a constant succession of seasons turning the years round, migrating birds counted home, that first swallow heard twittering high over the garden before Archie saw it dipping down into the old stable, swooping into the musty space, flickering up to a cobwebbed nest in the rafters, the nest the bird had left with stumbling flight seven months before.

Another summer, with cricket matches struggling through raining days to find a finish, endless mowing of wet lawns, weeding flower borders, eating crisp salads from the garden ignoring grains of dirt on washed leaves and sitting on the terrace he had built a few summers back. Then the swallows flew south again, the leaves turned and it was dark when he left his desk to motor home and another year was gone.

No daily trains ran between Northhill and Tonecastle since the Beeching axe closed the line. Later, saved as a heritage scheme, it was run at weekends by volunteers to bring in the tourists and enthusiasts. Buses seldom ran to his timetable. Archie used his car, a Harptree company car, one of the privileged few who had a parking space reserved in the company yard.

Archie's twenties, his thirties and forties had gone by. Staff had come to Harptree's and departed, the ranks of suited men returned from wartime adventure had given way in most part to a female sales force. No one other than Oscar Harptree, the doyen of

Tonecastle's business world, knew the intricacies of the department store's day-to-day activity in the detail Archie knew it.

'Did I see Sammy in the yard earlier?' Sammy – chauffeur, bagman, even occasional caddie to the store's owner – was known to staff throughout the store. 'I thought Mr Oscar wasn't coming in this week.'

It was hard for Archie to drop the habit of a past generation; not many staff called the owner 'Mr Oscar' these days.

'You know how it is, Archie. He keeps popping in. It can't be easy for Edward with Oscar keeping his eye on him all the time.' Lorna was two years older than the apparent heir to the business and thought well of Oscar Harptree's grandson, Edward Turner, a graduate in history. He had been in the company's management for almost a year. 'Oscar is a hard act to follow.'

Archie knew much of the Harptree family's comings and goings over the years. He knew how much Oscar had wanted his son, Andrew, to follow him in the business, in the end accepting Andrew was better placed training in racing stables than he ever would have been as a presence behind the scenes of the traditional department store. The excitements of Newmarket and Ascot were Andrew's adrenalin, not pre-Christmas stocks for the toy department, calculating order quotas for plastic-wrapped toys sourced from Hong Kong and South East Asian factories. That said, Andrew was no stranger to the clatter and excitement of the Far East, he knew it well, travelling frequently scouting for deals between overseas and European racehorse owners.

Oscar Harptree waited into his old age before welcoming his grandson, Edward, son of his divorced daughter Mary, into the business ignoring Andrew's obvious annoyance anxious over his inheritance.

'Has Mr Oscar gone to the Country Club?' Archie asked.

'He said he would call in there on his way home. Do you play golf, Archie?'

'It's not my strong point.' Archie had taken advantage of Oscar's invitation to have free lessons when a Harptree-owned farm diversified to build a golf course and club on its less rewarding land. 'I doubt I'll ever play like he does, even now in his eighties. It may only be a few holes on the par three these days. He can't see the green from the tee, yet he seldom veers off the line Sammy gives him.'

Word reached the office in mid afternoon. Edward came into Archie's room, his face white. Before he spoke Archie guessed.

'He'd just sunk a long put, gave the putter back to Sammy and said he wanted to sit down. Mother rang me.'

'Edward, I'm so sorry.'

'It's bad for all of us, Archie. We'll have to keep everything going here. It's awful.'

'Edward, don't worry. We'll cope here. Have you told Lorna?'

The young man shook his head.

'Get off home, Edward. Mary will need you at the house. We'll look after the store. We'll brief the staff and close early today.'

'Thanks, Archie. Should I say something, I mean to the senior staff?'

'It would be welcome, but it'll delay you getting away. They'll all want to speak. You'll best be getting home to be with Mary.'

Archie followed the young man out to the lobby and saw him to the lift. They both knew Oscar would have used the stairs. The lift doors opened, Edward paused.

'I'd better not,' a knowing smile flickered as he turned to take the stairs.

Archie knocked on the accountant's office door. 'Lorna,' she was on the phone. 'It's urgent,' he mimed, pointing to his room.

An announcement in the Tonecastle Gazette informed the town Harptree & Ellis would be closed on the next Friday morning. Staff came in for ten o'clock, at half past ten the house flag – a Celtic harp in gold on a green background, designed by Oscar fifty years before – flying at half mast on its flagstaff on the roof of the building, was raised then dipped in salute. The staff lined the pavement with bowed heads.

With an escort of two police horses the ancient Rolls hearse, unused for ten years and stored in the company's garage by the undertakers department for such an occasion, drove slowly by bearing a coffin made from estate timber by Tommy Henshaw in his basement workshop. Traffic was stopped behind the cortege, the occasion coming as near as a market town could to honouring a favoured son with his own municipal funeral.

Little of consequence had happened in Tonecastle over sixty years without Oscar Harptree having a hand in it. From St Mary's Church tower of rich red sandstone, looking out over late Georgian and Victorian houses, now mostly offices for solicitors and estate agent companies, came a peal of muffled bells. The carved saints of the stonework, depleted by the rain of centuries, reflected weak sunshine. In the nave the pews were already packed to overflowing.

A Cadet Corps honour guard stood to attention as the coffin was carried in through high oak doors. The County Cricket Club, the Town Football Club, the Rugby Club were represented. The Chamber of Commerce, political parties – Oscar had never confined his donations to any single party – local dramatic societies, charities and senior staff from the company were there in ranks seated behind the family pews.

Archie had stood with the others outside the store as Oscar's coffin went by, his head bowed. His thoughts not only of a benevolent employer, but of the man who had encouraged him back from the uncertainty of trauma, who'd been his father's first commanding officer and who he had known as a friend.

When the cortege had passed the store, Archie hurried through back alleys to join his mother at St Mary's. She needn't have come to the funeral, he would have represented her. But Dorothy was adamant, only too aware of the strength Oscar had been in their lives.

Archie knew change was coming at Harptree's, more fundamental change than a computer systems taking over the company's sales and accounting, displacing the Lampson pneumatic tubes whistling their sales slips and change around the sales floors. There had been days when Oscar came into Archie's office and talked, not seeking any response, working through ideas in his own mind. The independence of Harptree & Ellis was a matter Oscar held dear.

Requiem for Private Hughes

Territorial soldiers shuffled into position after the formal service to take up the old man's coffin and progress out of church for a private family burial. Archie feared the store's independence was going with them. Oscar told him many things, he knew that ownership of the company would now be split three ways between Oscar's children. Edward it turned out, though groomed for the business, was not Oscar's material heir.

The Harptree family filed out of the church uncertain of their precedence, disorganised by the unfamiliarity of the occasion, seldom meeting in such numbers. It was the first time since art college days that Archie saw Jane, resident for the last ten years in California, meeting with success as a movie set designer and nominated in a team for an Oscar, amusing her namesake father.

She looked worn out, her complexion hardened by sunshine, her hair an unnatural red shade. With oversized dark glasses masking her eyes, she seemed older than the early fifties he knew her to be. There had been a husband, or two, and occasional flurries into gossip columns, even an exhibition of her work in London before she went to live in America. Archie had been up to Town to see that show, unannounced and unimpressed by the garish work he saw.

Mary, from her hat and veil to her laced shoes, was a figure in black. He often saw her calling into the store to speak with her father. She would look in with a friendly word, knowing Oscar wanted Edward to learn from Archie.

He knew Andrew only from his appearances on television at race meetings. Oscar had been proud when the Daily Telegraph had a picture of Andrew being introduced to the Queen Mother in the winner's enclosure at Royal Ascot.

There were ranks of red-eyed grandchildren and two unknowing great grandchildren dressed in coloured clothes, none of which had been purchased at the family store. Jane, Andrew, Mary and Edward walked behind the coffin, eyes fixed on the heels of the military pall bearers.

The store re-opened at two o'clock, it was quiet on the sales floors; Archie, already behind with his reports, worked on in the calm of his office. He was surprised when there was a tap on his door.

'You're working late.'

'Lorna? I thought you'd gone home.'

'I set out to go, but I started wandering round the sales floors. There is so much to do here if we are to succeed. The store is so old fashioned, Archie. We must be the last store in the land to have a central cash booth with sales notes whizzing round the store in the vacuum system.'

'Not quite the last. There's one in London and another in Yorkshire. It works well, it never breaks down and it gives us an up-to-date central monitor of all our sales.'

'Point-of-sale online tills would be better.'

'Our customers are happy with the way we run the store.'

'You like it, don't you.'

'It all works. That's what I like about it, Lorna. You may be right; there may not be a place for a store like this in ten, twenty years time. I don't think I can change, you have the ambition. The likes of you and Edward will be the future of Harptree's.'

'It has to change, Archie.'

'Well, we won't sort it out tonight, that's for certain. Would you like a drink before we head home?'

'Where shall we go?'

'I've got the key to Oscar's cabinet. I don't think he'll begrudge us a drink to his memory before we go home, on this day of all days.'

It was ten o'clock before they said goodnight to the caretaker and climbed into the waiting taxi ordered over their second bottle of Chablis. Oscar had taken great interest in Food Hall buying and was proud of the variety and quality of their French wines. He'd been told by Archie and by others the wine market had developed with competitive wines from producers all over the world. The old man stood his ground serving a hardcore of longstanding county customers maintaining wine cellars stocked by Harptree's.

Archie sensing a phase closing knew something had to open. All his working life had revolved round the enterprise run by Oscar

Harptree. Now he had said goodbye to his mentor, probably more easily than had Oscar's family.

Lorna drank her wine quickly; she saw his raised eyebrow.

'I lived in France for two years, my father was a journalist.'

'Was?'

'He took off, left my mother in Paris. I haven't heard from him in ten years, somewhere in the States, last I knew.'

'I'm sorry, Lorna.' He refilled her glass.

'I think we were better off without him.'

Archie replenished his glass and swirled the wine round to sniff the bouquet.

'I lost my virginity in France. I always drink to that when I drink a good wine, and this is good.' She looked at Archie a smile on her lips.

'There were many things I might have expected you to say, Lorna; that wasn't one of them.'

'He was beautiful - I never saw him again.'

'Do you miss your young lover?'

'He wasn't young.'

'You are full of surprises, Lorna. May I ask if you have a boyfriend? I know nothing about you, apart from your skill as an accountant.'

'Thank you. No, it's just me and a cat in my not very nice flat.'

'And your mother?'

'Mum died three years ago, far too young. She had a stroke. It wasn't serious, but it annoyed her when she couldn't do everything on her own. Then she had another and it was massive. That's why I have a cat at home.'

'I'll get a second bottle.'

Lorna looked up eyebrows raised.

'Oscar would approve, even if there won't be any more work done this evening.'

'You always called him Mr Oscar.'

'People did when I joined. I suppose I'm the last.'

'It's like a Charles Dickens novel.'

'Am I a total fogey to you, Lorna?'

'Not in any way, Archie. You've kept the place running, despite its old-fashioned ways. You're rather modern really.'

'I'll get the second bottle while I'm still ahead.'

He watched as her animated fingers played music in the air and she told him where she wanted to get to in her life: to establish her business career then to have a child, a child on her own, suggesting any partner would be an encumbrance. Perhaps it wasn't a surprise seeing how organised she was. Might a daughter of his have been like Lorna? She was the sort of child he would have wished for, to be a pride to parents in her school days, independent, making her way and with great ambition.

The company's accounts were forgotten while they talked. With the second bottle open, Archie doodled on the pad of plain paper on his desk, his pencil working to pick up Lorna's looks.

'Are you an artist, Archie?'

He smiled. 'I went to art school, long ago, before you were born.'

'No one has ever drawn a picture of me. Is that how you see me?'

'It's only a scribble; I think it has your look. I've left your heavy glasses off. You have an elegant face; the glasses do you no favour.'

'I thought they would make me look older, more serious.'

'You don't need to do that. Have you tried contact lenses? I understand they're good and easy to use nowadays.'

'I don't like the idea of fiddling about in my eyes. I could get some different frames.'

'Make certain we can see your eyes, get something light. There you are.' Archie held up his sketch, pleased it had come together so easily, pleased she liked it.

'I'm flattered, Archie. Is that really how you see me?'

'Take off your glasses.'

She looked at him, then took the spectacles from her nose, her eyes a mix of green and blue, shimmering in the light.

'Yes, I think it's you.'

'Can I have it, Archie?'

'If you want it, it's only a doodle.' He tore the sheet off the pad.
'Did you have an accident, Archie?'
He looked up from his pad to question her meaning.
'On your arm, the scarring. Am I being nosey?'
'You are. Yes, I was burned when I was young.'
'And you've still got the scarring?'
'It could have been worse.'
'Was it at home?'
'No, in the army.'
'I didn't know you were a soldier, either. What happened?'
'It was all long ago. Let's just say it was an accident. Now I must get home. My mother will have something to say at my being kept out late by a beautiful young lady.'

Despite his repartee, she could see sadness in his eyes. 'I bet your mother is a lovely lady. You live out in the country, don't you?'

'Yes, a cottage with a large garden and the remains of an orchard. My mother has gradually annexed much of the orchard into the garden. Near Helecombe, off the Northhill road, there's a bypass now, it's very quiet.'

'It sounds lovely.' She looked at the wine in her glass, a few mouthfuls lingering, not wanting the evening to end. 'Were you ever married, Archie?'

He picked up the pad from his desk and put it into the briefcase Oscar had given him. 'It's time to go.'

'Do you mind my asking, Archie. I don't know why I want to know. We've worked together for months now, yet I know so little about you.'

'Perhaps it's better that way.' Archie tried to look stern to little effect.

She lifted her eyebrows, feigning innocence. 'Please, I'm not being nosey.'

'It's not something I talk about.'

'I think you were married, I think you had a secret wife, and maybe a mistress in a house in deepest Somerset, up on the moors.

I can't imagine you haven't been snapped up years ago, a lovely man like you.'

'Now it must be time to get home. That's the wine talking.'

'It isn't. It's me, I want to know.'

'I was engaged once.'

'And?'

'It didn't work out.'

'She must have been horrible if she hurt you.'

'No. She wasn't horrible. I was naïve.'

'How old were you, Archie?'

'I don't know, maybe twenty, or so.'

'Oh, Archie, you silly fool. Everyone falls in love at twenty. Look at me and my lover in Paris. Then nothing, and I found out he not only had a wife, he had a mistress as well.'

'So what's happened since then, Lorna?'

'Touché.'

'Come on, get your things, there's a taxi waiting. I'll drop you off.'

'You won't come in for a nightcap?'

'No, Lorna.'

'It was worth a try. What's your cottage called? I bet it's called Thistledown Cottage?'

'Hawthorne Cottage, it could be Thistledown judging by the amount growing in the garden.'

'Do you poison thistles?'

'Certainly not; the birds enjoy them, I slash the worst of them down.'

'I wish I lived out of town.'

'Come and see us one day. Come for lunch one weekend.'

Standing behind him Lorna put her arms round Archie's shoulders holding him in his chair and kissed him.' Thank you, Uncle Archie. I just wanted to know.' She picked up their wine glasses and the two dead bottles to take them to the pantry.

After dropping Lorna at her flat, a converted furniture depository, his taxi covered the familiar miles home faster than Archie

Requiem for Private Hughes

ever drove even with an empty road. He'd called a taxi for his mother after the funeral service, told her he would be late back home. She'd looked frail, she never complained of ill health yet the sparkle wasn't there, her dynamo was running down. She'd found it awkward getting into the taxi looking small in the back seat as it drove away.

Every year she'd been busy in the garden, working on her borders, getting ahead with the vegetable garden, planting early potatoes, sowing seed, setting summer cabbages in their rows. But the jobs normally done by April were not done. The garden didn't matter he could do the hard work. Dorothy had lost interest. If he suggested a check-up with the doctor, she protested the surgery would be full of sneezing children. Perhaps he could persuade the doctor to call. Or should he talk to Ivy? She knew his mother best, she knew how her energy was failing, that she was a shadow of her former bundle of energy.

'Can you collect me in the morning?'

The taxi driver sat immobile. 'I won't be on till midday.' Archie looked at him. The journey was on the Harptree account. 'I'll tell the office. What time in the morning, guv?'

Archie asked for the taxi at nine. It was later than he would normally go in to work, even on a Saturday. He wanted time to talk with Dorothy.

The light was on in her bedroom, this wasn't the time to talk, at breakfast it would be better. He waved the cat off the kitchen table. It objected with a hard stare. He slid the kettle across to the hotplate, wanting hot chocolate after what must have been a whole bottle of Chablis, although he thought Lorna had got ahead of him.

Muffled sounds of radio came from his mother's bedroom. He took her a cup of tea, taking care on the creaking staircase, but she was asleep. Archie put her book onto the night table, took off her glasses, askew on her face, pulled the cover over her hands, and turned off her light and the radio.

'Good night, Son,' she muttered as he left the room, the tea still in his hand.

Back downstairs Archie cut cold beef from the last of a roast joint and spooned chutney onto his plate, eating it as he stood by the kitchen work top installed the previous summer.

Archie took the office pad from his briefcase, holding it so the light put a shadow across it. There was the faintest of an outline; with a pencil he traced the lines, remembering her face, the way she held her head. He had it again. From a cupboard he took a large sheet of cartridge paper and using the sketch he worked on a full picture, carrying it down over her imagined body, guessing as he worked. He dug out water paints, mixed gentle flesh tones and put a wash over his sketch, sensing Lorna's figure, enjoying the shapes he stole, secrets he could only imagine. He put highlights onto the paper, the greenish blue of her eyes, the pink of her nipples and her flat stomach leading to a curl of hair.

In the morning, he woke to find Lorna still smiling out of his drawing across his bedroom, propped where he had left the sketch against his dressing table. Out of bed Archie took a folder from a high shelf in his wardrobe adding the portrait to those of his other imagined models, conjured from magazines bought in petrol stations, accumulated over the years in his private moments. Last night's sketch was the latest, the oldest being his painting of Maggie; the Maggie of that wild day in the summerhouse.

The collection of drawings he might have had, if he had kept up the pace of his art school year and his time in Malaya before the ambush, would have been huge. Even if he had done only one painting a month, as well as working in his sketch books, there would be three to four hundred paintings, one and a half thousand if he had done one a week. Yet this furtive folder was all he had to show for his youthful skill. Acrylics, he had never used acrylics; many painters used them now. After his morning working in the office he planned a trip to the art supplies shop near the library. He had no idea what paints would cost; he would buy a range of acrylic paints, some canvas boards and new brushes. He would need to take his cheque book.

After a bath and shave Archie dressed, went down to put the kettle on; there was no sound from his mother's room.

The taxi arrived as he was taking tea to her bedroom, the smell of burnt toast preceding him as he the climbed the stairs. The driver would have to wait – he couldn't leave without seeing she was all right. Ivy had told him there were days Dorothy didn't get out of bed till after nine. After a lifetime of being the first in the household downstairs and getting the household routine moving it was another sign things were going wrong.

'Thank you, Son.'

One look was enough for Archie to realise he shouldn't go in to work. Ivy was always busy on Saturdays; it would be unfair to ask her over to sit with Dorothy. He should never have let her go to Oscar's funeral. She'd insisted, and his fifty years counted for nothing when Dorothy made up her mind.

When Archie dismissed the taxi driver with apologies he was about to make a remark, but sensing the concern in his fare's face he turned his taxi on the gravel and headed back into the town, knowing the frustrated journey was on Harptree & Ellis's account. Provided Dorothy was all right on Monday and Ivy was over for the morning Archie could catch the bus to be reunited with his car, left behind in the Harptree car park.

Chapter Ten

A VACUUM cleaner churned in the room next door, a muffled note changing as it swept to and fro, an occasional thump as it connected with furniture, louder when it hit the adjacent skirting. Someone, a chambermaid no doubt, shouted in the corridor.

It was five months after Oscar's death. Archie felt numb, this could not be happening, it wasn't right. Did he understand what he was being told across the green-baize table in the sparse hotel meeting room?

Andrew Harptree was talking, but looking beyond Archie, avoiding eye contact, telling him what was going to happen at Harptree's. Lorna Curtis, her mousy hair tinted a much fairer shade, wearing designer glasses, sat next to Andrew, shuffling papers on the table, her head down, saying nothing.

Things were bound to change; Archie knew there would be change. He didn't expect to play a major part in the future of the business; the years ahead were for the younger generation.

'Close down the store? It's unthinkable. You can't do that.'

'We're building a new business, Archie. Moving on, moving with the times.' Andrew couldn't meet Archie's glare.

'There are things to bring up-to-date. I accept that, but close it down? How can you?'

'It's time to move on, Archie.'

It seemed the scheme had been put together outside the office in the months since Oscar's funeral although how long before that the planning had started he could only guess. How long had Lorna known Andrew Harptree? She'd been out of the office in recent days. Archie was surprised when she'd booked two weeks' holiday during such a busy period and without Oscar at the helm. He hadn't guessed.

The High Street site value of Harptree & Ellis proved to be the store's undoing. Archie was told that Oscar's daughters, Jane in California, and Mary in Somerset, were being bought out of their inheritance with prompt cash settlements.

A well-known retail chain, keen to have a presence in the town at a prestigious location, had agreed to take a lease over the ground and basement floors, which were to be stripped out and redesigned to provide modern sales space. The upper floors were to be refurbished and divided up for letting as high-tech office space, while the warehouse and yards would be cleared to make way for development of top-of-the market town housing.

Andrew pushed an architect's sketch towards him. Archie took no interest in it.

Under Andrew's chairmanship, Lorna Curtis was to be chief accountant of Harptree Property & Investments (1985) Limited. The closure appalled Archie. It went against everything he'd worked for during thirty years in the business.

The essence of these developments was told to Archie in the County Hotel, a Victorian building with a lingering four star rating flattering its hospitality. He had been summoned to the hotel from his top floor office by telephone.

It was the opening day of the home cricket fixture against Yorkshire; Archie had hoped to get away from work by mid-afternoon to watch the after-tea session. He was at the game before lunch, his desk cleared and his mind numb.

He avoided the members' bar. There were too many people he knew enjoying beers and wanting to chat. He didn't trust himself to talk to a soul. If he opened his mouth his anger would pour out. On this first day of the fixture, a working Friday, the spectators were few, most of the open stands were unoccupied. The ground, small by county cricket standards, with its new clubhouse, overlooked by the hills beyond the town, on the northern boundary and the two sandstone church towers behind the old stands on the southern side ready for the weekend crowds. Today it was quiet.

As a boy Archie had watched the county's leading batsman hit Ray Lindwall, back over the frustrated Aussie fast bowler's head for six, into the churchyard. He didn't expect such excitement today.

Archie sat alone on a damp bench seeing the white clad figures moving to unheard rhythms in the field. Occasional flurries of applause came from the thin crowd, sometimes a shout echoed from one of the public bars.

The letter was in his pocket, his hand felt it as he smoothed his jacket; there would be an early pension paid to reflect his years at Harptree's. He had never earned a great salary, but with Dorothy's war-widow's pension they got by. There would be less money coming in and he would have time on his hands, his own time to do other things. What could he do?

Andrew Harptree had asked if he would work on for a period to help in the closedown. He'd refused. Did he owe it to other staff members to help? It was too much to ask. There were things he should have said to Andrew. Maybe, in the long run, it was right and the time had come. The Harptree's he knew was reaching its natural end, yet the manner and timing of their plan was brutal.

Oscar could have realised the property value of the Harptree site on many occasions in recent years, but he chose to keep the store going. He saw it as a community before being a business, not his business, a staff enterprise. There had even been talk of a staff partnership once, the lawyers made heavy weather of it and the idea withered. A staff partnership would've put an end to these ideas.

Despite his anger Archie knew he would never write any letter to Andrew; such things were best left unsaid.

Lorna, silent throughout the interview, had followed Archie down the stairs to the hotel vestibule.

'Archie, I'm sorry; I didn't want it like this.'

For a moment Archie wished he was thirty again. He'd not seen her like this before, subdued, not in control of events. He thought of his scribbled drawing on the pad of office paper the evening after Oscar's funeral only months before. He wondered if she'd kept his drawing.

What insight into the store and its workings had he given away that evening as they talked? What information had she been able to add to Andrew's plotting?

'Tell me, Lorna, how long have you known Andrew Harptree?'

'It wasn't my idea, Archie. I promise. I just wanted to modernise the store.'

'But how long have you known him?'

'The firm I worked with before I came to Harptree's, where I did my articles.' Her longer hair and its colour suited her, and her eyes, no longer obscured behind her spectacle frames, shone out. 'We did advisory work for race horse syndicates. He trained most of the horses. One of the partners proposed me to work here. It was an opportunity for me.'

'And you were good, Lorna, have no doubt about it. Oscar admired your work. He wouldn't be impressed now.' Archie shook his head. 'So you were the Trojan horse and we took you in.'

'Archie, that's unfair, it wasn't like that. I'm just so sorry it has turned out this way.'

'Don't be sorry for me, Lorna. There'll be many staff members far worse off than me; folk loyal to Harptree's, who won't easily find other work. And young Edward, what happens to him?'

'He'll be offered a job.'

'I doubt he'll take it, unless he was in on the act as well.'

'No, he wasn't... I mean there wasn't an act, Look, Archie, Harptree's needs to move on.'

'Move on, maybe, but die, no. That's what this is: the end.'

Archie knew he was right, he could see she was upset. There was no triumph in her demeanour.

'And Lorna, take this advice from me if nothing else. Be wary for yourself, you're in the lion's den now. From the little I know about Andrew's connections they play hardball. Watch out it doesn't all blow up in your face.'

Archie wanted to draw her again, this time to paint her in acrylics, a large canvas, even life-size, to paint the vulnerable Lorna he saw in front of him, to paint something to eclipse the life drawing classes long ago at college and his sketches hidden in the wardrobe. Was this so absurd? His lifetime employment had come to an end, in part at her hand, yet he wanted to protect her, to portray her vulnerable naivety onto a canvas. The feeling was overwhelming.

Lorna looked away, unable to hold his questioning gaze. She hesitated a moment, putting out her hand, then turned and ran back up the wide carpeted staircase.

The cricket plodded on into the afternoon, the home side batting and losing wickets as the sky clouded over. Archie shivered on his isolated bench. His knee clicked sharply as he straightened his leg, a throb of pain shot up his thigh. It happened all the time now. Sometimes, as he lay in bed, his right knee locked and there was an awful pause, knowing he had to push to get his leg stretched out down the bed, waiting for it to hurt. Oscar had both his knees and a hip operated on; Archie didn't want that. The cricket meant little as his mind churned on thinking there had to be an opportunity, a frightening opportunity opening up for him.

Archie left the county ground walking along the riverside path to get his car. He stretched his frame as tall as he could, he was determined to show no limp from his hurting knee. Ducklings scurried in a calling parent's wake, trying to keep up, dashing away to check a piece of flotsam, then a frantic swim with flapping wings to be in their school again. He passed a man sitting motionless on a canvas stool amongst the reeds below the path, surrounded by plastic boxes of maggots and what seemed to be sandwiches, watching his line in the river. Did he ever get his boxes muddled?

Could he slip unseen into Harptree's yard, get the car and leave? It wasn't his car, it belonged to the company; Andrew had told him to keep it, hardly a big gesture. The Triumph Herald was ten years old and nursed through its modest mileage by Archie, no one else had driven it other than mechanics on service days.

Requiem for Private Hughes

An envelope was stuck under a wiper blade, in handwriting he recognised. He tossed it onto the passenger seat and drove out of the yard for the last time, sensing he was being watched from the fourth floor and wondering what had been said to other staff. Amongst the possessions on the back seat gathered up from his office in the morning was the oak perpetual calendar. Oscar had given it to him, not just for decoration in his room.

Since the bypass was built, the road to Helecombe passing the lane up to Hawthorne Cottage had little traffic. Archie drove by the turning to the cottage not ready to explain everything to Dorothy. Turning off further on, down the dead-end lane to Helecombe Halt, he found cars parked in the yard where they'd once loaded their belongings onto Vellacott's cart on their wartime moving day. A crowd of people were gathered on the platform of the refurbished station. He left his car and wandered over. A buzz of welcoming excitement stirred the air. They had cameras, mostly men checking their watches.

Now called 'Stationmaster's Cottage' by private owners and announced on a carved slate plaque, the house stood on the slope above the railway line. Archie looked up at the once familiar windows in part obscured by trees grown tall in the intervening years. The window on the right looked out from his parents' bedroom, the room in which he had first screamed out the joy of new-born breathing. The window to the left had been his bedroom. He'd watched so many trains pass through the station from that window, held in his mother's arms, then standing on a chair holding the window sill. From that window he had witnessed the Helecombe platoon with his father in its ranks entrain for war, a boy excited at their adventure and proud of the tall men in their uniforms.

Hawthorne Cottage, home ever since the station house was requisitioned, was two miles away as the crow flies, three through the lanes. Archie rarely ventured to this old haunt, he'd never travelled on the weekend steam trains run by the railway society volunteers.

He'd come to see the line once, after British Rail had closed the branch down. The summer growth of weed had claimed the permanent way – ragweed, nettles and brambles had grown up as the seasons passed. Even saplings and buddleias had forced through the ballast between the rusting rails.

The railway seemed lost, yet here it was alive with its lingering smell of paint, grease, creosote on the palings and flowers in pots along the platform.

Archie detached himself from the crowd checking their watches and adjusting cameras as they waited for the train, a steam excursion from the Midlands, he was told. He found the wicket gate at the platform end, pushed through and walked down into the woods on the steep hillside below the line, trees reaching up from a carpet of faded grasses. The wood had changed over the years, grown different and new, yet there was a familiarity. He found a wooden seat in a small clearing which was new. Archie sat down.

Even at the cricket, and all the way driving from the store to the station, his mind had been composing the letter he ought to write to the company directors, if there were any in place from the old company. The main text was clear in Archie's mind.

Gentlemen,

Harptree & Ellis is a well run business, it stands out in the county as a sound enterprise valued by both customers and staff. Over four family generations it has been developed to become the key business in Tonecastle.

The late Oscar Harptree understood the true worth of the business not only as the asset he owned, but also as the enterprise of its loyal and longstanding staff. He recognised the pride they have taken in the success and good standing of the store in the eyes of its customers.

Had the late Mr Harptree so wished he could on more than one occasion have realised the inherent asset value of the store, yet he was ever mindful of the store's value to the community of customers and staff.

The plan I have heard outlined today by Andrew Harptree is a selfish asset-stripping breakup of a sound enterprise, and places no value on the longstanding goodwill and commitment of the staff. It is being done to benefit narrow self interest and is likely in the long run to fail.

I deplore the action being taken...

Requiem for Private Hughes

Should it be an open letter putting his opinion in front of the store's customers and staff? Yet even as he thought of that bold step Archie realised his letter would never be sent, never get further than the words in his head. He sat in the dappled woodland light mesmerized by the shimmering light on the stream running through the wood below him.

A small boy in shorts and a V-neck grey sweater played in the water. He'd taken off his socks and, holding a bending bough of a willow, was working his way into the stream. He had a stick in his free hand, and when he'd got his stance firm he let go the tree and started to push the stick under rocks, looking for little water beasts fleeing their cover. There was a home made net attached to the other end of the stick and on the bank a preserving jar taken from the larder when no one was looking half full of stream water and weed.

The boy sought a prize to take home from the stream, a water beast to live in the jar on the chest by his bed. He planned to watch through the night as the beast wriggled round his makeshift tank. He'd have to hide his trophy when he took it into the house fearing his mother would throw it out and give him a row for taking the preserving jar.

The train, its steam engine panting from the gradient, rumbled along the line, slowing into the station, breaking into Archie's nostalgia.

He walked back up the path to the wicket gate, teasing himself he might see a driver's face he knew, even hear his father's shout on the platform calling out for arriving passengers. Standing with a hand on the gate that had been inches higher than the child carrying home the fish caught in the stream, Archie watched the excitement amongst the passengers in their compartments enjoying their day's excursion – old men reliving times past, their grandchildren impatient to get to the seaside at Northhill to dig forts in the sand and nag parents for ice creams. The train was full of happiness.

Archie braced himself. It was time to get moving.

Dorothy knew he would be late after watching cricket, now he would be early. It would be best to go Ivy's cottage and have a chat, to talk about the situation at Harptree's and to have her advice on what and when to tell his mother. Ivy understood Dorothy. They had been friends going back to Ivy's early teens, coming over to the station cottage most days to look after Archie, taking him off on long country rambles, almost as if he was a doll to treat as her own infant.

Ivy had been there for Dorothy when things went wrong. She was there when the telegram came from the War Office. In the forces, Ivy was at home on leave after a period of illness. She had common sense, she knew how to cope. She got the sad household through – Archie aged eight, Dorothy facing the chasm of being alone when other soldiers came home, and Archie's grandmother bottling up her shock at the repeating tragedy of her grief for Dorothy's father, his last letter from the trenches arriving days after the advice that he was lost in action, presumed dead.

Age had crept up on Dorothy, if anyone could it would be Ivy who would persuade Archie's mother to confide in the doctor, Ivy must persuade her to take it easy, leave all the gardening to Archie, now that he would have the time.

Ivy was out, but her cottage was unlocked. Archie let himself in calling out in case she was about then went through to the garden behind the cottage. She would see his car and not be surprised he was there, but after half-an-hour there was no sign of her. There was nothing for it, but to go home.

Dorothy sat deep in the kitchen chair. 'I thought you would be at the cricket.'

'It rained. I got cold.'

'Haven't seen rain here, garden needs it.'

'Would you like me to cook supper tonight?'

'I'm not hungry.'

'Not an omelette, a cheese omelette? It would be good for you.'

'We've no eggs, Son.'

'I can get eggs.' Archie grabbed at the chance of going out again. 'Why don't we keep chickens, like we used to do? You enjoyed having them about.'

'They take a lot of doing.'

'I could do the hard work.'

Archie didn't want to tell her, not yet. He would explain it in the morning, when he'd seen Ivy.

'I was thinking of getting out my new painting things. I haven't done any drawing for an age.' Archie thought of his sketch of Lorna, his imagination of a naked Lorna, hidden on the bookshelf. He would have to think of a place to hide any larger portrait.

'That'll be good, Son. I like to see you painting; you were always good at it.'

Chapter Eleven

THE mass of junk cleared out of the summerhouse was piled up on the lawn and Archie had painted a coat of white emulsion round the inside wooden walls; it didn't look a professional job on the rough timber boards yet it gave the place more the feel of a studio, Archie's studio. He put up two runs of narrow shelving to display finished and half-finished pictures against the back wall, including his sequence of experimental paintings, building a portfolio of Exmoor landscapes.

There were shortcomings, yet he was beginning to find a style much as he had in jungle days, releasing tension after patrols. Avoiding the obvious tourist sites, he sought out the subtlety of the landscape in its colours and shapes, his view of the shades and proportions of the rounded hills and wooded valleys.

He'd re-visited a bend on the River Barle below Withypool he'd known as a boy. It triggered some of the excitement the jungle had given him. He'd found the only sketch book saved from Malaya. Leafing through the pages he wondered if he would ever go back to Malaysia. The weekend papers advertised the country as a holiday destination. It was strange to think of it as a place for a ten day break.

Archie had exhibited pictures with others in a small gallery in Tonecastle, an upstairs floor over a craft shop, a contact through a friend of Dorothy's in Helecombe. Pleasant remarks were left in the gallery's guest book from those who climbed the steep stairs to view the pictures. But there were no sales of his paintings. Two fellow exhibitors had sold enough to keep them happy; they'd been showing for years locally and knew what would sell. Archie didn't think their work of greater merit than his own. That was the rub, they sold and he didn't.

Heavy clouds were building to the west. Before it rained he had to sort out the rubbish piled on the lawn. There was no point in re-stowing broken stuff that had lain unused in the summerhouse for years, things that should have been cleared away earlier during the strange months since his Harptree's days had ended. Those were long months of adjusting to a different pace of life and trying to use the cramped space of the summer house as a studio. A rotted tennis net; they'd never had a tennis court, he'd picked it up in a job lot at a sale, broken sunshades acquired over the years, deck chairs with ripped seats and one-time garden gadgets that had outlived their inspiration. Archie pulled the sofa back into the summer house, still something to keep despite its ripped lining after years of wintering mice. A studio needed a sofa.

By the time the rain came, pattering drops on the windows until it was drumming on the shingle roof, there was only rubbish left outside. It could wait; a trip to the recycling yard would be needed to get rid of it, a task long overdue. He decided a kettle, bottles of water, a jar of tea bags and a tin of biscuits, together with a camping stove would make for comfort in his studio.

Archie sat on the old sofa, lumpy and uncomfortable, surveying the effect of his morning's labours. In grandmother's day, when he and Dorothy came back to Hawthorne Cottage, the sofa was important in the parlour, next to the heavy dresser where the best china was kept, used only if a guest of rank in his grandmother's eyes was entertained, the vicar or the doctor.

Pride of place on the parlour dresser was the glass dome that held two long-dead Mandarin ducks. The ducks had been a source of wonder to the kindergarten boy. It was years since he'd thought about those ducks, he didn't remember their going. He'd drawn them many times for his portfolio to get into the art college. Archie guessed Dorothy had sold them when he was in the army.

He rocked the sofa, the frame was sound. A good upholsterer could work new comfort onto its Edwardian style and get rid of the flapping arm where the mechanism had failed. He leaned back on its good end as the rain drummed down, but not wanting to stay in the summerhouse too long. Dorothy spent much of her time in bed these days. She liked a cup of hot Bovril and a thinly sliced tomato sandwich for lunch. If it didn't stop raining in a quarter of an hour he would have to make a run for the house.

Hawthorne Cottage had seen changing times: his childhood, his years away, his years at Harptree's and now the new order of their life since the demise of the department store.

Not to forget the day Dorothy set fire to the orchard. It was something to laugh at now, at the time it was terrible. Archie thought the cottage would go with it. The ex-Army flame gun was a curse, but Dorothy thought it a good tool to keep the weeds in check. He hadn't realised what use she made of it when he'd been away working. She zapped the first weed growth on the paths, in the driveway, everywhere she wanted to keep clear.

He'd told her he would look after weeding in the garden, he hadn't realised how quickly the June sunshine forced their growth. The weeds got away and the orchard was turning to hay. On a day he rode his bicycle with its baskets fore and aft into Helecombe to get groceries from the shop, he'd pedalled along the quiet road, a pleasure to take the exercise now the bypass had been cut through the far side of the valley taking the traffic with it. As he cycled home he saw smoke billowing up. There had been little rain through April and May, last winter's dead grass was dry at the base of the summer growth. He was puzzled there was a bonfire burning. Dorothy would never light a fire if she thought birds were nesting.

The fire engine caught up with him half a mile from home. The retained firemen from Helecombe recognised the figure on the bicycle.

'It's your orchard, Archie,' they shouted down. 'You'd best jump up.'

He dropped his bike at the roadside. The smell of oil in the cab, the roaring engine, took him back to his days of troop wagons on army service. There was an excitement as the men strapped on their gear, the siren sounded without any need, other than announcing they were on their way.

They turned up the lane to Hawthorne Cottage. 'Best go past and back into the gateway. What's happened?'

'Ivy rang, didn't bother with the 999, she rang me at the shop.' Eustace Miller ran the ironmongers and delighted in any break from his routine. 'She said your mother had been using the flame gun on the weeds.'

'I told her to leave it alone,' said Archie.

It was three hours before they were satisfied the fire wouldn't flare again. The wind had whipped it towards the house, and the old hen house, unused for years was burnt down. The huge clump of pampas grass that could cut a finger if you let your hand brush against it, was reduced to a rump, several shrubs had gone and the Bramley apple tree, their source of cooking apples for the autumn, looked bad, its blackened bark reaching up, only a few green leaves and roasted baby apples left on one side.

Dorothy was annoyed as much as frightened by what she'd done. Ivy set her to making sandwiches, getting out the large enamel teapot and putting the kettle to boil. The snack was welcomed by the firemen after their exertions.

Luckily Ivy had heard the crackle of the flames as the fire ignited into the long grass. She'd led Dorothy to safety, extinguished the flame-thrower and called Eustace at his shop, all in double quick time, but the smoke had got into Dorothy's lungs in those first few moments. When it was over she spent the rest of the day in bed and the doctor called in the evening, telling her she had to take things easy. As the weeks passed Dorothy went downhill and her grip on routine at Hawthorne Cottage slipped.

Archie could not go out unless Ivy was at the house, so Tuesday and Friday mornings became his time for excursions. On the occasions he was exhibiting, when Archie had to take his turn at manning the gallery desk for a couple of tedious hours each day, Ivy came in to sit with Dorothy. Archie didn't enjoy his duty in the gallery, desperately trying to read a book as people looked at his pictures, with his ears alert for every whisper.

Ivy and Dorothy talked about times past on those days, but the old lady would fall asleep in mid sentence. It gave Ivy the chance to stretch her legs and make a fresh pot of tea.

Activity at the Cottage changed as the pattern of nursing Dorothy mirrored her decline. For months her routine dictated their pace of life filling each day, not only for Archie, but also for Ivy, who cycled over even on the wettest mornings. Nurse Williams looked in twice a week and occasionally the doctor dropped by if passing on his rounds. It was understood Ivy was competent both as companion and as untutored nurse, and Archie was there to do the lifting. God knows, Dorothy weighed little more than a child in those last weeks.

The curtains in Dorothy's bedroom hardly parted on bright days. Archie read to her in the afternoons, her questions and comments fading. She no longer took up the words of poems to speak the lines learned decades earlier at the village school. Her favourite poet was Keats, once word perfect just as it had been with Zebedee Vellacott. They were both taught at Helecombe School in the days of Mr Anstey his syllabus unchanged when Dorothy went to the school in the teacher's old age.

Zed had spoken to the cows on winter milking evenings:
"St Agnes' Eve – Ah, bitter chill t'was!
Th'owl, vorall 'is feathers was a-cold;
Th' hare limp'd tremblin through th't frozen grass,
And silent wus th't flock in woolly fold."

Archie had revelled in the rich Somerset recitation on the days he worked with Zed in the milking parlour, and recalled how Dorothy sat by his childhood bed, reciting the same stanzas before he was tucked up on winter nights. Yet in those last days she slept through Keats's words. On a dark afternoon threatening rain he read to her with the realisation it was for the last time.

Archie held her hand and Ivy held his. They sat in silence together after her wheezing stopped. The doctor came, then later a colleague to issue the death certificate. They called Mr Foster in Helecombe whose joinery business included duty as funeral director. He came to perform a routine task, yet at Hawthorne Cottage it witnessed the passing of an era.

Mr Foster and his assistant took Dorothy from the house in which she had been born seventy-seven years earlier, years that had seen her father march off to Flanders and never return; her husband, proud stationmaster Donald, buried in a war-torn Italian mountain village; and which had so nearly cost the life of her son in the Malayan jungle.

Chapter Twelve

ARCHIE kept busy in the days afterwards. Ivy had little to do once she had cleared up Dorothy's bedroom, returning it to a neutral place. She busied herself in the kitchen, needing to grieve on her own, planning the menu for those coming back from the church after the funeral. Archie put a notice in the Gazette and discussed hymns with the churchwarden, as there was no vicar attached to the parish. The Reverend Andrews had retired two years back to live with his daughter in Norfolk, and the authorities were yet to appoint any new incumbent, the living already shared with its neighbouring parish.

Dorothy had spoken of Mr Andrews taking her funeral, his leaving forgotten and Archie hadn't reminded her. There was no chance of getting him back to Helecombe to take the service. The churchwarden, himself a newcomer, promised a vicar would be there on the day to take the service. Archie wondered how many would come, as most of Dorothy's contemporaries had gone before her or moved away to live with their families.

There was work to be done in the garden. He mowed lawns, hoping he wouldn't have to do so again before the year end, raked up leaves from the paths and gave a final hoeing to the vegetable beds. Everyone coming to the church would be invited back to the house. Archie didn't want them thinking the garden in which Dorothy had spent so many hours had been neglected.

Archie woke on the funeral morning with a feeling of impending invasion, knowing the house would be filled with guests, some of whom he wouldn't recognise. He went by taxi early to the church where he and Ivy had spent the previous afternoon decorating Dorothy's window, the broad windowsill she had taken over from her mother to decorate with flowers at Easter, and with trails of ivy and holly at Christmas. Archie checked the decoration wasn't disturbed. He spoke with the Churchwarden, laying out printed Order of Service sheets in each pew, then went outside wanting to welcome those arriving and keen to be seen before he followed Dorothy's coffin into the church.

While Archie shook unaccustomed hands filing into the church, Ivy busied herself guiding people into pews. A chauffeur-driven car stopped at the church gate. Archie recognised the figure as soon as she was out of the car. He hadn't expected anyone from the Harptree family, although one or two of his erstwhile colleagues had taken their place in the church.

Oscar's daughter smiled as she walked up the church path.

'Mary, it is good of you to come.'

'Archie, it was the least I could do. Dorothy was such a loyal friend to all at Harptrees.'

'She was certainly proud of the store and my years with the company.'

'Not with the way we treated you all in the end. Archie, it wasn't what we wanted, things happened too quickly. Andrew persuaded us it was best for him to buy us out, he never let on he planned to close Harptree's down. I'm ashamed of it.'

'Mary, it happened, we all have to move on. I thought it was an awful decision for the business at that time... maybe it would have run its course before too long.'

Mary held his hand, neither of them letting go, sharing the emotion.

'How's Edward, Mary?'

'He's in America and enjoying himself, from the little that filters back to me. He's lecturing in European History at a university in California.'

'I'm glad he's found his feet.'

'Andrew offered him a job, but he was having none of it.'

'Good on him.'

The Churchwarden walked down the path pointing to the gate and nodding to Archie. A hearse followed by a black car was coming to a stop. A clergyman stepped out of the car and moved towards the hearse. Mary followed Archie's gaze.

'I mustn't detain you, Archie. We'll speak some more.'

'Thank you for coming, Mary; you'll come back to Hawthorne Cottage afterwards?'

Mary nodded and turned toward the church porch.

Archie swallowed and clenched his hands before moving toward the gate where the Churchwarden introduced him to the visiting vicar, Reverend Clements.

The undertaker's men shouldered their modest burden and with the vicar leading, his crumpled surplice blowing in the wind, they set off into the church.

After a wavering first verse the congregation took heart, the hymn sounded round the beams of the old nave, as had so many hymns over hundreds of years. Archie's thoughts drifted to his Sunday school days, the church cool in summer yet freezing in midwinter, the children not justifying keeping the stove burning into the afternoon after Matins.

'Dearly beloved, we are gathered here in the sight of God to give thanks for the life of Denise Middlebrook.'

A second of silence hushed the congregation, Archie stared at the vicar.

'My mother's name was Dorothy.'

Mr Clements looked up startled at the interruption.

'Of course... the life of Dorothy Middlebrook.'

Ivy reached along the pew to take Archie's hand. As the clergyman continued, Archie heard nothing, fighting back a lump in his throat. He felt in his pocket for the slip of paper on which he had written his prompt for the few words he wanted to say to honour his mother and then had to check in the Order of Service whether his place was before or after the next hymn. It was before.

He gave Ivy's hand a squeeze, as the congregation settled into their seats, he edged past Dorothy's coffin and took his place between the choir stalls, rather than at the lectern as had been suggested. Ivy smiled and gave him a double wink, the secret sign they'd used together in the years when teenage Ivy had taken young Archie on summer walks.

"My mother, Dorothy, sang in the choir from these stalls as a child, as a teenager, as a mother and as a widow; she was baptised in this church in the few months before her father died on the Western Front, she was married here and in this church she grieved for her stationmaster husband, Donald, who rests where he fell in the heat of battle in Italy. Dorothy was of this village and it is fitting we say goodbye to her here in the church at Helecombe."

Archie went on to thank the many people for being there and to recount the times of fun Dorothy had enjoyed in her life.

As he spoke the heavy latch of the church door gave a metallic clunk, the hinges creaked, many turned in their pews and a figure in a fur coat and sombre hat came into the gloom at the back of the church. The woman held up a gloved hand toward Archie in apology for the interruption as she slipped into a place, where others squeezed up to let her in. Archie stopped what he was saying and only remembered once back in his pew to turn and invite people back to Hawthorne Cottage after the service.

He was surprised Maggie had come. He looked at Ivy, she nodded. Ivy knew something.

Archie had dreaded the prospect of the hours at the church and entertaining those that came back to the cottage. He stood with Ivy at the graveside in the far corner of the churchyard close by his grandmother's grave, which he'd found overgrown since Dorothy had ceased caring for it. Now the grass was cut, the stonework was washed with fresh flowers placed in a new vase a few days earlier. They were joined by some of the mourners as the clergyman ran through the committal service and Ivy tossed flowers over the coffin being lowered into the ground.

On their way to the cars Archie thanked the undertakers, the Churchwarden and Mr Clements. He was not disappointed when the clergyman said he had a further appointment.

Neither Ivy nor Archie spoke as Jack Horsefield, the grandson of the taxi owner who'd brought Dorothy and Archie home from

Jellalabad Barracks after Malaya, drove them to Hawthorne Cottage to welcome their guests.

It was only later when most had departed that Archie found Ivy alone boiling up yet another kettle in the kitchen.

'Did you know Maggie was coming, Ivy?'

'Dorothy made me promise to let her know. I didn't think she would come.'

'How did you find her?'

'Dorothy had kept in touch on and off over the years. I should have told you, Archie.'

'Just as well you didn't. I was nervous enough over the day. When she came in I lost the place, probably for the best.'

'Let's hope this is the last pot of tea. Believe it or not we're nearly out of tea bags.'

'Have you seen Maggie here? It's a long way to come if she's come down from London, just for the funeral, and missing most of that. Has she come far?'

'Around London some place, Dorking, I think the address was. No, I haven't seen her, Archie. She never replied to my letter.'

Archie puzzled over Maggie's abrupt arrival and seeming disappearance as he said farewell to Janet, long retired from the Harptree switchboard, an operator who had taken great pride in recognising most of Oscar's callers from their first words. To many outside the business she had been the authentic voice of Harptree's.

Glancing out of the window Archie saw a figure in a fur coat wandering across the lawn making her way toward his summer-house studio.

Ivy had her hands in the sink. 'Ivy, don't do that. I've got all evening to sort things out. You must get off home while it's still light.'

'I'm in no hurry, Archie.'

'I could run you back.'

'I've got my bike. I'd rather get this sorted out.'

'I've just seen Maggie out on the lawn. I'd better go and find her.'

'I'm glad she's come, Archie. Dorothy would have liked that. It didn't work out for you two, but your mother was always fond of Maggie. Her mother was a special school friend to Dorothy before the family upped sticks and went away.'

'I'll go and find her.'

On an impulse Archie picked up two glasses and an open bottle of white wine as he went out into the garden.

The lawn was damp with evening dew. He walked towards the summerhouse leaving a trail in the wet grass. There was no sign of Maggie, or anyone else; he couldn't have imagined seeing her. Then he saw another trail in the grass and noticed a dull red spot of light brightening then fading inside the summerhouse.

'Hello, Archie. Am I welcome?'

'Of course you are, Maggie. I didn't know you were coming.

'I didn't know whether to come or not. I'm sorry I was late. I thought I could creep in, that door latch made a ghastly noise.'

'Let me put these down and light a candle.'

'Wine, brilliant, I need something to cheer me up.'

Even in the fading light of the day Archie had no problem laying his hands on matches; once the first candle was lit he took a taper and lit more candles to give a gentle light in the summerhouse.

'Archie, you've turned this into a studio. Are all these paintings yours?' Maggie seated on the old sofa looked round the walls lined with work, mostly finished, others barely started.

Archie poured out two glasses passing one across. 'Good health, I'm glad to see you, Maggie, and yes, these are all mine.'

'They're great.'

'If only the picture-buying public thought the same.'

Later Archie fetched two more bottles down to the summerhouse, one of Cabernet Sauvignon and one of Merlot; he preferred red, even knowing there would be a penalty in the morning.

They put away more than they should have drunk. His relief the dreaded day had passed led him into excess.

Layers covering the hurt of three decades had peeled away with the wine, silent for long periods as they both remembered the excess of their time together. Archie's anxiety, sprung on him when he saw Maggie entering the church, dissolved as the candles burnt down and the bottles emptied.

Maggie, with a blanket wrapped round against the cold, lit up cigarette after cigarette masking her own nervousness; from time to time she coughed. She shrugged when Archie admonished her.

'No stationmaster to greet me when I got to Tonecastle. The train was packed, it took me an age to find a taxi; and then he wouldn't let me light up. I'm sorry I was so late. I had to have a ciggy when I got to the church. I could hear you were speaking as I waited outside. I really did think I could slip in without a sound.'

'You should have told us you were coming, we could have arranged something.'

'I didn't know if I would be welcome. I was horrible to you, Archie.'

'I was naive in those days, Maggie.'

'And you have never married, Archie?'

'I've led a quiet life, I guess.'

'God, you were a ram that day we had together here in this old summerhouse, and on this same couch. I was stupid to let you go.'

After more than thirty years the hurt of the awful night in London whirled through his mind, they stared at each other until Archie shook his head.

'We were young. Now let's change the subject.'

'Give me a kiss, Archie.'

Archie made Maggie drink black coffee when he got her back to the house sitting her down in the comfy kitchen chair where the dog put her head on Maggie's lap looking to have her muzzle stroked as her tail wagged. Archie checked the spare bedroom, turned on the electric blanket and made certain there were towels put out.

'You're sending me to bed, aren't you?'

He helped her up the stairs and into the bedroom.

'Are you going to undress me, Archie? You've done it before.'

'You are incorrigible, Maggie. You need a good sleep. Get yourself undressed and into bed. Turn out the light and I'll see you in the morning.'

'Yes, Sir. Have you milked the cows this evening, Sir?'

'Maggie, into bed, I'm going to take the dog out and get to bed myself.'

Archie let time pass after he came in from the garden.

He saw the spare room light was out as he came upstairs and looked in to be sure Maggie had got into bed. She was breathing deeply.

'Night, night, my Farm Boy,' she muttered as he shut the door.

* * * * *

After a dawn stroll round the garden with Patch, Archie gazed out of the kitchen window, seeing the morning mist gather on the hillside beyond Greenings Plantation.

Apart from the two glasses and empty wine bottles he'd brought up from the summerhouse, the kitchen was as tidy as Ivy always left it. Ivy had done all the washing up and putting away, the chairs in the sitting room, pushed back to make room for their visitors were restored to their usual places and it looked as if the carpets were vacuumed. Ivy never left any place untidy.

With his elbows on the kitchen table and his mouth dry, despite two glasses of milk, Archie didn't regret his excess even for the night of his mother's funeral.

Later he would go to the church to be certain everything was in order. He would have to arrange matters with a stonemason for a gravestone. It would need room to add Dorothy's father and her husband, his father. The decision could wait a few days.

There were many things to plan, the things he'd wanted at Hawthorne Cottage, always resisted by Dorothy never wanting change to her childhood home. Central heating for a start even knowing the disruption the installation would cause. If he got on with it getting a plumber over in the next few days it might be done before winter sets in with frosts and bitter mornings. And the conservatory; he'd had that planned for years, measured out, even specified and quoted, but Dorothy had refused while agreeing it would be pleasant to sit out in its shelter on stormy days. "It'll make me idle, Son," she'd concluded setting her mind against his idea.

Maggie and three husbands, who would have thought it; one of them knighted so she'd been a 'Lady' at one time. Three husbands, three divorces and a lover or two besides; Archie recalled a society scandal over a junior minister who took his mistress to a United Nations conference in the Maldives. With only her married name in the press he'd never made the connection.

She'd smoked cigarette after cigarette, the stale tobacco odour mingling with the oil smells of his paintings. This morning he'd opened all the summerhouse windows to let the autumn breeze waft through.

It was time to cook breakfast. He wanted a fry up; there was black pudding and bacon in the fridge, the last of the summer's tomatoes and he hoped there was a homemade loaf left after yesterday's entertaining.

The back door latch woke the dog lying on the warm slates beside the range.

'Ivy... I didn't expect you this morning.'

'It's hard to break my routine, Archie.'

'Thank you for everything yesterday, Ivy. I think it went off as it should.'

'You did you mother proud, Archie.'

'I couldn't have done half that without you, Ivy. I was about to make breakfast, will you join me?'

'A bit late for me, but I'll get a brew going. I could do with a cup of tea.'

'We'd better take a cup up to Maggie.'

'She's still here, Archie? I saw you had candles burning in the summerhouse when I left. I didn't think she would be staying.

'Ivy, we talked and talked, lost all track of time. It was almost midnight when we got up to the house, far too late to send her off to a hotel.'

Ivy's look questioned Archie.

'It was just talk, Ivy. Her lifestyle is a million miles away from all of us down here in the country. She's in the spare room.'

'Lucky the bed was made up. I hope it was aired.'

'I put the electric blanket on for her.'

Ivy was still looking at Archie.

'It would be best if you took her up tea, Ivy. I'll get breakfast going.'

With the bacon, black pudding and tomatoes sizzling on the stove Archie got out another frying pan for the eggs and he cut bread to toast.

Ivy came into the kitchen.

'I think Maggie has seen a lot of life since she was last in Helecombe. I hope she gets her makeup on before she comes down. Just toast and jam, she wants, nothing cooked.'

PART THREE
1992
Chapter Thirteen

ARCHIE braced himself on the hedge bank working his handsaw, mindful of the lessons Zed taught him in hedge craft. Hand milking twice a day had been the routine farm work. Archie chuckled, doubting any child in Helecombe these days knew how to milk a cow. Yet of everything he did that winter after Malaya it was hedging he'd taken to most, outside in the fields, whatever the weather.

Over years Archie had worked long hours in the Hawthorne Cottage orchard. Once the cider apple trees had stood close by the cottage, those nearest the house had grown old and barren. He'd cleared them for firewood, digging out roots making space for his mother's herbaceous borders and vegetable garden. But he was proudest of his work on the orchard hedge banks; they were in as good shape as any in the parish. At intervals over the years he'd tackled the three boundaries with their neighbouring farmland, each in turn. Now he was back laying the first hedge for the third time after thirty years.

Archie stopped his work and stood up, breathing heavily and anticipating the brief, dizzy moment that accompanied any rapid movement these days. His sweat-soaked shirt clung cold on his back in the mean February wind. He owned a chainsaw and kept it maintained for use with heavy work. He preferred to use a handsaw whenever he could, finding it easier to control the cut, better able to pick the moment to press the slant-cut stem down along the hedge-bank on the line he wanted it to rest, finishing the bank with an even spread to sprout new summer growth.

There were trees standing along the bank chosen from saplings on earlier workings. Once there had been great elms amongst the sycamore, the beech and ash trees, until hit by disease in the seventies and felled. They'd sprouted and grown for a few years more before the voracious beetle returned. Archie cut out the dying saplings for burning.

It was a half after two in the afternoon, still a good light yet Archie needed to quit having forgotten to wear his back support; it made it harder to bend, but eased the strain on heavy jobs. It might be the third time this run of hedgerow had been laid, but now every yard of it found him out. In days past, employed in Tonecastle, he'd worked on the hedge over winter weekends revelling in the break from accounting office routines. Dorothy had brought out sandwiches and ale, putting on stout gloves to gather up the off-cuts and brashings to build a huge burning pile. Later Archie would gather the cordwood and cut it for winter logs, splitting the bigger logs for best burning. Now he was alone and home all the time, he had all day, all week, to work on the hedge and he took his time.

Archie weighed the billhook in his hand, ran his finger along the blade sensing the keen edge and felt for the initial 'V' carved into its handle. Vellacott gave it to him telling how he'd learned his craft from his father using that same billhook. Zed taught him how to sharpen it and how to use its weight, not his strength, to strip the branches. Archie's mentor had been a man of sinew and fond of his cider. In those days, older than Archie now, he wouldn't have stopped his day at half after two. Zed did field work till four o'clock, summer and winter, before calling the cows in for milking.

For Archie it was time to pack up. He wiped his tools with an oiled cloth and hesitated looking down from the bank; years ago he would have jumped down, not today. He reached into the hedge to find a handhold to ease his way off the bank. Unbalanced, he lifted his foot, snagged it against a stump of wood and tripped, tumbling over to fall heavily to the foot of the bank, sprawling onto soaking grass.

Archie stared unbelieving at the billhook, the hook of the blade embedded in his leg, then blood ran red over his hand and pain shot up his spine, nausea churning his stomach. His mind numb, the instinct of the battlefield dragged him back to the cottage, blood trailing across the lawn.

He dialled the phone leaning on the hall wall. Ivy, a mile away in her cottage, answered in her quiet telephone voice, always cautious over what she might hear.

'Ivy, thank God you're there. I've had an accident...' Archie's knees buckled, he sank to the floor, slumping in a pile on the hall slates as blood seeped from his tight grip on the slashed trouser leg. The telephone handset hung down the wall, swinging on its cable.

'Archie, Archie, are you there? What's happened?'

He pulled at a scarf hanging from a peg close by, tied it round his thigh twisting it into a rough tourniquet trying to staunch the bleeding. 'I'm bleeding,' he shouted towards the phone. 'I need help.'

Ivy dialled 999, and pedalled her bicycle as fast as she could to Hawthorne Cottage arriving just ahead of the ambulance. The paramedics worked fast telling Ivy it would have been worse, even fatal, if he'd not been able to get the tourniquet in place.

Five weeks went by before he was free of the plaster cast; not only had he sliced into a vein in his thigh, he'd damaged an ankle ligament, hence the cast and for three weeks after his stay in hospital he'd used a pair of crutches. He was eased through exercises set by the physiotherapist team to strengthen his ankle and banish his limp.

The episode was an embarrassment. His stupidity in ignoring the obvious risk of getting down from the bank with the billhook in his hand was plain for anybody. It was a tool he took such pride in keeping sharp,.

When Ivy collected him to bring him home she'd looked at him sitting in a chair waiting. She shook her head, glad Dorothy was spared the worry over his antics.

The tendon had taken too long to heel; the hedge remained part laid well into spring. By the time the physiotherapists were satisfied that he had got back full use of his muscles, the blackthorn was in blossom hinting at an autumn harvest for sloe gin.

* * * * *

Months later, on a September evening, Archie cooked scrambled eggs for his supper, a quick favourite. The egg from his wandering hens was served on late spinach pulled from a ragged row sown as he'd reached at an awkward angle with his ankle in plaster. He grated cheddar over the steamed spinach, added anchovies and a sprinkle of nutmeg. A bottle of red wine had been standing on the kitchen table during the day. Archie was tired not having slept well for a week. Two glasses of red wine with a glass of water between and an early night was his tonic for a sound sleep.

Not tonight.

After undressing letting his clothes drop in a pile on the floor, he'd slipped naked into bed. In bed before ten his mind rambled on, worrying about his paintings. He'd built up a portfolio of landscapes to take round galleries, and after weeks confined to the house and garden, not confident to drive although officially permitted, the first outing proved fruitless. The gallery hadn't wanted to take any of his work. They weren't poor pictures – the proprietor said they were competent – backhanded praise if ever there was. Archie knew he could paint better, but his paintings lacked spirit, they didn't rank well alongside the bold colour and confidence of the exhibition the gallery had on display.

The sounds of the night broke into his thoughts, a fox barked and a tawny owl called to its young. He lifted his head from the pillow, frustrated and wide awake well after Radio 4 had switched to the World Service. Through half-closed eyes he sensed a flash on the wall opposite his open window. Archie counted seconds passing – eight, nine, ten – before the rumble came – ten miles away. Eyes now wide open in the black night, he waited for the lightning to come again.

White and magenta flashed through the bedroom, bouncing from the long mirror, flashing across the ceiling, flickering for an electric moment. To the west beyond Hegly Beeches, beyond King's Beercombe, somewhere over Brendon Hill, he guessed. Six, seven… it was coming closer.

There was no point in trying to sleep. Archie went down to the kitchen, wearing a towelling robe, confident of every step in the dark. He opened the remaining wine, rinsing out Grandmother's old stemmed glass in the pulsing light from the microwave display. He poured wine close up to the brim. The electricity had been interrupted by power surges spiking down the lines, tripping distribution switches, and there was no point in resetting anything until the storm passed.

The dog, as had others before her, was lying on the warmed slates close by the stove, just a rapid beat from the tip of her tail against the dishwasher telling of her anxiety.

In the conservatory pulsing rain drummed across the roof. A steady dripping percussion reminding him of the damaged roof panel, already a month since the supplier had promised to courier a replacement. Patch, head down, followed him and pushed against his chair.

Music, the storm needed music, loud music blasting from the CD player. No chance, the power was off again.

The conservatory roof creaked in the buffeting wind, the first proper storm to test its construction. A huge blue flash backlit the umber and pink of heavy clouds, reflecting palely on his towel robe as he tensed in his chair.

Had he shut up the chickens, dropped their pop-hole door? It was too late to worry about them; the fox he'd heard earlier was unlikely to be prowling with the storm beating down. The dog whimpered, lightning and simultaneous thunder cracked overhead, flood lighting the garden with galloping shadows. Archie sat in his high backed rattan chair, wine glass in his hand, and watched the storm move through.

Would Dorothy have approved the new conservatory, despite her reservations? Surely Mother would have liked it once it was done; hated the upheaval and the casual familiarity of the builders. They took over the place for three days, staying in a Helecombe B&B and gaining a reputation in the pub. She would have liked the finished thing, the chance it gave to grow new plants and enjoy sheltered winter sunshine.

Central heating had been his top priority in renovating the cottage. At first he regretted the upset, carpets and floorboards up, ugly pipes running down the walls; in the first winter it proved its worth. Central heating and a dishwasher, his mother would no more have had a dishwasher than go abroad. No dirty crockery ever lingered, everything was washed up before she got on with her next task. Ivy had prevailed on Dorothy to get a washing machine; once Ivy was in her fifties she insisted there would be no more hand washing on Fridays.

He'd tried for years to get his mother's agreement, but she didn't want to change anything about the cottage. Though not born at Hawthorne Cottage, it had been his home for most of his life and he did want change. The night he was born, in the bedroom at the stationmaster's house at Helecombe Halt, had been one of thunderstorms. Dorothy told him the midwife arrived on her bicycle, puffing from the steep hill, soaked through in the downpour, trembling as she came through the door. She'd needed a brandy to steady herself. Dorothy had joked Archie delayed his arrival for the midwife to recover.

As the storm rumbled on Archie recalled those last weeks of his mother's illness, at first too proud to admit her infirmity then confined to her room with the awful business of the commode, struggling on her own, forbidding her son to help her on and off. Then overnight it all changed, she accepted everything; she was at peace with the final onset. Much of the day she slept, other times he read her poems, but most often they talked. Long, rambling chains of thought unwinding in her mind, telling him things she hadn't shared in the years since his father went to war.

Archie hadn't known his father had a weakness for drink, had been violent at times. The father he knew, always the immaculate stationmaster, was a war hero; he grew up knowing his father had won a bravery medal. His father's weakness with drink explained why his mother was upset whenever Archie went drinking as a young man, why it was awkward having wine with their meals. She wouldn't drink alcohol; she went quiet if he helped himself to a second glass.

The dog shivered uneasy at the storm thundering overhead, just as other storms had played out thousands of miles and a few decades away, watched from his clammy hospital bed under the ceiling fans in the British Military Hospital in Penang. Clouds piled high capturing the flaring lightning, flickering till it burst into the atmosphere, rumbling thunder echoing to the horizon, rain teeming onto the hospital veranda roof. It was not quite the same on a late summer night in England without tropical heat to sponge away the rain.

Swallows had come back in numbers, all summer they'd been about, wheeling and twittering in their faultless aerobatics then as evenings drew in they'd spent a few days congregating on telegraph wires and unnoticed at first they weren't around anymore their migration started. Every year Archie tried to remember which day it was he saw the last swallow of summer; he was never certain. The first swallow in spring was an excitement, eagerly awaited, that flicker in the sky. Was it? Wasn't it? Then there was no mistake as one, maybe two together, curved in a great arc round and over the cottage before banking into the old stable onto the beams and their nest of the previous summer. Every year his mother had written the date down in the kitchen diary, sometimes in the first week of April, more often for the middle of the month.

Archie had never seen a swallow in March, yet his mother had seen a March swallow. During the war, on her birthday, 20th March 1944, only days after she'd received the War Office telegram.

That was another thing she told him in those last days, convinced the March swallow was a final token from his father, lying cold in a freshly dug grave high in the Apennines. She believed in her heart that particular swallow had come directly to her, from the olive groves and vineyards of Umbria to the greening fields of West Somerset. When she told Archie her long held secret that she knew the March swallow had brought his father's last fond kiss, Archie wept. Birds migrated oblivious of man's war, in their thousands they ebbed and flowed across the battlefields of Europe. It could so easily be true; why not? Swallows had to come north by some route, why not across the sea from Africa to Sicily, up the spine of Italy where his father died, round the Alps, across the length of France and over the Channel to West Somerset? Swallows return to their nesting place each year. Why should it not have been that a swallow hatched under the beams of their stable had flit across the Umbrian sky on its homeward journey from Africa as Pioneer Corps volunteers dug a meagre grave to take the body they had collected from the shelled building?

Loom from a half moon broke through the storm clouds as the thunder drifted away. Archie put a fresh tin under the drip from the conservatory roof and listened to it changing note as the base of the container flooded.

Dorothy had said Donald was violent. Did she mean his father hit her? He didn't want to believe that. Archie had gone through school boasting about his father, convinced he was happy with the glory, yet with no man at home he envied the boys who had dads, even ordinary dads; they didn't have to be war heroes.

After Mario had gone back to Italy there had been Uncle Jack, not a real uncle, but he had been good to Archie, looked out for him, he came to school concerts and plays. He spent much time at Hawthorne Cottage until he married a woman a lot older than his mother, much older than Uncle Jack, and he'd moved away. It was said she had money. Dorothy never had a special friend after Uncle Jack.

There had been talk when the stationmaster married and their son was born months later. Donald was a respected man, he took a stand against Sunday working on the branch line choosing his duties as a Sidesman at Matins greeting worshippers and taking round the collection plate leaving the Sunday platform in the hands of Helecombe Halt's porter.

Requiem for Private Hughes

Donald Middlebrook's years of grieving for his brothers lost in the trenches when he was a schoolboy was eased being in a family again. As war brewed in Europe he joined the volunteers and was in France early in 1940. In his absence his duties at the station were taken up by his aging porter.

Donald's posthumous Military Medal, awarded for his action destroying a German sniper post in a fortified building high in the Italian Mountains, opened doors for Archie doing his national service. It ensured he had a place in his father's battalion. Two long-serving soldiers had been Donald's contemporaries in Italy. They worked in the back echelons at the depot by the time Archie got to the battalion, they kept an eye out for him, sheltered him from the more pointless training activities that filled up the hours of daylight.

The wine bottle had stood too close to the stove. Archie charged his special glass, the wine warm and a touch bitter as he cupped the glass in his hand, wondering on what other nights the ancient glass had given comfort to drinkers. Mother said it had been gifted from her great-grandmother. For as long as he could remember his mother had filled it with warm milk and taken it up to bed with her. He never used the glass when she was alive. Now he always drank evening wine from it, enjoying its heavy shape in his hand, the unevenness of the blower's work two centuries before, the still sharp place under the stem where it had been broken from the glassblower's rod.

The leak dripping into the tin had run its course, eased its dripping, leaving suspense in the air, the chance another drop might fall. Archie opened the double doors into the garden and breathed in the damp air, its smell distinctive after many dry days.

Memories of young men running naked under tropical rain pressed into his thoughts, young soldiers he'd never seen again over the years.

'Come on, Patch. Let's see what the storm has done to the garden.'

The dog rolled onto its back, her tail sweeping the floor tiles.

'You're keen enough to be out when I want to stay in.'

Archie stepped out into the garden, realised how wet the grass was, kicked off his slippers, and walked bare foot across the lawn. It was too dark to make out other than the shapes of shrubs and borders. He stood still a moment, hearing sounds of the storm now only a distant rumble in the night. On an impulse Archie stripped off his towelling robe, letting it drop onto the lawn and with arms outstretched, the limp from his hedging accident only a memory, he walked briskly round the well-known plot of his garden, brushing rain from the shrubs over his tingling body. A tawny owl hooted, Archie laughed. He forced his way through where the sodden shrubs were bent down with rain. The wet on his naked body excited him, the tingle on his skin, the chill that shivered into his soul. Patch barked from the safety of the conservatory doors puzzled by the cavorting shape of her master, now running round the perimeters of the garden.

Pausing only to wipe himself over with the roller towel hanging on the kitchen door, Archie went back to bed, his damp body finally drying against the sheets, shivering to warm himself, fulfilled by the storm and its aftermath. The conservatory doors were left gaping open. As his head hit the pillow he knew he should have had a pee. He seldom got through the night these days without a befuddled stagger to the bathroom, certainly not after drinking almost a bottle of wine. He lingered a moment waiting to make the effort to get out of bed.

Chapter Fourteen

ARCHIBALD Harold Middlebrook, bachelor of Helecombe parish, of fifty-seven summers, living on his own at Hawthorne Cottage, stirred from his deep sleep as daylight filtered across the garden, mopping up the night's deluge.

The rising sun projected through his bedroom window onto the wall above his bed steadily crept down the flowered wallpaper until it reached his pillow and his eyes blinked. He'd slept late, he woke to a dull feeling something was wrong with the day.

Damage from the storm was not as bad as Archie had feared. The summerhouse, for all its aging timbers, looked in reasonable shape, other than a fascia board he'd repaired before was broken away lying on the ground. On the far side of the lawn, a newly planted crab apple tree was loose from its stake and bending under its ripening harvest. Archie made a temporary repair to the fastening, something more substantial was needed and headed back to the house to get a hammer and nails to fix the facia.

A patch of stone wall on the cottage gable end caught his eye. A rambler rose he'd been training up the wall had come away, bringing down an area of render. The surface was broken and more would fall away as rain and frost got in behind it. He needed a builder on it before winter.

His waking premonition of storm damage meant a trip into Helecombe to see Eustace Miller, the ironmonger. His son, a builder and jack-of-all-trades, would get the render job done. Rather than phoning, it was best to see Eustace, as he needed to pick up heavy duty tree ties from the shop's crowded shelves. Mr Miller's days leading the retained fire crew in Helecombe had ended with the closing of the fire station. Word had it the Millers were going to retire from the shop before long. There was little chance of any ironmonger's business continuing once they sell up.

After he'd dealt with facia board and eaten breakfast of toast and marmalade, Archie made out a shopping list, took his bike with its wicker baskets from the shed and set off for Helecombe.

It was time he bought an up-to-date bicycle. He'd looked in shops, not for a lightweight sports bike, for something better suited to his aging legs, with proper gearing and modern brakes. It would no doubt be expensive, but not so great an investment as when he'd bought his Raleigh Roadster to cycle into art school in Tonecastle. It had cost all his saved money.

Ivy's cottage was not far ahead on the road. He would call in and see if there was anything he could get for her in Helecombe.

Blackbirds picked at berries along the hedgerow, rooks were gleaning in the fields and as he rounded a bend a crow tugged at the broken corpse of a rabbit hit by an early morning motorist. Archie pressed down on the pedals, weaving as he accelerated the creaking bike, trying to reach the crow pulling at its prize before it flew off.

A car raced past from behind him before he heard it and the slipstream hit him blasting him off balance and juddering off the road. The driver glanced back and the car swerved, clipping the far grass verge. In slow motion it launched into the air turning end over end, landing inverted against the hedge with a horrific crunch.

Archie threw down his bike and ran toward the car, rocking as it settled, its front wheels spinning in the air.

In the fields and hedgerows no bird sang, no cow or sheep moved. It was silent, save only for the stalled engine hissing.

Archie grabbed at a spinning wheel, needing to get hold of some moving part, to do something to restore order at the awful scene.

The driver's side lay against the hedge-bank. Archie gagged at the stench of leaking petrol as he forced his way into the broken hedge, nettles stinging his hands, briars clawing through his trousers, the wet grass and mud soaking his clothes. No window was broken, he peered in through the windscreen at the inverted driver strapped into the seat, her hands rigid, gripping the steering wheel, a ghastly stripe of blood dripping through dangling blonde hair.

Archie banged on the driver's window, there was no response. He had to get her out; he hit the window with his fist as hard as he could. He searched in the mangled hedge levering at a branch, but it wouldn't twist away. He found a stone in the banking and pulled it out, the edge cutting his fingers. With the stone in his hand and trying to warn the driver he hit the window with all his force. Again and again he hit the glass as stinking petrol seeped onto the ground.

The driver's window exploded into a myriad pieces, Archie reached past the shattered glass into the car, stretching for the seat belt fastening to free the upturned woman. She stirred, her blood dripping through her hair and on to his face and in to his eyes. He couldn't reach the end of the seat belt.

With his face close to hers an awful certainty struck him. The woman with once short mousy hair grown long and dyed blonde, was the Harptree's accountant, Lorna Curtis.

Loose debris, flung round the car as it had cart-wheeled off the road lined the inside roof. Her head was bleeding from a wound, he couldn't see. The reek of spilled fuel was in his nose and throat.

The car jerked, subsiding into the hedge and trapping Archie half in and half out of the car window. Strapped into her seat, Lorna hung down like a puppet, her knees wedged in the steering wheel, her arms flopping over her shoulders. A low moan and choking gulp gasped from her throat.

'Lorna, speak to me, say something.'

He heard a motorbike. It was stopping. It revved again. Archie screamed out for help. There was an answering shout. The motorbike roared away to summon assistance.

'Hold on, you're going to be all right, help is coming.'

He held Lorna's shoulders, trying to ease the weight of her body in the seat belt strap. He rocked her body and stretched again for the seat belt fastening, but found nothing.

'You must stay conscious, you must hang on. Help is on the way. You've had an accident. You're going to be all right.' He squeezed her shoulders. A sob broke from her gurgling mouth.

Amidst all the chaos, Archie sensed a calming force, a long mourned presence in the car with him, urging him to talk to her. He had to keep her awake, she mustn't let go.

A dog rose was pressed up against the windscreen.

'See the rosehips, Lorna. Count the red rosehips, you must count them.'

Lorna's eyes flickered, her lips parted.

'Come on, Lorna; count. One, two, three, look at them, there must be six, a dozen, count them, Lorna.'

When would help come? Why were there no more cars passing? Someone must drive past.

He shook her. 'Come on, Lorna, you must keep awake. What on earth were you doing speeding along this road. Lorna, it's Archie, speak to me, Lorna.'

Time ticked away, no vehicle went past. He heard a blackbird giving an alarm call, and the heavy breathing of a cow peering over the hedge before it saw his legs move and shied away.

Far off he heard a siren.

'Please, Lorna, talk to me,' Archie was shouting. 'Say something, Lorna.'

The awful reality of her giving up, of her slipping away from life in his arms overwhelmed him and he shook her to keep her with him.

'Count the red hips, Lorna. Count with me, blast it, one, two, count, Lorna, please, I beg you, count.'

More sirens getting closer.

Powerful engines drew close, voices approached and he heard running feet.

Ivy's panting tones shouted to the rescuers.

'The man rang 999 from my house. I live up the road.'

The rescue team worked on the car. Archie was eased clear.

'Oh grief, it's you, Archie. What on earth has happened?' Ivy clutched his arm.

'She's in there, the driver, you must get her out.'

A paramedic led him stumbling toward an ambulance to whisk him away from the scene.

After hours spent at Tonecastle General A&E being treated for cuts and bruising, cleansed of Lorna's blood and wearing borrowed clothes, his ruined garments sent to the incinerator, Archie told a police constable what he remembered of the crash.

He was told Lorna was in Intensive Care, said to be stable under observation. She'd been hit on her head by some item flung round the car. He told the hospital staff all he could about her, confirming he knew of no next of kin. He left them with his contact number.

The constable gave Archie a lift home. Ivy was waiting at Hawthorne Cottage, a casserole on the stove and hot water bottles in his bed. With the constable they sat at the kitchen table.

'I can only guess. I think she was trying to find her way here' She must have overshot our turning, it's easy to miss if you don't know it. I once worked with her at Harptree & Ellis,' he told WPC Jane Simons.

'Do you mean the place that closed down?' she queried. 'My mum used to take me there for school uniform, those horrible pinafore dresses.'

'That's the one. I thought our school uniforms were good value.'

'Value, they may have been, the height of teenage fashion they were not.'

'I left when it closed down; Lorna Curtis was appointed Chief Accountant of the replacement business. I told her at the time she was in for a rough ride. I don't know; something must have gone wrong. I can't think why else she was driving wildly into the country unless things had gone wrong.'

WPC Simons offered Ivy a lift home. Although she had her bike at Hawthorne Cottage she accepted once Archie persuaded her he was fine and would get to bed as soon as they were away.

There were candles and matches on the kitchen shelf for the all-too-frequent power cuts, as in the storm the previous night.

Requiem for Private Hughes

Alone, Archie lit several candles, turned out the kitchen lights and slumped down into the upholstered chair by the kitchen stove.

Anxious over storm damage when he'd woken, the day had brought horror and emotion leaving him washed out. And he'd never reached the ironmongers to organise the repairs to the gable end.

The candles projected light through the stems of flowers on the table sending dancing shadows onto the walls. Patch stretched out where she lay by the stove at last relaxing after a disturbed day.

Archie didn't want to go to bed. He pressed back in the chair. He had to ring the Intensive Ward in the morning to ask after Lorna. She would be all right; she had to be all right. He wasn't sure in his mind what had been said about her condition when the doctor spoke to him, there was something about an induced coma. Did he say they might put her into a coma, or they had done so? He'd have to find out in the morning.

Archie's eyes closed, but he blinked them open to see the candle-lit shadows dancing on the wall. In his mind he heard a voice, a soft Welsh tenor voice, not in the room from somewhere else, singing above the wavering whine of a well tuned military engine. The shadows on the wall reached high into the sky, great trunks of trees reaching up from the jungle floor as the rattans twisted and curled around them.'

Archie closed his eyes. 'Geraint, you were with me, you were there; I know you were there with me in the hedge bottom squeezed into the car. We saved her with the stench of petrol waiting to explode. Geraint, you and I, we got her out of disaster.'

Archie slept a dreaming sleep.

The dog stretched, looking at her master, her head set on one side. He didn't move. The dog curled herself back down on to the warm slates.

Two candles had burnt out, but one still flickered in the dark. Archie woke with a start, leapt up, and grabbed a sweater, pulling it over the shirt borrowed from the hospital. He thrust his feet into already-laced shoes and set off for the summerhouse, leaving the back door open. Patch watched him depart before she got up and followed.

Archie lit camping lights, the gas hissing through their fragile mantles and casting a bright white light onto the walls of the studio. Archie reached behind a stack of old canvases and pulled the largest stretched canvas out, fastening it to his main easel. Patch watched through the open door as Archie got paints and brushes from the shelves before boldly stroking paint onto the canvas.

A half-full whisky bottle stood on the shelf. Archie took a tot direct from the bottle, rinsed it round his mouth and swallowed. He stood back from the canvas, looking at the bold paint invading the canvas, then went back to his palette to work more paint onto his brush.

Patch wandered away into the garden.

* * * * *

Hours later WPC Simons found Archie asleep on the couch in the summerhouse.

She'd driven out from Tonecastle in a police van, bringing his bicycle collected from the accident scene. The door of the cottage was open. She'd called inside, but met only the dog, at first growling then remembering her from the evening and wagging her tail. With no-one in the kitchen she looked round downstairs and eventually into the bedrooms. The house was empty.

'Mr Middlebrook.' She eased his shoulder, taking in the array of paintings, the muddle of pots, paints, brushes and an empty whisky bottle on a window sill. On a wooden easel a big canvas was painted with a flurry of greens of every shade, with browns, reds and blues interwoven into a great scene of jungle flora.

'Mr Middlebrook, it's time to wake up. Archie, wake up.'

He stirred.

'You haven't been to bed have you?'

Archie rubbed his eyes. His sweater and hands were covered in paint. He was unshaven with paint smeared on his cheeks.

'I've had a sleep.'

'Not a very comfortable one by the look of things, and not for long, I would guess.'

'I had to do the painting.'

'It looks like a jungle.'

'You're right, the jungle in Malaya, Malaysia as it is now. But this was back then.'

'It's good. Have you done all these?' Jane looked round the summerhouse shelves stacked with his paintings.

'All of them.'

'Do you sell paintings?'

'Not enough of them, hence they pile up in here.'

'Have you ever been to Malaysia?'

'Yes, decades ago and younger than you I'd guess. I was there for my national service in the 1950s.'

'You haven't been back and you did this painting from memory?'

'I did drawing after drawing of the jungle out there. I loved the jungle.'

'I can't see any other pictures of the jungle. These are Exmoor and around here, aren't they? And that's the bridge in Tonecastle and the beach at Northhill. All round these parts.

'I haven't painted the jungle in the years since I came back.'

'Why was that?'

Archie hesitated. What was it to her? It was years ago, not of her generation. She wouldn't know what had happened in The Emergency, of the communist terrorists fighting to get rid of the colonial power and pave the way for Chinese minority rule. Why should she care?

'I don't know much about Malaysia. My grandfather was out there, but he would never talk of it. He was a prisoner of war of the Japanese,' she added.

Archie needed to tell someone so it might as well be this young woman.

'We were fighting terrorists in Malaya after the war. We went on foot patrols into the jungle, it was frightening, yet it was fantastic. I loved the jungle, so huge, full of sounds, yet every living thing invisible until you were right on it, but it was dangerous with the CTs – the terrorists – all over the place. Then we had to do road patrols escorting supply wagons using armoured scout cars. That wasn't much fun. My scout car was blown up and the driver was killed. Geraint was my closest friend in the army.'

'I'm sorry. What happened to you?'

'I was in hospital, mostly burns, I was there for weeks, then it was over and I came back to Somerset. I should have gone to see Geraint's parents. They lived in Cardiff, not far away. I could have gone on the train. I never did. I couldn't face them. He died because I couldn't get him out of the scout car. I failed to get him out.'

There were tears in Archie's eyes. The constable saw Ivy standing by the summerhouse behind Archie. She was listening.

'I didn't see the accident yesterday. I came only to the hospital. I was speaking to the guys at the station this morning. They said you were incredibly brave. They said the car was flooded with petrol and it was a wonder it didn't go up. You saved the young woman's life risking your own.'

'It wasn't just me. Geraint was with me. I know he was with me. I'm tired, Jane. I'd better go to bed.

'I'll help you into the house... and Ivy is here.'

Archie looked round trying to get himself off the couch.

'Morning Ivy, don't get cross with me. I didn't get to bed and I've already been told off by the police. Anyway I've done the best painting ever and PC Jane here likes it.'

'Come on, Archie let's get you into the house.' Ivy took an arm to help the constable get Archie moving. 'I've rung the hospital. They said the young lady is doing as expected and will be kept sleeping all day. We can go in to see her tomorrow.'

'Well done, Ivy. Always a big sister looking after me, doing the things I forget to do. And I'll do more painting when I've had a sleep. There is so much to do. I'm going to do so many paintings for Geraint, these are going to be my best ever paintings.'

Chapter Fifteen

ARCHIE slept from mid-morning into the evening, overwhelmed by exhaustion. When he woke he ran a deep bath and lay soaking as he worked through ideas in his mind. He had to do large paintings, canvases that could stand together needing major gallery space wherever they were shown, paintings to honour Geraint Hughes. A collection of paintings in remembrance of a young man killed in circumstance beyond his grasp, far from his home and his family.

Ivy was calling from the top of the stairs.

'Archie, have you had a proper sleep?'

'Ivy, have you been here all day?'

'No, I've come over to see you're all right, not out painting again... or drinking whisky.'

'I've slept as deep a sleep as in ages, only been in the bath quarter of an hour.'

'Glad to hear that. I've brought over some sausages. I'll do supper when you're out of the bath.'

'You don't have to, Ivy.'

'You need a meal, and have you got the hospital dressings wet?'

'Oh...'

It wasn't long before the smell of frying onions and sausages wafted into the bathroom. Archie hadn't eaten since last night's casserole.

He brought a sketchpad into the kitchen to plan out the ideas for his series of paintings. He drew three rectangles on the paper, putting a legend beside each of them – BMH, Penang, Jungle and Ambush. Then in each of the spaces he blocked in basic shapes, pulling ideas from his long-frozen memory. He turned the page to do a similar exercise on the next three pages expanding the ideas roughed out on the first page.

'You're busy.'

'I'm planning a series of paintings; it's going to be something special, Ivy. Supper smells good.'

'Not ready yet. You'd better take Patch out, Archie then I'll have it on the table.'

'Come on, Patch. Nothing I can do here, Ivy?'

'I assume you're hungry.'

'Ravenous, Ivy, all the more so with these smells wafting around the house.'

'Off out with Patch then, ten minutes and it'll be on the table.'

Archie tried to interest Ivy in his scheme of paintings, already planning a shopping expedition to Tonecastle to buy new supplies. He decided to make six foot by four foot frames, to fix them with hardboard then stretch canvas over them and coat them in gesso, but before he could paint on those he would have to work up each idea on smaller canvases. Ivy didn't rise to his excitement, only saying Dorothy would have been glad to see him enthusiastic over his painting again.

Ivy was brooding.

He ate the sausages and mashed potato and onions served up by Ivy. He checked whether he should be ringing the hospital to ask after Lorna. She told him to ring in the morning after ten.

'If she is progressing you should be able to go in to see her. Also the police want you to tell them exactly what you saw. There's a number by the phone for you to ring.'

'I told them in the hospital, after A&E let me away.'

'I expect they want you to go through it again now you have had a chance to relax.'

'Don't see the point of that. I want to put it out of my mind just as long as Lorna recovers.'

Ivy looked at Archie. She'd heard him say more about Malaya in the summerhouse, talking to the constable, than he'd ever said to Dorothy, although she'd guessed most of it.

'Archie, just who is Lorna?'

Archie had a cut of sausage on his fork. He stopped at the unexpected tone of Ivy's question. 'Lorna, from Harptree's, I told you, I worked with her. She was made the Chief Accountant of the new company, Harptree Ventures, when I left, when I was kicked out and they closed the store.'

'Should it have been you had that job?'

'I would never have closed the store, you know that. It was vandalism dumping long serving staff on the scrapheap. Not everyone, word has it a number got better paid jobs in the chain store that opened on the ground floor.'

'How well do you know the young lady?'

'I worked with her best part of a year. She's a qualified accountant, and good, and we worked well together. Of course, she's much younger than me. She can only be in her thirties now.'

'And she got the top job.'

'It wasn't pleasant at the time. I didn't realise she was working with Andrew Harptree on his scheme after Oscar died, maybe even earlier.'

'Have you been seeing her since you left?'

'Not since the day I went. I've got a few contacts who've told me the business has been having difficulties. Their housing redevelopment in the old warehouse buildings hasn't been a success. There were long planning delays and now they aren't selling, rather cramped and pricey, too greedy by half.' Archie took a slice of bread and wiped his plate clean.

Ivy picked up her own plate and the empty dishes. She looked out into the garden seeing a rain cloud gathering.

'I must get off, it's going to rain again... if you haven't seen her for six or seven years, why was she coming out this way?'

'Ivy, you have as much idea as I do. Come to think of it I did bump into her once, a year or two back. I was coming out of Igor's Coffee House and she was going in with someone. It was awkward for both of us. I think the other person was a business connection. It was a brief hello and no more.'

Ivy collected up her things and put on her mackintosh. 'Will you ring me when you've spoken to the hospital? I can come with you if you want.'

'Ivy, what's bothering you?'

'I just wondered. It seems odd she should be driving out this way.'

'Ivy, there is nothing to wonder about. I don't know why she was out here. I didn't recognise the car or her until I was in the car. She had short hair when I worked with her, not long blonde hair. There's been nothing going on, Ivy.'

'Not my business if there was.'

'Ivy, I was fond of Lorna, I am fond of her, perhaps a little protective, but in a brotherly, an uncle sort of way, given our age difference. I thought from the beginning she was getting into a vipers' nest and, as I said last night, I think she's got hurt. I don't know if she was trying to come here or to go to Northhill to run on the sand and shout at the sea.'

Ivy was fiddling about with the dishes on the worktop.

'Come on, Ivy you must get off before it rains. I'll clear everything away and I promise it will be early bed tonight'

'You'll give me a ring in the morning?'

Archie got up from the table and held Ivy's shoulders before kissing her on both cheeks.

'Archie, stop that nonsense; I'll box your ears if you don't behave yourself.'

'You would, too. You've done it before. Do you remember the time you got wet in the pond on one of our walks?'

'You were a cheeky boy, Archie Middlebrook. I know you fell in on purpose. I should have left you to get out on your own.'

'Ivy, you wouldn't have. Of course I want you to come and see Lorna tomorrow.'

Ivy couldn't suppress a smile.

'You'll like her, Ivy; her mother has died, she's an only child, her father ran off to America when she was young. If she hasn't got a boyfriend, or a husband, and I don't know why not, we'll have to look after her when she gets out of hospital. She can't be on her own.'

'That's a decision for you, Archie. I'll be off now.'

He watched Ivy leave, realising her bicycle was the same one she had ridden ever since he could remember.

They both needed new bikes and it reminded him the telephone at Hawthorne Cottage needed updating. It looked dated besides being in the wrong place. There was a darkened patch on the floor slate by the phone in the hall, where even Ivy's cleaning skills had not removed the bleeding stain when he'd cut his leg.

Archie decided to add to his list of things to do in Tonecastle - a shop stocking telephones and all the ancillaries to go with them. A wall mounted phone in the kitchen and another by his bed. He would need many feet of cabling.

Despite speaking to one of his contacts who still worked in Harptree Ventures, he learned little of what might have gone on at the company in the last few days, other than there had been altercations in the management office. Gossip had it that Lorna had walked out. There was no connection of her storming departure with the local report of the accident with the overturned car. Archie said nothing of it to his contact.

Next morning the duty sister on the intensive care ward asked Archie to come by in mid-afternoon. Lorna's sedation was being eased, she would be undergoing a series of tests during the morning, and if all was going well she would be moved to another ward next day. When Archie contacted Ivy she told him she couldn't visit in the afternoon, she was going to a WI meeting.

Archie slowed his car to a halt where the hedge was broken. The grass was trampled with deep ruts where a heavy machine had planted metal feet to lift the wrecked car onto a recovery vehicle. Archie switched on his hazard lights and got out to survey the scene. Traces of gunge from fire retardant foam lay on the grass, the smell of petrol still hung in the air; overhead a buzzard circled hanging without effort on the wind as it hunted. Its mewing called over a second, he guessed one of this year's young. Archie held his arms to his side in military fashion and stood a minute.

'Thank you, Geraint. You were here,' he whispered.

Seeing his hazard lights a passing car slowed. He acknowledged the driver, giving a wave with his thumb up. The motorist drove on. Archie got back into his car pausing a while before starting the engine.

At Millers Ironmongery in Helecombe, Archie found the heavy duty tree ties he needed, explaining away the scratches on his face with his struggles to reattach roses knocked off their trellising during the storm.

Mrs Miller smiled. 'I heard about the car that turned over, Archie. Just as well you were passing by and called the firemen to sort it out. I gather there was a young woman in the car.'

'There was, Mary. The fire brigade had all the rescue equipment, they soon got her out. I wouldn't expect anything less. Can you ask Jack to call me? I've got damage to the gable end of the house after that storm the other night.'

'I heard they took you to hospital and all. Were you knocked off your bike?'

'No, but I did see it happen. The gable end needs fixing before the winter months.'

Mrs Miller wrote a note, tore off the sheet and pinned it to a notice board. 'It may be a few days, before he can get to you, Archie.'

The artist's supply shop in Tonecastle couldn't provide the width of canvas he needed for his planned six by four paintings, so they put it on order for him. It wasn't urgent – it could be weeks before he was ready to tackle the big pictures.

At Gregory's timber yard, he found the wood he needed to make the backing frame for the canvas and, taking advice from Eric Gregory, decided on marine ply rather than hardboard to go under the canvas. Eric who had often worked for Archie in his days at Harptree's agreed to make up the frames and deliver his order out to Hawthorne Cottage.

'I'll be out your way after the weekend, I can drop them off, too big to get in your car.'

'Is business ticking along, Eric?'

'Tell the truth, Mr Middlebrook I wish you were still working at Harptree's.'

'It's a different business these days, Eric. Not like in Mr Oscar's day.'

'That's for certain.'

'Have you got problems with them, Eric?'

'I always got paid promptly in your day. You were strict over standards and prices, always paid accounts on the dot. I regret getting the contract, if the truth be told, Mr Middlebrook.'

'What's the contract?'

'We're doing the kitchens in the workshop conversions. Fact is we've done it, finished months ago. I say it myself we did a good job, yet the account is unpaid. I've been into the office myself, got nowhere. I'll have to get a solicitor involved and that'll be another cost.'

'Forgive my asking, Eric, but is it a large sum?'

'Eighty thousand and a bit. That Andrew drew up the contract, so I had to take the first cost of all the white goods. I should never have touched it. And we aren't the only one out of pocket. They owe money all round town.'

'I hadn't realised. I'm sorry, Eric. Oscar would be mortified to have the name disgraced in that way.'

'Not what it used to be, not at all, Mr Middlebrook.'

* * * * *

The bruising took Archie by surprise. Lorna looked as if she'd been fighting a bare knuckle bout – black eyes spreading down into her cheeks and part of her hair shaved to reveal stitching to her head wound. A drip was linked into her arm and a machine with a monitor screen was beeping by her bed.

'She is conscious, Mr Middlebrook, but she is woozy from the sedatives and remembers nothing of what happened. She knows she was in a car accident, none of the detail.'

The nurse had taken him aside before he went into Lorna's bed space. 'She won't remember you found her in the car. We haven't tried to explain to her, best to leave that to later as we see what she can recall.'

Archie stared at Lorna lying with her eyes swollen.

'Are you all right, Mr Middlebrook... Mr Middlebrook?'

'Sorry, I'm fine. I hadn't really thought about how she would look.'

'I'll take you over and check all is well. She hasn't had any other visitor, just medical staff. I'll be interested to see if she recognises you. You do know her?'

'Thank you, yes, I do.'

There were other beds in the intensive ward, screened off, with other machines beeping their progress. The nurse led Archie one side of the raised bed and stood on the other side with her hand on Lorna's shoulder.

'You have a visitor, Lorna.'

Lorna turned to look. Archie put his hand on hers lying outside the covers.

'Archie, why are you here?'

'I've come to see you, Lorna.'

The nurse nodded with a smile. 'Only a few minutes, Mr Middlebrook.' She went to look at another patient.

Archie gave Lorna's hand a squeeze searching for words. Lorna's gentle touch responded.

'I've had my head shaved. Do I look funny?'

'You look lovely, Lorna. There isn't much shaved off.'

'I don't know where I've left my car, Archie. I think it's damaged. I hope it doesn't get towed away, it costs so much to get a car back from the pound. I don't know where it is.'

'Don't worry about your car, Lorna. I know where it is and there is no fine to pay.'

'Is it badly damaged? I don't know how it happened.'

There was no point in telling her about it. 'Not too bad. I'll look after it for you. You get yourself better, Lorna then we'll sort things out.'

Later, Archie sat in his car in the hospital car park, tears rolling down his cheeks, tears of relief, of anger or of fear he couldn't tell. The nurse was pleased with Lorna's progress. Archie had expected to talk to her about the accident and why she was on that road. It would have to wait.

He turned the ignition to set off home before deciding to call at the Cricket Club. Once a week when the season was over there was an open evening in the clubhouse. He wanted to hear if there was any gossip about Harptree's.

It looked as if there was a decent turn out judging by the car park. A light rain was falling as it grew dark. Archie made his way to the bar and ordered a gin and tonic before joining a group talking about the past season. The County had got into the top third of the Championship, a better result than for several years.

Archie saw him first. Andrew Harptree was sitting on the far side of the room talking intently with a man Archie hadn't seen before, probably from out of town. The conversation between the two men lapsed. The man looked at Andrew, seemingly waiting for an answer. Andrew hesitated, looked round, then reached into a pocket and took out a slim package, which he gave to the man, who put it in his briefcase, got up and left, without shaking Andrew's hand.

Andrew looked at his empty glass and got up. Archie watched as he crossed to the bar.

Andrew saw Archie and stopped as Archie raised a hand in greeting. Andrew put down his empty glass on a table, turned away and hurried out of the room.

Andrew's car was awkwardly parked and he had to reverse a couple of times to exit the space. Archie tapped on the driver's window and Andrew let down the glass.

'Do you not want to say hello, Andrew?'

'Hello. Now out of my way, I'm in a hurry.'

Archie put his hands on the open window. 'You weren't in a hurry just now. I was going to buy you a drink.'

'Get out of the way.' The engine revved. 'Get your damn hands off the car.'

'I wanted to ask you how Lorna Curtis is, Andrew, how things are going in the business.'

'None of your damn business. Now clear out of the way.' The engine revved again and the car started to move.'

Archie reached in, turned off the ignition and grabbed the key. The car stalled, the wipers stopping in mid sweep.

'Don't drive off when I'm speaking to you.'

'What the hell do you mean by this? Give me my key.'

'Answer my question. How is, Lorna Curtis?'

'I'm going to call the police.' Andrew reached for the mobile phone attached to the dash.

'I had a meeting with the police earlier today.' Archie had meant to call in as requested, but it had slipped his mind in his hurry to get to the hospital on time after his shopping. 'I'll ask you again. How is Miss Curtis, Andrew?'

'How the hell should I know? She is a total incompetent and I've sacked her.'

'Do you know where she is now?'

'I neither know nor care.'

'If I were to tell you she is in Intensive Care in hospital would you care?'

'What the hell has it got to do with me? Give me the key or I'll...'

'Don't worry. I never did like you Andrew. Now I'm beginning to understand why.'

Archie tossed the key back into the car, turned and walked away. As he strode toward the building he heard the car revving and a metallic screech as it scraped a car before speeding away.

Back in the safety of the building, Archie sat on the stairs, his pulse racing.

There were voices at the top of the stairs on the floor above. He stood up his legs quivering as he held the banister. He took a couple of deep breaths before going back to the bar to order a double brandy.

An hour later, his mind turning over all the experiences of the day and after another double brandy, he ordered a taxi and went home leaving his shopping with his car in the car park.

Archie rang Ivy as soon as he got back to the cottage.

'Sorry to ring so late, Ivy. To tell the truth, I was shaken. She looks rough, bruised with drips and monitors. I didn't expect it.

She's been heavily sedated. The good news she is she is talking and knew who I was. But she doesn't know what happened and doesn't realise I found her, not yet. The medics reckon she is making as much progress as they hoped she would.'

'It is bound to take time, Archie. It may be a long recovery.'

'They reckon as well as the forces she will have experienced as the car flipped over, even strapped in her seat belt, she was hit by loose things flying around in the car. There was a briefcase, shoes, water bottles and all sorts lying around in the car. They look harmless enough, but I guess can do a lot of damage in those circumstance.'

'She recognised you, Archie. That's good, I'm sure she will make progress.'

'It was a near thing, Ivy.'

'They had to cut the car open to get her out.'

'She has no idea her car is a write-off. She thinks it's in a pound, with a fine mounting up to get it out.'

'Will you go in tomorrow, Archie?'

'Yes, in the afternoon again, they may have moved her to a less dependency bed if she keeps up her progress. Will you come in with me, Ivy?'

'From what you say, it's still a bit early to introduce new faces. Best if I wait a few days, Archie.'

'Maybe.'

'Thanks for ringing, Archie.'

'Sorry it was so late, Ivy.'

'Sleep well, Archie and don't start drawing. Get a good night's sleep and you'll be fresh in the morning.'

Chapter Sixteen

AUTUMN arrived with storms and gales, the leaves turned yellow and gold, piling up on the lawns and in drains. Discharged from hospital, Lorna was driven home by Archie to Hawthorne Cottage, the day improving until there were few clouds in the sky. She was fragile after her time laid up.

Archie wanted to give her his mother's old room it being more convenient for the bathroom, but Ivy was having none of it, insisting she should be in the spare room like any other visitor. Archie got no change from Ivy.

At least the spare room was a warmer room, facing south with two radiators. He'd set the heating going full-bore in the morning before he left to fetch Lorna. Ivy turned the heating off when she arrived to set up lunch, although she doubted Lorna would be eating much.

Archie feared Lorna would react badly on the road she'd travelled before her accident. At least they wouldn't pass the site of her crash, still obvious from skid marks and the broken hedge.

She'd begun to remember what had happened in the hours before the car turned over, recalling the vitriol poured out by Andrew Harptree. She'd told him urgent steps had to be taken to address the substantial amounts the company owed and she doubted they had sufficient funds in hand to pay end-of-month salaries.

Andrew had put all blame squarely onto her shoulders, prompting her to tell him she was going to set up a meeting with their bank and if they were unwilling to help they must at once have a meeting of directors to discuss the company's ability to continue trading. Without town house sales their cash flow was inadequate.

Their exchanges led to the row in the office. Quite whether Andrew had dismissed her or she had resigned on the spot was not clear to Archie. Lorna had stormed out of the office to drive out of town seeking a breathing space then finding she was going toward Helecombe, she'd decided to seek out Archie.

Archie turned the car into the lane up to Hawthorne Cottage.

'I missed this turning, in fact I wasn't looking for it. I was going to ask in Helecombe. I knew you lived somewhere nearby.'

'It's easy to miss the turn.'

'I was driving too fast.'

'You shouldn't say too much of that, Lorna. The police want to talk to you about the accident. I've managed to put them off for a while. Someone will be in touch over the next few days to arrange an interview.'

'But I was speeding.'

'You don't need to emphasise it.'

'Then I swerved to pass a bicycle. I looked round, thinking it might be you, and lost control.'

They travelled up the rest of lane in silence, the high hedge-banks tunnelling the light.

'I don't know what happened after that.'

Archie turned the car in through the cottage gates.

'Is my car a complete write-off, Archie?'

'It is.'

'I'll have to tell the insurance company.'

'All done, Lorna, nothing for you to worry about, at least until you get into the swing of things. Ivy will have a light lunch for us and afterwards you're to go to bed. The hospital said to take everything at a slow pace for weeks rather than days.'

'Archie, why are you doing all this for me? I might have killed you.'

'You missed.'

'Archie, be serious.'

'Here's Ivy. I'll help you out.' Despite the sunshine there was a wind blowing through the yard. Archie put a coat over Lorna's shoulders and held her arm as she walked from the car. Ivy took the other arm.

'Thank you, Ivy. You're both so kind. And thank you for coming into the hospital. It was such a break to have visitors, and you didn't even know me, Ivy.'

'Any friend of Archie's is a friend of mine, dear.'

Tears rolled down Lorna's cheeks. She tried to hide them before giving a sniff and a whimper.'

'Come on, dear, we'll get you sitting down inside.'

'I'm just so happy.' Lorna gulped for air as she was settled onto a chair in the kitchen. 'Everything was awful, now it's wonderful.'

Ivy passed her paper from the kitchen roll to wipe her eyes and blow her nose. Archie took her case upstairs, containing the few things she had with her in hospital, mostly things he and Ivy had taken in during recent days. He didn't hurry wanting the two women to be together.

Patch eased herself up from her customary place in front of the stove coming over to inspect the new arrival with her clinical smells. Lorna fondled the dog's muzzle.

'Anything I can do to help, Ivy.'

'No, you sit tight where you are. I'll get things on the table. I don't suppose you want much do you, dear.'

'It's a long time since hospital breakfast and I only had a piece of toast and jam for that. I'm ready for something.'

Pleased to hear them chatting, Archie called the dog over. 'I'll take you out, Patch.'

'Archie, I have to get off as soon this is dished up.'

'Ivy, you must have lunch with us.'

'I'll get away, Archie. I have a pile of things to do.' Ivy turned to Lorna. 'You'll be all right to get yourself into bed, Lorna?'

'Thank you, Ivy.'

* * * * *

As October days shortened into winter, Lorna grew restless at Hawthorne Cottage, picking up the pieces of her interrupted life.

During the first few days of her stay, Archie insisted she be treated as an invalid, waking her each morning with a cup of tea, running baths for her and doing all the cooking. In between times, when he had settled Lorna in the conservatory with the radio and a book, he went to the summerhouse to work on his paintings.

Archie needed to paint a celebration of the national service days in Malaya – in the jungle on patrol, even of the awful unfolding of the ambush, and above all a portrait of Geraint Hughes, showing his joy when he first got to drive the scout car.

It was a tall order. The more he worked on the sequence, the more aspects he found to illustrate delving back into the times frozen in his mind. Archie needed to get it all out, to remember everything. Yet one thing was missing. He had never been to Geraint's resting place, the plot in the cemetery in Ipoh, were his friend was buried. One day he would go, sometime when he'd brought all his ideas together and his paintings were ready he would exhibit them to the public in homage to his friend, then go to Malaysia.

In the meantime there were practical things to worry about. The summerhouse, while good for his current work, was too small for the large paintings he was planning. He decided to use the garage, get it cleared out, with the accumulated junk of years to be thrown out or housed in the unused loose box. The garage had good space for the six by fours, but it didn't have the light he needed. When Jack Miller gets in touch to repair the gable end he would ask him to put roof lights into the garage.

After two weeks, Lorna put her foot down and told Archie to stop running about after her. She was quite capable of cooking meals for them both and to do things in the house. The weather had turned stormy, which precluded venturing outside for too long, although she enjoyed taking Patch out for short walks in the lane.

Late one morning Ivy found Lorna on the Helecombe road, standing by the broken hedge staring at the place where her car had flipped over. If Patch hadn't pulled at the lead, Lorna, transfixed at the sight, wouldn't have noticed Ivy standing behind her, holding her bike.

'Sorry, Ivy; I was day dreaming.'

'Are you all right, dear?'

'Archie hasn't let me come here before. Don't let on, Ivy. I think he will be cross with me. I don't know why he doesn't want me to see it. I'll have to go past here sometime.'

'You look cold, Lorna.'

'I should have worn a thicker coat. All my things are in the flat in Tonecastle. I must get Archie to take me in to collect a few things.'

'It's one of Dorothy's old coats you've got on, dear. My cottage is down the road. I'll get us some hot soup and give Archie a ring to come and collect you.'

'He's in the summerhouse painting. I told him to spend the day at it. He keeps talking about the pictures he's working on, then interrupts himself to do something for me.'

'Come on then, we can walk.'

'Do you always ride your bicycle, Ivy?'

'As much as I can. I've got a car I can use for longer journeys, but mostly it's the bike or buses. The bus used to come on this road before they built the by-pass. Now I have to walk or bicycle to catch the bus in Helecombe to get to Tonecastle.'

At her cottage Ivy lit a fire in the room that was both kitchen and family room. As it caught and started to warm the room, she opened a tin of soup to heat on the stove, brought a homemade loaf from the larder and unwrapped a slab of cheese.

'Who is this in the picture, Ivy?'

'That's Jilly, my daughter. She lives in Essex now.'

'She's beautiful, and a lot like you, Ivy. I should have guessed. Is there a 'Mister' Ivy?'

'You're full of questions.'

'Sorry.'

'There was once, a lorry driver he was, maybe he still is. He has another family in the North-East somewhere. Jilly knows where.'

'And is Jilly... yes, this looks like her wedding.'

'Older than you, she is. Her boy is at university now, bright lad. I don't understand what it is he does, but he enjoys it.'

Requiem for Private Hughes

'Does he come to stay at Helecombe with you?'

'Not this summer, but most years he's been down to see me. Now let's have some soup, it'll warm you through.'

The kitchen was crowded, open shelves full of pans yet everything had its place. On the kitchen table there were rows of jars newly labelled; damson jam, apple and rosehip jelly, green tomato chutney and others Lorna couldn't read.

'Are all these yours, Ivy?'

'I make a lot every year. It's wonderful what you can find from the hedgerows and in the garden. Always tastes good in winter.'

Her visitor might have been asking the questions earlier, but after their soup and cheese it was Ivy who'd wanted answers. In the course of their talk, Ivy learned something of Lorna's life story, understanding how much she regretted the part she played in the events surrounding the demise of Harptree's. Lorna felt even worse when Ivy told her how it had affected Archie.

Lorna hadn't realised the full part Archie played in her rescue from her wrecked car. As Ivy spoke, a vision of Archie holding her shoulders as she hung strapped into her seat woke in her mind, a vision of him counting red rosehips, telling her to count with him, urging, forcing her mind to focus.

Lorna sat by Ivy's fire silent tears on her cheeks.

'He's fond of you, Lorna. Don't do anything to hurt him; he's had troubles enough over the years.'

'I won't, Ivy.'

'And don't lead him on. It's wonderful to see him painting again with the verve he had years ago as a teenager. He lost all his interest in painting after his trouble in Malaya. He was doing so well at college before he went into the army. Try as she might his mother couldn't get him to go back to it when he came home. It was a tragedy – he really had something'

Lorna dried her eyes and asked Ivy what had happened in Malaya. At first Ivy didn't want to talk about it, but she relented and told her what she knew of Archie's melancholy over his perceived failure to save his fellow soldier from the ambushed scout car.

It was mid-afternoon before Ivy got her car out to drive Lorna and Patch back to Hawthorne Cottage. She'd rung Archie, but there had been no answer; they assumed he was busy in the summerhouse, far from the phone.

Archie was in the yard whistling for Patch when Ivy drove in from the lane. He saw Patch on the back seat and Lorna with a nervous smile, sitting by Ivy.

'Where did you two get to?'

'I've been to see Ivy's house. She gave me lunch, have you had anything to eat, Archie?'

'I don't want anything thanks. I haven't seen you for days, Ivy. Have you been busy?'

'Making jams and chutney; I'll bring some over when I get back.'

'Get back, where are you going?'

'Up to see Jilly. Her Robin has started at university again, so she's feeling a bit on her own.'

'You're not driving, are you?'

'Taking the train.'

'When are you going?'

'Friday.'

'I'll take you to the station, Ivy.'

'And you can take Lorna in to her flat, Archie. She needs to get things. She had to wear Dorothy's old gardening coat this morning.'

Little was said over supper after Ivy left. Archie insisted Lorna must have something to eat, despite her telling him she had done well at Ivy's. Archie made them both Welsh rarebit, lacing the cheese with Worcester Sauce. Lorna found it too strong, leaving half of hers for Archie to finish up.

'I'll wash up, Archie. There's not enough for the dishwasher. Then I'll make coffee and we can sit in the conservatory as it grows dark. I'm sorry I was away so long. It was great hearing about Ivy's family.'

Archie told her he had a job he must finish in the summerhouse. He'd broken off when he realised she was out with Patch. He promised not to be long.

Requiem for Private Hughes

Lorna put the plates and cutlery onto the drying rack before setting about making milky coffee on the stove. She hadn't meant to upset Archie, but she needed space and there were important things to resolve. It was five weeks since she had stormed out of the Harptree office. Archie had told her of his confrontation with Andrew in the cricket club car park. Whether she was still an employee or not was unclear. The situation had to be resolved. And there was the matter of her car – she needed to get the file closed. As for the police, it appeared they were satisfied and would not be pursuing the matter. She'd had her interview with a constable who came to the house.

Lorna took the coffee through to the conservatory in a flask to keep it hot, set two rattan steamer chairs so that they could sit and look out over the garden as light faded, and brought two candles from the kitchen for later. There were lights in the conservatory, but they were too harsh.

She needed to have a talk with Archie. She knew little about him, yet here he was organising her life.

Daylight had faded by the time Archie returned from the summerhouse. Lorna was sitting in the dark with Patch beside her chair, pleased to have an attentive friend.

'Why do you call her Patch, Archie?'

'They've all been called Patch. The first Patch I had as a boy, a black dog, had one large chest patch of white. She grew old and another one came, he had a patch, not much just a bit of white on his chest. I don't think any of the others justified the name.'

'Have you always had a dog?'

'Most of the time; there were a couple of gaps in between and an overlap or two.'

'What was the second called when you had two?'

'Probably just Puppy until it inherited the name. You are full of questions tonight.'

'I've got many more.'

Lorna struck a match to get a flickering light from the candles and poured Archie his coffee.

'I can heat it up if it isn't hot enough.'
'It's fine, how I like it.'
'You haven't tried it.'
'It's still fine.'
'Archie, tell me about the army and what happened.'
'I think I told you when we were working together.'
'I want to know what is driving your painting activity. It's important to you... and to me.'

Archie watched the candle reflections on the glass shutting out the night, recalling the incessant noise of the jungle, the myriad of insects communicating, the occasional call of a bird or a gang of monkeys going about their business in the high canopy. It was hard to bring it to life on canvas, yet he felt a touch of its mystery was in his paintings, something of the anxious thrill he'd felt as they'd weaved a path into the steaming depth.

At last, after years, he needed to relive every second of that drive to disaster. It was the fatal assumption that the scout car assignment was an easy option, not the real thing in comparison to jungle foot patrols.

Geraint had been keen to get on the road again, impatient at the holdup of the overheating radiators on the Bedford trucks. Away from the bulk of the convoy, they could motor home as they wished, deliver the two trucks they were leading then backtrack to team up with the sluggards and get them back to base. In the evening it would be beer and chips in the NAAFI, recounting and exaggerating the thrills of the day. Geraint had found his great passion driving the Ferret. For every mile they travelled he was singing into the intercom, not bothered with the stifling heat in his driving position.

On NAAFI evenings they'd talked of the adventure awaiting them in the nightspots of Singapore prior to embarkation home, that's if Geraint didn't pursue his threat to sign on to continue working with scout cars. They were going to break their duck, going to 'do it' and go home true men at last.

All their dreams ended in the blinding flash and thunder of the explosion, the terror and anguish locked in his mind for impotent decades, wanting to speak of it, wanting to illustrate it, wanting his release from not saving Geraint from the wreckage. Now after the wreckage of Lorna's car it was coming out onto canvas and confidence gripped him.

'Stop me if I'm boring you, Lorna.'

'It's what I want to know, Archie.'

'I thought you were going to die in that car and it was going to be my fault, my fault you lost control, that the car flipped over and that I couldn't get you out to safety.'

'You saved my life, Archie.'

'That was the emergency services, the firemen who got you out, the paramedics who got you to the hospital.'

'You realise I went to the crash site today, Archie. I know you didn't want me to go, but I had to see it. Then I remembered, you made me count the rosehips pressed against the windscreen, you made me see them, concentrate on them, count them.'

'I didn't think you were seeing them.'

'I saw them. I saw them for days afterwards as I got better in hospital, dream after dream there were branches weighed down with rosehips, hundreds of them and I always had to count. I've counted scores and scores of rosehips. I found the rosehips in the hedgerow where I crashed. I think I was counting them when Ivy came along on her bicycle.'

'And you went back to her cottage?'

'I was cold, she made me soup and I sat in front of her fire to get warm.'

'I'm sorry about the coat. We can go in tomorrow to get things from your flat.'

'You said you would take Ivy in for the train on Friday. That'll be soon enough.'

'Do you want to move back to your flat?'

'Not really, unless I'm outstaying my welcome here.'

'Not at all. It's quiet here on my own. I know I spend hours in the summerhouse, but it's good to have you here if it isn't too boring for you.'

'Archie, you must let me do more in the house. I'm up to it, I promise. I've got an appointment to see the doctors next week. I'm sure they will give me an all-clear. I admit I'm a hopeless cook. I'll bring my recipe books back from the flat. It would be good to get some practice, if you don't mind being a guinea pig.'

'I'll chance it. Do you want more coffee?'

'I'll make some for you, Archie. I don't think I'll have any, I'll be awake in the night.'

'That's an old wives tale.'

Lorna came back with more coffee. 'I've made it extra milky. It smells good, so I'm having half a cup.'

'Was Ivy chatty this afternoon?' Archie smiled.

'Chatty?'

'Was she asking questions?'

'What about?'

'About how you are getting on, who you are, even.'

'Not really. I think it was more me asking her things.

'What about?'

'You mostly.'

'Me.'

'Yes, Mr Mystery Man. I don't know what makes you tick, or why you are doing so much for me. We worked together for some months before everything went pear shaped and I did the dirty on you.'

'It was long ago.'

'You realise Andrew was afraid of you, he knew you'd had the ear of his father. He thought you knew too much not only about the business, but the family, too.'

'He was right about that.'

We haven't seen each other for years and now you are looking after me as if I was your daughter. And I don't know why.'

'And what did Ivy tell you in answer to all your questions?'

'Not a lot.'

Archie watched the reflection of the candles on the conservatory glass, one of the candles losing its battle to stay alight, sputtering into an ever smaller flame.

'Ivy hasn't been over much since you've been staying here.'

'Have you been to see her?'

'Not really. It's always been her coming here.'

'She may feel neglected. I think she is uncertain why I'm staying here, who I am, why you are doing all this for me.'

'Where else would you have gone?'

'My flat, that's what other people have to do when they leave hospital.'

'Is that what you want to do?'

'No, Archie. I told you, I don't, not yet. I love being here. I fear Ivy has reservations. I don't know whether she trusts me.'

'How do you mean?'

'Oh, Archie. She sees me as a young unattached woman who has ambitions to get my claws into you, seduce you and run off with all your money... or something.'

'I doubt it.'

'Do you think I'm not capable of doing that?'

'You women, you do dream things up.'

'I don't think you realise how fond Ivy is of you, Archie. If I were to upset you in any way she would tear me limb from limb.'

'Ivy's always been family.'

'She's thrilled you are busy painting. She sees me as a distraction.'

'Truth be told, you are the reason I'm painting.'

'You'll have to explain that to me in the morning. I'm falling asleep. Will you do something for me, Archie?'

'If I can.'

'I'd like a painting of rosehips.'

'I don't get commissioned every day. But I thought you were having nightmares counting rosehips.'

'Not nightmares. I want to see rosehips when I'm miles from here in London, when I have to fight my way through busy streets and travel on the Tube, I want to be able to go home and count the rosehips in a picture.'

'How many do you want?'

'Be serious, Archie.'

'I'll do you a painting: 'Rosehips, the portrait'. Are you planning to go back to London?'

'Sometime, I don't know. I'll have to start earning money soon.'

'There's no hurry.'

'I can't live off your hospitality much longer, Archie.'

'I like having you here, Lorna. Don't forget you are the reason I've started painting again.'

'And don't forget my rosehips.'

Chapter Seventeen

ARCHIE left Ivy and Lorna chatting as they waited for the London train, billed on the departure display to be 'on time' and due in ten minutes. He strolled along the length of the platform to the furthest end of the station, almost expecting George Sanderfoot to catch him up to exchange pleasantries. It must be years since Sanderfoot retired from the railways, he would be an old man today in his nineties if he was still alive.

Archie watched the two women talking as they whiled away time. Ivy had said little in the car on the way in to the station, insisting on sitting in the back, leaving Lorna in the passenger seat beside him. Ivy had been distant these last few days, as Lorna had been getting more active.

By his watch the train was due in three minutes. Archie strode back to where they'd estimated Coach D would stop. Ivy had a booked seat.

'How will you get across London, Ivy? Take a taxi?'

'On the bus, Archie, number 23 will get me from Paddington to Liverpool Street.'

'That'll take an age.'

'I've got plenty of time and it's good to look out at the crowds and remember why I live in the country, away from the bustle of London.'

As the train, an early morning departure from Penzance, pulled in, it was packed and had people standing. Archie told Ivy he would go on board to make sure she got her seat.

'Don't worry, Archie. No-one will make me stand.'

Archie gave a chuckle picking up her surprisingly light suitcase. It would need the grip of a limpet to outsmart Ivy over a booked seat.

As the train pulled out, Archie was glad he wasn't travelling to London. It would be a difficult journey, with blocked corridors and unusable lavatories.

Archie had been up at first light for the last two mornings. First he had wandered around the hedgerows, with Patch trailing along behind, unsure of her master's purpose, repeatedly stopping with his sketch pad in his hand. The hedgerows were full of rosehips after autumn had stripped away the leaves of summer. Back in the summerhouse studio he worked up his composition, using many shades of green for the grasses, putting late leaves on the hedgerow against the stark contrast of cascades of scarlet rosehips, tempting birds and animals to raid the hedgerow larder.

Lorna was a late riser. She would wander down to the summerhouse as his painting morning progressed to see if he wanted any hot drink or sandwiches. She was curious, for ever asking about the work he was doing and the bric-a-brac lying about in the studio, bird skulls picked up in woodlands, misshapen driftwood from the seashore, pebbles from the beach.

By nine o'clock on each of the two mornings Archie had stopped painting the rosehip picture, concealed it behind old works propped against the wall, and turned back to another of his jungle works.

'You haven't made much progress on that, Archie. You were doing that the day before yesterday.'

'I've had to rework a large section of it. The picture was unbalanced.'

'It seemed okay to me. In fact it hasn't changed much.'

'Having changed it I've been working it back much as it was. I have days like that.'

The rosehip picture was ready. He knew how many hips there were in the picture, some partly concealed as the thorny dog rose tendrils weaved through the hedgerow stems. In a corner he'd painted in Hawthorne Cottage a field away. He planned to bring the picture into the house and set it up on an easel in the conservatory to surprise Lorna when they got back from visiting her flat in Tonecastle.

'Can we park at your flat?'

'My space is temporarily available for your use.'

Despite Lorna's jest her parking space was occupied.

'That's a liberty, that couple are always doing that. Park behind the BMW, Archie, and block it in.'

At the front door, Lorna searched for her keys.

'I didn't think to check.' Her handbag was one of several items returned by the police from the wreckage of her car. After unzipping various pockets she found the spare key to her flat, 5D, St Magdalene Close, a onetime furniture depository converted to four apartments on each of its two upper floors, the ground floor housing offices.

'There was a separate bunch of keys; I put them on the dressing table in your bedroom, Lorna.'

'I forgot to bring them. My keys are always in my bag; I didn't think. Thank heavens for the spare.' Unlocking her front door she had to push it open against a pile of mail. 'Look at all this junk.'

'You'll need a wheelbarrow to get that away. I should have come over earlier and you could have sorted it at home.'

'This is home, Archie, humble though it may be.'

'At Hawthorne Cottage.'

'My other home. Let me get the kettle on; would you like a cup.'

'Please.'

Archie picked up the post. 'Shall I sort out the rubbish, Lorna?'

'If you want, there's a table in the sitting room.' Lorna pushed open a door.

The curtains were drawn. She must have left in a hurry that morning. Archie pulled the curtains back, flooding the room with daylight, and began sifting through the mail for flyers and other "To the Occupier" envelopes – in the end the largest pile. Those that looked like bills addressed by name made up the next lot, which left three personal letters one hand written, the other two typed.

'Sorry,' Lorna called through from the kitchen, 'it's instant and solid in the jar, and there's no milk. Would you like some Red Bush tea, caffeine free and fine without milk?'

'If you're having some. Out of all this lot behind the front door there are just three letters that look interesting.'

Lorna brought two steaming mugs through. 'It's amazing what comes through the letter box. I hope I haven't missed any payment dates, most accounts are on Banker's Orders.'

'You've got good high ceilings here. I remember when this was a furniture depository. It was owned by Harptree's once.'

'I didn't know that.'

'There was a separate house removal business. Oscar sold it in the late 1960s to a national company, who sold off the depository. The conversion to housing went rather better than the latest effort of Andrew with the Harptree warehouse. From what I've heard it is somewhat of a disaster with hardly any sold.'

'None sold, if the truth be told.'

'Nothing sold?'

'Not a single one.'

'It's no wonder tradesmen haven't been paid. Do you mind if I look around.'

'Help yourself. I don't suppose it's tidy.'

There was a small balcony set outside a floor to ceiling window, which had once been a freight door, through which goods had been raised to the top floor level outside the building. Above the window, the original steel beam remained in place, on which the lifting tackle had hung. From the balcony a wide perspective over Tonecastle was laid out, the red sandstone tower of St Mary's prominent in the foreground.

The phone rang. Archie heard Lorna talking in the next room as he watched the town going about its business on a November day of unexpected sunshine. In a strange way, he felt nostalgia for his office days at Harptree's, working long hours in his office above the store, going out in his meal break to run errands in the town for Dorothy or himself.

Leaning out over the rail, he could see past the corner of the building to the department store building and the window of his one-time office on the top floor.

'Careful, Archie, what are you gazing at?'

'Trying to see the old office,'

'Guess who that was on the phone.'

'No idea.'

'A florist; they say they have been trying to deliver here for the past week and were checking if I was in. She wouldn't say what it was, just that they would be round in the next hour to deliver, and could I wait in.'

'You must have an admirer.'

'Not one I know about. We'll have to hang about, is that all right, Archie?'

'There're a couple of things I could do in town if you don't need me here. You could sort out what you want to take back to Hawthorne, and I'll give you a hand getting it down to the car. I won't be out as long as an hour.'

There was nothing particular Archie needed in town, but he preferred not to hang about in the flat waiting for the florist to call.

In the town centre he stopped off for a coffee. There were always newspapers to read at Igor's Coffee House, yet he wasn't concentrating. Why was the florist delivering to Lorna? There was no-one she had mentioned while she'd been staying and she had no relations, unless her long-lost father had emerged from the States. She had made no mention of him.

When Igor's wife Marie brought over his latte, he was drawing in his notebook, working out shapes for more jungle paintings.

'Is this for another exhibition, Mr Archie?'

'I hope it will be, Marie.'

'You want to put more pictures on my walls?'

'You never sell them, Marie.'

'I like them, Mr Archie. Why should I sell them?

'So I can afford to pay for your expensive meals.'

'Away with you, Mr Archie, you are rich man I'm just poor cook.'

Their exchange ended with its usual laugh and Archie got back to his sketch planning as Marie went round clearing plates.

Requiem for Private Hughes

When Archie looked at the clock he saw he had been away over an hour. Hurrying back to St Magdalene Close, he called into a food store to buy cheese and a crusty loaf. He hadn't baked bread for months, and added strong flower and yeast to his basket. It would be good to bake again.

No flowers had been delivered when he returned to the flat, yet Lorna was bubbling with excitement.

'Archie, where have you been? Look at this; it's from Charles Stapleton. Lorna handed him one of the three letters.'

'Stapleton, the name rings a bell. Do I know him?'

'He's an investor in the company, a significant shareholder. Read what he says.'

'There was a Stapleton colleague of Oscar Harptree. I remember meeting him on occasion; he would have been Oscar's age.'

'Charles is in his forties. Read the letter, Archie.'

'Maybe a son of the man I knew.' Archie took the letter over to the light by the window. It was written from a private address and, by the style of it, from a house of some standing: Drayworth Manor. Drayworth was a sought after village to the east of Tonecastle, favoured by people retired from the services. Admirals and generals were thick on the ground.

Archie scanned the letter, typed by an expert hand he guessed, a secretary rather than by Charles Stapleton himself.

Dear Miss Curtis,

I was concerned to hear you have been involved in a road accident and have spent time in hospital. I understand you are making a recovery and are away for a time convalescing. I trust you are soon returned to good health.

There are matters pertaining to the company that are giving me and my fellow non-executive directors concern in relation to funding in the light of current trading.

I would be grateful if we could speak on the matter and would ask you to contact me on a private basis on the phone number given in the address above.

Yours sincerely,
Charles Stapleton

'How well do you know this Charles Stapleton?'

'Only from directors' meetings; he isn't in the office much, yet he has a good grasp of what is going on. He listens to what others have to say, unlike Andrew who's impatient and not interested in the opinions of others.'

'Are you going to get in touch with him?'

'Yes.'

The door bell rang. Lorna answered it, returning in seconds with a huge cellophane-wrapped bouquet of orchids. Attached with a ribbon was an envelope and Lorna tore it open.

'You do have an admirer.'

'Hardly, the cheek of it, I've half-a-mind to send them back.'

'There were orchids like those in Malaya, they grew everywhere. Why do you want to send them back?'

'I don't believe it.' She held out the gold-edged card. 'Look.'

The card read: Trust you are getting better, Andrew Harptree.

'I suggest you ring Stapleton without delay, something is afoot.'

Lorna told Archie she needed to clear her mind to be certain what she knew and what she remembered of the events before she fled the office. They set off home in mid-afternoon, having had no lunch. Archie told Lorna he would find something in the deep-freeze urging her to make her call before evening.

Lorna insisted she had to have time to think. When they got home she called Patch, put on her coat and the winter boots recovered from her flat, and went out for a walk in the lanes. While she was gone, Archie brought the painting of rosehips into the house, setting it on an easel in the conservatory, but unsure whether it was an appropriate time to give it. He wanted her to be thrilled, yet there was much on her mind.

He'd persuaded her to ignore the origin of the orchids and not throw them into the wheelie bin outside the flats. He retrieved them from the back seat of the car to take them to the summerhouse, wanting to work wild orchids into his jungle painting.

When she returned from her outing, Lorna was smiling, her cheeks flushed and hair wild. She'd been running.

'Can I ring Stapleton before we eat, Archie? I've geared myself up for it and must do it now.'

'Of course.'

'You don't mind me using your phone, only I can't get a signal on my mobile. In fact I'm not certain it works properly. I'll pay for the call.'

'Don't be daft. You make your call and I'll start to dish up. You may need some warmth, the central heating isn't on. There's a blower heater near the phone, or go up to my bedroom and use that phone.'

'I'll use the hall phone.' Lorna took Stapleton's letter from its envelope and went through to the hall.

Archie looked at the old dog slurping water from its bowl. 'Made you run, did she?' The dog wagged her tail before going to her bed in the corner.

Five minutes later, Archie heard Lorna call out from the conservatory.

'Archie, Archie, it's wonderful.' Lorna came running into the room. 'It is my painting isn't it, it's just what I wanted.' Lorna threw her arms round Archie, kissing him on both cheeks. 'You lovely man, I didn't know you were going to do it. When did you paint it?'

'When you were still in bed in the mornings. Have you rung Charles Stapleton?'

'Yes. We are going over to lunch at Drayworth Manor tomorrow.'

'We?'

'Yes, both of us. Remember the doctors said I shouldn't drive until I've got the all-clear.'

'I can take you, but I'll find a pub for lunch.'

'Oh no, Archie. I told him I wanted you to be there, that you were my mentor at Harptree & Ellis and I'm staying with you during my convalescence.'

'But the company affairs are not my business, Lorna.'

'He said he remembered meeting you and he is very happy for you to join us.'

'Will anyone else be there?'

'I don't think so.'

Checking one of the many Ordnance Survey maps from the sitting room bookcase, Archie found the village of Drayworth, some fifteen miles east of Tonecastle, with the Manor marked down a long drive. Lorna suggested they go via her flat, as she wanted to stop off to collect things she needed for her meeting.

* * * * *

Next morning Archie waited in the car hoping she wouldn't take too long, they were running late.

'Sorry, I'd forgotten where I'd put them.' She was holding a zipped bag smaller than a handbag.

'Anything exciting?'

'Back-up floppies, I think he wants to talk figures. These may be a bit old, but they could be useful, assuming I can run figures off on his computer.'

'I never liked things being taken out of the office.'

'It's important to keep back-up discs at another location.' Lorna chuckled. 'I'm going to have to teach you about computers, Archie.'

'My paper and pen systems worked.'

'I don't deny it, even so...'

'Come on, seat belt on we must be on our way.'

A mile out of the village they found a gatehouse, drove in past the open wrought iron gates, along an avenue of fine trees to a wide curl of gravel before a Georgian frontage.

'Do you think this is where we are supposed to park? The car makes a drastic alteration to the symmetry of the place.' Archie hesitated before turning off the ignition.

'I can see why Charles Stapleton must be worried over his investment in Harptree Ventures.'

There were steps up to a portico, double wooden doors standing open, inside which there were further double doors set with glass panels. As they approached, the glass doors opened and Charles Stapleton came out to greet them. Archie recognised him from one of Oscar's long ago receptions, also from the cricket club.

'Miss Curtis, I am very pleased to see you recovered from your horrible accident. Welcome to Drayworth.'

'Please, Mr Stapleton, I'm Lorna.'

'Lorna it is. And you are Mr Middlebrook. Don't I recognise you from visits to the cricket?'

'A reasonable season, given the days we lost to rain.'

'It has been good, now less formality. I am Charles, we have Lorna...'

'And this is Archie.' Lorna chimed in smiling as he hung back.

'Your mentor, as you put it. Archie I'm glad to see you here. I hear you witnessed Lorna's accident, you were the first to get there and did great things until the Emergency Services reached the scene.'

'I was there. I don't know how you know about it.'

'The Chief Constable lives in Drayworth. I've been making enquiries. Now let's all get into the warmth, it's a fine enough day, but a sharp wind.'

Over lunch Charles Stapleton apologised that his wife, whom he referred to as Angie, as if they already knew her, was not joining them. She was in Bristol discussing a project in which they had a financial interest.

Lunch was provided and served by the daughter of the publican of The George & Dragon in Drayworth, a free house with a reputation for good food. Providing meals out was a new venture and Charles had been waiting for an opportunity to try the service. All three of them agreed it a success, to the obvious relief of Nancy serving them.

After lunch Archie was interested to hear something of the history of the house. Before they started their business discussion, Charles showed them round with an enthusiastic pride, explaining in a previous generation the house had been used as a school, after war time service as a convalescent home for US soldiers evacuated from the D-Day landings. It had taken several years and a fortune to restore the house as a home.

Their tour ended in an elegant room with a high ceiling, fine plasterwork cornicing and inside shutters on its tall windows. Now used as an office where Charles and his wife together with Molly Rogers, their secretary, monitored the several business enterprises in which the Stapletons had a stake. Lorna explained she needed to run off spreadsheets for their discussion. Charles ushered Archie through to a sitting room, leaving Lorna with Molly Rogers downloading files needed from the floppy discs.

While they waited for Lorna, Charles asked Archie about the abrupt end of Harptree & Ellis, the department store. It was clear to Archie that Charles interest in Harptree's had come after the store had closed down, so he felt free to air his opinion. Charles said little, listening to Archie's views.

When Lorna joined them, it was apparent the picture painted by Andrew to his fellow investors was optimistic in the extreme. Lorna had generated a series of trading assumptions based on different sales of property and trading scenarios. Charles was aware of only the most favourable assumptions; real trading had been falling well short.

Lorna reminded Charles that she had been away from the office for almost six weeks suggesting things may have improved in that time although she thought it unlikely.

* * * * *

Back at Hawthorne Cottage, with Patch given a run in the garden, the chickens shut up for the night and two gin and tonics on the table, Archie questioned Lorna.

'Will you go back, Lorna?'

'I might spend a while part-time with Harptree Ventures getting things back on track, as long as the immediate funding issues are being addressed and, as Charles implied, Andrew Harptree will no longer hold an executive position. It will depend on the outcome of their meetings next week.'

Archie was impressed with what they had seen. 'Those Stapletons have considerable wealth, their business interests are in all sorts of activities and not just locally. He said his wife was involved in a restaurant opening shortly in Bristol and a hotel in Bath. Must have been the restaurant she went to today.'

'How he came to be dealing with the likes of Andrew I don't know; he was being misled, that's for sure.'

'So you might go back?'

'Not permanently. You were right all along, Archie. It was not a good day when I got involved. I should have listened to you.'

'Once Oscar had gone, I don't think there was a prospect for the store. I've thought about it a lot. Even with modernisation, it was probably on the way out. It is sad to think so after its many years.'

'Let's take our drinks through to the conservatory. I want to be able to sit and admire my painting and count the rosehips again.'

'Is it good for you to be reminded of that day?'

'I'm not worried, Archie. Counting the rosehips has been like finding my way back from catastrophe, the golden thread to lead me out of the labyrinth. Now I can count them with pleasure. It will always remind me of these recent happy times. Beside which, it is a great painting. Tomorrow I want you to show me everything you are doing in your studio. I want to be the first to see your exhibition.'

'I'm glad you like the picture. Everything is at sixes and sevens in the summerhouse. I must make progress getting the garage prepared as a studio to paint the big pictures. I'm ready for them now.'

'It'll be freezing in the garage in winter, Archie.'

'I have a plan. I've got an ancient wood-burning stove hidden away in one of the outhouses; I bought it at an auction years ago. If I can set that up and get Jack Miller to put a chimney through the roof it will be as snug as anywhere. There is a good supply of logs in the woodshed. I want him to put lights into the northern roof slope, and once the walls are whitewashed it will be a proper studio.'

'I'll help you, Archie. I can paint walls and help you sort out the wood burner. I must do something to help.'

'You're not to overdo things, Lorna.'

'I'm fit, I promise. The doctors will sign me off next Tuesday, I'm sure of it.'

Chapter Eighteen

LORNA was given a clean bill of health and complimented on her robust recovery. They started work on the garage. Jack Miller soon had the roof transformed, with a couple of opening windows giving an easy northern light on to the space below and a chimney set up to bring the old wood burner to life, transforming the garage into a studio. Jack was the source of gallons of white emulsion and with the aid of a scaffolding platform moved round the walls on its lockable wheeled feet, Lorna slapped several coats onto the walls so that even the roughest surface reflected light back into the space.

All the time she was asking Archie questions.

He was reluctant to answer, yet bit by bit his friendship with Geraint Hughes and some hint of their homeward ambitions in Singapore, their conversion to scout car operations, the ambush, Geraint's death and Archie's injuries were told and repeated. Lorna, always sympathetic, learned something of the puzzle that was Archie.

Lorna insisted on getting a bolt of cheap white lining material and securing it under the rafters to complete the studio space, providing a baffle against the fall of dirt and insects from the tiled roof. Shifting Jack Miller's scaffolding tower round the studio, she used the staple gun she'd found in Jack's tool kit to secure the cloth.

Meantime, she decided what time she would give to Harptree Ventures on her terms until Christmas. In the New Year she intended taking up with contacts in London. She had been offered use of a bedroom in a flat shared by two others while their third sharer was away for a year. Lorna was confident she could find freelance accounting work in the capital.

'Tell me about Ivy, Archie.'

'What about Ivy.'

'I know she was close to your mother, she's told me what a lovely lady your mum was. Were they related?'

'No, though many in Helecombe are. Mother's family came from Northhill way a generation ago, but she was born here.'

'Do you mean in this house?'

'Born here and died here, but we lived at the stationmaster's house at Helecombe Halt when I was young, my father being the stationmaster.'

'Is he the one in the photo in the hall, the man in uniform?'

'That's the one. I was only five when he went off to war. In my memory he was always in uniform either for the railway or in the Army.'

'And he didn't come back.'

'He came back after Dunkirk, but not the second time. In his late thirties when he was killed, in Italy.'

'I'm in my thirties. That's awful.'

'It's strange to be so much older than your own father. I missed him as a boy. It was all very well having a hero father, but I just wanted a dad to be at home.'

'Have you got his medals?'

'They're with Mother's things. It was an all female household with my grandmother, Mother and Ivy.'

'And now you've got me hanging around.' Lorna was sitting on the scaffold platform swinging her legs as she questioned Archie.

'I like it now. It's good to have a female touch about the house.'

'But never a Mrs Archie?'

'You've made a good job of that roof curtain, or whatever you call it. This is a proper studio now. I have no excuse to delay the paintings now.'

'Hawthorne Cottage would be a lovely home to bring up a family. It's a shame there has never been a Mrs Archie.'

'Time to pack up, it'll be dark soon. Did you speak with Charles Stapleton this morning? You were going to ring him, weren't you?'

'I'm going in to the Harptree office for a day next week. Then if it all makes sense I'll do two or three days a week up to Christmas.'

'And then?'

'See how it works out; I won't go back full-time. I might try my hand at freelancing in London for a while.'

'I'll miss having you around.'

'Forgive my asking, Archie; why does Ivy come over to Hawthorne Cottage a lot?'

'It's partly habit, also my mother paid her to help in the house for all those years, and when she was settling her affairs she provided Ivy with a lump sum allocated out of the trust inherited from her great grandfather, a sort of pension, not a large amount. I think Ivy feels an obligation to still look after things at Hawthorne, and I enjoy her visits.'

'She does as well, I'm sure of that.'

'Ivy is ten years older than me. As a teenager she took charge of me spending hours taking me out on rambles, or playing cards and reading to me. We wandered all over the place then she went into the ATS, the women's Army. She was home on leave when the telegram came from the War Office. She got my mother through that first week, got her over the shock. They were always close after that.'

'How about you, Archie?'

'Father was remote. He'd been away much of my life. It sounds callous, but I was not very upset, it was a badge of honour to have a father who was killed in the war, then there was his gallantry award. It was later that I felt it, when other children had their fathers back home.'

* * * * *

'I wish you were coming with me, Archie.' Lorna held a spoonful of porridge halfway to her lips as he checked eggs and bacon in the frying pan.

'No, you don't. I would make a fuss about the old days. It's for you younger generation to pull this one out of the fire. And I want to see your contractors paid, in full, maybe with interest on overdue payment. It's a scandal the way Eric Gregory and the others have been treated.'

'Yes, Sir, I'll see to it.'

'End of lecture.'

'Perhaps it is best you aren't coming.' Lorna finished up her porridge, put her plate in the sink, and reached over to Archie kissing his cheek. 'I know you're right and I will insist it gets done.'

'That's my girl.'

On a fine Thursday morning in the second week of November, with a sharp frost showing the myriad of cobwebs decking the shrubs in the garden, Archie paused from his preparations in the garage studio, opening the stove for a full burn to eliminate the overnight cold, sending an unbroken column of wood smoke high over the outbuildings.

He watched Lorna as she got into his car and prepared to drive off. She had taken it out with him as passenger the previous afternoon wanting to prove she had no lingering anxiety after her long layoff - even driving by the crash site as a deliberate gesture. Lorna waved over to him after fastening her seat belt.

She'd promised to be back by late afternoon to make supper for them both.

Her meeting with Charles Stapleton in the Harptree Ventures boardroom at eleven gave her the chance to go to her flat in St Magdalene Close to gather her final thoughts and papers.

Charles had told her the other outside investors would be there, that he would chair the meeting and that Andrew Harptree would also be attending. There had been a note sent giving the current state of apartment sales, of Company out-standings and credits as at the previous Friday evening.

*****

For four weeks the daily patterns changed at Hawthorne Cottage to long weekends, with three or four midweek days when Lorna stayed in Tonecastle, spending long hours at Harptree Ventures working closely on Charles Stapleton's behalf frequently meeting with him on the company's refinancing. Andrew Harptree played no part in this process. He had retreated to his racing interests. After investors had put in new funds, Andrew retained only a token shareholding in the venture.

A couple of times Lorna took Archie's car with her into town, other times Archie dropped her at her flat, collecting her later in the week. Back at the cottage Archie worked in his studio.

At the weekends they cleared the garden from autumn's impact, raking up and piling leaves into wired enclosures to rot over the winter, or when the weather was bright they went walking along the coast or onto the moors. At Steart, the promontory edging the Bristol Channel to the west of the mouth of the tidal River Parrett, they strolled with teeth clenched into the wind in the shadow of the two square nuclear power station concrete blocks. Shellduck and waders fed below the tide line, while inside the sea defence wall, on grazed fields, curlews and lapwings grouped and regrouped as the occasional alarm unsettled their feeding. On the days they ventured onto Exmoor, Archie took Lorna on a series of walks along the River Barle, seeing dippers working the boulders and telling her stories of past moorland residents and happenings long ago.

Lorna was adamant she was stopping work with Harptree Ventures by the third week of December. Archie had pressed her for an answer to where she would spend Christmas and at last she confirmed she wanted to be at Hawthorne Cottage. Together they persuaded Ivy to join them and were delighted when she told them her grandson Robin would be with her, his mother, Jilly, spending Christmas with her new partner and his family, a prospect Robin wanted nothing to do with.

'What on earth are you doing, Archie?' Lorna, back earlier than expected one afternoon, found Archie pouring a boiling liquid into a muslin bag suspended from a wooden tripod on the kitchen table. Steam billowed into his face.

'Can you get my glasses off, I can't see a thing; careful this stuff is scalding.'

'Are you all right, Archie?'

'I'm fine, I just can't see.'

'What's the sludge?'

'Sludge. I'll have you know, young lady, this is going to be the finest rosehip jelly in the kingdom, or if it doesn't set it'll be rosehip syrup.'

'How cool is that. Does everyone make jam in the country?'

'It's a bit of a new challenge for me.'

Lorna bent down to look at the liquid draining into a glass bowl. 'It's a wonderful colour. Will that be what it's like when it sets?'

'If it sets; I don't know if I got it hot enough. It should set there's some on the plate which looks sticky enough. Get a spoon.'

'And it's just boiled rosehips?'

'With crab apples and sugar.'

'Is it hot?'

'Not off the plate.'

Lorna scooped the sticky residue from the plate.

'That is so good, Archie. I've got to take some with me to London. I'll sit in my bedsit with your rosehip picture on the wall and eat jelly with a spoon.'

'London is definite then?'

'Fifteenth of January and I've got a three month rolling contract.'

Archie drained the last of the boiled fruit out of the jam pan to put it through the muslin bag. 'We'll miss you.'

'Archie, I'm not going away forever, I promise. I'll be back for weekend breaks. I'll be sick of London in no time. You spoil me; I'll miss it.'

As the shortest day approached Christmas became competitive, not with the presents they were buying, but their planned menu and table decorations. Lorna started the competition, having read in a newspaper how to make crackers. She purchased the snap-pulls in Tonecastle, sourced bright papers, made festive hats, found trinkets in shops she hadn't known existed and set about writing her own riddles.

Archie reserved the job of cooking a joint, but not being the most ardent turkey fan, he planned topside of beef and all that went with it. Ivy had for years made Christmas puddings well ahead of the day, making three so that after Christmas another could be in the larder for Easter. And if folk were minded one was left to be served sliced cold with homemade ice cream in mid-summer. She never put coins in her puddings, yet in secret gave way to Lorna's pleading, using Edwardian silver sixpence pieces kept from her childhood. And it was not only the puddings she made – a Christmas cake was on the larder shelf waiting to be iced, and in the week before Christmas a supply of mince pies came from her kitchen. Once the mince pies were discovered, Lorna took to walking Patch to Ivy's cottage in the afternoons to sample the latest batch, always taking a couple back to Archie for his tea.

Ivy planned a traditional icing on the cake, white with a few sugar flowers. Lorna persuaded her they should challenge Archie's artistic skills and build an icing model of Hawthorne Cottage with a snow-covered roof. Their first attempt didn't look recognisable as a house, not in the least like the cottage. The two women spent an afternoon practising and the final version was a good model of Hawthorne Cottage, even having the conservatory and a whiff of smoke from a chimney.

PART FOUR
1993

Chapter Nineteen

'YOU get one heck of a view up here.' Robin, sitting alongside Lorna on the coach top deck, speeding along the M4 bound for London, was mesmerised by the traffic approaching on the opposing carriageway.

'Our combined speed must be a hundred and fifty, even more.'

'I don't want to know that, Robin.'

'Sorry.'

'We'll be early at this rate.'

'It'll slow down as we get near London. When are we due in?'

'Half twelve at the Hammersmith Bus Depot – that's only three hours from Tonecastle.' She checked her watch.

Lorna had planned to travel by train before discovering Robin was already booked to London on the same day on the coach service, so she decided to try it. Archie got them to the pickup point with only minutes to spare. Ivy stayed home, already missing her grandson after his three weeks in Somerset. Seeing how close Ivy was to Robin, Lorna felt her lack of close relatives.

'Are you happy to be going back to your studies?' Lorna asked.

'Can't wait.'

'Will you commute from home?'

'I'm going to sort out digs near the college. I can't stand this bloke Mum's hooked up with. I bet he's moved in by now. Don't understand what she sees in him.'

'Can you afford digs? Everywhere is so expensive these days.'

'Don't tell anyone, but Gran is subbing me.'

'Well done, Ivy. Wish I had a fairy godmother.'

'You're an accountant; you must earn a fortune, top whack.'

'If only, I'm apprehensive about this new job. It's going to be a challenge.'

'You'll do it, no problem. Uncle Archie says you're a high-flyer.'

'He's exaggerating. Have you always called him Uncle Archie?'

'It's what Mum calls him.'

Lorna took a cab from Hammersmith, not wanting to struggle with two suitcases on the Underground, while Robin preferred to get straight onto the District Line and out to Upminster. He wrote down Lorna's telephone number, promising to get in touch when he was settled to meet up for a theatre and a meal. Robin suggested an Indian restaurant he'd discovered near Covent Garden.

Lorna checked her new address in Shepherds Bush from the note made before leaving Somerset and the taxi driver nodded. No more taxis after this, the Tube and buses would be the order of the day, at least until she had some idea of what everything was going to cost. London in 1993 was going to be expensive after her weeks at Hawthorne Cottage.

Her future flatmate had sent her a key in the post, warning there would be nobody in till late. Lorna tried the key, but the door stayed locked, and it was beginning to rain. Minutes passed as Lorna tried to ease the key a fraction in and out of the lock, hoping it would work. The rain got harder and she looked around the street to see if there was a nearby cafe or pub for shelter.

The neighbouring door opened and a young man came out.

'Got a problem?'

'Wretched thing. I know it's the right key.'

'Jenny always struggles. Moving in are you?'

'If I can get in.'

'It's a double lock. The second turn is dicey. This one is the same. It seems only the local burglars are adept at opening front doors, all us tenants struggle.'

'I'm getting soaked.'

'Let me try. I'm Harry.' He stepped over the low brick wall dividing the two terraced dwellings, the coping stone studded with metal stumps from railings removed in wartime. There was a modest space between the houses and the pavement, once a sliver of garden for a shrub or potted flowers now occupied by rubbish bags. Harry worked the key. There was a click and the door opened.

'At last. Thank you, Harry; I could have been here for hours if you hadn't appeared.'

'You'll get the hang of it. Must dash; see you sometime.'

'I'm Lorna.

'Bye, Lorna.'

Lorna lugged one wet suitcase into the lobby, keeping a foot against the door in case it swung back as she reached for the second case. On a table in the hallway she found an envelope addressed "LAURA – hope you had a good journey".

'That's all I need.'

As it grew dark Lorna drew the ill fitting curtains on her single window overlooking the neighbouring property, where an unlit matching window looked back to her. Her curtains were thin not reaching to the bottom of the window. She'd unpacked her two cases, fearing the rain had penetrated through to her clothes. As she put everything away into the narrow drawer space in the sole dresser in the room, all appeared to be dry. In pride of place on a shelf with a mirror above it she put the rosehip picture, alongside two jars of Archie's jelly, set well despite his fears. Lorna sat in the 1940s utility upholstered chair beside her bed and counted the rosehips in the picture.

There was a bulb in need of a shade in the centre of her ceiling. It wasn't going to be the lure of home comfort that was going to bring her back to her digs each evening in the coming weeks.

Someone was at the front door. Remembering Harry's quip about the skill of local burglars with the troublesome door locks Lorna remained in her seat, listening.

'Laura, are you there?'

She relaxed, 'Jenny?'

'Great, you've found your way; I was worried about the directions I sent you.'

Lorna went into the hallway. 'Hello, Jenny. I took a cab and I'm Lorna, not Laura.'

'I'm sure your letter said Laura.'

'Perhaps my writing wasn't clear.

* * * * *

Back at Hawthorne Cottage Archie pottered in his garage studio, looking at the jungle painting on his easel, adding nothing to it, from time to time taking up a brush, touching the still soft oil to make a minimal alteration to yesterday's work. He went over to the six by four foot frames faced with marine ply Eric Gregory had delivered in late December.

'I guess I've got you to thank, Mr Middlebrook. The Harptree payment came through last week, with an interest payment for late settlement, not a large addition, but a good gesture.'

'Not me, Eric.'

'There are rumours, Mr Middlebrook. There have been changes for the better at the company.' With that Eric had gone on his way, a happy man. Archie hadn't asked Lorna about the contractor payments certain the matter was being addressed.

The art shop had advised the canvas he needed to stretch over the frames would be delivered in the third week of January; he would be ready with the canvases prepared to work the first of the large pictures come February.

Now the time was approaching to work the big pictures the spaces looked huge. He had never painted any picture so large, he needed to be confident the ideas he had sketched and painted in smaller sizes could scale up and retain their dynamic. Archie looked at each of his three main themes already finished in groups of pictures hung on the walls. The first of these was the jungle, with only the hint of a foot patrol in its depth; the extension of his endless sketches done on days off as the tropic heat sapped the energy of the men. It was the scene with which he felt most at ease, the candidate for the first of the large canvases.

The second he wanted to scale up was a portrait of Geraint Hughes. By the time he had worked it onto the large canvas it would be a full-length, three-quarter life-size portrait, with him wearing his oil-stained overalls standing by his Ferret Scout Car, the one he'd polished, caring for every square inch of its camouflage painted metal, until it was blown up into twisted burnt metal. Lorna had researched military magazines, sending off for articles written by enthusiastic owners of veteran Ferrets. The pictures were pinned to a cork board on the studio wall. An old photo from his army days was enough to confirm the exact model of scout car they were working with on their convoy patrols.

Archie had to leave to last the picture of the ambush. His sketches for it lacked the desolation he wanted to portray. He couldn't decide whether or not there should be a figure in it representing himself. And if there was where the figure should be, either trying to open the driver's hatch after the first explosion or lying injured in the jungle edge? The best of his sketches was the point of the concealed mine's explosion, adding gunfire coming from the terrorists' hideout, although in reality the gunfire and grenade came later.

He looked at the wall clock. The coach to London would be on the M4. When next he looked they would be through the Hammersmith depot, or maybe Lorna would have found her lodgings. He'd asked Lorna to ring when she was settled. He closed down the wood burner and crossed to the cottage in light rain that had fallen all day.

'Never mind the rain, Patch, let's go and see how Ivy is getting along without Robin.'

The dog, eager to be the subject of attention, stretched and went to the door. They walked along the road past the crash site still evident with the broken hedge. Next summer's growth would disguise the site. Patch was happy to trot along the road margin, having learnt over the years to get on to the verge and sit down if a vehicle passed. The rain eased as they reached Ivy's cottage.

'Hello, Archie. I don't see you here for a while then twice in one day.'

'Sorry we had to rush away this morning. We were cutting it fine; in the event we got to the pick-up point by the old Odeon only a few minutes before the coach. Hope you had time to say farewell to young Robin.'

'Muddled boy, I trust he's had something to eat on the way; he missed out on his breakfast.'

'He's a grand lad, Ivy. I've seen him grow up over the years, but I feel I got to know him better over these past three weeks. You'll miss him.'

'You'll stop for tea, Archie?'

'Any mince pies?'

'I'm so cross with that daughter of mine, Jilly. She shouldn't be chasing after men at her time of life. Robin needs her, now he'll have to find digs near the college if that man moves in.'

'That'll set him back a bit.'

'I told him I would help with the cost and it's too late for mince pies. I've made a ginger cake.'

Over the weeks of February and March the large canvases came to life. Archie struggled with the ambush scene, revising the composition several times. He found in scaling up his earlier sketches the scout car got lost in the background and had to be pulled into the foreground, demanding greater detail of the equipment attached to the vehicle, which taxed his memory. At last he was able to take photographs of the three large canvases and a selection of the smaller pictures; once the photos were processed in Tonecastle he was ready to start his round of visits to galleries, seeking an exhibition. He chose twenty photos that best showed his smaller pictures and the large showpiece pictures, the fundament of his *Requiem for Private Hughes,* and set them into a wallet album convenient for showing to gallery owners.

He had two sets of prints made and sent photos of the three key paintings to Lorna. She rang him the evening she got his letter, telling him the photos were sitting on her shelf alongside his rosehip painting. Even Ivy, never the most ardent fan of his paintings, praised him for his perseverance.

Archie started his round of local galleries, first in Northhill, then in Tonecastle and ran into the same problem every time. The proprietor of Painters in Tonecastle was interested in his smaller paintings and offered to take them to display alongside two other artists. The six by four foot canvases were too big for every place he tried. It was hard to argue against, as even where there was the wall space to hang them, there was no room to stand back to view them. Frustrated, Archie travelled up to Bristol to seek interest at a regional gallery. One asked him to leave his album with them, but he decided to keep the album and return home to have another word with the owner at Painters in Tonecastle, trying to persuade him to give him a one-man slot without the large paintings, even if only for a week.

He'd concentrated all his efforts on getting his paintings on to canvas, assuming that exhibiting the works would follow. He wrote to Lorna and felt better when she rang, saying she would be down in Somerset for Easter in the second week of April, staying for ten days. She planned to hire a car and motor down with Robin, as he preferred to be in Somerset with Ivy for the break to three weeks with his mother in Upminster. He'd tried to get an Easter job in a holiday camp, but nothing was forthcoming.

During November Lorna had helped Archie plant a sack-full of mixed daffodil bulbs in places round the lawn and on the edge of the lane by the turn in to Hawthorne Cottage. Archie watched the bulbs shoot during February and March. When April came there was a dramatic display of yellows and gold to greet Lorna driving into the yard.

'Is this from our planting, Archie?'

'Most of it, there are some from earlier years, but nothing like the number flowering now.'

'I never thought it would be such a bright display. It was freezing doing the planting, this is recompense in plenty.'

'You look in good heart, Lorna. Journey all right?'

'I feel good now I'm home.' Lorna looked at Archie and laughed. 'Well, you know what I mean.'

'And Robin?'

'Ivy was thrilled to see him.'

'Ivy wants us both for lunch on Easter Sunday. Is that all right with you?'

'Excellent.'

'Another thing I want to do is to take a trip along the railway. There'll be several steam hauled trips over the next couple of weeks and it's the best time to see the country from the train, with primroses in the hedge banks and before the trees are in full leaf. I'll show you the stationmaster's house where I was born.'

'Is that where we'll catch the train?'

'No, we'll go to Northhill and do a there-and-back trip.'

'Can I smell supper, I'm ravenous. We didn't stop on the way.'

'It's shepherds' pie.'

'Great. Am I in the same room?'

After they had eaten Archie and Lorna sat in the conservatory, with coffee and a bottle of wine passing the occasional comment on their happenings since Christmas. Archie relayed his frustrating discussions with gallery owners casting his net as far north as Bristol and to Exeter in the west.

'Truth is I don't know where I go from here. Maybe that's as far as my Requiem will go and I'll have to store the paintings and hope for better things another day.'

Lorna watched the flickering light from candles she'd insisted they light as the spring evening darkened, fading the landscape from view. She felt at home after testing times in London. She'd settled into her digs having set up her room as she wanted, with new curtains, brighter bedding, an electric blanket, a rug on the floor and a more comfortable easy chair bought in a local auction room. She'd come to terms with the intricacies of the front-door-double-lock and with the alarming thumps when lighting the Ascot water heater in the shared bathroom.

There were three of them in the house – her bedroom downstairs with the other two bedrooms upstairs. As the most recent joiner she had had to thread her routine into those already established by the others. The gauntlet of the chilly stairs to get to the bathroom upstairs was a challenge. After a few days, Jenny had proved to be good company, going a street away for a drink in the Crown & Sceptre, announced on the street front as the Crow & Sceptre with the 'N' of Crown fallen away. Lorna saw little of the third member, Helga, who hailed from Hannover and spent time away from London. She worked in a film crew out of town most weekdays.

Lorna was not sure whether to tell Archie or to leave it until she was able to get a stronger indication from Nathan, the director of a gallery, a client she was advising. She had shown him the photographs of the three big canvases and he'd been interested, saying he would like to see more of the paintings and know something of the back story. She didn't want to set another hare running, just to find there was nothing at the end of the course.

'Strange thing happened the other day.' Archie broke into Lorna's thoughts. 'I was watching a TV documentary about Ancient Greece when they interviewed an Oxford professor, and it was a chap I was in the army with in Malaya.

'And you recognised him.'

'He seemed familiar – but he had long grey hair, a bit thin on top and a beard, nothing like he was in our youth. I hadn't been following the programme too closely, pottering in and out of the room and I'd missed his name, yet his voice was familiar. It turned out he was the officer in charge of our platoon, James Peterson, also doing his national service. He was on the convoy patrol when we were ambushed.'

'Have you seen him since Malaya?'

'He was good to me afterwards, he came to see me in hospital, then his national service ended, as did mine, and our paths went separate ways. Strange thing is that when I went through Mother's bits and pieces I found an old shoe box with letters in it, some from my father in the war, some from me when I was abroad, and there was a Christmas card in the box from James, the first Christmas I was home. I didn't remember it at all, a posh card with a crest on the front and a ribbon with a photograph inside of his Oxford College. He'd written in it, quite chatty about how cold it was after the tropics.'

'He was with you on the day of the ambush?'

'He was the officer-in-charge. He must be quite an expert on ancient Greece these days, not only a professor, but knighted as well – Professor Sir James Peterson, it said on the credits.'

'I bet you he'd want to see your paintings.'

'He got me to do one for him when we were on jungle patrols, said in his card he had it on the wall in his room and looked at it when it was snowing.'

'You must contact him.'

Archie reached over to fill her glass.

'I don't know whether he would remember me.'

'Of course he would, Archie.'

For a while nothing was said. Outside the conservatory, nothing could be seen beyond the reflected flames of the candles. Archie topped up his glass, then poured another coffee and held the pot up, asking Lorna.

'Not for me.'

* * * * *

After Ivy's Easter Sunday lunch, Lorna and Archie walked back to the cottage with Patch trailing along behind, snuffling into her world of scents and signs along the lane-side hedge.

It had been a long lunch as they caught up with each other's comings and goings of the last three months – Robin's move into digs, Lorna's plan to sell her Tonecastle flat and see if she could afford something reasonable in London and Archie's round of galleries in search of his exhibition.

'I need this walk after that feast,' said Lorna. 'You know the photos you sent me, of the Requiem canvases.'

'Keep hold of them, they'll be a historic document one day.'

'I have shown them to someone, he's in the business, I've been doing work for his gallery. He liked them.'

'I'm glad.'

'Archie, he runs a gallery in London, the Chiswick High Road Gallery, it's quite important.'

'Sounds impressive, but can it hang large pictures?'

'I've seen huge ones on the walls, modern abstract paintings. They are a go-ahead lot. Nathan Willoughby is the driving force, in his thirties and he's quite a looker.'

'I see.'

'Archie, don't mock. Judging by things I've seen in their books they do big deals, in tens of thousands for top works.'

'I hadn't thought about selling. I just want to get 'Requiem' exhibited and recognised. Not many people remember the Malayan Emergency, with all that's happened since the fifties.'

'The two go together, exhibiting and selling. Think about it, Archie. There's nothing to lose by our putting a portfolio of information together, photos of you and the pictures, notes about you and the events in Malaya. I can take it to Nathan and get him interested. If it doesn't click nothing is lost... or gained, I accept. He might want you to come up to London.'

'I guess you are right. Let's talk in the morning, I'll sleep on it.'

So Lorna's Easter holiday progressed. Once they'd decided to pursue the possibility of London, they spent hours putting together a portfolio to make the case to Nathan Willoughby. Photos were taken of all the paintings and early jungle drawings, Archie was photographed on his own and working in his studio. In Dorothy's box of letters Lorna found a photograph of Archie and Geraint together in Malaya sent home in a letter six months before the ambush. Archie was reluctant to put too much down in print about his national service days, but Lorna insisted.

Lorna then set off to her flat in Tonecastle where she had her computer – one of the reasons she'd hired a car over the holiday was to take her PC with her to London. Archie was happy to talk about his purpose behind the paintings, all of it went into the document before Lorna sat up most of a night editing the draft into a concise and, Lorna felt, compelling case for an exhibition to be staged. Archie realised his sales efforts with local galleries had been well below par. Once Lorna had the bit between her teeth she lost her worries of the approach to Nathan being a dead-end.

When they felt the portfolio was in a presentable form they used Ivy and Robin as guinea pigs. Lorna's hard sell overwhelmed their audience, Archie watched as they sat in silence through the lecture.

'I know nothing about galleries; give it a whirl, Uncle Archie. How about it Gran, do you think they deserve it?'

'London is a strange place, but I know one thing. Dorothy would be so proud of you, Archie. She always wanted to see you succeed as an artist and now you have.'

'Thank you, Ivy. Maybe a success if we get an exhibition. Fingers crossed for Lorna when you go to see Willoughby.'

'I've spoken with him on the phone. I'm taking the presentation round on Thursday next week,' said Lorna.

'Well good luck, dear; we all wish you well.'

'Thanks, Ivy. They may sit on it for quite a while. I know the gallery is booked through into next summer.'

'We'll have to bide our time, as Dorothy always said.'

'Who is for a train trip tomorrow?'

'Where to, Uncle Archie?'

'On the Heritage Line, steam hauled to my father's old station. We can get off at Helecombe Halt and take a walk round the places we explored all those years ago, Ivy. You'll come won't you?'

'What do I want to go gallivanting round the country like that for? I could walk to Helecombe Halt from here if I was minded.'

'Come on Gran, you'll love it. I've never been on a steam train.'

'That's a date then; I'll check the timetable; I think there is an 11.20 train. That'll be the best bet for a trip from Northhill to Helecombe Halt, a walk on the paths along the river below the station that might just lead us to The Royal Oak for a sandwich and a beer. Then the train back to Northhill in time for a cream tea in the Old Beachfront Cafe. They do a good spread I'm told.'

Chapter Twenty

NATHAN gave Lorna a fair hearing, spending half an hour listening to her presentation of the case for a major exhibition of Archie Middlebrook's *Requiem for Private Hughes.* She told him about the experience of the young men on their national service in Malaya, the terrorist ambush, its aftermath, Archie's inability to return to art college studies and the years of subconscious grieving for Geraint Hughes, his part in Lorna's rescue, his inspiration after Lorna's crash and his return to painting.

It was a speech she had conjured up from her conversations with Archie over Easter at Hawthorne Cottage, not the one she would have spoken to him and not the commentary she had rehearsed with Ivy and Robin.

Nathan listened, looked in detail at the written presentation, the photos of the paintings and of Archie including the pictures she had found of Archie and Geraint together in uniform.

'It's a lot to think about, Lorna. The gallery has a full schedule over the next twelve months. I like what you've told me, so leave your documentation with me. I'll give it thought and discuss it with the exhibitions committee. If we think of taking it further I'll need to meet Middlebrook.'

'That will be no problem.'

'In Somerset, so I can get a feeling of the man in his own environment.'

Lorna rang Archie that evening to give him the news as far as it went. 'We will have to be patient, Archie. It could be at least a year before it happens.'

'I've waited the best part of forty years to get as far as this, so another year or two won't make much difference.'

Apple trees blossomed, exciting bees into hive duties, while serving the trees to set fruit for the summer months. Roses bloomed and sweet peas climbed from their trench up the brush cut stakes to flower and be cut many times a week, to stand in vases, perfuming the house. Swallows returned soon after Easter, by mid May they had made good their nests and were sitting on eggs. Before long, mid-summer had passed and sunsets were creeping earlier every week. The juvenile swallows ventured along the beams from their nests and the first hatched tried their wings and flew.

In Archie's enthusiasm for painting every day, he'd done little in the garden over the summer months. As summer days shortened into autumn, he worked hard outside in the garden, even on days of rain, and when the apples were ready he gathered the best of the crop and set them onto shelves wrapped with paper in the old summerhouse hoping they would keep well into the winter. The windfalls he was happy to leave for the birds and other scavengers.

There were days when he didn't visit the garage studio to browse the paintings, and sometimes even a week passed without checking the pictures to wonder if there were themes he had missed. Maybe there would be an exhibition, maybe there wouldn't. While it would be an achievement if the London show happened, Archie came to realise it wouldn't be a catastrophe if it didn't come off. The paintings were done, the project was finished. Maybe the paintings would stand in the garage as he grew old, and some day someone would have to decide what to do with them. Maybe he would do it himself, building a bonfire in the garden as the final chapter.

What mattered now was that the garden looked good, a place Dorothy would be proud to see, something she would respect, whatever she would say about the conservatory on the side of the cottage and the expense of a central heating system. On a few days over the summer Archie had gone into Tonecastle to watch the county playing cricket. He'd enjoyed his hours at the ground in the days when he worked at Harptree's, but his enthusiasm for watching cricket had waned. He found himself wanting to get back to the cottage to finish a garden task left over from a previous day.

Requiem for Private Hughes

On a quiet mid-week afternoon, when a rain interrupted game was working itself to an inevitable draw on the final day, Archie sat with a pint of beer in the members' bar. He was looking at the numbers on the scoreboard working out which of the two competing county sides had the better scoring rate per over, when someone sat down next to him.

'Mind if I join you? It's Archie, isn't it?' The man held out his hand. 'Charles Stapleton.'

'Hello, Charles. You caught me calculating scoring rates. Can I get you a drink?'

'I can't stay long, I have a meeting in half an hour in town, I just looked in to see what's happening; not too exciting by the look of things.'

'Almost the end of the season just one more match and that is an away game, both sides playing for a draw. I'll head back home soon and get mowing if the rain keeps away.'

'Even mowing sounds more interesting than my meeting. Good to see you, Archie, keeping well?'

A round of clapping interrupted the conversation. A batsman was trudging back toward the pavilion, trying not to catch anyone's eye, knowing he had played a rash stroke.

'Never know; a few quick wickets and there could be a result yet.'

'It's the first one to fall today,' Archie told Charles.

'By the way, I'm sure I have you to thank, Archie, for persuading Lorna to come back to Harptree's before Christmas. Things might have run out of control without her input. As it was, it was a close call and we will have to see how the next few months work out.'

'Much as I resented the closedown of the old store I wouldn't have enjoyed seeing the new company collapse.'

'I saw Lorna a couple of weeks ago.'

'In Tonecastle?'

'In London, she's been doing work for me.'

'I don't know what she does in London. She was down at Easter and all seemed to be going well.'

'She works in a management consultancy company. I've had dealings with them over the years and gave her a reference when she told me she wanted to go to London to find work. I would have liked her to stay on with Harptree's but she was adamant she wanted change.'

Archie had been thinking of Lorna earlier in the day as he'd motored in to Tonecastle, knowing in a few days it would be a year since her crash, a year since his life had surged forward with his painting, the trigger to the wealth of paintings now hanging in the balance, waiting to see if they would go further than Hawthorne Cottage. And that prospect depended on Lorna and what she could persuade the gallery over his pictures.

'I expect she was in good heart. She found London difficult at first even though she'd worked there doing her Articles. To tell the truth, Charles, I half hoped she wanted to come back to Somerset.'

There were spots of rain on the windscreen as Archie drove home. He abandoned thoughts of getting the mower out and called in to see Ivy. On the lawn in front of the house there was a wheelbarrow part-filled with weeds pulled from her herbaceous border with garden tools lying on the grass beside a kneeling mat. Ivy was nowhere to be seen. Archie went round to the back of her house calling out. With no sign of her at the back he tried the kitchen door and found her with tears in her eyes sitting on a chair. There was a letter open on the table. Archie recognised the writing. It was from Jilly.

'Ivy, is it bad news?'

'Oh, Archie, you read it. I've never had such a horrible letter and never before a cross word between us in all these years, other than our differences when she was a child.'

Archie sat with Ivy as they drank tea. He'd read her letter. The cutting words had shocked Ivy. Jilly was accusing her of trying to come between Robin and her, blaming Ivy for Robin's attitude toward her partner. She told Ivy she was going to marry the man next month – and Ivy wouldn't be welcome at the wedding.

'Am I wrong, Archie? Truth is I haven't met the man, I don't know him. I've taken Robin's word and his side in the matter. And why does she want to have another man at her age? In my day you had to be content with your lot. When her father went off I had to accept it. As a child she was hurt by his behaviour, and now I see her doing the same to Robin.'

'Time will tell, Ivy. I should wait awhile, don't do anything in a hurry. She has written in haste and no doubt will regret it.'

'Robin wouldn't put me wrong, Archie. I'm sure of it.'

'There's bound to be sides to it. He's a sensible lad, he wouldn't tell you wrong, Ivy.'

Over more tea and a cake, Ivy told him her fears for what the future might hold and her thoughts to move from Somerset to be closer to Jilly, not to live with her, just to be nearby as she grew older. All that now looked in jeopardy.

It was late when Archie got home. Patch, in since the morning, was keen to be out of the house. The dog was hours late for her only meal of the day.

Archie pottered between the kitchen and the cool larder on the north flank of the house, trying to decide if he wanted to make an effort and cook something for supper or to have a sandwich and make up for it in the morning.

Ivy had always been there, a friend to his mother, a constant figure in his life, a reliable friend, yet she was uncertain of where her life was leading. Not yet in her seventies, she shouldn't be concerning herself with her later years. The letter from Jilly had shaken her. Ivy often told him of the visits she'd made with Dorothy around Somerset to see country houses, mostly with Ivy driving or on occasion with others as a WI coach outing. It was getting late in the season, already September, there would be places still open. In the morning he would plan an expedition with Ivy. She needed cheering up.

A few days later, Archie took Ivy to Wells Cathedral, driving across the Somerset Levels, they had lunch at The King Alfred, at Burrowbridge, where Ivy ate little. She needed no input from the cathedral guides telling Archie all she knew of the great building, the threatening weight of the central tower solved with the huge scissor arches built underneath, still looking modern yet standing their ground since the 14th Century.

Together they stood under the clock as the knights rode round and the figure struck the quarters and they inspected the west front, Ivy wandering off to the cathedral shop to buy mementoes of the day to give to friends in Helecombe, while Archie stood at the edge of a tourist group, listening to their guide before they were rushed off to find the unique octagonal Chapter House, once the strongroom of the cathedral.

Archie suggested they have tea in the cafe, but Ivy knew better and took Archie through a series of side alleys to her favourite teashop.

'I would never have found this place, Ivy.'

'Dorothy discovered it one day when we got lost looking for the coach park.'

'Good chance judging by the cakes on the counter.'

'It's been a good day, Archie. It would have been nice to hear the choristers, but we can't have it all.'

Archie amused himself after the trip to Wells drawing the dramatic facade of the cathedral from the sketch notes he'd made. He sketched the mellow stonework of the cathedral sheltering its multitude of carved stone figures, looking down on tourists staring up, the whole west front reflecting the warmth in the sky in late afternoon. Sitting in the conservatory, Archie painted the scene in watercolours, applying the colours the tour guide insisted the statues and stonework were painted when built in the 1400s without the two towers completed later. He put his painting aside to show to Ivy later.

It was October and nothing heard from the Chiswick Gallery. It had been worth a try and good of Lorna to pursue the chance; a gallery of their standing would have plenty of opportunity to keep busy with young and contemporary painters.

Archie missed his hours spent in the studio, the smell of paint and varnish, the excitement of building a new concept into a picture scheme. He looked for the poetry he had read to Dorothy during her illness. Her frequent request was *The Eve of St Agnes* scenes of feasting in the castle, the freezing evening, Madeline's bedchamber and the anticipation of St Agnes's eve when virgins dream of husbands to be. The bedchamber cried out to be a painting. As the evening grew dark Archie turned up the studio lights and sat with the volume of Keats poems his mother had kept and read since her schooldays and a sketch pad. He was still working up ideas when he noticed the studio clock showed two in the morning.

A week went by and Ivy appeared at Hawthorne Cottage bringing a casserole in the basket of her bicycle she'd pedalled round the district for a generation. Her instinct told her Archie was not getting proper meals and she was right. Apart from a few breakfasts, he had again thrown himself into a series of paintings done at speed until he got his idea clear, always a precursor for careful studies changing tack between the castle feast and Madeline's chamber. He showed Ivy his watercolour of the rainbow colours of the original west front of Wells Cathedral. Ivy dismissed it as not her idea of what it was about.

Archie laughed. 'I promise, Ivy; this is what the guide told us. I've made my own guess at what was coloured what; it was something like this.'

'Now you get yourself washed and I'll get the casserole on the table. It's always the same when you get painting, Archie Middlebrook. You neglect yourself and look at this kitchen. You haven't cleaned up for days.'

But he'd achieved much in the studio.

The smell of the casserole on the stove set his taste buds running. He was hungry. He found bottles of stout in the larder and poured two glasses expecting Ivy to resist; she said nothing. Ivy's casseroles were always delicious, thick brown gravy and tender meat.

Archie cleared his plate as Ivy sipped at her beer and took a few mouthfuls from her lightly laden plate.

'More, Archie?'

'No need to ask, Ivy, one of your best. I'll get the house shipshape after lunch. You must see the paintings I'm doing. It's all going well.'

Lorna rang as Archie was clearing the table after persuading Ivy to sit down and put her feet up a while. She was ringing from the gallery in Chiswick.

'Nathan wants to come down to Somerset to meet you and see your paintings, Archie. How are you fixed next week?'

'No problem, any particular day?'

'Thursday, he'll motor down and I'll come with him.'

'Wonderful, will you be down by lunchtime?'

'Maybe late lunch, if Thursday is OK, I'll tell him. I'll ring again tonight, Archie, must dash.' And she rang off.

Archie looked at Ivy. 'This may be it, Ivy. The gallery man wants to come down from London to see us, Lorna with him.'

'And you said lunchtime?'

'A late lunch most likely.'

Ivy immediately started to think up a menu for next Thursday, pleased to have something definite to plan, knowing Archie will be enmeshed with his pictures.

Lorna rang in the evening. The gallery were interested, nothing confirmed and subject to Nathan's decision when he meets Archie and sees the pictures. There was an exhibition slot from first week next September for four weeks. With good fortune, Archie would be exhibiting his *Requiem for Private Hughes* in London in ten months.

After he'd made the kitchen tidy Archie took a bottle of red wine across to the studio, lit candles and sat in the easy chair looking at his trio of big canvases in the flickering light: the jungle patrol, the ambush and the portrait of his lost friend. It was a good likeness, a reminder of lost youth; Geraint never growing old, Archie combed his fingers through his thinning hair, felt the skin blemishes on his scalp, sensing the tingle from his long-healed burn scars.

Archie fell asleep only waking when Patch licked his hand as the candles sputtered out.

'They're good paintings, Patch, old friend. We'll get to London, I know we will.'

* * * * *

Meanwhile, Lorna had another mission. She'd written a letter to Professor Sir James Peterson. Almost by return she was invited to Oxford. The following weekend she caught a train from Paddington to have lunch at the Randolph Hotel with Sir James and Lady Peterson.

Sir James was an inch or two taller than Archie, with his hair turned white and thinning. Because of their shared national service he would be much the same age as Archie, in his late fifties. By contrast, his wife Bridget, a casual yet beautiful woman, had to be many years his junior, even still in her thirties. Lorna met with her hosts in the Morse Bar, Bridget insisting on first names and no formality.

'Lorna, your letter intrigued us, well James mainly, as you spoke about times past well before my time and I guess yours.' Bridget came at once to the point of their meeting as James returned from sorting out drinks at the bar.

'Tell me about Archie today. It's on my conscience that I should have persevered and kept in contact with him after Malaya,' said James who sat down opposite Bridget and Lorna. 'Sometimes these things don't happen when they should. And how come you got in touch with me, Lorna?'

'Archie spoke about you; he'd seen you on the TV.'

'On that dreadful programme about Ancient Greece.'

'It wasn't that bad, Bridget, it paid for our trip to the States last year.'

Over drinks and lunch, Lorna told her hosts why she'd got in touch, about Archie's giving up on his painting for so many years, her car crash and his bravery getting her out alive, his inspiration to paint again and his ambition for his hoped-for exhibition to honour his friend Geraint Hughes. By then they were having coffee, and James had added some insights to what she knew and told Lorna he had kept contact with Geraint's family over the years.

'Life hasn't always been good for them. His young brother Huw went off the rails as a teenager, got into all sorts of trouble, Borstal and drug problems. However, through the help of a wonderful woman, he married and they have a daughter, Megan. Huw died in an accident at work, probably his own fault. With Megan's grandparents, Geraint's parents, both gone life has been a struggle for Geraint's niece, and for her mother.'

'Was she the young Welsh girl who came to see you about careers last year?' Bridget asked.

'Yes, in the summer, she's at an art college now.'

'From what he has told me, Archie felt he ought to get in touch with Geraint's family after he got home from Malaya, yet somehow he never could.'

'I can understand. It was easier for me as Geraint's immediate commanding officer. It was almost a final military duty, having written to them after his funeral.'

It was late afternoon by the time Lorna caught her train back to London, having told James she would tell Archie of their meeting. James said he would write to him after a couple of weeks and try to go down to Somerset to see his paintings.

'He told me he did a picture of the jungle for you.'

'He did, it hangs in my study to this day.'

Lorna meant to phone Archie as soon as she got back from Oxford, but let it wait for a couple of nights.

'Don't be cross with me, Archie. I know I should have asked you. I've met James Peterson.'

'James Peterson, the James Peterson I told you about? Why?'

'He wants to meet up with you. He's pleased to hear about your paintings and he has had contact with Geraint Hughes's family over the years.'

'Hang on, Lorna. What's this all about?'

'He is very keen to see your paintings, Archie. He is charming and has a wife who must be twenty years younger than him – and I don't think she is his first wife.'

'Lorna, are you sure this is a good idea. Our paths crossed a long time ago.'

Chapter Twenty-One

THE deep-throated throb of twin exhausts announced the arrival of their guests, the man from the Chiswick Gallery and Lorna. Archie hadn't expected them to arrive in a classic sports car. Lorna was beaming, her blonde hair straggling back from a white Alice band. There was a hint of Daimler style in the furrowed marking over the radiator grille. Oscar Harptree always ran a Daimler; never any model such as this.

'Archie, this is Nathan... Nathan Willoughby.' Lorna struggled to catch her breath.

'Welcome to Somerset, Mr Willoughby. Has Lorna guided you well?'

'Nathan, please. Never a missed turn I would have been searching all day on my own. You are hidden away here.'

'I'll go and find Ivy. I can smell cooking and I'm famished,' Lorna disappeared into the house.

'This is a fine car, Nathan.' Archie gazed at the coachwork.

'My father's, he let me borrow it for a couple of weeks. I'm on my way down to Cornwall to return it.'

Was his visit for convenience on his way to see his parents, not primarily to see the pictures? Archie studied his guest, younger than expected, taking off leather gloves and tossing them into the open car.

'Is it a Daimler? A classic, I'd guess? Don't think I've seen one of these before.'

'1963 Daimler SP250, or Dart, as they wanted to call it.'

Lorna came from the house with Patch circling round in greeting. 'Come on in. Ivy has lunch on the table and doesn't want it to spoil.'

Requiem for Private Hughes

'Oscar Harptree, he was my employer some years ago,' Archie remarked. 'He had a number of Daimlers over the years, nothing as sporty as this, always chauffeur-driven.'

'Was that Sammy?' Lorna asked.

'In the fifties and sixties it was Sammy's father. Now we'd better not keep Ivy waiting.'

Over lunch Archie told Nathan the facts of his time in Malaya and the terrorist ambush, before they headed for the studio.

Archie had arranged and rearranged his pictures. There were more than he realised; selecting those he wanted for the exhibition, let alone for Nathan to see, had occupied two days. He'd dithered over whether to leave any other work on show. In the end he decided against, other pictures would complicate the situation, they were not what he wanted the exhibition to be about. He'd questioned Lorna on the gallery space, but she was vague. He needed photographs, yet in the end they would say what they wanted, if anything. Eventually Archie had set up the three large canvases on the back wall, put another twenty pictures in groups on the side walls, and left a pile of canvases propped against the wall near the door.

He took Nathan through the order of his paintings, explaining his motivation in painting the Requiem sequence. Nathan said little. He had a black bound notebook and wrote in it from time to time, and kept his Polaroid camera working. He asked if he could take one of the smaller paintings with him, he couldn't take more as he would be going back to London by train after delivering the car to his father. He took Archie by surprise in suggesting he should paint at least one much larger canvas to be the focal point in the exhibition. He left the subject matter to Archie.

He confirmed the gallery wanted to run the exhibition. It would be next September, and that the gallery would write to Archie with a proposal on commercial terms.

A hundred questions raced through Archie's mind. 'I would like to get a feeling for the space in the gallery.'

'I'll send you photographs. No, even better, come and see us, Archie. I'll be back in Town next Wednesday, so give me a ring and we'll fix a date. Time will go by and we'll have a lot of publicity to organise. We want to go big with this, Archie. There's a lot to discuss.'

After a cup of tea with Ivy's scones and fresh made cream, Archie stood in the yard, listening to the roar of the Daimler's twin exhaust fading away. Contracts, London, publicity, a larger painting to do, and of what he had to decide. This was bigger than he'd expected.

'It's going to happen, Archie.

'All thanks to you, Lorna. Archie put his arm round her shoulders and gave her a squeeze. 'Did you hear him say I had to do another even bigger picture?'

'That's wonderful.'

'If I can do it. I thought I'd gone as large as I can.'

'You'll do it, Archie; what'll it be.'

'I don't know, at least there are months in hand; he wants to get started on publicity, a catalogue and things like that, even some prints and postcards for people to buy if they don't fork out for a painting. I haven't even thought of paintings being sold, I don't know what the gallery do and what I will be expected to do.'

'You'll be in your element, Archie. Think of the January sales you organized at Harptree's, always a success.'

'I knew what I was doing then. This is different.'

'You do the painting, Archie. I can help with admin if you want.'

'Bless you, Lorna; I need your help.' Archie squeezed her shoulder again, pulled her close and kissed her cheek. 'You're a star. How long can you stay?'

'I'll go back on Monday. Has James Peterson been in touch, Archie?'

'I don't know about it, Lorna. It's forty years since we knew each other.'

'Isn't that the point of the Requiem exhibition? It was a long time ago, yet Geraint Hughes is remembered. James Peterson will want to remember him, too.'

'Will he? A man in his position may not want his past paraded in public.'

'Archie, I've talked with him, he has kept contact with Geraint's niece and her mother, the past is not forgotten. Believe me, Archie, he wants to meet you again, he wants to see the pictures.'

It was growing dark as they went back to the house to join Ivy.

'Proper gentleman, that Nathan, he liked my scones. I put a few in a bag for him to have on his journey.'

'You made a hit there, Ivy,' laughed Lorna.

* * * * *

A couple of days after Lorna went back to London a letter came for Archie from James Peterson. Archie read through the two hand-written pages, skimming to the end. He put the letter down, went out to the garden, walking round and looking at the lingering roses persevering against early frosts. Back in the kitchen, he made a mug of coffee and sat down at the kitchen table to read the letter in detail.

James was uncertain where Lorna came into the equation as she didn't appear to be related to Archie. He was glad Archie was painting full-time, reminded him of the picture he'd done for him in Malaya, telling him, as he already knew, it hung on the wall in his study and many people had remarked on it over the years. James had kept up with some members of their battalion, he mentioned Major Willocks, now long since retired with the rank of Colonel, living near Warminster, where he had for years worked as a stalwart of the British Legion.

Peterson's letter also told Archie of his contact with Geraint Hughes's niece, Megan, and her mother in Cardiff.

Archie sat gazing into the fire, the flames lapping up the logs. He was uneasy with this voice from his past reminding him he should have got himself to Cardiff to meet Geraint's parents, now long since passed away. Why wallow in his own pity when he could have helped them? He had survived; they had lost a loved son. And from what Lorna, not knowing any of the people involved, had told him a second son who, without the guidance and example of an older brother, had got his life in a mess and suffered a fatal accident.

Unhappiness on unhappiness had built up for the Hughes family, while he had sat in Somerset feeling self pity.

Peterson talked of coming down to Somerset in the New Year. He wanted to see the paintings. Was this right after almost forty years had gone by? James, Second Lieutenant Peterson, now Professor Sir James Peterson, lived in a different world from rural Helecombe. Yet it was James who had forged the link with Geraint's family. And wasn't that what his *Requiem for Private Hughes* was about – a remembrance of things that happened, and no longer to be only a private gesture. It was going public, on exhibition to the world.

He must write to James, inviting him down and to get him to share in the venture. His endorsement would be good. Once again Lorna's instinct was right.

One o'clock; he put on his walking boots, found gloves, a winter sweater and a scarf, picked up his waterproof coat to go walking on the coast, along the sea wall separating the low lying farm land from the mudflats, to watch the winter birds and settle in his mind all he had to say to James.

※ ※ ※ ※ ※

Lorna met Archie on the concourse of Paddington Station shortly before midday. The station was crowded with pre-Christmas shoppers. The appointment with Nathan at the gallery was at two. Lorna suggested a taxi to Chiswick, where they could get something to eat. Archie preferred the Underground. It was years since he had been in London and ridden the Tube. Lorna used it getting to work and had no enthusiasm for its crowded carriages standing pushed close with other commuters. Conceding it wouldn't be too bad in the middle of the day, they set off to catch the first arrival on the westbound platform, a Circle Line train to pick up the District Line at Gloucester Road for Turnham Green.

'Thank you for coming with me, Lorna. Now things are real, I'm nervous. I've been trying to get my pictures into an exhibition for so long, and to get this scale of showing is daunting.'

'You'll be in your element, Archie. It would never have fazed you in your Harptree's heyday.'

'This is different.'

'I enjoy being a go-between.'

'Perhaps I should appoint you as my agent. When it is all done I'll paint you a special picture.'

'That'll be perfect.'

The Circle line carriage was at once familiar with its rattling jerky ride, yet strange. Archie had been to London many times on Harptree's business, to buy goods or visit commercial exhibitions on behalf of Oscar Harptree, yet in recent years he'd not strayed from Somerset. When the District Line train they'd changed to emerged into daylight, Archie watched the backs of houses with their competing gardens closed down for winter.

Leaving the train at Turnham Green, Lorna took him to a restaurant she used on occasions. As they went in she pointed out the gallery, a building further along Chiswick High Road, on the other side of the road.

'Is it an old church?'

'It was a Methodist Hall.'

Archie wasn't hungry and opted for soup and a roll. Lorna made up for her missed breakfast.

As they ate, Archie spoke about his exchange of letters with James Peterson, their plan to meet up in Somerset in February, and James insisting Archie must meet with Megan before long. Lorna grinned at him as he spoke.

'Yes, you were right about James. I guess it's what an agent does, call the shots and get it right... most of the time.'

At the Chiswick gallery, Nathan showed Archie photographs of previous exhibitions. Nothing was on display as they were currently between shows, but the bare walls called out for large paintings. At one end of the huge floor space iron columns supported a mezzanine floor. The high windows were blacked out giving a strange light in the hall until Nathan got an assistant to show Archie how the exhibition space could be lit in a variety of ways.

'That gallery, Lorna, I can't get over its size, and they promised, didn't they the whole space will be used to exhibit my paintings; nobody else?'

'That's it, Archie, all for you.'

It was obvious now why Nathan had asked for a bigger painting to be the centre point of the exhibition. His problem was going to be at home, setting up and manoeuvring much larger surfaces, let alone painting them. He'd discussed with Nathan the idea of painting the largest work on a number of panels to be locked together for exhibition. Nathan and his staff saw no problem in that. However he was going to have to get cracking; it was going to be difficult to get the idea and scale right first time. One thing he was adamant over - any figure in the huge painting should not be greater than life size. He didn't want giants.

'You deserve this exhibition, Archie. You've invested so much effort and emotion into your project. It will be a success.'

'I hope so. If I can succeed with a huge canvas it will be good. I understand what Nathan means having seen the photos. In truth it is our project, Lorna, yours and mine. If it wasn't for your efforts here in London the pictures would most likely have been stacked away in the studio at Hawthorne to rot when I'm long gone.'

'Don't be so maudlin, Archie. Let's go to a theatre, and we must have a celebratory meal. We both deserve it. You don't have to go back to Somerset this evening, do you? I'm sure Ivy can look after Patch. You can stay the night in my flat. Helga is away, I'll use her room and you can have my bed. It isn't the best bed in Town, but you'll manage for one night.'

'I can't, Lorna. I'm always putting upon Ivy.'

You must, I want to see Alan Ayckbourn's play at the Gielgud Theatre... Communicating Doors or something like that, it's had good reviews. Archie; we deserve a celebration. Please, Archie, my treat, I really want you to stay, just for one night. I'll ring Ivy.'

After the theatre, they picked up a bottle of Merlot at an off-licence. Back at Lorna's Shepherds Bush house Archie sat at the kitchen table as Lorna searched in a cupboard, telling Archie she was certain she'd bought a jar of olives when she last went shopping. They were nowhere to be found.

Lorna's housemate joined them wrapped in a dressing gown.

'Sorry, did we wake you, Jenny?'

'No, I was reading and heard you chatting.'

'Jenny, this is Archie. Get a glass and join us. We've been to the theatre.'

'So you are the famous artist Lorna has been telling me about.'

'Hardly famous, I dabble with painting.'

'That's not what I hear, Archie. You're going to have an exhibition at the Chiswick High Road Gallery. That's only for the elite.'

'We've been there today to have a first look.'

'More than that, Archie, it was our first planning meeting. The exhibition is set for September, Jenny,' said Lorna.

'I'll put that in my diary. Did you meet the mysterious Nathan at the gallery, Archie?'

'Mysterious?'

'Lorna spends a lot of time at the gallery, she tells me she is working.'

'I am, Jenny, I've been sorting out some pretty poor bookkeeping for them.'

The exchange between the two women had a piquancy confirming what he'd supposed since Lorna arrived in Helecombe in Nathan's sports car. He guessed Nathan might be younger than Lorna, yet both in their thirties. Nathan wouldn't be a bad catch and it was time she found someone, although visits to Hawthorne Cottage would be missed if she settled into London family life. It was not his business. Jenny was changing the subject.

'What did you go to see this evening?'

'I saw all two acts of Ayckbourn's play Communicating Doors at the Gielgud. I think someone I was with only saw parts of it.'

'Sorry, Lorna; did I snore?'

'Heavy breathing I'd call it with your chin on your chest.'

'A large glass of wine and a rich meal before the theatre isn't the best idea for an alert evening at my age.'

'The play was a bit weird; people were going back and forth in time.'

'I'm glad you said that, Lorna, I thought my episodes of shut-eye caused the confusion.'

'I don't suppose nodding off helped.'

Lorna explained that Archie was staying the night; she would use Helga's room for the night. Jenny told her things had moved on and the room was hers if she wanted to move upstairs; Helga had gone home to Germany, her father had had a stroke

'I'll have to find someone else for your room. I don't think Ginny, who had the room before you will come back, she hasn't been in touch.'

They talked on well past midnight about the play, about Archie's exhibition and how difficult it would be to find a compatible third sharer for the house. Eventually Archie stretched deciding it was time for bed.

'I'll leave about half seven in the morning, Archie. Suit yourself when you go, there's cereal in the cupboard or there's Dino's cafe on the Green. He'll give you a bumper cooked breakfast. Paddington is easy from here, catch a bus up to Lancaster Gate and you can walk through or get the Hammersmith and City line from Shepherds Bush. '

'Best wake me. I'll leave when you go, Lorna. Thanks for this evening, I've enjoyed myself. I'd better buy a present for Ivy as a peace offering.'

'Archie, she was fine on the phone, you know she doesn't mind. She likes it that you can call on her when you need a helping hand.'

Chapter Twenty-Two

A MORNING spent with a carpenter's rule, working out how to set up for painting the large picture divided into sections, tested Archie's patience. He changed his mind several times as he worked out what was manageable in the garage studio space. By afternoon he was in Tonecastle, seeking out Eric Gregory to make ply panels that could be joined together for the exhibition and if the picture ever found a permanent home.

Archie decided he needed six panels each four foot square. Set up two on two on two, the assembled painting at twelve foot high and eight foot wide was going to be a challenge. The size of it made him anxious, having never contemplated working on such a scale. Yet after seeing the space in the Chiswick gallery, he knew making a success of one huge painting would create a stunning centrepiece at the exhibition.

Eric was intrigued as Archie explained what he was planning, and was pleased he would be contributing to the focal point of a London exhibition.

Archie left Eric to prepare the panels and went back to Hawthorne Cottage to work on sketches for the huge work. Eric promised to deliver the panels to Hawthorne early in the coming week.

The weekend passed with nothing achieved. Countless sheets of drawing paper littered the studio floor, all marked out with scaled eight by twelve panels, all with soft pencil ideas and designs, all reflecting jungle and scout car shapes, but nothing that suggested an idea worth working up into a picture to dominate the exhibition. And Archie didn't want to scale up any of his existing primary pictures. To do so would mean discarding something from the trio of major paintings, around which the exhibition was originally based. Perhaps he would ring Nathan and tell him there wouldn't be a major new work for September.

Archie turned the lights off in the studio and crossed to the house. Patch pushed past him dashing out onto the lawn as he entered the kitchen. The dog hadn't been out since the morning and hadn't been fed. Archie followed Patch calling after her. Old as she was the dog ran in circles round the vegetable beds, emptied of last year's winter cabbages and not dug over for this year's planting. As Archie surveyed the neglected beds he remembered James Peterson's letter and the mention he made of the jungle patrol drawing he had given his platoon commander, seen by generations of undergraduates attending tutorials. Archie recalled Peterson had said something about the day on patrol when they had broken clear of jungle to discover an abandoned tin mine not marked on any maps. At first they had feared it was a terrorist camp. It was deserted, but they did find arms.

Leaving Patch now wandering round the old apple trees catching up with the scents of the garden fading into darkness, Archie went indoors to find Peterson's letter. An idea was forming in his mind. They had seen a number of tin mines on their patrols, yet there were none in his paintings. Geraint had told him about the slag heaps he explored as a boy in the Welsh valleys, comparing them as giants with the lesser piles of tailings from the tin mines.

As the new day's sun rose Archie was dozing in his once smart now battered chair, its upholstery tattered and paint-stained, in the garage studio. In front of him on an easel an A3 drawing pad displayed his emerging composition, combining a patrol emerging from the jungle chancing upon abandoned tin workings. Archie had cracked it, this would be the centrepiece.

He was still dozing when Eric found him having looked for him in the house.

'You haven't been to bed, have you?'

'Not to bed, Eric. I've had some sleep and I know what I have to do.'

'See what you make of the panels I've made for you then.'

Requiem for Private Hughes

Together they unloaded Eric's van. Each of the panels had a wrapping of bubble wrap, was numbered and bore a set of dowel pins in its joining sides at varying spacing, so that the panels could only be joined in one unique sequence. Once assembled they locked together to make a perfect whole.

Archie had cleared space under one gable end of the studio. Working with Eric, it didn't take long to assemble all six panels on the frame Eric had made, holding them a foot off the floor. The frame was organised to double as an easel, so Archie could work on two adjacent panels at any time, without having to bend or stretch unduly.

'Eric, this is a perfect design. You must have worked all hours to get this done.'

'It'll do the job,' he replied, content he'd met his brief.

'What do I owe you for this, Eric?'

'One ticket to your exhibition will do nicely.'

✳ ✳ ✳ ✳ ✳

'It's coming on for forty years, Archie.'

'You wouldn't think it to look at you.'

'I got to Tonecastle in good time; it's the last few miles that were the puzzle. I didn't know you were hidden away like this, I went through Helecombe twice before I found the right road, then I missed the turning up the lane.'

'It's good to see you, Sir James.'

'No formality, Archie.'

'I always called you 'Sir' as my platoon officer.'

'And a few things else, I'd wager.'

'When did you set out?'

'After an early lunch, that M5 is a bit of a clutter around Bristol, down to a crawl at one stage.'

'Friday afternoon, people getting away for the weekend, anyway come on in, I'll show you where everything is, so you can freshen up, then we can have a drink before a bite to eat. You are staying the night aren't you?' James didn't appear to have any luggage.

'If your offer of a bed still stands. And I must see your paintings before it gets dark.'

Archie took James to the spare room, showed him the bathroom telling him he would be downstairs. Ivy had left potatoes, carrots and peas ready in a steamer to put on the stove, the joint was cooked and resting in the bottom oven. Archie decided to leave things a while and took wine and glasses through to the conservatory where he'd set up two easels with paintings he hoped would bring back memories for James.

There was a call from the kitchen. Archie went through.

'Can I see the paintings, Archie?'

Archie let his visitor go ahead of him.

James stood staring at the two paintings, looking from one easel to the other, from a patrol scene showing a vanishing file of soldiers working their way deep into the jungle to the other picture of two Ferret scout cars on a laterite track passing a rubber plantation, with tappers at work in the background.

James was silent. Archie waited.

'James, red or white? We're having a leg of lamb for supper.'

There was no answer; Archie waited for a hint of recognition within the pictures. He poured himself a glass of Merlot.

'Merlot or Cabernet Sauvignon, James?'

James stood unmoving, apart from his head turning from one picture to the other.

'James?'

Archie waited a bottle in hand.

'It was red last time we dined together in that club in Penang.'

Archie poured Merlot into the second glass and took it to James. He was blinking back tears.

'Are you all right, James?'

'Sorry, Archie, I was unprepared for this.'

'I didn't mean to upset you.'

'You haven't. Suddenly everything since those days fell away. I was back in uniform in Malaya, in the jungle and the rubber plantations. What were we doing there, Archie? Why were we plucked off our comfortable streets and sent half-way across the world for this?' He pointed at the pictures. 'Why?' James fumbled for a handkerchief and wiped his eyes.

'Are the pictures all right, James?'

'Archie, these are tremendous. I've been back to Malaysia a couple of times in the last ten years. It's never had this effect on me. These are powerful. Don't they get you that way, Archie?'

'In the beginning it was emotional. I couldn't make progress, but I've lived with them for months now.'

'We got a lot right in our bumbling way, Archie. We achieved a foundation for Independent Malaysia. Let's drink a toast to those who came back... and to those who didn't.'

Nothing further was said as the two men stood in silence, their lives so different over the years after the shared experience of their national service in a strange tropical country, bonding fears and loyalties. James stood looking at the pictures, his reawakened youth pressing into his thoughts.

'But you do like the pictures? They are true to our time out there?'

'Without a doubt. You have more, don't you?'

'They are for tomorrow.'

It was a while before they sat down to eat, the leg of lamb could best be described as 'well done'. Both men ate heartily. They had trawled up the names and memories of long ago, as if their friendship had no interruption. Archie was determined to keep his exhibition pictures for the next day, not wanting to overwhelm James's emotions. He'd lived with the pictures so long, building up the composition stroke by stroke; he was immured to their impact. He hadn't expected James's tears.

Over the space of an hour, as they finished the bottle of Merlot and switched to the white over dinner, James told Archie of his visits to Cardiff, the first soon after he arrived back from his course in India. He'd decided to wear uniform to make it a formal visit, in case Geraint's parents had not wanted to meet him. They had been welcoming, sitting him down in their best chair and bringing rich cake and sandwiches to refresh him after his journey. He'd brought a photograph of Geraint's grave in Ipoh Cemetery with him intending not to give it to them if they were too upset. It was welcomed, telling him it was the only thing they had that connected them with their late son in Malaya.

'I went back to see them a few years later, having exchanged letters. They had grown old before their years not helped by Geraint's young brother, Huw. He went off the rails in a big way.'

James told Archie of Huw's escapades, his time in Borstal and of Jane, who, when she had the pick of the field, had married Huw and brought him onto the straight and narrow until he had his fatal accident at work.

'I feel bad at never going to Cardiff, James. I should have gone; it's no distance away. It would have been the right thing to do. I chose to wallow in my own problems, and then it was too late.'

'If your exhibition is what I feel it will be, you are providing a proper memorial to Geraint. I'm going to introduce you to Jane and her daughter Megan. She wants to be an artist and she will be thrilled by the exhibition.'

'Let's wait until you see the pictures tomorrow.'

Next morning James had to be in Salisbury for an afternoon meeting. Archie gave him a large breakfast before suggesting he take his coffee over to the garage studio and browse round the pictures Archie had set up for him. Archie made his excuse of tidying in the house, leaving his former platoon commander to inspect his Requiem, including the huge six-panelled painting finished in the week before James's visit. James was the first to see it although Archie had sent a photograph to Lorna, asking her to show it to Nathan and to let him know any reaction from Chiswick.

Ivy pedalled into the yard, puffing from her exertion. 'That hill gets steeper every week, Archie, I swear it does. And how was the roast last night?'

'Excellent as usual, Ivy. We ate late and it was delicious. I've tidied everything in the kitchen. You needn't have come, Ivy, although it's always good to see you.'

'I had to come, Archie. Not every day of my life I get to meet a real 'Sir' is it.'

'James is looking at the pictures. Here he comes now.'

'And you must be the famous Ivy keeping this man in check.'

'I don't know about that, Sir.'

'I've heard of your work here over the years. Archie spoke of it when I knew him as a soldier.'

'Ivy's face beamed as she looked at the two men.'

'Pleased to meet you, I'm sure. Now can I make tea or coffee for you both?'

'That would be much appreciated, Ivy. I want Archie to give me a tour of the garden or maybe a walk up the lane to get my bearings of the countryside round here, then a coffee would be excellent to set me up for my drive up to Salisbury.'

'I've got some biscuits here I cooked this morning.'

'Even better.'

'And when Ivy cooks biscuits she means real biscuits. You won't be disappointed, James.'

They paused on their walk along the lane, each side high banked topped by hedges. They leant on a field gate overlooking meadows and the last old apple trees of its original orchard surrounding Hawthorne Cottage. James was silent, gazing out over the countryside. Archie didn't want to speak first. He needed James to say something, even if it was to condemn his pictures. He'd been chatty with Ivy as he came away from the studio, so why silence now?

'Sorry, Archie, I'm mulling it over. I had no idea the paintings were going to hit me so hard, even after seeing those two last night. Have you had any contact with others of the platoon?'

'Nobody, I got detached from the unit after my sojourn in Penang. I never met up with any of our Battalion, just a mass of strange faces in transit in Singapore and on the troopship home. I wallowed in my problems for months.'

'Depression is a crippling thing.'

'I know you got in touch and I didn't reply. I found your Christmas card not so long ago. It was with my mother's things.'

'Everyone who witnessed that day will be hit-hard seeing your painting of the ambush. It brought it back to me. I was there again, in that scene, when we topped the rise in the track and found you. Even knowing there had been a disaster hadn't prepared us for the carnage.'

'I haven't set out to upset anyone. The series of pictures is meant as a belated memorial to Geraint.'

'Don't get me wrong, Archie. You've captured the essence of those times and the likeness of Geraint Hughes. The paintings bring it all vividly back. You've achieved something wonderful and a thing that needed to be done. I guess you have worked this through your system for months. Seeing it in its final form, suddenly confronting it, is awesome.'

'Should I pull out of this London exhibition, is it my pride that wants to be on show?'

James didn't answer. He stared out over the fields. Archie looked for Patch who'd followed them up the lane and wandered off. James turned from the gate, blinking with the sun or the emotion, and gripped Archie firmly on his shoulders almost hugging him.

'No, Archie, the exhibition is the final act of the adventure we young men shared years ago. You owe it to the platoon, to all who served out there. And above all to Geraint's family, to those he never knew, his niece Megan and sister-in-law Jane.'

'Thank you, James. I want your endorsement.' Archie looked at his watch. 'Now let's get back for coffee and Ivy's biscuits.'

As they walked down the lane Archie felt impatient for September and the exhibition. It was still six weeks before the pictures would be moved from Somerset to the Chiswick Gallery.

'Your niece told me there has never been a Mrs Archie Middlebrook.'

'My niece?'

'Yes, Laura.'

'You mean Lorna? She's not a relative.'

'I'm on my second marriage. The first was a mistake, but we're still friends.'

'I thought I was going to get married soon after we got back. My mother asked a goddaughter of hers to stay to cheer me up. It was a passionate encounter, I misunderstood her signals. She was a London girl, somewhat ahead of the swinging sixties. It wouldn't have worked out. She came to Mother's funeral and appeared to have lived a very full life.'

'Who is Lorna, then?'

'I suppose I am a sort of uncle to Lorna, in the non-family sense.'

Archie told James of the events at Harptree's and his falling out with Lorna, his former much younger work colleague, of his witnessing her accident and his certainty Geraint's spirit had been there, helping to save Lorna in the crashed car.

'That night I got the inspiration for these pictures. It has worked up from a single moment in her crashed car; Lorna has had a big hand in it. She found the Chiswick High Road Gallery and got them interested.'

'She's certainly a spirited soul. I was intrigued when she got in touch.'

'I was annoyed at first. I thought you wouldn't want to know. She was right I should have been in contact with you long ago.'

Back at Hawthorne Cottage over coffee and biscuits in the kitchen, James told Ivy he enjoyed cooking and persuaded Ivy to tell him her biscuit recipe. With Ivy well pleased at his interest, James told them more about Megan and her ambition to pursue an art degree after she completes a Foundation Year at College. It was agreed James would get in touch with Megan and her mother to arrange a meeting with Archie. He was sure they would want to see the exhibition, yet thought it best they should know and understand the works before seeing them in a public setting.

'They only have a few blurred photographs of Geraint as far as I know.'

James spent a few minutes taking photos in the studio to send to Megan then it was time to set off for Salisbury. The two men looked at each other uncertain how to part, reached out to shake hands before embracing in a bear-hug.

Requiem for Private Hughes

* * * * *

With three weeks still to drag by before the paintings were due to be packed and relayed to London, Archie found it hard to cope with inactivity. The feedback from Chiswick on the centrepiece picture was positive and he was trying not to do any more to the many paintings. He'd twice been up to the gallery seeing current exhibitions, and despite Lorna's urging him to stay a night or two he insisted on day trips, using the coach service from Tonecastle, the Hammersmith terminus being convenient for Chiswick High Road. On the second visit he'd walked the mile-and-a-half between the coach station and the gallery.

Archie had seen the draft version of the exhibition catalogue and insisted on a number of changes to the text, in particular over the account of service in Malaya, wanting to downplay the hyperbole creeping in concerning national service conscripts and emphasising the long periods when nothing happened in the tropical heat between the highs of jungle confrontation.

There were voices outside in the yard. Archie, pottering in his studio, listened but couldn't hear what was being said. Through the studio window he saw two young women; maybe Young Farmer members looking for sponsorship. It was amazing what youngsters get up to these days, events as gruelling as any he had taken on in his army training.

He watched them at the cottage door. The taller, blonder girl was knocking, before calling out for Mr Middlebrook. The other girl, with dyed curly pink hair, wore a baggy sweater despite the warm day, and jeans. She seemed less sure of herself, hanging back. The blonde girl wore a flower pattern summer dress, harking back to fashions of decades past. She called into the house, pushing open the front door stepping into the hall. The pink-haired girl stayed where she was, turned and saw Archie at the studio window. She called the blonde girl. Coming back into the yard the girl smiled and half-waved.

'Can I help?'

'I'm looking for Mr Archie Middlebrook.'

'You've found him.'

'Oh, hello, I'm Megan Hughes, you won't know who I am, Professor Peterson told me and my mother about you, about the pictures you have painted...'

As she spoke a sharp picture of Geraint came into Archie's mind, triggered by the family resemblance. They looked at each other in silence.

'Mr Middlebrook?'

'Megan, you are Geraint's niece. Of course I know who you are.'

'This is Rachael. She's a fellow art student. She helped me find where you live.'

Archie looked round, looking for a car.

'How did you get here?'

'Train from Cardiff, then a bus from Tonecastle.' Megan's expression was anxious sensing rejection. 'Then we walked from Helecombe.'

'From Helecombe? It's a hot day, you must be thirsty. Come into the house and I'll get you something to drink.'

Archie led them toward the house before pausing to face Megan. 'You have your uncle's looks, but you're taller than Geraint. Forgive my hesitation I wasn't expecting you.'

'Sorry. Do you mind us coming?'

'Not at all.'

'There you are, Rachael, I said it would be all right. Can I call you Archie?'

Summer drinks were followed by sausage and mash, not ideal on a hot day. The girls needed feeding, having had no breakfast in the rush to catch their train. Megan had told her mother she and Rachael were going to Bristol for the day.

'Have you any photos of your uncle?'

'There's one of him in uniform, and Dad used to speak about him. Dad was proud of him; my grandparents never spoke about him. It was too sad for them.'

'Do you know what happened?'

'He was in the army and died in Malaysia.'

'My paintings go further than that.'

'It was in an accident.'

'An ambush, our scout car was blown up. I was thrown out, Geraint was trapped.'

Archie told the girls about national service, about Malaya, about the Emergency and what his platoon was trained to do, with James Peterson also a national serviceman as their officer-in-charge. He told them about the scout cars and how they were set to escort supply convoys – only the ambush happened on the first day when Geraint was driving. Archie was going to say he should have been keeping an alert look out. His voice choked and he had to turn away.

Megan came round the kitchen table and held his hand as he swallowed and took deep breaths.

'I'm sorry, Archie. We didn't mean to upset you. We'll go away if you want us to.'

Archie shook his head without trying to speak. He looked into the caring face, an echo of Geraint of those years ago, conscripts together, who had been going to go to Singapore on their way back to Blighty to come of age.

'I would like to see some of your paintings before we go.'

'Of course you must. Sorry, ladies, the past caught up with me for a moment. Come on, Patch, we must take our visitors over to the studio.'

Archie asked them to wait in the yard for a moment. He had rigged up a high curtain he could draw over the six-panelled picture when he'd seen the evening sun coming in to light up the top four panels. He'd spent too long setting the distance and perspective tones in the picture to risk sunlight fading it in any way. Archie drew the curtain across the huge painting to await the two art students' verdict on his work. He pointed them to the original series of jungle patrol paintings and told them to leave the painting behind the curtain until he returned. With a sharp whistle he called Patch over and left his visitors in the studio.

Later Archie drove the girls to Tonecastle after they realised they'd missed their intended train home Archie asked them what styles and studies they worked on at college. Rachael wanted to work with abstract sculptures, although at this stage in their course they were doing mixed media exercises in landscape and life drawing. Archie was puzzled: he'd presumed their foundation year had ended. They told him they'd come in on an Easter entry and still had eight months to do.

'I'm doing the same as Rachael at the moment.'

'Megan does really cool townscape work, drawings of small shops in urban backstreets.'

'Best capture what you can, Megan, while there still are small shops in backstreets.'

'How on earth did you do that huge picture, Archie? I know it's on separate panels, but to work on that scale is incredible.'

'It's a first for me. Even the middle sized ones are bigger than I would normally do. I was taken aback when the gallery insisted on the big one. I agonised for days how and what to do.'

'You're a good draftsman; it shines through in the little canvases.'

'Thank you, Rachael.'

Archie turned the car into the short term waiting area outside the station and went in with them to find out if there would be long wait for a Cardiff train. Luckily there was a Bristol train in ten minutes; changing at Temple Meads they could catch a train on to Cardiff without too much delay.

'Will your mother be worried where you are?'

'I'll ring her from Bristol.'

Chapter Twenty-Three
September 1994

THE gallery booked a serviced apartment half-a-mile distant as his base for the week during the hanging and exhibition preliminaries, building up to the public opening. To his surprise they sent him an open first-class return rail ticket – Archie had never travelled first-class. From the brochure he received in the post the apartment had two en-suite bedrooms, a kitchen and a lounge-cum-diner.

He queried Lorna on the phone about the apartment. It seemed extravagant and he hoped he wasn't paying. She told him she would be staying there with him for the week. It would be a busy period of long hours back and forth to the gallery. He still thought it a waste of money.

'And why the rail ticket, first-class at that? The coach is much simpler and drops me off only walking distance away.'

'You're the star, Archie.'

Lorna was right. They worked long hours with the gallery staff, hanging the exhibition and making all the arrangements for the opening. Time and again minds were changed and the placing of paintings altered in relation to the fixed centrepiece of the huge panelled painting. Gradually, a consensus was reached so that a numbering sequence was agreed and a pricing list prepared. A third of the paintings, all the major works, were not for sale. Archie was adamant he wanted to keep the core of his work together with further exhibitions in mind. Nathan was at first reluctant to keep works back before he agreed to the principle, provided that his Chiswick gallery retained an interest in the core pictures in the event of any final sale.

On their way back to the apartment each evening Archie and Lorna stopped off for a pizza or curry, depending on their mood, then it was back to the apartment, a nightcap and bed before another early morning and a busy day. When everything was done and there were only hours to the opening, Archie left the gallery in mid morning to walk down Devonshire Road to the Hogarth roundabout underpass, the traffic racing overhead. He found his way to Hogarth's House – walking in the great painter's footsteps would be an omen for the opening in the evening.

Although he had been warned, Archie was unprepared for the questioning he received from the press and critics who came to the High Road Gallery, delving into his motivation for the paintings. Endlessly he posed in front of paintings as cameras flashed, mostly in front of the jungle scenes, sometimes of the ambush and once as a special request alone with his portrait of Geraint Hughes.

James Peterson and his wife had travelled from Oxford, bringing Megan Hughes with them. A photo was taken of James, Megan and Archie with the portrait of Geraint. Yet Archie wondered: was this gala evening with the press and celebrities a fitting memorial?

As the evening wore on Lorna found Archie sitting alone on the mezzanine floor overlooking the exhibition space above the bustle and excitement of the invited crowd.

'It's a huge success, Archie. All your endeavours are being recognised here this evening. Art critics, collectors, everyone who is anyone, they are all here tonight to acknowledge what you've done. Just look at the champagne flowing.'

'I am overwhelmed, Lorna; it's more than I expected.'

'Enjoy it, Archie. You deserve their acclamation.'

'I'm thrilled to see people think well of my painting, of course I am. But this is for Geraint. I want it to be his memorial.'

'Believe me, Archie; it is for Geraint. I've been talking with Megan she is thrilled with all you've done. She told me her Uncle Geraint lives for her now.'

'If I have achieved that, it's reward enough.'

'She wants to ask a favour of you, Archie. She wants to work in your studio with you later on her course. Students are encouraged to work with established artists for a practical part of their course.'

'I imagine they mean proper artists.'

'You are a proper artist, Archie Middlebrook. Just look at all the people here tonight. They are here for you, Archie, for no-one else.'

Archie looked down into the space below. The crowd was thinning out, but there was a knot of people around the sales desk. A secretary, her hair cascading onto her shoulders in ringlets around her pale face, was busy responding to guests. Archie had noticed her during his week at the gallery. She was an ideal model for a portrait.

As the crowd lingered someone looked up at the gallery. The face was familiar, but he couldn't place it.

'Come on, Archie,' Lorna took his arm. 'People want to see you. You can't hide away up here. And by the way Nathan has invited us out for a meal with a few others, important clients mainly.'

'Do we have to, I'm exhausted?'

'Yes, you do, Archie.'

'You're coming, too?'

'Oh, yes.'

Later at the restaurant, Archie struggled to hear conversations round the table against the chatter of diners at other tables. Nathan dominated the proceedings talking at length about the gallery's exhibitions, mostly about past exhibitions and the programme for the next year. Archie didn't attempt to join in being content to watch the secretary from the selling desk, the Pre-Raphaelite girl sitting watching Nathan as if his words were all that mattered to her. Her wan looks were crying out to be painted.

The meal looked tired – a fish terrine of uncertain origin, followed by lamb with a vegetable couscous of North African provenance or the choice of a second fish serving, fillet of sole with out-of-season asparagus. He guessed it had been standing around before serving. Archie chose the Moroccan lamb; it could have been better spiced.

Requiem for Private Hughes

His eyes were getting heavy. He'd been drinking wine, first champagne, whisky, and now red wine, since five in the afternoon. He blinked looking at his watch, it was close to eight o'clock, or maybe it was nine – the numerals on his watch were indistinct. Archie examined the Pre-Raphaelite girl still gazing at Nathan. Lorna was looking at him, a frown on her face. Archie smiled, looked at his watch again and shrugged his shoulders.

They'd used taxis to get to the restaurant, standing on the kerb to leave in the chill evening air, as the doorman waved at cabs, he asked Lorna if they could walk instead. Her reply was a curt and negative. He fell asleep in the cab, waking to find Lorna already out on the pavement paying the cabbie through the window.

'Must have nodded off.'

'You were leering.'

'I was doing what?'

'Leering, at that girl from the gallery office, Imogen, or whatever she calls herself. You were leering at her all evening.'

'I was thinking she would be a good model.'

Lorna was up the stairs, leaving Archie to climb the two flights at his slower pace. There was a lift, but it was small and claustrophobic. By the time he reached their door she was already in the apartment, her coat tossed over an armchair, and at the sideboard pouring a gin and tonic. Archie closed the door dropping the catch, before he shed his coat to hang on a coat rack by the door. He went to the sideboard.

'Self-service tonight, is it?'

'I would've thought you've had enough, the rate you've been putting it away this evening.'

'Lorna, Lorna, don't get narkey at me. This has been the big day of our success.'

'Your success.'

'No, both of us. I'm in your debt for tonight.'

Lorna said nothing, sitting with her legs tucked up on the sofa. Archie relaxed into a chair.

'When did James and his wife leave? I saw them one minute, but when I tried to find them they were nowhere to be seen.'

'They said to tell you they had to rush for a train back to Oxford, they slipped away when you were tied up talking to journalists.'

'Was Megan with them?'

'Yes. I thought her mother would come, she was invited.'

'I want to meet her. Maybe she has reservations. I suppose she never knew Geraint, maybe Huw, with all his problems was overawed by the memory of his older brother. At least Megan wants to share in his memory. Do you think she does want to come and paint at Hawthorne Cottage? She's not just being polite.'

'I'm certain she does. She needn't have said anything, it's her idea.'

'I've never had a pupil, I'm not a teacher.'

'You taught me plenty at Harptree's.' Despite her mood Lorna had to smile. 'If I'd paid heed to you I might not have ended up working for Andrew.'

'I was old school, Oscar's pupil as it were. Did you know he was the Honorary Colonel of the Regiment when my father was in Italy?'

'When your father was killed?'

'Oscar was good to me when I got back from Malaya. He'd done his homework, had all the information from my army records. He knew all that had happened. He helped me through those first years, not ostentatiously, always there, encouraging and promoting me up the tree. There were some who resented it.'

Relaxed at the apartment, his weariness abated, Archie no longer felt the need to get to bed. He was tired, yet it was a day he didn't want to end. Days, weeks, months – in truth decades – had led to his exhibition and Archie didn't want the day to be over.

It had four weeks to run, and then there would be the task of getting everything back to Helecombe. One more day in London and he would be setting off back to Somerset. Ivy had offered to come in to the station to meet him, but she didn't need to, he would get a taxi. He would ring her from Paddington. He knew she would be cooking him a meal. He guessed it would be one of her shepherd's pies.

It was time to get a new painting project up and running, maybe his sketch ideas for *The Eve of St Agnes*. Requiem had brought him peace of mind, made contact with James Peterson after so many years and his introduction to Megan. If she did come to work at Hawthorne Cottage he must pursue a scheme of work, it was time to move on.

Lorna was getting herself another drink from the bottles on the sideboard, Archie held out his glass.

'I thought you were asleep.'

'Thinking things over after a day I never thought would come.'

'Thinking about Imogen, I bet.'

'No.'

'I'm surprised she didn't object to the way you were staring at her, undressing her.'

'She is certainly fascinating. In my judgement she only had eyes for Nathan.' Even as he said it Archie wanted to bite the words off in his mouth. He hadn't meant to rile Lorna.

'That's rubbish. You were leering at her like a dirty old man.'

'I would like to paint her.'

'Nude, no doubt.'

'Why do you say that? I've hardly painted a life model since my days at art school. It was very stilted back in the 1950s. And it was usually a male pensioner wearing his drawers; only a few times a female model.'

'What did females wear?'

'Probably nothing, they were very remote coming in when we were all at our easels and slipping off a dressing gown when they were seated.'

'What do you mean "hardly" painted a life model? Who have you painted?'

'You've seen the portraits of my mother.'

'Yes, but life drawing or whatever you call it, naked. Who?'

'If you must know I did a full length picture of you on one occasion.' He should have said nothing.

'When? Was it after the crash?'

'No, years before that.'

'You drew a picture the evening we were working late after Oscar's funeral, but I have that, I got it framed, it's in my digs.'

'I guess it was that evening, it was only my imagination. I had enjoyed drawing your picture in the office, it was the first good drawing I'd done in years. I drew you again when I got home that evening; I let my imagination do the rest, probably nothing like you. I shouldn't have said anything.'

Lorna stared; she knocked back the rest of her gin and tonic, shook her head and went again to the sideboard to fill her glass.

'I don't know what to say, Archie Middlebrook. You are a dark horse drawing young women in the dead of night for your private gratification. Who else have drawn?'

'I shouldn't have said anything.'

'Why not, I'm entitled to know, it was me you were drawing. Had you been watching me in the office?'

'It wasn't like that. It was done on a whim, I'd enjoyed the evening, it was the first time we'd talked about ourselves I liked working with you. We were a good team.'

'Have you still got the drawing?'

'Probably.'

'What do you mean – probably? You either have or you haven't. You might have told me.'

'Lorna, I don't know if I still have it. You know how Ivy throws things away. Now please give me another whisky, and I'd like a glass of water while you're up.'

'Don't tell me Ivy has seen it.'

'No, she hasn't. I do know where it is.'

Lorna splashed another whisky into his glass and went to the limited kitchen, described in the brochure as a galley kitchen. She returned putting the water on the table by his chair, and left the room.

It wasn't how he'd wanted the day to end. How had it got to such a ridiculous exchange? Archie looked at the picture on the wall, a print, a scene on the Thames. After the exhibition some of his prints, even the originals, might be hung on walls in people's houses. Nathan said there had been good sales. He was glad he had insisted the large pictures were not for sale. Maybe one day.

Lorna was shaking his knee, he blinked himself awake.

'You're snoring.'

'I drifted off. What time is it?'

'It's long past your bedtime, unless you want to do some drawing. I bet I have a better figure than that Imogen woman you are so interested in.'

Lorna stood in front of Archie, undid the dressing gown loosely tied at her waist and let it fall to the floor. They stared at each other.

'Lorna, you are beautiful. I have never doubted it.'

'Come to bed, Archie.'

Archie drained the last of his whisky from his glass.

'Come to bed with me, Archie.'

He gazed at her, unashamed to look at the body standing before him, the girl he'd worked with, who'd played her part in the ending of his career with Harptree's, who'd been searching for him when she crashed her car, with whom he had shared those awful dragging minutes trapped in the petrol stench of her upturned car. This was woman he had brought home to Hawthorne Cottage to recuperate, of whom he had grown so fond.

'Lorna, this isn't right; apart from the fact, as you have pointed out, that I've had more than a fair measure to drink today. I'm fond of you, Lorna, you have brightened my life, I dare not think what I would have done if you had died in that crash. I love you, Lorna, but this isn't right.'

Archie pulled himself up out of his chair, reached to pick Lorna's dressing gown off the floor and put it over her shoulders, looking at her figure as he wrapped the gown round her. Archie held her in his arms and hugged her with an emotion he had never felt before.

Embracing they stood gently rocking. As he hugged her he felt the warmth of her tears on his cheek.

'I love you, Archie. You must get your rest. You're falling asleep again. We have more work to do tomorrow.'

'I intend to sleep in tomorrow.'

'That'll be a first for you, Archie Middlebrook.'

'Or is it today?'

A few hours later she knocked at his bedroom door. Then she was shaking his shoulder. She left him half awake and pulled the curtains open. Even with the view limited by the buildings across the street, sunlight streamed in. Archie blinked himself awake.

'Come on sleepy head. It's almost nine o'clock. I've been out to the newsagent on the corner to get newspapers. There are some reviews of the exhibition, even a photo of you with Megan and James so you're in the big time, Mr Archie Middlebrook, famous Somerset artist.'

'Where did you say you've been?'

'Archie, wake up, to get papers from the corner shop. And I have had my breakfast and brought you a cup of coffee.'

'What time did you say?'

'Nine, Archie. Time for you to be up and out.'

'I've not got the clearest head.'

'No surprise at that.'

'Do you have to be so chirpy?'

'Archie, I'm off out. I've got an errand to do. Then I'll go to the gallery. I should be there before noon. See you there.' With that she left the room.

Archie sat up, paused a moment, grabbed his dressing gown and chased after Lorna. She was already going down the stairs.

'Lorna, where are you going?'

'I have other business than the gallery to see to, Archie.'

'Of course, but where will we meet.'

'The gallery, I'll be in time for lunch and you'd better do up your dressing gown or you'll be scaring the neighbours.' And she was gone.

Archie pulled his dressing gown round his naked body and ducked back into the apartment before anyone saw him.

He breakfasted on black coffee and charred toast – the first effort was underdone, so he pressed the control again and the bread burned. There was marmalade on the table, but he couldn't find butter so he did without, spreading lumpy marmalade as best he could; the toast crumbled as he ate.

By ten after two mugs of coffee Archie was in touch with the world. He'd never got on with showers, but the one in bathroom off his bedroom was powerful. After a long massaging of his body in the pummelling shower, he felt ready for whatever the day brought, and sorted out fresh clothes amongst those still unpacked in his case. He dressed and went through to the sitting room to dip into the newspapers Lorna had left in a pile on the coffee table. The papers had changed in size and style since the days when Archie had the job of stacking the kiosk on the ground floor of Harptree & Ellis, three months learning the ropes in the kiosk, always busy in the mornings as office-goers called to buy their papers, cigarettes and pipe tobacco – pipe smokers lit up at their desk in those days.

Lorna had left the paper with the photograph of him standing between Megan and James on the top of the pile. There was a brief piece with it explaining rather than praising the pictures. Another paper gave him a good write-up although dwelling on his age, almost sixty, for his first major exhibition.

After he had been through them all and put them aside he looked about the room. Lorna had been busy tidying the place since their night-time bickering. It was hard to not have a glass in his hand through the hours of the exhibition, as he had to keep repeating his purpose, and to get people to understand he wanted the pictures to be a memorial for Geraint.

Archie stared at the sofa where Lorna had sat with her legs tucked under her watching him then of a sudden standing before him letting her dressing gown fall to the floor, challenging him to come to her bed. Would it really have been so wrong to sleep with Lorna? She'd been in a truculent mood, furious over his interest in the girl from the gallery, and it was plain enough the girl was hanging out for Nathan. That was the point, Nathan was in Lorna's sights, and his comments riled her.

Lorna had been born after he'd done his national service, after the ambush, after his wild affair with Maggie. Good grief she was the age of any child they might have had. That was Lorna's generation.

But he did love her; he'd told her he loved her. Was their age difference so great, twenty four years, there were hundreds, thousands, of husbands with a twenty or more age difference over their wives? Had he been stupid?

There would be other times nothing should be rushed.

Archie picked up an unfamiliar redtop he'd missed in the pile. Its front page carried a link to an inside page proclaiming "Ambush in Malaya – who was to blame?" Inside, the front page headline was repeated above a photograph of his portrait of Geraint.

He scanned the article, which trumpeted a needless waste of a young man's life, telling of the disorganisation of the forces in Malaya shortly before the 1956 amnesty, and the inexperience of the national service soldiers, poorly trained for their tasks. It quoted a retired regular soldier who'd served in the Malayan Emergency: Major Alan Brewer.

Archie froze. Could this be Sergeant Brewer with whom he had such difficulties over trivial things, the Sergeant Brewer whose wife had come on to him in Singapore?

The statements in the paper were outrageous. It was malicious; the paper shouldn't print this rubbish. Was Brewer the face he had seen amongst the cameramen, the paparazzi as Lorna had called them, a brief glance to wonder if it was someone he'd seen before? There had been half remembered faces amongst the guests. Could one have been Brewer? And how on earth was he Major Brewer? He was an incompetent sergeant in Malaya in the days they clashed.

Archie grabbed the phone to dial the gallery number. The call rang out, there was no answer-phone picking up, yet he knew there was one in the office. He dialled again and a strange voice answered.

'Who is it?'

'Archie Middlebrook. Have you seen the article about the ambush?' Archie was shouting into the receiver.

'Who is it, please? Did you ring just now when I couldn't get to the phone? Mrs Pemberton is out.'

'Archie Middlebrook, I'm calling about...'

'I think you have a wrong number, young man.' There was a click and the receiver reverted to the dialling tone.

He grabbed his coat from the stand by the front door, stuffed the newspaper into his pocket and left, tripping on the stairs in his haste only saved as he clutched at the banister.

'Careful now, we don't want broken legs.' The concierge was behind his desk.

Archie jogged until he was out of breath, stopped for a moment, then tried to keep up a fast walk. The pavement was damp as a light drizzle fell. He crossed the road, not seeing a cyclist, who swerved and shouted at him. He hurried on. They'd taken a short cut down this side street many mornings, only it wasn't the same street. Archie stopped, he'd turned too early. He swore and retraced his steps, but the next turn was wrong too. He saw a tube station sign ahead and hurried toward it only to find it wasn't Ravenscourt Park which it should have been. It was Goldhawk Road wherever that was.

He was lost. There was nothing for it, but to retrace his steps to the apartment block and to set out again. They'd done the journey on foot every day over the past week, but he must have turned the wrong way out of the apartment block door and kept turning in the wrong direction.

There was a phone box ahead, Archie felt in his pocket for coins; in his hurry he had left his loose cash on the dresser in his bedroom. He could buy a paper to get change from a note, then realised he hadn't picked up his wallet either. He could take a taxi and get the gallery to pay. There was no taxi in sight – there never was when you need one.

A black cab turned into the street, he waved at it, but it swept past. He pushed on walking as fast as his breathing allowed the rain getting heavier hoping at every turn in the street to see something familiar, a pub or one of the curry houses they'd used. And he hadn't got his key. The concierge was usually there all day – hopefully at his desk, not at lunch.

At the gallery Lorna and Nathan were wondering where Archie had gone.

'I said I would meet him here at lunchtime. Have you rung the apartment?'

'Yes, more than once and left messages on the machine,' Nathan replied.

'Archie isn't very machine minded. I'll try him again.'

'Will he have seen that article in the paper?'

'He may well have seen it – I can't think how I missed it. I left the newspapers for him when I went out. He'll be hurt, even if it is rubbish. I spoke to James Peterson as soon as you told me about it. I read it over to him, he said it was wholly malicious and that the chap whoever he was...'

'Brewer.'

'Yes, Brewer was a regular who had it in for Archie, knowing Archie was the better soldier. James has contacts on Fleet Street, so he said he would see what he could do to quash that rubbish.'

Nathan shrugged his shoulders. 'It's all publicity for the exhibition at the end of the day.'

Lorna dialled the apartment.

'There's no answer again. I hope Archie is all right. He put away a lot of booze yesterday. He was up when I left after I woke him.' The answer-phone clicked on with its anodyne message. 'Archie if you get this stay in the apartment, I'll keep ringing and we'll speak.'

The concierge was at his desk when Archie staggered into the building.

'I saw you rush out earlier and said to myself, "I bet that gentleman has forgotten his key", so I hoped you would come back with the young lady, or I would have to be going up to the second floor to let you in.'

'I'm most grateful. I had to leave in a hurry.'

'You look as if you've been running and all. Now we'll have to use the lift. It's my knees; they don't do stairs no more.'

'If you let me have your key you needn't come up.'

'Can't do that; I never let my keys away; more than my job's worth.'

A light was flashing on the telephone answering machine, Archie pressed buttons, the messages appeared to run over each other, but he heard Lorna telling him not to worry about the review, to wait and she would ring.

There was only bread in the fridge. He was hungry and put two stale slices into the toaster, waited for it to pop up, and pressed it down again before going to find the offending paper. It wasn't on the table.

He was flicking through the papers when the kitchen smoke alarm went off. Blue smoke was curling across the confined space. He grabbed a tea towel and fanned the alarm to get it to stop. The windows in the flat had locks, there were keys on a hook in the kitchen cupboard. When the alarm was silent, he managed to get a window open. The toast was beyond redemption. He threw it in the waste-bin, decided to try the gallery again and searched for the number on the letters he had from Nathan in his suitcase.

Clutching one of the gallery's letters, Archie started to dial then remembered the offending newspaper was in his coat pocket. He put the phone down, found his coat and pulled the offending paper out, to read it again, the misery of the ambush aftermath spinning in his brain. It was lies, it was unfair and malevolent.

The phone rang. Archie dropped the paper and rushed across the room. He stumbled and the room spun round. He grabbed at the phone pulling the receiver off as he fell to the floor, into an awful cold blackness.

Chapter Twenty-Four

'HELLO, Lorna. How's it all going in London? Is Archie with you, my dear?' Ivy's calm greeting from the gentle pace of Somerset eased the hectic sense of traffic going about its business in the street outside the window.

'The exhibition is going well, Ivy. I'm ringing from the Brompton Hospital. Archie has had a turn.'

'Lord in Heaven, whatever has happened?'

'Ivy, you mustn't worry, he's in safe hands getting the best of care; they think it could be a mini stroke.'

'A stroke? That's serious. My dad had a stroke and he was all squiggly, and couldn't speak proper.'

'Archie has spoken, a bit slurred, and he's confused. They have a lot of tests to do, Ivy. He will be here for a couple of days.'

'Should I come?'

'No, Ivy. Could you get Hawthorne Cottage ready as they'll probably send him home before long?'

'He can't travel like that.'

'Ivy everything will be fine, I'll arrange it all here, it'll be a proper patient transfer and I'll come with him. What did you mean "squiggly", Ivy?'

'My father, dear; he were all lop-sided after he had a stroke and couldn't say a word.'

'Archie won't be like that, Ivy. They're saying it is minor and he will make a good recovery.'

'Just when it was all going so well for him.'

'Ivy, I must go. I'll call you again this evening and in the morning. If the tests are going to take days, I'll let you know, and you may want to come up and see him. I hope he'll be home within the week.'

'And you'll come too.'

'Promise. I'll be with him, Ivy.'

The days ran into a week, then into a second. Even after many tests the doctors were uncertain of the cause of Archie's condition, but steps were made for his transfer back to Somerset. It was proposed he should go to the cottage hospital outside Northhill, but Ivy was adamant he would be best looked after back home under her care with the district nurse calling. Half-an-hour talking with the hospital doctor persuaded him it would be the right course.

Lorna linked arms and guided Ivy across the road to the coffee shop she had been using over the past week.

'What do you think, Ivy?' Lorna waited until they were settled.

'We'll manage. I'll move up to the cottage and I'll get help in to get his bed set up downstairs for the time being.' Ivy stirred her coffee watching the rotating pattern. 'I thought he would be worse, even though you'd been reassuring me. After they needed more time I was worried. Let's hope it doesn't happen again. He'll be happy back home.'

Lorna reached over for Ivy's hand. 'You're the tonic he needs, Ivy. You've always been there for him.'

'He's got into some scrapes in his time, has Archie. There were always cuts and bruises in his young days, then the trouble in the army and us, his mother and I, miles away. We feared the worst, what with his father killed in the war, then him not talking about it when he came home. All bottled-up inside, it was. I thought he'd at last got to terms with all that.'

'He has, Ivy. This isn't back to square one for him. He has talked about the article in the press and the newspaper has printed an apology over the implications of its piece. That counts for a lot with Archie.'

'They should be a lot more careful.'

'I'll stay in Somerset as long as I can, Ivy; I will have to get back to London.'

'He'll settle as soon as he is home. We'll get him up and about in no time.'

'Ivy, the exhibition isn't far away. I know you've seen all his paintings, but it's great to see them set up for the exhibition.

'When's my train, dear. I don't want to miss that.'

'Don't worry. I'll get you to Paddington for that, Ivy. I'll ring Nathan at the gallery. You remember him coming down to Somerset, Ivy? I'll tell him we are coming over.'

Ivy patted Lorna's hand. 'Is that Nathan your young man, dear?'

The direct question caught Lorna unawares, and her blush gave the answer.

* * * * *

The journey to Somerset was beset by traffic hold-ups on a day of frequent rain. The medical transfer vehicle was driven by a volunteer and equipped with a special airline-type seat for the patient. Lorna sat in the front, with Archie reclining in the back alongside a nurse. There was an oxygen cylinder with other resuscitating equipment.

By chance a Malaysian art collector had been in the gallery, finalising the purchase of one of Archie's jungle pictures, when Lorna was with Nathan discussing getting Archie home. They agreed to use the purchase monies, both Archie's and the gallery's portions, to underwrite the cost of the transfer pending insurance clarification.

Archie asked they travel on the A303 route, which he preferred to the M4 and M5 journey on his coach travels between Hammersmith and Tonecastle. Near Stonehenge, the traffic slowed to a crawl before standing stationary. The driver explained that if delays became too difficult he could call his operator on the radio to ask for a police escort to get them through the worst jams.

Lorna had asked Archie how much he remembered about his stroke, but he'd been vague. As they travelled, he started to speak of it in his disjointed delivery. He remembered the phone ringing, thought he caught his foot against the sofa and tripped rushing for the phone, then after he hit the floor Lorna came in and was kneeling by him.

Requiem for Private Hughes

It had taken Lorna twenty minutes in her rush from the gallery, getting a taxi which got stuck in traffic then running up the stairs into the apartment to find Archie prostrate and shivering on the floor, the phone still in his hand. Within ten minutes the paramedics were on the scene, closely followed by the concierge, always ready for local excitement and determined to relay his account of Archie's morning excursion and his forgotten key.

After Stonehenge the road cleared and by the time they reached Tonecastle, travelling through the town past the Harptree's building, lying empty with sale notices posted along its road frontage. The store renting the two commercial floors had moved to new premises.

'Look at Harptree's, Archie. What has it all come to now?'

But Archie was sleeping. Lorna smiled at the nurse beside Archie and turned to look ahead.

They arrived at Hawthorne Cottage in mid-afternoon. Ivy, waiting at the door, came over and peered in through the darkened car windows.

Archie only woke when the car stopped. Lorna opened her door without a sound and greeted Ivy. The nurse used a flannel to wipe Archie's mouth. He pushed her away and, seeing Ivy he waved. Between them Lorna and Ivy each taking an arm helped Archie into the house. He made a fuss at being taken into the sitting room converted to a bedroom.

'No. Stairs, upstairs,' and he pointed to the ceiling.

'It's all ready for you here, Archie. This will be comfortable for you. Lorna will be here and I'm staying to settle you in for a while. Then we'll get your bed back upstairs once you've settled down again.'

'No, no.'

'Archie.'

It was the look of admonishment that had ended many a tantrum in the days when teenage Ivy took young Archie out for country walks, the days when his father was keeping the trains on schedule and Archie was risking his reward of a lift onto the footplate when they got home after their walk.

The nurse, who Lorna had only known for the journey, went through the packages of drugs Archie was taking, marking each off a list while giving information on dosages. There was also a letter for the doctor, who'd been asked to call next day.

Lorna and the nurse left Ivy to settle Archie and joined the driver waiting in the kitchen and eyeing the table heavy with cake and sandwiches, as the kettle boiled. Lorna made tea. The nurse and driver were making the return journey and were grateful for the meal set out on the table.

'Archie is an artist, isn't he?' the nurse asked.

'Yes, that's his studio across the yard. Ivy will have a struggle to keep him away from it.'

'No harm in getting active; provided he doesn't overdo things.'

'You can see his exhibition at the Chiswick High Road Gallery. They've extended its run for an extra week.'

'I like a good picture. Not too abstract is he?'

'He was a national serviceman in Malaysia in the fifties. The exhibition revolves around his experience there.'

'I've been on holiday to Malaysia. I'll go if I can.'

'It wasn't a holiday for Archie – they were fighting terrorists.'

Lorna stayed in Somerset for ten days, helping Ivy to get Archie's bedroom installed back upstairs and spending time with Archie sitting out on fine October days. Archie made progress, but was frustrated it was not more rapid. He was often confused, even on one occasion thinking Lorna and he still worked at Harptree's.

Lorna set up an easel for him sitting in the conservatory. He was keen to sit and paint, yet got upset when his right hand would not grip the brush effectively and his arm made wild movements. Lorna encouraged him to try a double handed approach. Archie persevered and on the day before Lorna was due to return to London completed a painting of the autumn trees seen from the conservatory. They were thrilled to see it finished. Ivy asked if she could have it at her cottage and Lorna took a photograph of Archie at his easel.

'That's the first step, Archie.' Lorna kissed his cheek. 'You are on the road to a good recovery.'

He beamed. Painting was going to dictate his recuperation and now, a month after his fall at the apartment, it was going well. There had been out-patient appointments at Tonecastle Hospital endorsing their good opinion.

The physiotherapist had persuaded Archie to use a stick to assist his getting around. He was reluctant, but agreed.

Lorna kept James in the picture on Archie's progress. He arranged to visit during the week after she returned to London. Nathan was in touch with cheering news that the exhibition was closing with the best count of visitors the gallery had seen in its ten years amply reflected in the sales figures.

'I want you to sign that autumn picture you've done for me, Archie. I'll need proof that it's a genuine Middlebrook,' teased Ivy.

'You wait until I get going on my St Agnes Eve paintings, I'll aim to get another exhibition going in a year or two.'

'I'll hold you to that.' Lorna laughed. 'Keep him working, Ivy.'

'I'll put you in it.'

Lorna caught his eye with a questioning smile.

'What time are you off in the morning, dear?'

'I'll try for an early afternoon train, Ivy. I've got to see the solicitors in Tonecastle at noon to make certain all is teed up for the completion of the sale of my flat.'

'Why are you selling your flat, where will you live?' Archie blurted out.

'You know I'm selling the flat, Archie. I work in London now; I'll be down to see you in three weeks and again to stay for the Christmas holiday. I don't need my flat any more.'

Archie ignored her reply as he tinkered with his painting.

✳ ✳ ✳ ✳ ✳

New Year's Day was greeted with snowfall, looking as if it would all be gone by the evening. At lunchtime it snowed in earnest and by mid afternoon was deep and drifting in the wind. Lorna had gone back to London for a New Year party two days earlier.

Ivy had been spending as much time as she could at her cottage, yet when she saw the first of the winter's snow she went back to Hawthorne Cottage, leaving tracks through the settling snow, her car slipping as she turned in through the Hawthorne Cottage gates.

She was furious to find Archie shovelling a path across the yard from the house to his studio. She drove over his path and took the shovel from him. Archie looked at her, about to argue, but one look from Ivy and he knew he was off-side. He had always kept paths open across the yard in winter. This winter was going to be different. Luckily he'd got logs in for the fires during the morning.

Over tea they said little. Archie wanted to be over in his studio, determined to make progress on his St Agnes series of paintings. He'd worked out a sequence and had already got the first picture well under way: the Watchman reciting his beads in the cold of the evening. He was keen to get on with the scene of Madeline in her bedchamber. He was at last fully into the spirit of his project although he found he could not concentrate for long in a session.

'Ivy, I'm grateful for all you do for me. You've got me through a few scrapes in these last few years.'

'Since you were a boy, Archie; mind I don't want you doing any more digging. Snow won't be here for more than a day or so, and the last thing I need is you going over again or getting pneumonia.'

'Ivy, I'm ten years younger than you are. I'm not the only one who needs to be careful, you driving around in the snow. I saw you slide when you were turning the car into the yard.'

Their spat was over, calm was restored. Archie went through to light the fire in the sitting room glad there was a shed full of logs for the winter.

He kept busy as time passed until Easter, pleased with his latest picture of Keats's Madeline. Ivy had seen the painting as Archie worked on it and thought it a poor likeness of Lorna, despite Archie's insistence. She didn't say as much.

Archie was adamant Lorna must come down to Somerset for Easter at the beginning of April. Weeks had gone by since her Christmas visit and he had a whole series of paintings to show her.

He was determined not to send her photographs of what he was doing despite her repeated requests. It would give her an excuse to stay away.

Lorna rang up late in March, saying an Easter visit would be difficult. Ivy sent her a postcard, asking her to come down if she could, saying Archie was in good heart yet still fragile and would be upset if Lorna didn't come.

It wasn't easy. Lorna had good reason to be in London over the Easter holiday. Then everything changed for her in the space of a single day.

Archie had not been cleared to drive and Ivy was happy to act as his driver on occasional shopping trips into Tonecastle. With Lorna due on Maundy Thursday Archie fussed over getting provisions in, finding it hard to decide what joint they should get in for Easter Sunday lunch. Then when he decided to have a turkey – what wine he should buy? Ivy admonished him over alcohol, reminding him the doctor had advised moderation, if any at all.

Ivy drove in to Tonecastle to meet the train, but Archie stayed behind, wanting to finish a detail on the painting he had done for Lorna, her image as Madeline on St Agnes Eve. He wanted her to be thrilled.

'Archie will be pleased to see you, Lorna. Thank you for coming, I know you had other things to do, dear.'

Lorna gave Ivy a wan smile.

Nothing was said as the familiar landmarks of the town passed by and they ran out into the country.

'You're quiet, dear.'

'I'm tired. I'm glad to be back in Somerset. Other things didn't work out. I would have been on my own.'

Ivy guessed there was a young man involved somewhere amongst the 'other things' and from her mood nothing had gone as Lorna had hoped. She didn't want Lorna depressing Archie.

'A week in good country air will do you good, dear.'

Lorna gazed ahead, saying nothing.

'I want to stop by my cottage to pick up supplies. Archie made a fuss about getting everything in for breakfast and things got forgotten.'

Lorna said nothing and stayed in the car. Inside Ivy went into her front room and looked out at the car and her quiet passenger. Things were bad for her; Ivy had a notion what it might be. She filled a basket, locked up and carried the provisions out to the car. Lorna was staring out from the car not noticing Ivy until she opened the door to put things on the back seat.

'Ivy, I'm sorry I'm being an awful drip. Thank you for coming in to meet me, and the train late and all. I could have got a taxi.'

'You don't want to do that, dear. It would cost a fortune to bring one of those city cars out into the country.'

Archie was waiting in his studio, but Lorna left the car and took her case straight into the house. In the bedroom she dropped her case threw herself face down on the bed and wept.

Ivy busied herself in the kitchen laying plates on the table, filling the kettle and setting it to boil on the stove, getting the cake from its tin, finding jam and butter, getting a loaf from the larder and a bread knife to start making toast. Archie appeared from his studio grasping the back of a chair with his unwanted stick in his other hand.

'Where's Lorna?'

'She's in her room, Archie. She had a bad journey and needs a few moments.'

'The picture is ready for her.'

'Let her have a bit of peace, Archie. She's tired and needs refreshment. Let it rest a while.'

His impatience showed and his hand was shaking. He looked at the table went to the end of the table where he most often sat, but getting his stick between his legs he landed heavily on the chair.

Lorna got up from the bed and looked in the mirror above the basin. Her eyes were puffy. She washed her face, combed back her hair she'd let grow over the past few months, found dark glasses in her bag and straightened herself up, tilting the mirror to see herself again.

'Get a grip of yourself, girl. It isn't the end of the world.' She was getting weepy again, squeezed her nails into the palms of her hands and counted. 'One, two, three, four...'

'Tea is ready,' Ivy called up from the foot of the stairs.

'Coming.'

Archie struggled in his chair. 'Lorna.'

'Archie, sorry to keep you all waiting.' Lorna crossed to his chair, gave him a hug, kissed his cheek and stood back. 'You look so well, Archie.'

'Why the dark glasses, it's dull today.'

'I've got a headache, the train was stuffy. It'll soon go with this fresh country air. Wow, Ivy I haven't had a tea as good as this since I was last down.'

'Get sat down, dear and have some cake.'

'No, the picture, you must see the picture, Lorna. It's set up and ready for you on the easel in the studio,' insisted Archie

'Let her have a cup of tea first, Archie.'

'No, picture first.'

Lorna looked at Ivy, shrugged her shoulders and stood again.

'I'll have a quick look, then tea and wonderful cake, then a long look at what you have been doing while I've been away.'

Lorna went to the door, but Archie struggled to get up his stick falling to the floor. Lorna turned to retrieve it, but Archie pointed her to the door. She smiled and went ahead to the studio. Archie followed on and reached the yard as a scream came from the studio.

'No, no, not that bitch!' Lorna was shouting.

Ivy overtook Archie in the yard. They found a hysterical Lorna, a studio knife in her hand slashing at the painting. 'Bitch, bitch...' invective pouring from her lips until the painting fell from the easel. Archie, strength flowing into his arms, dragged Lorna back, tears streaming down her face, her whole body shaking. Ivy grabbed the knife and Lorna's glasses as they fell to the floor, Archie kept a tight hold on her as she struggled, went limp, turned her face into his shoulder and sobbed.

'Lorna, dear Lorna, what is it, what has got into you?'

Lorna, wrapped in Archie's arms, couldn't speak, and her body shook as she gulped mouthfuls of air.

Ivy came over to take one of Lorna's arms. 'Archie and I will walk you back to the house and you can tell us all about it.'

At last she could find some words. 'Archie, how could you. That isn't me. She's that cow from the gallery, the girl you were ogling all through that wretched meal. It's Imogen. The slut Nathan has dumped me for taking her off to the West Indies on holiday.'

'Lorna...' Archie looked at Lorna, at the remains of the painting lying ripped on the floor and back to Lorna. 'I...'

Ivy put her arm round Lorna. 'Come on, let's get you back into the kitchen and get tea and cake inside you. Then it will be early bed.'

Archie was puzzled by Lorna's wild actions. He'd painted Lorna. He knew he had - not that girl whatever her name was. It was Lorna. He knew what he had painted. Maybe the hair was wrong, the face, but it was Lorna, perhaps not the best likeness, maybe. Was it the other girl? Why would he paint her? Archie turned out the studio lights, pulled the door shut leaning on his stick and went to join them in the kitchen.

Ivy and Lorna sat in chairs facing each other by the stove. Ivy was holding both of Lorna's hands, moving them rhythmically up and down as Lorna looked at the floor, not wanting to speak. Archie came in and Ivy glanced across at him, frowning lest he speak. He remained silent, looking at the two women. Ivy nodded her head toward the sitting room. Archie went through, sat in one of the armchairs before lowering himself to his knees, reaching for matches to light the fire. Archie watched it take before closing the doors of the woodburner. He twiddled the draught controls and soon the fire was pulling flames flickering behind the glass panes. Archie got back into the chair and waited.

He was dozing when Lorna came through, bent over him to kiss his forehead.

'I'm so sorry, Archie. It was unforgiveable. I should never have done that to your painting.'

'I got confused, Lorna.'

'I know.' She stood in the dark room lit only by flames from the fire dancing their light out into the room. 'Let me get you a cup of tea and you'd like Ivy's fruit cake. It's delicious as always.'

'Tea and cake, that's good.'

'Then we can talk.'

The two women brought in his tea and a slice of cake. An occasional table was placed beside his chair.

Lorna sat by the fire, looked at Ivy, then Archie.

'You may have guessed I have been having a relationship with Nathan. It was casual to start with, in recent weeks it became intense. I hadn't moved in with him, I thought about it, and I thought I would, he seemed to want me to move in and I was falling for him.'

Archie looked at Lorna as she spoke. He had no claim over her, yet in his heart he felt aggrieved.

'At the weekend I found Nathan and that girl snogging together at the gallery. I challenged him and he told me we were finished, he'd been carrying on with that Imogen tart behind my back. I felt so foolish, I should have realised. Then he said he was taking her with him on holiday. It was over.'

'Maybe it is for the best, dear.' Ivy's gentle tone eased the tumult in Archie's mind. Now it would be back to normal, with Lorna treating Hawthorne Cottage as her home away from London.

'It isn't straightforward, Ivy. I'm pregnant. I don't know what to do.'

'Does the young man know?'

'I was going to tell him at the weekend, I had to be sure.'

'And you are sure?'

'As sure as any tests can be, several tests and I've missed two months.'

'Are you going to tell him?'

'I don't think I love him, Ivy. I'm thirty-six, I so want a baby. It's as if it is a last chance for me. I don't know.'

Archie was rocking in his chair and tapping his stick on the carpet, excitement in his eyes. 'Lorna, come home, live here. You can have your baby in Somerset. This can be your home. It can be, can't it, Ivy?'

'It's your home to decide, Archie.'

'Lorna, I want you here, have your baby here, Ivy will be your baby's aunt and I can be an uncle. You don't need anyone else; it will be a perfect family.'

Lorna looked at Archie then at Ivy. Ivy nodded and Lorna burst into tears. The flames flickered up as a log settled in the fire. Archie eased himself forward onto his knees, picked up the gauntlet lying on the heap of logs beside the woodburner to open the doors, and put more logs in to the fire. Lorna pulled out a handkerchief and wiped her eyes. Archie eased himself back into his chair.

'I am so happy, you are the sweetest, the best people on this earth. I love you both.' Lorna jumped up from her seat, kissed Ivy, kissed Archie and ran upstairs.

They heard the sound of feet running on the floor above, then silence. Archie looked across at Ivy, who leaned her head on one side, with a questioning gaze.

'Good news, Ivy, it is good, isn't it?'

'It's your choice, Archie, it's your house.'

'It is good with the two of us, Ivy; with Lorna here and a baby it will be a family here. It will be good for all of us.'

'Everything will change, Archie. Your routines, your rooms, everything you do will change.'

'We must do this for Lorna, Ivy... mustn't we?'

'Don't get me wrong, Archie. I'm fond of Lorna. It hasn't always been that way, once I thought she was using you, but she has done much for you, you have been so happy with your painting. She was the one got you your exhibition. I realise we are the nearest she has to family.'

Ivy picked up the plates and took them out into the kitchen. Archie stared into the fire worrying over the things Ivy had said. What would change, not Ivy, not him, not... well Lorna would change - she would be a mother. That was all. What did Ivy mean? Archie picked up a cup and saucer and carried them through.

'Archie, give me that before you let it drop.'

'Ivy, we must do it.'

'I am not against it, Archie, it's your home. There hasn't been an infant here since your mother was a baby. Even you were a lad when you and Dorothy came to live with your grandmother. Don't underestimate what a whirlwind will go through this house if a baby arrives.'

'When... the baby, when's it due?'

'I don't know, but from what she has told me I guess October, maybe November.'

'Am I getting it wrong, Ivy?'

'No, Archie, you're not wrong. I'm none too certain it is as an uncle Lorna needs you, Archie. Come the day she'll want you for more than that.'

Ivy got on with the washing-up, rattling plates and making it clear she would say no more.

Archie went out into the darkening evening and crossed to the studio. With a single bulb lit, he picked up the remains of the St Agnes picture and examined the ripped canvas. Perhaps it was the looks of that other girl. He turned off the light and sat back in the paint stained armchair. There were things to consider.

It was past eight o'clock when Ivy tapped on the studio door shinning her torch to see Archie was all right.

'Come on, Archie, high time you were indoors.'

'So much to think about, Ivy. So much, so exciting.'

'Sitting here all night won't get things sorted. Take my arm, Archie, we'll get locked up, I'll stay over tonight.'

'We'll have to think about bedrooms... and a playroom.'

'Not so fast, Archie. It will be months before you need to sort any of that, and then only if Lorna does come to live here. Things can change. Lorna and her young man may get together again. He is the baby's father, after all.'

Chapter Twenty-Five

ARCHIE was up early and downstairs pottering about, first going to the studio, where he got rid of all sign of the offending picture and set up another on which he had barely started. He went back into the house, looking into all the downstairs rooms, thinking what rearrangement would be necessary when a baby lives in the house. He looked about each neat room, with scant understanding of what might be in store.

When Ivy came down she went out to her car. She hadn't locked it with all the confusion of the previous day, not only was it not locked; the key was in the ignition. Back in the kitchen, she told Archie that if Lorna was settled she would go back to her cottage once they had breakfast and leave the two of them to look after each other. She promised she would be back in good time on Easter Sunday morning to cook the turkey.

Archie was keen to take tea up to Lorna. Ivy worried at him going upstairs with a mug of boiling tea. He was having no problem with the stairs on his own and he could carry a mug of tea well enough from one room to the other with little if anything spilt. He had not tried to combine the two – stairs and a hot mug.

'But if you aren't here I will have to do it on my own. Look, I'll reach it up to a higher step, get myself up a few steps then place the mug on a higher step again.'

'Does she want tea, Archie?'

'I always took her a cup when she was here before, well not at Christmas, but I'm in good shape now. You come and watch.'

The kettle was ready to boil. Archie got the biggest tea pot, the one his mother had bought as a memento on a seaside trip to Poole, got tea bags from the caddy and poured the water over leaving it on the stove to mash.

'Milk and one sugar for Miss Lorna.'

His plan worked, although it took a few moments to sort out the sequence at the top of the stairs and a little of the tea was spilt, not so you'd notice. Lorna was awake and watching the apple trees blowing in the wind wondering when they would blossom. Last year she'd asked Archie to do her a painting of apple blossom. He was too busy with his Requiem paintings to do it, maybe this year.

'Wonderful, Archie, good old West Country service, as ever.'

'Did you sleep OK?'

'On and off.'

'Was it the bed?'

'No, the bed is fine. Just me and getting over the journey, the train was packed, people standing in every carriage. I was lucky to get a seat.'

'You should have preference in your condition.'

'Archie, I hope no-one noticed. I'll have to go back to London next week. It'll take me a while to untangle my London arrangements and to finish my current workload. At a time like this it's good to be freelancing.'

'I never did sort out what it was you did.'

'I don't think I'll even bother to try and explain it, not today at any rate.'

'There'll be breakfast, a big breakfast when you are ready for it.'

'Not a big breakfast, please, Archie.'

With that Archie left her. Back downstairs he started getting things from the larder, eggs, sausages from the Helecombe butcher made to a traditional recipe, tomatoes and mushrooms. Ivy watched sitting at the table with her second cup of tea.

'She'll not be hungry, Archie.'

Breakfast was cooked and plated up long before Lorna came down. Ivy only ever had a small breakfast, but Archie piled his plate high aware of Ivy's disapproval, with the doctor insisting he limit his intake of rich meals while he was on the drug routine, even though that was diminishing. Archie ate with enthusiasm, enjoying the familiar flavour of the Helecombe sausages off his menu for months.

Archie hadn't heard Lorna coming down stairs, he was wiping his plate clean with bread when she came into the kitchen and sat down. Ivy knew at once.

'Had a lie in then, breakfast has been waiting.' Archie got up from the table to get Lorna's plate.

'Just a cup of tea for me, Archie.'

'That's not a breakfast.' Archie brought the plate from the bottom oven.

Lorna took one look at the plate piled high and rushed from the room.

Archie turned to Ivy looking puzzled.

'I did tell you, Archie.'

Ten minutes later Lorna came back. 'If there was any doubt about a baby, there isn't now.'

'Sit by the fire, dear. I'll make a fresh pot of tea.'

* * * * *

At the end of April Lorna was back in London, uncertain whether to keep the buzz of the capital or to settle for the rural pattern of Somerset as soon as she could. She knew Archie and Ivy would look after her and Poppy – after she'd been persuaded to go to the doctor she was convinced her child would be a girl.

The job was not a problem, working within a co-operating group of accountants and lawyers on business development and rescue projects. They told her she would be welcome to return later if she was minded to work again in London, part-time if she wished it. There might also be opportunities opening up in the West Country as some clients had widespread interests.

The question of Nathan was the problem. How could she find out the lie of the land without making contact? The chance came unexpectedly as she dawdled over latte and pain au chocolat in one of the many US style coffee houses invading the capital.

'Hi Lorna, where have you been hiding? We haven't seen you at the gallery for weeks.'

'Hello, Gerald.' Lorna kept her seat, not wanting to stand up and give anything away. 'Pull a chair over.'

Gerald was an assistant at the Chiswick gallery. He was knowledgeable, but often in their bad books as he was forever turning up late and disappearing when needed.

'Can't stay long, I'm meant to be minding the shop, but Jenny will cover for me.'

'How goes it all?'

'Requiem broke all records at the gallery. How's Mr Middlebrook getting along?'

'He's well on the way to good health.'

'Painting?'

'Not easy, but he's getting into the hang of it again.'

'That's good. Are you up with the gossip at Chiswick?'

'Tell me.'

'Nathan has gone.'

'Nathan... why, how... when?'

'He had a row with the directors. Word is that after Requiem he was getting a bit too big for his boots and taking decisions without reference. They took him up over it at the board meeting two weeks ago and he stormed out, saying if he wasn't wanted in Chiswick he wasn't short of offers in the States.'

'Has he gone to the States?'

'No one knows.'

'Are you in line for promotion, Gerald?'

'Some chance, I'm always getting bollocked for something or other. No, I'll drift along for a bit, see what any new person is like and make my mind up then.'

'I'll give Nathan a bell.'

'Be careful.' Gerald knew most of the secret goings on at the gallery. 'Dreary Imogen left last week – you can guess why.'

'Ah.'

* * * * *

James had been in touch with Archie by phone several times since the exhibition, regretting he couldn't get down to see him with commitments in Oxford before he went off on a prolonged lecturing-cum-holiday trip to the Far East. By the end of May he was back and drove down to Somerset. James brought Megan with him, picking her up at Gordano Services on the M5. She wanted to see Archie again to discuss spending six weeks at his studio in the summer. They arrived for lunch planning to motor back later in the day. Archie persuaded them to stay the night.

Megan was impatient to get into the studio and left the two men to chat, sitting on chairs under a sunshade on the terrace looking out over the lawn. Ivy stayed in the kitchen.

'You're looking good, Archie. I was expecting you to be using a stick. You kept telling me you were going on fine. I thought it was your customary modesty.'

'I set a goal of getting rid of the stick in April. I'm well, mostly thanks to Ivy.'

'Hope you don't mind Megan coming along. She was hard to refuse once I told her I was coming to see you. She's very excited about coming to work here in the summer.'

'I hope it lives up to expectations. I ought to have a word with her tutors to find out exactly what she should be doing. I hope they don't expect an academic input.'

'I have a proposition for you, Archie.' James took a drink from his iced water, having expected to be driving home later. Once persuaded to stay he said he would wait until later for wine.

'Well.'

'As you know I have been away in the East for much of the past two months.'

'I want to hear all about that. You must have got to a good few places.'

'We did, but Bridget was relieved to get home again after so many hotels. This is something special. And I haven't spoken to anyone else about it as I wanted to get your reaction first.'

Archie waited, and it took time to get James to the point, explaining the connections he had built up based on contacts with Malaysian students at Oxford. Over the years these contacts had become formalised into an association – the United Kingdom Malaysia Alumni. Many of the earlier members were now in senior positions in commerce and the professions in Malaysia and other countries. James had made contact with Association members during his tour of the East.

'The upshot of all of this, Archie, is that there is a gallery in Penang that wants to put on an exhibition based on your Requiem.'

'In Penang? You're kidding.'

'No, it's true. The owner, a very rich lady, bought one of your paintings from the Chiswick exhibition last autumn. She and her husband have a house somewhere in Kensington and business interests all over the place. We got talking at an Alumni do in Penang. She was excited when she realised I knew you and had been involved in the original events. It's her idea and she wants to hear back from me when I have had the chance to talk to you.'

'Much of the exhibition is dispersed now and we could never ship the big stuff out there.'

'Her gallery is a lot smaller than Chiswick. The main interest is your jungle paintings. She didn't believe me when I told her you hadn't been back to Malaysia since the 1950s.'

'I must have got something right.'

'I've had time to think things through, Archie, since that first conversation and I have seen her gallery.'

'Have you got any photographs?'

'I never thought to do that. We can get her to send some if you are interested. My idea would be to concentrate on your smaller pictures, even painting more, including a portrait of Geraint and a picture of the ambush to keep the exhibition in perspective.'

'How do we get everything out to Penang?'

'That can all be left to the gallery owners. They trade goods back and forth all the time. It's no problem to them.'

'Exciting.'

'There is one other thought. What would you think if Megan were to contribute some work to the exhibition?'

'Have you talked to Megan about it?'

'No.'

'She knows nothing about Malaysia.'

'I thought, if you agreed, she could do pictures of Wales to tie the two countries together, Archie.'

'It's a good thought, James.'

'And another thing.'

'More?'

'How about the three of us - you, I and Megan – go out to Malaysia to visit Geraint's grave in Ipoh, even go to the ambush site if you wanted, and to be at the opening of the exhibition.'

In the kitchen Ivy was making sure everything was on the table ready for lunch. She looked out through the window seeing Megan coming away from the studio. It struck her the girl was not much older than Archie was when he came back from his national service. Megan looked over toward the terrace, where the two men were talking, hesitated and came into the kitchen.

'Lunch smells good, Ivy.'

'Hope it doesn't spoil with them nattering away.'

'Do you mind my calling you Ivy, only I don't know your surname?'

'Ivy'll do, dear. We don't stand on ceremony here.'

The girl asked if she could help as she nosed around lifting lids and looking in the dishes. Ivy was amazed when Megan told her she couldn't cook and her mother only bought ready meals and tins. It struck her as strange to be going out into the world and unable to cook. Even Archie could cook.

Megan smiled when Ivy told her she would teach her to cook in the summer. Archie could teach her painting and she would teach her housekeeping, and for good measure she could have a bedroom in her cottage for the time she was working in the studio.

Ivy said nothing, but knew Hawthorne Cottage would be full if Lorna came back with a baby on the way. Lorna had phoned a day or so ago. Archie was sure she would come back to Somerset. Ivy sent Megan out to tell Archie and James the lunch was waiting and would spoil if they didn't come soon.

It wasn't until later Archie mentioned a possible exhibition in Penang and suggested it might include Megan's paintings. She jumped at the idea and by the evening Archie was helping Megan with ideas that could stand alongside the jungle and ambush paintings. It was important to make the connection between Megan, Wales and her uncle. She reminded Archie she had been doing drawings of the fast disappearing old shop fronts in Cardiff. Geraint's parents, her grandparents, had been shopkeepers. Their shop had gone long ago, bulldozed for a car park, but she was sure there was an album at home with photographs of the shop with its flat above where Geraint had lived as a young child. In any case it would be enough to guide her with pictures of surviving shops and research in the public library.

Later James floated another suggestion, one he was not certain Archie would be happy with, but he needn't have worried. A student at Oxford was the grandson of Bee Chin, the communist imprisoned for life for many incidents against the British during the Emergency. Although the evidence had been circumstantial, it was probable that the Ferret ambush was one of those many incidents. Bee Chin was an ailing man by the time he was tried. He died in custody three years later.

James asked Archie if he would be prepared to meet Bee Chin's grandson, now a young businessman in Kuala Lumpur.

Chapter Twenty-Six

LATE in September there was a gathering at Hawthorne Cottage to celebrate Megan's summer of tutelage in the studio and the kitchen. Megan, under Ivy's watchful eye, was cooking supper. James and Bridget had motored down from Oxford. Archie was trying to contain his excitement at the prospect of the Penang Exhibition, having superintended the packing and departure of thirty paintings of the jungle and tin mines in Malaysia, together with three larger paintings of the ambush, Geraint's portrait and of a Ferret Scout Car with three young national servicemen - James, Geraint and himself standing proudly in front of the vehicle. These paintings were accompanied by five pen and wash drawings and five acrylic paintings of 1950s shops and streets in Cardiff, work started in Wales by Megan working from old photographs and finished during her summer weeks in Archie's studio.

Lorna was moving slowly from room to room, finding her pregnancy wearying, impatient for Poppy to arrive, even with three weeks to wait. She'd given up her work, made a permanent move to Somerset and reconciled herself to a future as a single mother. Nathan was thought to be working in America unaware of imminent events. He had Imogen in tow as reported by Gerald at the Chiswick Gallery.

'You owe us an explanation, Megan,' James smiled at the young student, but she was apprehensive as to his meaning. 'When we motored away from here last May you were saying what a wonderful cook Ivy was and how no-one cooks in your household – and then you produce this feast for us tonight.'

'Much of it is Ivy's doing.'

'Not a bit of it, my dear. It's you doing supper tonight. You decided what it would be and you've done the preparation and cooking.'

'You were checking what I was doing, Ivy.'

'Only so that it all got done.'

Megan had started serving in the sitting room after Archie lit the fire against the chill of the evening. Megan produced plates of mixed canapés and, once they sat down round the kitchen table, mackerel pate as an entree, a steaming steak pie to follow and crème brulee for pudding, with Helecombe Cheddar to round the meal off.

'You can't stay with Ivy and not get hooked on cooking.' Megan looked at the empty plates relaxing at her success.

'And you were a diligent apprentice in the studio. You can be proud of your work we sent off today.' Archie took round a bottle to top up his guests' glasses, wanting to wish the paintings bon voyage. 'They certainly knew how to pack the pictures for this adventure. They told me they would travel in a temperature-controlled container until they were unloaded into the air-conditioned store room at the gallery awaiting hanging in January; not like the troopships in the fifties, eh, James.'

'At least I got to fly back and see India on the way.'

'You're quiet tonight, Lorna. Is everything OK?' Bridget looked across; Lorna's plate was the only one with leavings.

'I think things could be starting.'

Archie stood, bottle in hand. 'There's three weeks yet.'

'Maybe there isn't.'

'Please say it wasn't my steak pie.'

'Megan, it was magnificent. I'll go and stretch out on the sofa if you'll all excuse me. I'm not very comfortable.'

Ivy led Lorna through to the sitting room, She'd been sure for a while the baby would be coming earlier than Lorna had been told, but not this early.

Archie sat back in his chair. Even Ivy had had a couple of drinks, so they would have to get a taxi or phone for the ambulance if things were starting. James read his thoughts.

'Our taxi is booked for half eleven to take us to the hotel. We may have to give way.' He smiled at Archie.

'Things will be a while yet,' Bridget suggested.

'There's best part of a month to go yet,' Archie told them.

There wasn't.

Poppy was born half an hour after midnight. They hadn't planned a home delivery, but once started they realised they would never make it to Tonecastle.

Archie and James were dispatched to the conservatory with strong coffees, while Megan acted as go between relaying progress from upstairs to the men downstairs.

Under Ivy's lead, not her first experience of a home birth in the parish, and Bridget's backup, the baby came.

Chapter Twenty-Seven

POPPY gurgled as she lay on a floor mat decorated with cartoon characters from the Jungle Book. The infant kicked out her legs and arms wrapped from neck to her toes in her baby grow suit. It was Christmas Day and already the cottage was taken over by the three-month-old child from the night times, when she woke impatient for Lorna's attention, to daylight hours when Archie pushed her in a refurbished pram round the garden and along the winter lanes. She had taken her first breath at Hawthorne Cottage eighty-five years after Dorothy had been born in the same bedroom. There was nothing the three month old needed for Christmas, yet there was a stocking hung at the end of her cot, filled with soft toys and a cloth book poking out from the top.

'When did Santa put that stocking on her cot, Archie?'

'You were both fast asleep. You could have left out a glass of sherry for Santa.'

'And have him over the limit driving his sleigh.'

Ivy and her grandson, Robin, were busy in the kitchen. Archie sat in his old chair, with its arms worn through, as Lorna picked Poppy off the floor mat to feed her before they sat down to lunch.

'Now, little madam, I hope you are going to be good and go to sleep after your Christmas lunch, not that it is anything different from every other day.'

'She's a demanding soul. Will you be getting her onto made-up milk soon? I'm looking forward to giving her bottles,' said Archie.

'Maybe by the time you get back from Malaysia. It'll be quiet around here with you all away.'

'Ivy will be around.'

'Just me and Poppy in the house.'

'Are you worried?'

'No, not at all, but we'll miss you.'

Logs crackled in the wood burner with its doors open and a stout guard clipped to the wall against any mishap.

The baby suckled with a hungry rhythm, fingers flexing and eyes bright.

Archie beamed at the contented scene. It was a very special Christmas. Lorna lifted Poppy onto her shoulder and patted her back. She obligingly gave a baby belch. Archie passed a cloth to Lorna.

'Haven't you got the best home in the world, Little Miss? And Archie is going to go on a long trip away, so it will be just you and I to look after each other.'

'I'll be back by the end of January.'

'Back from the tropics, while we all shiver through the winter. Come on, Poppy love; time for your sleep. I think Robin is hiding. He hasn't got his mind round babies yet.'

'Poppy will be old enough to enjoy Christmas next year.'

'It'll be a few years yet, Archie. I don't want her growing up too fast. In no time at all she'll be a teenager and sulking because we don't live in a town.'

'She'll be busy pushing my bathchair by then.'

* * * * *

As the cabin staff readied the plane for landing, the Malaysia Airlines 747 descended through a cloud layer, looking solid from above, yet no more than a haze looking up from underneath. The rippling blue sea lay far below, with its pale hints of shallow coastal waters. A toy-like ship trailed its wake, rounding the northern tip of Sumatra, heading out into the Indian Ocean, as had the Empire Georgic with its burden of troops four decades earlier. The jumbo was losing height toward the coastline of Malaysia on the far side of the Malacca Strait.

Archie had slept much of the journey after eating dinner as their flight journeyed through the winter dark across Europe out of

Heathrow. The Penang gallery owner had been generous with return business class tickets, Golden Club as the airline called it, for Archie, James and Megan.

He'd watched the routine of the flight attendants, marvelling at size of the jumbo's cabin, something he had never appreciated from the vapour trails high in summer skies drawing white lines over Somerset's landscape. There were headphones and films available, but he'd slept as the world turned below, the deserts of the Middle East giving way to the huge population of the Indian Sub Continent, going about their business through the night hours and into daylight.

He wondered about Lorna and Poppy. Leaving was hard, even when facing the adventure of returning to the land that had so marked the life ahead of him. Christmas celebrations last month had been a great success at Hawthorne Cottage, Lorna was over the difficulties of Poppy's sudden birth, Ivy was in her element with her grandson Robin staying, and he had come alive when Megan joined them for New Year. Both the youngsters were musicians, skilled at the piano, spending hours together playing and laughing over the keyboard.

Archie looked across the upper cabin from his window seat to the port side where Megan and James were finishing their breakfast. Megan had been granted a special leave of absence by her course tutor, hard to refuse with her paintings featuring in the Penang exhibition.

They were coming in over the coast. A huge drift of river mud flowed out into the clear blue water of the Malacca Strait, mangrove swamps stood at the sea edge before Archie's first glimpse of natural jungle, then palm oil plantations set in patterns following the contours, and rubber estates with their parade ground lines of trees. A highway with cars and trucks rushing about their business, clusters of newly-built houses and factories, the land seemingly coming up to meet the huge plane crossing the perimeter fence of the airport, and the jumbo was rolling along the runway its flaps and engines breaking the speed of their landing.

The passenger in the adjacent seat had slept, even through breakfast. He stretched out his arms and flexed his feet. 'Always good to be home,' he smiled at Archie.

They'd talked over dinner. He'd been on a business trip for two weeks. His family business had factories and he'd been looking for new clients wanting to outsource their European manufacturing to Malaysia. He was certain he would soon get new business.

Megan gave a cheery wave across the cabin. Archie checked his passport was handy – he'd checked it several times before.

At the door of the plane the chief steward introduced Sir James Peterson to a ground staff member, who conducted the three of them through a special channel swiftly processing Customs and Immigration, before being taken into a VIP lounge, where a stewardess came forward to pin an orchid corsage to each in turn. An army officer saluted and introduced himself.

'I trust your flight was satisfactory. I am Captain Halim bin Yusef. I will be your escort over the next few days to Ipoh and on to Penang.' After a brief glance to make certain he knew who each of the visitors was, he shook hands with them in turn. 'Sir James Peterson, Miss Hughes, Mr Middlebrook, welcome to Malaysia.'

'Captain Halim, thank you for greeting us.' James encompassed all three in his reply. Archie wondered if James had expected a VIP reception on their arrival. He'd said nothing to hint he was.

'Sir James, Datuk Paduka Aisha binte Mustaffa sends her warmest regards and is sorry she cannot be here in person to meet you. She is looking forward to welcoming you in Penang later in the week. Now we will go to your hotel where you can rest and prepare for your journey. Tomorrow is a rest day at your leisure. On the second morning I will collect you after early breakfast and we will fly up to Ipoh to visit the cemetery where your colleague rests.'

Captain Halim led the three travellers out of the air-conditioned complex into the day's sticky heat to a waiting limousine, asking them to check their luggage had been gathered and was waiting to be loaded into the second vehicle. How it had been brought so swiftly from the plane was a mystery.

Later, at the KL Hilton, they sat out on the mezzanine terrace as the tropical day faded into humid night and spirals of sweet smoke drifted from the mosquito coils. Megan and Halim sipped iced colas while Archie and James renewed acquaintance with Tiger Beer discussing the itinerary of their journey as told by Halim.

'I've already seen the paintings set up in the gallery in Penang, Mr Middlebrook. Your jungle pictures are excellent, Sir.'

'You must call me Archie, please, you are a regular captain, remember I was only a national service corporal.' Archie laughed, nodding at James. 'And Sir James there, he was a mere second lieutenant, so you outrank us both, Captain Halim.'

'Ah, you are senior gentlemen,' Halim replied.

'Do you like pictures, Captain Halim?'

'I've always enjoyed drawing. We had a good teacher at my school.'

Archie noticed Halim had with him a notebook. 'Is that a sketchbook you have, Captain Halim?'

'Only a few little drawings.'

'Might I look?'

Archie thumbed through the book, with Megan looking over his shoulder.

'They are only my doodles, Mr Middlebrook.'

The drawings were mostly of soldiers on exercise in the Malaysian landscape. Archie reached over and gripped Halim's hand. 'These are good, Halim. Whatever you do, don't ever stop drawing. Draw something every day. Even if you think nothing of it on the day, keep your notebooks and you will be building a storehouse of ideas for the future. I stopped for too many years, and it was a mistake.'

Captain Halim acknowledged Archie's compliment and stood up. 'Gentlemen and lady, tomorrow is your rest day here in Kuala Lumpur, the next day we will leave early in the morning, we fly up to Ipoh, I will collect you from the lobby at oh-six-hundred. Your wake-up-calls are booked for five o'clock, your account is settled, so just enjoy your breakfast and be ready for the airport, thank you.' With that Halim departed.

James stretched. 'I'm for shut-eye. Just hope our time clocks are not too disjointed. I suggest we meet up over breakfast and plan our day in Kuala Lumpur. There's much to see.'

'Hard to think we were still at Heathrow twenty-four hours ago. It took us weeks to be here on the troopship,' Archie smiled.

* * * * *

In common with graves tended by The War Graves Commission in home parishes, in the war cemeteries of Flanders, Archie's father Donald's grave amongst so many in Italy, and those in the stone-corralled Military Cemetery of Blue Beach at San Carlos in the Falklands, a simple headstone in the tropical heat of Batu Gajah Christian Cemetery near Ipoh, bearing the battalion insignia, marked the grave of Private Geraint Hughes, killed in a terrorist ambush on 10th August 1955.

Archie stood, his head bowed, in the heat of the day holding Megan's hand as James placed a wreath of interwoven orchids beside the headstone. Captain Halim, smart in his crisp uniform, stood a few paces away at attention, saluting. James stepped back and took Megan's other hand, the three of them standing together in silence with their thoughts.

Megan let go her two companions' hands, took a deep breath, clasped her hands together and in a hushed unrehearsed voice sang the opening of Cwm Rhondda in Welsh. Archie clenched his fists, hearing Geraint singing with her.

James and Archie watched Megan, her voice swelling as she sang. Only remembering English words from the first verse,

"Bread of Heaven, Bread of Heaven,
Feed me till I want no more, feed me till I want no more."

They joined, with Megan ending each verse.

When they turned away from the graveside, James gave the young woman a hug. 'Thank you, Megan, I didn't know you are a singer as well as all your other skills.'

'I'm Welsh, Sir James, all the Welsh sing. I was in the Cardiff Girls' Choir before I left school.'

'Your singing was beautiful, Megan.'

'My Dad sang, but they all said Uncle Geraint sang best of everyone in the family.'

Archie could only beam his gratitude to Geraint's young niece. He bent down and using a practiced thumbnail he took a sprig from the scarlet hibiscus growing on Geraint's grave.

He smiled at his watching companions. 'You never know, it might root if I manage to nurse it back home.'

Megan reached over, picked off a flower head and held it up to the tropical light. 'I'll press this in my diary for Mum.'

'We'll give you a few minutes, Archie.' With that James and Megan joined Captain Halim to stroll toward the gates of the cemetery.

Archie stood, clutching the Panama hat he had with him against the tropical sun, turning the brim in his damp hands. Megan's singing had brought alive the spirit of Geraint. He'd lingered long in Archie's deepest thoughts, flowering back to the foreground in the horrific crash of Lorna's car, urging him on, counting the rosehips, and always been with him in the long studio hours of the exhibition paintings.

'We were good friends, Geraint. You would have done great things. I hope I've done enough to honour your sacrifice. I've had many blessings in my life. Your friendship has been the chief of them.'

Archie stood, head bowed, reading the inscription on the stone, the simple facts recorded in military fashion.

'Farewell, good friend. Your genius lives on with Megan. She has all your spirit.'

Archie turned and walked over to the others.

James gripped Archie's shoulder. 'Well done, Archie; you've done your friend proud.' Megan reached up to kiss Archie's cheek. They turned for a final look toward the simple grave as Captain Halim stood to attention and saluted.

The military driver who had met them at Ipoh airport was waiting at the cemetery gates.

'We'll call at a hotel to freshen up and meet with Mr Danny Tan. I understand, Sir James, he is known to you.'

'Yes. He was at one stage a student of mine at Oxford. Archie, Danny Tan is the grandson of Tan Bee Chin, I mentioned to you. Are you happy to meet with him?'

'Thank you, James. Will he come with us to Lenggong?'

'Yes, if we are all happy, he will be our guide. Megan, our plan is to go to the site of the ambush where your uncle died and Archie was so badly wounded. Danny Tan took me there last year, it is unrecognisable, but he can point us to the place where the ambush happened. It's no longer the laterite track we witnessed, Archie. Now it's a metalled main road.'

They travelled in two vehicles, Archie going with Danny Tan in his chauffeur-driven Mercedes, the others following in the army staff car. They took the road from Ipoh along the highway toward Lenggong.

As they drove north through the increasing jungle landscape, Danny pointed out various places along the route. He told Archie that after Oxford he studied law and was now both a solicitor and a businessman, building up an import/export company with partners. They had satellite offices in Singapore and Bangkok.

Danny Tan had all the signs of success in his chosen career. He was expensively dressed and much travelled.

Well into the journey he spoke of his grandfather's life before and after the Japanese occupation.

'He was a man of passion and strong belief in what he stood for all his life. He opposed his colonial masters. When the British were swept out of the country by the Japanese invasion he fought against the incomers. He spent the three years of occupation living in the jungle, working in league with those that infiltrated from the Allied Forces. They were successful and skilled, but led a dangerous life. When the British returned, he continued his struggle, wanting to see a Malaya of the people, albeit he was fighting the communist cause, which he believed was the antidote to colonial rule. If he was wrong, I honour him as a courageous man, who fought for the cause in which he believed. By the time he was captured and imprisoned he was an ill man after his years of deprivation.'

Archie nodded. 'I understand. By the time James and I were here we were the opposing forces, but there is a truth in all of it. Your grandfather was pursuing his beliefs. We were called up to do a job and were uncertain of what our purpose was in your country.'

'Malaysia is in a good place now, a place to build a strong business,' Danny was confident of his place in the business community.

As their journey progressed, Danny told Archie about the research he'd done into the activities of the communists, the CTs as they were known, in particular of his grandfather's life through the forties and into the fifties finding the places he had been, some of it still in deep jungle. It was during his research he had established where the ambush of the Ferret scout car had taken place.

'As Sir James has said there is little to indentify the place, just a bend in the road at the top of a short hill.'

'Even so, I am keen to see the place again.'

'I look forward to seeing your exhibition of paintings, Mr Middlebrook. I have been told your depictions of the jungle and the old tin mines of the 1950s are an important record of those years.'

'I hope they do your country justice.'

Before Lenggong, they turned away from the highway on to a smaller road. After quarter-of-an-hour Danny told the driver to stop on the roadside. With both cars parked up the party walked forward to a place where the road curved and went down a hill. It was the hill the scout car had climbed, getting ahead of the two Bedford trucks on their way back to Ipoh, the road now a metalled main road. There was no sign of the events forty years ago, but Archie knew it was the place.

Danny carried with him a two foot long carved wooden stake. One end was shaped into a sharp 'V', the other, the top end, had a pewter orchid blossom set into the shank, where two dates were carved: '10th August 1955 and 22nd January 1996'.

He gave the wooden stake to James. 'This is a token to acknowledge your visit today.'

James beckoned Archie and Megan to join him and together they worked the wooden memento into the soft ground edging the road.

'It may not survive here long, but it marks the passage of time since that unhappy event.' Danny's voice was lost as a heavy timber lorry laboured up the hill, belching out foul exhaust smoke.

The party walked back to the cars, where they said good-bye to Danny, thanking him for the visit. James, Megan and Archie joined Halim in the staff car to head for Penang. Halim estimated they would be there by six o'clock.

'Danny talked a lot of his days in Oxford,' Archie grinned.

'Not telling tales, I hope.'

'Very interesting, James.'

Chapter Twenty-Eight

ON the morning of their first day in Penang they were asked to lunch at Datuk Paduka Aisha's house. Their army escort picked them up from The Eastern & Oriental Hotel in mid-morning and took them first to the gallery. The exhibition was due to be opened in the afternoon. Archie was pleased to see that Megan's pictures had been given good space, with a well presented introduction setting them in the context of Geraint's youth, living at his parent's flat over their shop in Cardiff.

After an hour they headed to the gallery owner's home. At the sumptuous house they were shown in to a spacious designer-decorated room. On the wall, in pride of place, was one of Archie's larger paintings, one of his jungle pictures, with a patrol just visible as they wound their way through the thick growth. It had been sold at the Chiswick Exhibition, one of the highest priced paintings to sell.

'That must make you feel good, Archie, to see it on display. It's one of my favourites,' added Megan.

Archie beamed and went over to examine it closely, as if he was expecting to find some blemish to correct.

A door opened on the far side of the room and their hostess appeared. She grasped James's hand. 'Sir James, you are here and in good spirits, I'm sure.'

'Certainly, Datuk Aisha, and grateful for the arrangements you have made for us under the guidance of Captain Halim. And you are well and as graceful as ever.'

'Always the flatterer, Sir James.'

'Datuk, may I introduce Archie Middlebrook, whose work you know so well.'

Archie was about to cross over to his hostess, but she was already by his side, holding his hand before he could move.

'Mr Middlebrook, it is an honour. Do you approve of the hanging of your picture?'

'Excellent. And please call me Archie.'

'Archie, it is.'

'And can I introduce Megan Hughes.'

'Megan, such a beautiful name. Your pictures have all been hung in my gallery, Megan, but you will have seen them already this morning. They are very exciting. I fear there will not be many of the old shop houses still standing in your home town. It is the same here, buildings ever upward, determined to have more floors than the last building.'

With the introductions over Datuk Aisha invited James, Archie and Megan onto a veranda, where they were given iced fruit drinks sitting in the shade on rattan chairs under ceiling fans. Halim had slipped away after the introductions.

James kept up the small talk. He was well respected by their hostess, it seemed she was instrumental in organising part of his lecture tours in the Far East.

Later they enjoyed a luncheon buffet of oriental dishes and satay, which appealed to Megan, who had tried most cuisines available to students in Bristol. With her new enthusiasm for cooking, she wanted to know more, wondering what Ivy would think of the spiced dishes.

After lunch they returned to The Orchid Gallery for the exhibition opening. The contrast between it and the Chiswick High Road Gallery was marked. The converted Methodist building, with its upper floor and huge hanging spaces, compared with the air-conditioned simplicity of Datuk Aisha's gallery on the mezzanine of a downtown hotel, impressed Archie. He had no problem with the end result in the smaller gallery – the lighting was excellent, showing off his paintings and Megan's work to good advantage.

His only regret was that Lorna was not with them. She had been such a large part of the Chiswick exhibition. As the days in Malaysia passed, he'd felt anxious at the distance between them. He kept thinking of the routine at Hawthorne Cottage, his home, but so fully lived in by Lorna and Poppy. He would be back within the week, but he missed his girls.

Halim joined them at the gallery. The opening of the exhibition passed in a blur of introductions, questions and iced fruit drinks. Archie enjoyed the afternoon, even happy to address the whole gathering, talking about the jungle and how it had excited him as a young artist far away from home.

Next morning, it was a day to look round the delights of the island only half remembered. James asked Halim if he knew where to find the one-time British Military Hospital. He went off to make enquiries and soon they were in the army car again, on their way to find the buildings, now part of the university. There were new buildings in the grounds, but the old building where Archie had begun his recovery from the horrors of the ambush was more real than the ambush site. They even found the bench, or perhaps a replacement bench, where James and Archie had sat at their first meeting after the ambush.

'Fitting that we should be here again, James.'

'It is the right place, I remember looking across to the main hospital building while we both hesitated on what to say next.'

'I guess it was the start of recovery. It was the first time I had faced up to what had happened. It has taken too many years to appreciate the reality, but these last few days have been wonderful, James. I am very grateful.'

'You deserve it, Archie.'

'Just two regrets.' Archie gazed across the lawns. Megan, who had learnt always to have a small sketch pad to hand was sitting cross-legged on the grass a distance away drawing a bougainvillea blossoming in tropical colours.

'And, will you tell?'

'The first is that I didn't respond to the card you sent that first Christmas. My apology, James, if it isn't too late.'

'Accepted, but you don't have to apologise, Archie. And the second?'

'I wish Lorna was with us.'

'I did ask her, Archie, but... '

'There was no chance after young Poppy burst into our lives. But I am missing them.'

'It won't be long, Archie.'

'Do you miss Bridget, James?'

'We are used to long absences, but she often travels with me. She had commitments this time. It would have been good for Megan if she had come, but she seems to be coping well on her own.'

'No children, James.'

'Not for want of trying, Archie. We've only been together for five years; she is in her late thirties so it could happen, although I'm not as young as I was. Being with Lorna and Poppy made her broody; both of us, if the truth be told.'

'I hope you don't mind me being nosey, James.'

'Not in the least. I'm jealous of how things are with you, to tell the truth.'

'I'll go over and warn Megan she might find herself in the path of ants. It never did to sit on the grass in the tropics.'

Back at the E&O Archie turned off the air-con, opened the French window on to the balcony and settled on his bed. It had been a wonderful trip, but it was time to go home.

What time was it in Somerset? He added seven-and-a-half hours, then realised he had to take time away. Eight thirty, breakfast over and the day planned, maybe a trip into town or a walk with the pram to call in on Ivy. Or was it a winter day with snow flurries and staying in all day with the log burner going?

Tomorrow back to Kuala Lumpur, next day their flight to Heathrow, just him and Megan. James had work appointments in Singapore.

Chapter Twenty-Nine

ARCHIE stood on the platform at Reading Station, feeling numb. A day in tropical sun, sixteen hours of awkward comfort in a crowded airliner, with meals appearing at intervals, the sharp cold of a Heathrow winter dawn, and a bus to the main line station left him disoriented. Megan had been with him through the journey, but she'd gone ahead on a train to Cardiff. He waited amongst a growing crowd to catch a Plymouth-bound train advertised with two stops before Tonecastle.

He'd telephoned Lorna using a pay phone at the airport, apologising for his early call. Poppy was crying in the background. He told Lorna not to meet any trains, he was uncertain when he would arrive, he would get a taxi.

As the train ran across the Somerset Levels Archie gazed out over flooded fields, surprised how quickly the fields had flooded; the pastures were green when he'd set off a week past. He got up from his seat long before they reached the station, keen to have his suitcase ready to leave the train. In the event they stopped outside the town, the train staff announcing a wait for the platform to clear.

The guiding hand of Captain Halim, with his help and know-how, was only a memory. No staff car was waiting to take him home, indeed no taxi was on the rank by the time Archie was clear of the platform. Another passenger said the driver of the last cab had told him more were on their way. Should he ring young Mr Horsefield?

Three taxis drove in to the station yard.

'Helecombe, where's that then?'
'Just head to Northhill; I'll guide you.'
'Been away?'
'For a week.'

'Hope it was somewhere warm. It's been miserable here.'

Back at Hawthorne Cottage, Ivy had the kettle on for tea.

'I could have come in to get you, Archie.'

'I had no idea what train I was going to get, Ivy. It wasn't too long a wait for the taxi, but it was expensive, a lot more than it used to be.'

'Everything is.'

'And how is the little one?'

'Full of beans, she's been a right little madam; I think she's cross with you for going away, Archie,' Lorna smiled. 'The little lady is asleep at last. I've told her I won't tell you how naughty she's been, if she is good tonight.'

'You look short of sleep, Lorna.' Archie gave Ivy a hug and Lorna a kiss. She held him not wanting to let go.

'We've missed you, Archie.'

'Come along you two, get sat down and have a cup of tea. I've baked shortbread.'

Lorna held his arm. 'We want to see lots of photos, Archie. And what about the exhibition? Was it as good as Chiswick?'

'Megan was our expert with the camera. She's promised to get a set of prints run off for us, it will be a few days.'

'Has she gone home to Cardiff?'

'For a couple of days, then she has to be back in Bristol for college.'

'I expect we'll see her here soon. Ivy says Robin is coming down for a break.'

'Are you two match-making?'

Lorna chuckled.

'Can I go up and see Poppy?'

'Give her half-an-hour, Archie. If she's not awake by then I'll fetch her down.'

Even as they chatted Archie fell asleep in his chair by the open log fire. Ivy took the plate from his hand smiling at Lorna.

He woke forty minutes later to find Poppy in her mother's arms, reaching out to be put on his lap.

Much as Archie wanted to be bright and tell them about the places he'd seen, of Geraint's grave, the ambush site and the Penang exhibition, he was exhausted.

Ivy announced she was going home.

Having played for a brief while with the giggling Poppy he was persuaded by Lorna to go to his bed.

Archie woke at three in the morning, squinting at the luminous hands on his alarm clock. He lay still for a while, working out the time in Malaysia. Ten-thirty in the morning was his guess. Was it all a dream? Yet the realities of the past week were evident enough, the past forty years, the exploits of a group of national servicemen on that tropical ground, his life in rural Somerset – these were all real. It was not a dream.

James would be away for several days longer in Singapore before coming back through India pursuing his busy academic life. Megan was home with her sketch book and photographs. She would be busy working her experiences into her Art degree tasks. Maybe Captain Halim had got something from his unusual duty escorting their party and was reflecting on their many conversations about painting.

Archie needed his own new project.

He was wide awake and he needed a hot drink. It was dark in the house. He didn't want to wake Lorna and Poppy. With caution he made his way down to the kitchen turning on a light over the cooker. Patch wagged her tail against the side of her basket.

There were envelopes in a pile, letters addressed to Archie. The top one had a gallery's name printed across it. The letters could wait until the morning. He made himself hot chocolate and sat at the kitchen table, wondering what his next project could be. The most obvious was his Exmoor landscape series. Ten years ago it had been his main work, yet was never successful in the local galleries.

Archie crept back upstairs. His bed was still warm, it was time for more sleep and with luck he could wake in his normal Somerset routine with his time reset to English winter.

He sensed a movement in the room. She sat on the edge of his bed as her hand searched for his head on the pillow.

'Have I woken you, Lorna?'

'I haven't slept.' She leant over to hold him. 'I'm so happy to have you back, Archie.'

He turned in the bed, freeing his arms to grasp her shoulders. Her tears were on his cheek and they held each other.

'Promise you'll never go away again, darling Archie. I need you so much, Poppy needs you. You must always be here.'

'Lorna, has something happened while I've been away? What is it?'

'No, nothing has happened.' She let out a big sob and gripped him hard leaving him struggling to breath. 'Everything's happened.'

Lorna leant back, pulling at the sheets to slip into his bed. 'Isn't it obvious, Archie? We need each other. We've got to be together. You're the father Poppy needs; you're the lover I must have. Please never leave us.'

'Lorna, I love you. I'll always be with you.'

* * * * *

Ivy's car came into the yard as they were lingering over breakfast coffee. Poppy was in Archie's arms taking milk from her bottle, only the second time Lorna had tried a bottle and much more successful than her effort the day before.

'I didn't think Ivy would be round today, were you expecting her this morning?' Archie looked at Lorna.

Ivy came in to the kitchen.

'Look, Ivy, Archie has cracked it, Poppy's taking her bottle and no complaint, and she slept through for almost six hours.'

'Just come by to see you two are all right. You looked like zombies last night, both of you.'

'We're fine, Ivy.'

'I'm off shopping. Robin has rung, he's coming at the weekend, and he's bringing Megan.'

Archie looked from Lorna to Ivy. She held his gaze.

'Ivy... Ivy, I want to say...'

'I know, Archie, I've known longer than the pair of you. Why has it taken you so long?'

Ivy went over to stroke Poppy's head as she nuzzled her bottle. She brushed a kiss on Archie's forehead and looked at Lorna. 'You look after him, mind, or you'll have me to answer for it.' She embraced Lorna, kissing her on both cheeks. 'Now I have Robin and Megan to think about.' And Ivy was on her way back to her car.

Archie passed the bottle to Lorna. Cradling Poppy, he went to the window. Ivy didn't look back.

'Ivy always knows.'

He watched as she buckled her belt and started the car. Poppy in his arms gazed up at Archie, a smile breaking over her face.

'I swear Ivy has second sight, little lady.'

THE END

ACKNOWLEDGEMENTS

The judges of the 2010 Yeovil Prize Novel Competition, who shortlisted, and highly commended, Requiem for Private Hughes, giving much encouragement to the writer to complete this novel, albeit on a slow burn.

Jim Bruce, of www.ebooklover.co.uk, for his editing and proof-reading of my manuscript and for formatting this book.

ABOUT THE AUTHOR

Chip Tolson came to writing fiction late in life, many years after schooling, national service in the army and thirty-five years in the shipowning industry, working in Liverpool, the Far East and Edinburgh.

Redirecting his energies, he gained a degree in Creative Writing at Middlesex University and is a member of Writing Groups in Somerset.

Chip and Clare live on Exmoor in a one-time farmhouse looking after twelve hilly acres of woodland and rough grazing.

Chip has twice won the annual Yeovil Literary Prize Short Story Competition and won the 2014/2015 Somerset Film Scriptwriting Competition.

OTHER WORKS BY CHIP TOLSON

The Battle of Slotterham Hall, AD 1929, published on Amazon in 2015, is a fable of tribulation and triumph: the pheasants resolve to challenge the shoot. It is a tale dedicated to the memory of all people wounded and lost in wars.

Pebbles is a collection of short stories to be published in 2016. Pebbles lie on the shore in their billions waiting to be found. Sometimes one or two are picked up, maybe even kept and taken home to be looked at from time to time. More often after a cursory glance, they are cast out to sea, perhaps bouncing and making a splash before they disappear.

In the hope that some of the words in the Pebbles collection will be noticed they lie waiting on the pages. It is hoped they will give enjoyment before the waves reclaim them.

Website: www.chiptolson.com

Printed in Great Britain
by Amazon